FOR THE LOVE OF JULY

A NOVEL

L. B. JOYCE

For the Love of July
ISBN: 978-0-9600311-6-0

ALSO BY L. B. JOYCE

Twelve Months, Twelve Love Stories

A Million Decembers

For the Love of July

February's Angel

Promise Me November

An Unexpected June

A January to Remember

September's Moonlight Serenade

Goodbye Heartbreak, Hello May

March, a Song and a Dance

Holidays in White Oaks Valley

A Grand Slam Kind of Christmas

This book is a salute to love. And to Cleveland, a baseball kind of town. There's no doubt about it, we have the best fans in the nation! And Jingle and Honey? A special thanks to both of you, from my heart to yours.

FOR THE LOVE OF JULY, BOOK 2

*"Love is the most important thing in the world,
but baseball is pretty good, too."*

~ Yogi Berra

CHAPTER 1

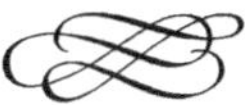

Progress involves risk...
You can't steal second base, and keep one foot on first.
~ Anonymous

"Welcome to Cleveland!"

The dealership guy had barely said the words before he jumped into the waiting car. Tires screeched, and dust swirled, leaving Kevin Kardell alone in the parking lot, the July sun warm on his shoulders and shiny new keys in his hand.

He looked down at the keys, then at the bold red Porsche Turbo S parked right in front of him.

Damn... she was gorgeous.

This car didn't just sit there—it announced itself, proud and impossible to ignore. He ran his hand over the glassy-smooth hood, a big grin spreading across his face. He'd said yes to the one-month loaner in half a second flat, and right now he had zero regrets.

Could this day get any better?

He snapped a quick photo and fired it off to his sister Katy with the caption *Jealous yet?* She was going to lose her mind. Girly as she was, she loved fast cars almost as much as he did.

The second he reached for the door handle, the headlights flashed and the locks clicked open.

He chuckled. "Show-off."

After he tossed his bags and gear into the trunk, he slid behind the wheel and sat there for a moment, hands on the steering wheel. The ballpark rose ahead of him like a cathedral, sunlight glinting off the stands, Lake Erie sparkling bright blue in the distance. A warm breeze carried the faint smell of hot dogs and fresh-cut grass.

As he adjusted the rearview mirror, he caught his reflection—twenty-six, sun-streaked hair, and that same cocky smile that had carried him all the way from Chicago Little League.

Major League Baseball.

You're here.

You actually made it.

Tomorrow night he would step onto the field as Cleveland's starting shortstop. Not a prospect. Not a call-up. The real thing. All the hard work, all the years of grinding through the minors—it had finally paid off.

A small flicker of nerves mixed with the excitement in his chest. One bad month could send him right back down. But he pushed the thought away.

Not today.

He hit the start button. The engine roared to life with a deep, satisfying growl that vibrated through his whole body as he pulled out onto Carnegie Avenue.

He knew he probably shouldn't… but come on.

He pressed his foot down on the gas.

Hard.

The Porsche shot forward, pressing him back into the seat. The city blurred past in streaks of steel and summer green, Lake Erie glittering like a promise on the horizon.

He laughed out loud, the sound mixing with the roar of the engine.

Look out, Cleveland… here I come.

This was it.

The beginning of everything he'd worked for.

And maybe—just maybe—the beginning of something he hadn't planned on at all.

Game on...

CHAPTER 2

"*P*lease...."

"*Pul-eeeeez...* I just need a little more, that's all. Come on, don't run out on me now."

Anxiously watching the icing oozing from the tip, Abby Evans squeezed the pastry bag as hard as she could. She was cutting it pretty close. But with only one cookie to go, things were looking promising.

With a dramatic flourish, she added the one last decorative swirl of icing. But it was only after she'd inspected every cookie lined up on the counter to make sure they were all finished to perfection, she tossed the empty pastry bag into the sink.

Thank goodness, it looks like you're finally done....

With this last batch of cookies now finished, the order for the four hundred wedding cake shaped cookies could now be checked off in her order book.

As she observed the glossy coated pink and white decorated cookies, she had to admit they were a beautiful sight.

And she never wanted to see this shade of pink again.

Nope, not in a thousand years.

A color fittingly named Princess Pink, mind you.

It seems nothing but the perfect shade of pink would do for

Lucinda Miller. Pretty in pink... even tickled pink. It looked like everything was going to be coming up pink for her wedding day.

At least it was nice to know someone's wedding day would be the day they had always dreamt about...

There was another whine from Poppy. Coming from the other side of the gate, blocking her from the kitchen, the little dog had been camped out there ever since Abby had discovered the remains of half eaten cookies scattered all over the pantry floor.

Knowing she would be pulled in by her big brown eyes, Abby had been ignoring her. After all, she was the reason for this all night frenzy of baking and decorating cookies to replace those that had been ruined.

That she'd been able to accomplish this?

She considered this a miracle.

She sighed. She didn't even want to know how many cookies had been gobbled up.

After a long stretch, she gazed around the room. Then, dropping her arms to her sides, she groaned. She had a huge mess on her hands.

One would think a gang of rowdy five-year-olds had been given free rein of her kitchen. Cupboard doors and drawers were wide open, the sink was piled high with dirty dishes and she'd swear there was a film of icing on just about everything in sight.

Again, it was all about pink.... Princess Pink.

She wanted to sink down onto the floor and cry. Or better yet, take a nap. But since she only had four hours until her promised noon delivery time, neither of these was an option.

Another whine filled the room, louder and more pitiful this time. Against her better judgment, she stole a quick glance over at the gate. Her front paws just reaching the top of the gate and her tail wagging like crazy, Poppy gave a little bark.

With a resigned sigh, Abby removed her apron and tossed it on the counter. She slipped past the gate and had only just sat on the floor before an ecstatic Poppy pounced into her lap.

She buried her face in the little dog's silky fur. "Poppy, what were you thinking? And how did you get into the pantry? I don't understand. You've never done anything like this before. Is it because you know they're for Lucinda? We both know she's never been very fond of you."

This was an understatement. If Lucinda caught even a glimpse of Poppy, she became hysterical, begging Abby to lock her up. As if Poppy was a ferocious attack dog, waiting to tear her to pieces. At a whopping ten pounds, Abby would bet most of the cats in the neighborhood were at least twice her size and ten times as ferocious. Trying to avoid the onslaught of wet kisses to her face, Abby laughed. "I take that as a yes. Well, don't worry. You won't be seeing her anytime soon."

She hugged Poppy close. "Not if I can help it."

She framed the little dog's face in her hands. "But it looks like we need to go over the rules again, don't we? Did you forget? You know the kitchen and any people cookies are off limits. You have your own doggie treats. And homemade ones at that."

Her only answer was another round of wet kisses before Poppy burrowed into her lap and settled in with a long, contented sigh.

Leaning back against the wall, Abby ran her hand through the little dog's fur. "I've been ignoring you lately, haven't I? But I thought we discussed this, how I need to work as much as I can if I want this business to succeed. Which means you'll need to be patient for a little while longer."

She smiled down at her. "I promise, later today, we'll go for a long walk. It will do us both good."

She continued to run her fingers through the little dog's fur until she knew if she didn't make a move, she'd fall asleep right where she was. Something Poppy appeared to have already done.

She carried the little dog to her dog bed, where she curled up into a ball and went right back to sleep.

It seemed any regret over her unacceptable behavior has already been forgotten. Which goes to prove, in your next life you should request to come back as a dog. A much simpler and stressful life, it seems.

Abby sighed, shaking her head. A hot shower was what she needed. Then she would deliver the cookies and erase the order, and the people it involved, from her mind. An order, had she not needed the money, she never would've agreed to take on in the first place.

When she returned to the kitchen after her shower, the frosting had set and the cookies were ready to be bagged. After she tucked each cookie in one of the elaborately monogrammed parchment bags Lucinda had insisted on, she gave an enormous sigh of relief.

She only had to print out an invoice, load the cookies into her SUV, and deliver them to the party center.

Then she could come back home.

And crash…

CHAPTER 3

I never understood how people could fall in love at first sight.
Then you came along.
~ Anonymously Yours

The cookies loaded in her SUV, Abby checked one last time to make sure they wouldn't slide around during the drive. She wasn't going to take any chances of anything else interfering with the delivery of these cookies.

She began to back out of her driveway, her eyes on the rearview mirror. Catching a sudden flash of red, she slammed on her brakes, cringing at the sound of the boxes bouncing around in the back of her SUV.

There was only silence.

No crunch of metal against metal.

No sound of breaking glass.

Thank goodness...

She turned her head to watch as a sleek red sports car raced down the street before it came to a screeching halt. With a loud roar, it made a sharp turn up the driveway of a condo two units down and across the street from her.

Music was blaring, the bass booming like drums.

She groaned, dropping her head down on the steering wheel.

You don't need this. Not today, and certainly not now.

Then she was angry.

Really angry.

In one swift move, she was out of her car and marching down the street. Someone needed to let this person know this kind of behavior would not be tolerated, and it might as well be her. This was a residential neighborhood, for heaven's sake. Not someone's personal racetrack. No matter what kind of fancy car they drove.

When she came closer, she saw the driver was a man. Now rummaging through the trunk, he was pulling things out and tossing them in a pile on the driveway. From what she could see, it looked like all kinds of sporting stuff.

You know, bats, mitts, jerseys and what not. All the gear men seemed to think they needed to have in order to prove they were men. The same stuff, even if they rarely used it, they carried around with them to prove that, yeah, they were as athletic as the next guy out there.

And from the collection this man had, it appeared he considered himself more athletic than most.

Great... just great. Another egotistical, wannabe athlete.

Again? She wasn't in the mood.

Observing him from behind, she couldn't help but notice his muscular physique, suggesting he frequented the gym regularly. He was tall, about a head taller than she was. And his hair, what little she could see that wasn't covered by his baseball cap, was a wavy, burnished gold, curling down the back of his neck.

The thought popped into her head he only needed a toga and he could pass as a Greek God. Or better yet, one of those Nordic warrior-hero-types featured on the cover of a racy Victorian romance novel.

What the heck are you thinking? He's no God... and certainly no hero. He's just a man. A man who nearly ran you over, and evidently believes rules are not meant for him. So, get your mind out of the gutter and back to why you're here.

She cleared her throat. Loudly. She did this twice, in fact.

He turned around just as he was pulling another bag out of the trunk. He dropped the bag on the ground, a look of surprise coming over his face. Then he leaned back against the car, and after slowly adjusting his sunglasses, he crossed his arms over his chest.

He smiled. "Well, well, well… hello there, Red. What can I do for you? Wait, let me guess. You're the one-woman welcoming committee of the neighborhood, aren't you?"

He held his hands up. "But wait a minute here, no homemade baked goods? Surely you intended to bring cookies or something, no?"

He shook his head. "I must say, I'm very disappointed."

She stared at him.

Red?

She decided right then and there, she didn't like him.

No, she didn't like him at all. His reference to her hair, which by the way was not red, but more of what she liked to think of as a strawberry blonde, had a lot to do with this. Then there was those mirrored sunglasses he was wearing. How was she supposed to get through to him when she couldn't even see his eyes to know what he was thinking?

And the comment about baked goods? She made a mental note he would never, *ever* be on the receiving end of anything baked, cooked, broiled or whatever, coming from her. No matter how much he begged.

She matched his stance, and crossing her arms, she glared right back at him. Her words came out fast and furious.

"First, *do not* call me Red. I don't like it and just to make it perfectly clear, my hair is not red. Maybe if you removed those ridiculous mirrored sunglasses you're hiding behind, you would see this. Second, you should be so lucky to have any 'baked goods' coming from me. Which, I can assure you, will never happen."

He opened his mouth to respond, but she cut him off. "And third, I don't know if you'll be living here or you're just visiting. Either way, I hope you haven't already assumed you can use this road as your own private racetrack. Because, if you think this will be a way to impress everyone with how fast you can drive this fancy car of yours, you've picked the wrong neighborhood."

She waved her hand towards her car. "And finally, you owe me an apology for almost hitting me as I was trying to back out of my driveway. While traveling at an extremely high rate of speed, I might add."

For a few moments, he was silent. Then he laughed. And as much as she hated to admit this, it was a very contagious laugh. Seriously, she had to fight back the smile tugging at her lips. After all, there was certainly nothing to laugh about right now, was there?

Again, get your mind back to where it should be. Starting with his outrageous behavior.

Still lounging against the car, he tilted his head towards her. As if he was studying her. But then who knew what he was doing? She had no idea what was going on behind those sunglasses of his.

He finally spoke. "I stand corrected. About your hair, that is. Even though, from where I stand, and in the sunlight, it appears to be a most glorious shade of red, a perfect match to this fiery temper you seem to possess. A temper I've now had the pleasure of experiencing first hand."

Then he grinned. "*Hmm...* aren't redheads also known for their passionate nature? I'd be very interested in finding out if this is true. Much more so than whether you can bake or cook. Or anything else you might do in your kitchen."

He paused, watching as the color slowly filled her face, bringing out the freckles that were scattered over the bridge of her nose and across her cheeks.

Funny, he'd never thought of freckles as being so alluring... or even sort of sexy. But on her? They were making him want to kiss each and every one. Between this, and the deep, almost emerald shade of her eyes, he'd have to say she was nothing short of adorable.

He gave her a lazy smile. "And come on... I almost hit you? Since I'm pretty sure I had the right of way, I believe it's more like you almost hit me."

Abby wasn't even listening. How could she, with his previous comments still bouncing around in her head?

Glorious shade of red? Passionate nature? Did those words really just come out of his mouth? Describing her?

Now completely rattled, she accidentally tightened the hold she had on her keys, setting off her car alarm. As the horn began blaring, she frantically began pushing the buttons on her key holder. But to no avail. The horn just kept going… and going…

It just wouldn't stop.

Just as she was about to throw the keys, it didn't matter where, just anywhere, he took them from her and within what seemed like a millisecond, there was silence.

Tossing the keys back to her, he smirked. "Calling in reinforcements?"

She stared back at him, frustration showing all over her face.

Could she possibly be even more embarrassed?

Or more furious?

This wasn't how she'd planned for this encounter to take place. It was supposed to be short and sweet. About how his car almost hit hers. And that he'd been driving too fast. He would apologize and she'd leave. She certainly didn't think she'd be dealing with of all these personal comments he kept throwing at her.

The color of her hair and whether she had a passionate nature were none of his business.

Why, he doesn't even know you!

She was tempted to turn around and leave, definitely what a sane person would've already done. But this guy was pushing her buttons like no one had ever done before.

And she couldn't walk away for the life of her.

She gave him a long, hard stare. Well, at least, this is what she tried to do. She was beginning to re-think her earlier opinion of his sunglasses. Right now, she would welcome the luxury of being able to hide all the different emotions surely showing in her eyes.

She spoke very slowly. "I don't need reinforcements. I am quite capable of handling this by myself. And getting back to what we really should be talking about, it doesn't matter who was at fault. What matters is you were driving too fast. If I hadn't been paying attention, you might not only have caused a lot of damage, but also destroyed all of my hard work. Something I can't afford to have happen right now."

She took a deep breath, and even though she knew she should shut up and walk away, the words just kept coming. It was obvious she was on a roll and there was no stopping her.

"And this so-called fiery temper you've accused me of having? Or this passionate-red-haired-fantasy-thing you've dreamt up in that typical male mind of yours? You'll have to go elsewhere to find out the answers to either of those."

There... that should shut him up, shouldn't it?

Her smile was triumphant. "So, now if you will excuse me, I'm already behind schedule as it is." She turned and began walking away.

He was silent.

She smiled. So, he had nothing to say, did he?

Good. Score one for you.

Then, the possibility he might be watching her, she quickened her pace.

And, of course, this was bound to happen...

She caught the toe of her shoe on an uneven part of the sidewalk and, with a loud shriek, landed face down in the bed of ivy lining the sidewalk.

He was next to her before she even had the time to process what happened. When he reached over to help her up, she panicked, pushing him away. Then she backed away from him, scrambling to her knees.

It was only when she went to stand, she realized she may have finally hit rock bottom. Because, not only had the beds recently been watered, leaving a trail of mud and ivy leaves plastered over her legs, any weight she put on her left foot sent a sharp pain shooting through her ankle and up her leg.

Her eyes squeezed shut, she willed herself not to cry.

His voice was too close. "Hey, are you okay?"

No. No, she wasn't.

But there was no reason to let him know this. Even though for some crazy reason, she wanted to turn around, go right into his arms, and cry her eyes out. Not only because of the fall, but because of everything else going wrong in her life right now.

His voice came at her again, more hesitant this time. "Are you hurt?"

She shook her head.

Hurt? No, obviously just very embarrassed.

He persisted. "Are you sure? You seem a little wobbly on your feet."

Okay, now she was starting to get mad.

Couldn't he just leave her alone?

After she batted at her legs to remove as much of the mud and ivy as she could, she sent him a quick glance, nodding her head more vigorously this time. "I'm fine. And, as I've already informed you, I'm quite capable of taking care of myself."

In an attempt to make light of what happened, she forced a bright smile on her face. Then she sent him a casual wave. "Again, I need to get going."

And with as much dignity as she could manage, which at this point was pretty close to non-existent, she began hobbling her way to her car.

Wow

For the life of him, Kevin couldn't seem to wipe the silly grin off his face. He'd heard redheads were temperamental, but this one?

Well, let's just say he'd swear he saw sparks flying from those gorgeous eyes of hers.

And now he wasn't sure what to do. Should he go after her? This seemed a little iffy. But as he watched her make her way down the street, he knew he couldn't let her go without trying to make amends.

He'd never be able to forgive himself.

Yeah, and something tells me you're going to regret it, but you've got to give it a shot.

His mind made up, he adjusted his hat and took off in a run after her.

"Hey, wait up."

She froze.

Oh, no...

Now what was she supposed to do?

If she turned around, he would see she'd begun to cry. Then he'd jump to the conclusion she was crying because of him.

But she wasn't.

Honest.

No, she was crying because of everything.

She was dead tired.

Her ankle was throbbing.

And she still had to deliver the stupid cookies to the party center. Where there was a good chance she'd run into the person who had stolen what she thought was going to be her perfect life.

Suddenly it was all too much. And none of it was fair.

Furtively wiping her eyes, she croaked out a response. "I told you I'm fine. So please, go back to what you were doing and don't worry about me."

After a short silence, he cleared his throat. "I don't know if this will make you feel any better, but I'm truly sorry. I shouldn't have kept teasing you. Maybe then you wouldn't have tried to run away from me."

He hesitated before he added his next comment, hoping she wouldn't take him seriously. "I've been told it seems I have that effect on women."

She didn't respond.

Ah... so it appears this isn't the time for humor.

Now beginning to feel a little desperate, he began moving closer. But the sudden urge to reach out and pull her into his arms hit him so hard, he took a step back, almost in shock.

His hand slowly going to the back of his head, he groaned.

What's going on here? Why are you letting her get to you like this?

After jamming his hands in his pockets, if only just to ground himself, or *God help him*, keep him from doing something entirely foolish, he cleared his throat. "So, I guess it's sort of my fault you fell. And from what I can see, it looks like you're limping. Which means you're far from fine."

When she remained silent, he persisted. He didn't know why, only that it was suddenly very important she didn't leave hating him.

"Hey, come on. Can't we start over? After all, it appears we're going to be neighbors, so it would be nice if we could at least be friends."

She turned, enough for him to see the telltale sign of tears.

Damn... he made her cry? He'd never meant to do that.

He pulled off his baseball cap and after running his hand through his hair, he jammed the hat back on again. Again he groaned. *"Oh geeez...* please don't tell me you're crying about this?"

As soon as these words came out of his mouth, he knew he'd made a mistake.

A big mistake.

Sure enough, she stiffened, those green eyes of hers throwing daggers at him.

Oh boy, here we go again...

He took a step back, his hands going up as if to ward her off. *"Whoa... what I meant..."*

Her fists clenched to her sides and, with an angry toss of her head, she cut him off. "I know exactly what you're insinuating. And for your information, I'm not crying. And even if I was, it certainly wouldn't be because of you."

She looked up at the sky, shaking her head. "Are all men full of themselves, thinking everything is about them?"

She'd had enough. It was time for her to put an end to this conversation. Limping her way down the sidewalk, she threw her final words over her shoulder. *"Please...* let's just pretend this whole encounter never even happened. And more importantly?"

She began walking faster.

"Just. Leave. Me. Alone."

Pretend this whole encounter never even happened?

Well, Kevin sure as hell knew he wouldn't be able to do that. Frustrated, he pinched the bridge of his nose, fighting the urge to run after her again.

But wait a minute... why would he do that? He'd already extended the olive branch. In fact, he'd gone out of his way to make things right between them. He couldn't think of anything he would have done differently.

Face it... she's crazy. Just all out crazy.

It was clear she had issues with every man who walked the face of this earth. And if there was one thing he didn't need right now, it was someone like her to complicate his life.

No, sir-eee... he wasn't going to get caught up n another woman's insecurities again.

Been there, done that.

He saw she'd made it to her SUV and was now backing it down the driveway to the street. This was at what could only be described at a snail's pace.

He shook his head. Did she just recently learn how to drive? Because he could walk faster than she was moving right now.

He continued to watch as she inched her way to the main road, turning the corner at a speed that was almost embarrassing to watch.

Why was she driving so slow? Maybe this explained why she'd made such a big deal about, what was it she said? Something about him using the neighborhood for his own private racetrack?

He smiled.

Yeah, those were the exact words that came so passionately out of those perfectly formed lips of hers. Lips, he'd been so tempted to silence with a kiss. This sent him right into thinking about her eyes, and how they'd flash with anger if she knew he hadn't taken anything she'd said seriously.

He chuckled. How could he? He was having too much fun teasing her.

But wait a minute... you need to get your mind off this woman. You're here for one reason. And this is to play ball.

This meant the less he saw of her, the better. Because it was obvious, even in the short time he'd spent with her, she was too much of a distraction.

But, as he removed the rest of his gear from the trunk, he couldn't stop thinking about that amazing hair of hers, glowing like a new copper penny in the late morning sun.

He stared into space, and his imagination taking over, he visualized running his hands through those soft curls, right before he would pull her face close to his and...

He groaned, slamming the hood to the trunk much harder than necessary.

What the hell are you doing? Remember? She has problems... big problems. Forget about her.

He gathered up as much stuff as he could carry and headed toward the condo.

He had things to do.

Important things.

Do not look back. *Do. Not. Look. Back.*

Even though these words kept repeating over and over in Abby's head as she hobbled away, everything inside of her was screaming the opposite. She couldn't shake the feeling he had some kind of hold on her, mentally pulling her back to him.

Briefly closing her eyes, she groaned. Of course, he wasn't. Why would he? If anything, he was probably relieved to be rid of her.

She started up her SUV and, after backing out of her driveway, she drove out to the main highway, traveling at a much slower speed than usual. But, with the way the past twenty-four hours had gone, she wasn't going to take any chances.

Granted, she was a little too cautious as she waited to pull on to the highway, but there was no reason for all the horn blowing and rude gestures from the guy behind her. Only after she glared at him for a good five-seconds in the rearview mirror did she finally pull out onto the main road.

Men... they're all the same, self-centered and egotistical. And right now, you don't like any of them.

She was confused. Never in her life had she been so irritated and riled up over something so incredibly stupid. She didn't understand. What had made her confront him like that?

She'd launched into him as though he was the worst kind of criminal living on this earth. It had to be his casual attitude about the whole situation. She wouldn't be at all surprised if he'd already forgotten about what happened.

Just like she should forget about him.

Yeah, Mr. Sports Car... a man way out of your league.

In fact, it would be best to avoid him at all costs.

Nothing good would come from it if she didn't.

Abby pulled up to the front entrance of the Regency Party Center, joining the queue of vehicles waiting to unload.

As she limped her way to the back of her SUV to open the trunk, someone called out her name.

It was Jason Bennett, the lead band member of the group, Banded Together. They had been friends since grade school.

She watched as he made his way over to her, a big smile on his face. And, as with every other time she saw him, she was amazed he was still single. If she were to describe him, she'd have to say he was a younger Johnny Depp look-alike, minus all the brooding Johnny usually had going on.

He was also terribly shy, most notably around women. Only when he was performing with his band did he become a different person, putting on a show only a superstar could pull off.

His smile faded. "Hey, what happened? Why are you limping?"

She shrugged. "Let's just say I should've paid more attention to where I was going. Instead, I wiped out. It still hurts, but as we both know, life must go on. This especially holding true with this wedding."

She cast a cautious glance behind them before continuing almost a whisper. "Are they here?"

He shrugged. "I don't know. Like you, I just got here. But, come on, you shouldn't be walking around, let alone carrying things. Go inside, get yourself a cup of coffee or something, and sit down. I'll get my guys to bring in your boxes."

"Oh Jason, you're such a sweetheart. I was told to leave them on the table right inside the entrance of the Grand Ballroom." She reached over to give him a big hug. "I can't thank you enough."

"*Aw...* you know I'd do anything for you." He winked. "And, remember... you can always re-pay me in cookies."

After she gave him a thumbs-up, she made her way into the building. The first person she saw was Jenny, the Regency Events-Coordinator. She was counting what looked like hundreds of pink and white roses overflowing the buckets lining the wall.

Good... she could give her the bill. Then she would be free to leave.

She headed in that direction.

"Abigail?"

Abby came to a dead stop, her heart dropping to her feet.

Oh, no... please, no...

There was only one person who called her Abigail and this would be Peter. The same Peter who, almost exactly a year ago today, told her he'd made a mistake. It was almost like an epiphany, he told her, coming out of the blue.

And the message he received? It turned out marrying her would be a mistake because she wasn't his true soul mate. Instead, he was destined to be with Lucinda Miller.

The same Lucinda Miller who, until then, had not only been her best friend, but had also signed on as her maid of honor.

And, just like that, with less than a month before the wedding she'd been planning for over a year, she lost both her fiancé and her best friend.

All in one heartbreaking and mortifying swoop.

But for some insane reason, this hadn't stopped her from taking on the job of making four hundred intricately decorated cookies for the wedding taking place tonight.

The wedding of Peter Benedict and Lucinda Miller.

If this didn't make her look like a fool, she didn't know what would.

"Abigail…"

He had now moved closer.

She pretended as though she hadn't heard him. But then he grabbed her arm. Resisting the urge to jerk it away, she came to a stop.

Closing her eyes, she waited.

"Abigail, I need to talk to you." His voice was low, almost a whisper.

Oh, no… why was he whispering? Was Lucinda somewhere close by?

Her eyes darting around the room, she was relieved to find that, no, Lucinda was nowhere in sight. But almost everyone that was, had stopped what they were doing and were watching her and Peter with interest.

But this was to be expected. Since everyone knew each other from working together at the party center, they also knew about the drama that went on when Peter had decided he no longer wanted to marry her.

She had to hand it to him, throughout the whole ordeal, he'd maintained the proper and reserved demeanor his career as a lawyer entailed, treating her with the utmost respect. Never had he talked to her the way this new guy in her neighborhood had, making comments that had her blushing, just thinking about them.

So now, with this desperate look on Peter's face, she found it hard not to feel a bit more forgiving.

After all, she'd been in love with him once.

At least she'd thought she was.

A resigned smile on her face, she tugged her arm from his grasp. "Peter, what do you want? If you're wondering where the cookies are, they should be in the ballroom by now."

She glanced down at the bill in her hand. She held it out to him. "I was going to give this to Jenny, but since you're the one who will probably be writing all the checks, I'll give it to you instead."

He stuffed it in his jacket pocket, his eyes never leaving her face. "As soon as I get home, I'll write a check and send it out. But this isn't why I stopped you. I wanted you to know I tried to talk Lucinda out of asking you to make the cookies. I told her it was pretty heartless to expect you to do this after what happened."

She laughed, surprising herself with how carefree she managed to sound. "Seriously? Now you're suddenly concerned about my feelings? How sweet of you. And in case you haven't noticed, yes, I'm being very sarcastic."

She backed away from him, her voice calm. "I need to go. I hope tonight is everything you've dreamed it would be. And give my congratulations to Lucinda, too."

He moved closer. "Abigail, please listen to me. I don't want you to think I'm crazy, but lately I've been having serious doubts about Lucinda. I'm beginning to think she only wanted to get married because she wanted this big wedding." He waved his hand around at the room. "Look at this, it's like a damn three-ring circus. It isn't even about us anymore."

When he reached out to touch her cheek, she cringed, backing away from him. A flash of pain crossing his face, his next words were barely audible. "Abigail... I made a mistake. I never should have left you."

She studied him for a few seconds. He had to be kidding, right? Now he was having second thoughts? On the day of his wedding? Wasn't he marrying the woman he'd so passionately referred to as his true soul mate?

And what does he think is going to happen? You'll throw yourself into his arms? Ecstatic and grateful he wants you back?

Suddenly feeling very weary, she shook her head. "I don't know what to tell you. Except it's probably a little too late to think like this. I also wonder if the real problem might be you don't want to get married. Period. After all, this is the second time you're changing your mind."

She was overcome with an urge to laugh. "So, what did it this time, Peter? Another epiphany?"

The laugh bubbling up inside of her, now almost on the brink of hysteria, she put her hand over her mouth. If she started to laugh, she wouldn't be able to stop.

They stared at each other until she finally looked away.

He was the first to speak. "Abigail? Say something."

She sighed. "Peter, I'm sorry. I don't know what else to say, except I really do need to leave."

She turned away, the sympathy radiating from everyone in the room following her as she limped her way out into the hall.

She leaned against the wall and closed her eyes. Could this day get any worse? If Peter had told her this same thing a few months ago, she would've been overjoyed.

But now?

The only thing she felt was a deep sadness. And pity for both him and Lucinda. It seemed like such a terrible way to start a marriage. Which meant there was a lesson to be learned here.

Forget about ever getting married.

As she headed for the main entrance, she thought of checking to see if the cookies had been delivered. But suddenly, she didn't care. In fact, if they never even paid her, she wouldn't care. Instead, she would write off the order as her wedding gift to both of them.

Because, the way she felt right now, all the money in the world wouldn't make her feel any better.

She started up her SUV and drove out of The Regency parking lot. Hopefully, these last twenty-four hours would be the end of what had been a very long and emotional year.

She was *so* ready to move on.

CHAPTER 4

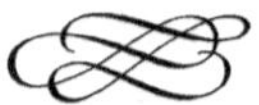

Kevin unlocked the front door to what would be his new living quarters for the next few months and pushed his way inside.

After he dumped his belongings on the floor, he glanced around the room.

Not bad... a bit more of a country theme than you would have liked, but since it's only temporary, it will do.

After a quick inspection of the kitchen, if only to make sure there was a microwave and his only claim to cooking, he gathered up his bags to go in search of the bedroom.

He found it at the end of the hall. As he went to throw his stuff on the bed, he caught the slightest hint of movement out of the corner of his eye.

After scanning the area, a startled laugh escaped him.

Holy cow... a cat.

It was, in fact, a rather large and ferocious looking cat. Perched on the arm of the chair, it was glaring at him through narrowed eyes.

He tentatively moved closer, holding out his hand. "Hey kitty, kitty..."

This was met with a loud hiss as the cat dove through the air and landed right by his feet, almost scaring him to death. The cat then raced out of the room and disappeared down the hall.

Scratching his head, Kevin laughed as he stared down the empty hall. "What the hell? You gotta be kidding me."

He sank down on the bed, shaking his head. He liked dogs. But he didn't like cats.

His one and only experience with a cat was when he was just a kid. His sister Katy had found a stray at the playground and insisted on bringing it home with her. But this was short-lived when they found out their mother was allergic to animal fur.

This had been fine with him. The cat had been so damn sneaky. Even now he shuddered, thinking how it would appear out of nowhere to pounce on him when he walked by.

So, yes… he could do without cats.

He pulled out his phone. Maybe Jake could explain this latest development. He was his go-to for any questions or problems about his move to Cleveland. He hit his number, and after setting the phone on speaker mode, began unpacking his bags.

After only two rings, Jake's cheerful voice filled the room. "Hey Kev, what's up? Did I give you the right directions to the condo? No interruptions or problems, I hope?"

For some reason, his thoughts went right to his encounter with the saucy little redhead. Would this be considered an interruption or a problem?

He would have to say neither. Then he grinned. If anything, it was almost more like a breath of fresh air.

This had him to wondering what the chances were he might run into her again. Something he'd really like to happen. Of course, this was only because, being new to town and all, he could use a friend. And it would be a lot more fun if that friend turned out to be a woman.

But what happened to all of that talk about staying away from her? She's got problems, remember?

He sank down onto the bed, closing his eyes. None of this was making sense.

"Hey, you still there?" The sound of Jake's voice, breaking into his thoughts, he ran his hands down over his face, shaking his head. "Sorry. Just a momentary lapse here."

Jake laughed. "At first, I thought jet lag, but you only came from Chicago, so that's out. And I know you couldn't have dozed off on me, since your adrenaline must be running pretty high right now. But getting back to why you called?"

Kevin laughed. "Yeah, about this roommate you've set me up with? I'm not sure we're compatible."

"Roommate? I know nothing about that." There was the sound of papers rustling in the background. *"Hmm... but let me take a look here."*

Then he laughed. "So, I take it you don't like cats? From what it says here, your current residence belongs to a woman who will be out of town for a few months because of a family emergency. Since the place we had for you needed some last-minute remodeling, this was suggested as a temporary alternative. But we can find another place if this cat is a problem."

The cat had returned and was now lurking right outside the door. When he held out his hand, it slinked into the room and jumped up on the bed, where it began grooming itself.

He smiled. "Nah, don't worry about it. Though I'm not all too sure about what to feed it."

He could hear more rustling of paper before Jake spoke. "It says here the cat is a female and goes by the name of Bella. A friend of the owner will stop by with food and instructions. But again, it's up to you. Whatever you decide."

The cat, or as Kevin now knew her as Bella, rolled over and began rubbing her head against his hand. As he ran his hand through her fur, she gave a deep rumbling purr.

He laughed. "I think Bella has decided for both of us. From what I've heard, cats require little care. So, for the short time I'll be here, I think we'll get along just fine."

"Good. Now, is there anything else?"

Kevin could hear the relief in his voice. "Nope. I'll come by the ballpark as soon as I finish filling out the mountain of paperwork you gave me. I'm eager to get into the swing of things."

Jake laughed. "Sounds good. Because until we have that paperwork on file, you're not supposed to pick up a ball or even step on the field. And hey, be careful with that car. It can bring out the beast in a guy and you don't want to be caught speeding. Remember, you'll be in the public eye now."

After they ended the call, Kevin wondered what Jake would have said if he told him he'd already been caught speeding. And how lucky he was to get off with just a lecture.

This brought back the memory of those green eyes.

There you go again... you need to stop thinking about her.

He headed for the shower.

The late afternoon sunlight coming in through the window blinds was what finally woke Abby. Sensing she was awake, and desperate to go outside, Poppy began showering her face with kisses.

Abby groaned, and after dragging herself out of bed, she was relieved to find her ankle felt almost normal. With Poppy dancing circles around her and giving excited little barks, she gathered her hair up into a makeshift ponytail.

She yawned. "Okay, okay... I get it. Let me find my shoes."

Her shoes located, they headed out the door.

It was the perfect summer afternoon, the sky a clear, dazzling blue. As Abby followed where Poppy's darting nose took them, it occurred to her this was the first time in the past week she could finally relax.

Well, sort of. Her encounter with Mr. Sports Car kept popping up in her mind, leaving her feeling unsettled. Almost as if what had occurred between them wasn't finished yet.

But this was crazy. What did she think was going to happen? And come on, hadn't she already decided, the last thing she needed in her life right now was another man? She was doing fine by herself.

A car passed by before turning into the driveway of the condo occupied by, none other than, Mr. Sports Car. A woman got out of the car and, carrying a shopping bag, she hurried to the front door.

Poppy pulled at her leash, giving an impatient bark. Startled, Abby turned and began walking back to her condo. If he answered the door, she didn't want him to think she was spying on him.

But in a way, you are.

She'd almost arrived at her condo when she heard the car start up. Within seconds, it pulled up beside her.

Uh oh...

"Hey… do you live near here?"

It was the woman with the shopping bag. She gave Abby a big smile. "If you do, I wonder if you can do me a favor. Do you know the guy staying there?" She pointed over at Mr. Sports Car's condo.

Whatever she wanted, Abby's intuition was warning her not to get involved. She shook her head. "No, I don't. I've seen him, but I don't know his name or anything else about him."

The woman kept smiling. "I promised my friend I would drop off this cat food. I guess he's staying in her condo while she's out of town. Since the cat needs to eat, someone's got to feed it. This means he's the lucky guy."

Abby smiled. A cat? She wondered how Mr. Sports Car felt about this? And suddenly, she was very interested in finding out. She held out her hand. "Here, I'll give it to him. I live across the street, so it won't be a problem."

The bag handed over, the woman shouted out her window as she as she drove away. "Thanks so much! Everything you need is in the bag, both the food and the instructions. Good luck."

Abby was grinning as she watched the car go down the street. She was really looking forward to delivering the bag.

For someone who claimed they never wanted to see this guy again, you've certainly changed your tune.

Oh no, she was merely curious to see how he was dealing with this new roommate. He just didn't seem like the cat kind of guy.

Back in her condo, she headed for the kitchen. Suddenly, she was starving. She opened the refrigerator to search for something to eat.

After all, a girl couldn't live on cookies alone.

Kevin ran his key card through the parking lot security scanner, grinning when the gates swung open.

After he pulled the car into the space marked with his name and sh off the ignition, he was tempted to take a photo of the sign as proof this space belonged to him.

Aw, go ahead. Do it.

So he did, his plan to send it to his family. Was there a better way to let them know he'd arrived?

He didn't think so.

Equipment bag in hand, he walked into the clubhouse and headed for the manager's office. He found Joe Conte at his desk, engrossed in the papers spread out in front of him.

At Kevin's knock, he looked up, a big smile lighting up his face.

"Hey, Kev. You made it. Come on in and sit down."

After Kevin gave him the forms he'd filled out and was seated, Joe leaned back in his chair and studied him for a few moments. He finally spoke. "So, are you ready?"

Feeling like he was in the principal's office and he needed to prove himself, Kevin found he was almost tongue-tied. Sitting up as straight as he could, he cleared his throat.

"Mr. Conte, I want to thank you for giving me this chance to be a part of the team, and I promise I'll do my absolute best to not disappoint you. I've been waiting for this ever since I played in my first little league game. So, yes… I'm ready. I'm more than ready."

Joe stopped him with a wave of his hand. "We're all on a first name basis here, so call me Joe. I know all about what you just told me. That's why we called you up. With your talent and a lot of hard work, we see a great future ahead of you. And we hope this will be with us."

Kevin grinned. "Thanks!"

Joe stood and, holding out his hand, he shook Kevin's in a firm grip. "Now I know you'd much rather be hanging around with the rest of the guys instead of an old man like me. So, go. But stop by if you have any questions. Or if you need to talk. My door is always open."

Kevin found the locker room and, after taking out his mitt, he stuffed his bag in the locker labeled with his name.

This prompted a few selfies in front of his locker. He knew he was acting like a kid, but he was just so damn pumped.

He ventured out to the field, where he found a few of the guys doing their own thing, their voices and laughter echoing in the empty stadium. At the crack of the bat, he stopped to watch a ball soar through the sultry July air.

He was searching for a familiar face when he saw one guy jogging towards him.

"Hey Kev! You made it!"

He grinned.

It was Alex, who he'd become good friends with during his time in the minors. With his winning personality, he made friends wherever he went. And true to his nature, he called everyone over, introductions coming at Kevin almost faster than he could think.

There was only one guy who had little to say. A big burly looking character who went by the name of Chester, he gave a nod in Kevin's direction, a mocking grin on his face. "So… married? Girlfriend? Or should I say girlfriends, as in more than one?"

This rubbed Kevin the wrong way. His first instinct was to tell Chester it was none of his business. But he had a feeling this wouldn't go over very well. So, he decided to go with a little humor.

He grinned. "No to all of those. Why do you ask? Do you have extras or something?"

A few of the guys snickered, following with a few comments. "He's only curious. He can't hold on to a woman, scares them away faster than you can count to three."

Another guy chimed in, "Yeah, we refer to him as strike-em-out-Chez."

After giving both guys a dirty look, Chester turned his attention back to Kevin, the mocking grin back on his face.

"Just curious. With your all-American good looks, every woman on the lookout for their own personal sports star will be coming out of the woodwork to claim you. You're open game now, so whatever you do, don't let your guard down. Unless you consider this as one of the perks that goes with the job."

Kevin didn't know what to say, making a mental note to ask Alex about him later.

And hey, women are the last thing on your mind right now.

Even a woman with gorgeous green eyes and hair that could drive a man wild?

Hmm...

Slowly shaking his head, he sent a grin around to the rest of the guys. "So, fill me in... what's the drill right now?"

A few hours later, he shut the door to his locker. Almost the last to leave, he gazed around the deserted room

Did this ever get old?

He couldn't imagine it would. At least not for him.

Nope. He was going to savor every moment.

It was late when Kevin turned on to the street leading to his condo. A grin began to grow on his face as he drew near to where the little redheaded beauty lived.

He pushed his foot down on the gas pedal, sending him thundering past her condo. As he made the sharp turn into his driveway, the satisfying screech of tires was magnified in the still night air.

Then, to bring it all home, he put the car in park and stepped down on the gas pedal once more, the engine giving a final satisfying roar.

He turned off the ignition, and dropping his head to the steering wheel, he groaned.

Seriously? What the hell was he doing?

You're acting like a teenager. What's next? Are you going to slap on half a bottle of cologne and go strutting back and forth in front of her condo?

Now feeling extremely foolish, he got out of the car, After he sprinted to the front door, he turned, sending a glance over at her condo. It looked like she was home, lights shining in her windows.

The key halfway to the door, he paused. Maybe he should play the good neighbor and stop by to see how her ankle was doing? Checking his phone for the time, he saw it was already pushing eleven. Not the best time to just drop in on someone.

Someone you hardly know.

There's also the possibility she might not be alone. She could very well have company.

Maybe there's a boyfriend.

Or she could even be married.

Suddenly feeling very irritated, he unlocked the door and shoved it open.

He was greeted with a very loud and angry meow.

Damn... the cat.

He'd forgotten all about it.

CHAPTER 5

The first time I saw you,
my heart whispered "That's the one."
~Unknown

Abby was feeling very pleased with herself.

Once she added the final details to the baseball cookies lined up on the counter in front of her, she'd be able to cross off another order in her books.

She'd just picked up the pastry bag filled with red icing when the late night silence was broken by the loud roar of a car as it raced past her condo.

This was followed by the sound of squealing tires.

If this wasn't enough, there was one last roar of an engine.... almost like a grand finale.

Or what sounded like to Abby as—*Hey Red, take that...*

She ran over to the window and peered out to see that yes, it was Mr. Sports Car himself.

Really?

Had he learned nothing from the conversation they had earlier?

Evidently, he hadn't.

She watched as he got out of the car and ran to his front door. Then he turned and looked right at her.

Oh, come on... why would he? You're imagining this.

But just in case, she ducked away from the window and slinked back to the counter, praying he hadn't seen her. She picked up the pastry bag of red icing and began piping the stitch design on the baseball cookies.

But it was slow going. She couldn't seem to concentrate. Instead, her mind was all wrapped up with him.

Was he just coming home from work? And what kind of job did he have to come home this late? After all, it was Saturday.

He might have been on a date, you know. He probably has his choice of girlfriends.

She slapped the pastry bag down on the countertop and, leaning back against it, she closed her eyes. This was ridiculous. She needed to stop thinking about him.

Again, he's way out of your league. You couldn't hold on to Peter, so what makes you think you'd have even the slightest chance with this guy?

She stared down at the cookies in front of her. If she were to compare them to a cookie, Peter would be the plain, unfrosted cookie. Maybe even a little too well done and crisp around the edges.

And Mr. Sports Car?

Obviously, he would be the ultimate cookie. Perfectly cut out, baked just right, and decorated to perfection. He was the cookie everyone wanted, the first to be snatched from the plate and most likely to be fought over.

But this was crazy? Now she was comparing men to cookies?

She gathered up her decorating tools and tossed them in the sink. As she began cleaning up the clutter on the counter, she came across the bag holding the cat food. She stared at it, frowning.

Why did you promise to deliver this?

She sighed. Since he was home, she might as well get it over with and deliver the bag now.

She caught sight of her reflection in the kitchen window. She certainly couldn't go over there looking so frazzled. A little make up and a quick fix of her hair was definitely in order. And her baggy sweat pants? She needed to change those as well.

But she was only doing this for herself, mind you.

After all, she did have her pride.

Bella wouldn't leave Kevin alone. After twenty minutes of her non-stop meowing, a sound he decided was very similar to fingernails scraping on a blackboard, he was about to lose his mind.

He'd searched through just about every cupboard, drawer and closet in the whole damn condo, but not a single can of cat food was to be found.

Massaging the back of his neck, he groaned. It had been a long day, and he really didn't feel like dealing with this right now. Where the hell was the person who was bringing reinforcements? Shouldn't this have already happened?

He stared down at Bella, but she didn't seem to have an answer to this. Instead, she gave him another desperate meow as she wove in and around his legs.

Running his hand through his hair, he sighed. There was no way around it. He had to go out and buy cat food.

He looked down at the cat. "I don't know the first thing about cat food, or even if you prefer a certain brand. So, I hope you're flexible. I'll be back as soon as I can."

Grabbing his car keys, he headed out the door.

Abby set her brush down on the vanity.

You need to walk away from the mirror. It doesn't matter how you look, right? It's all about the cat food, nothing more.

She went into the kitchen and picked up the bag.

Then she set the bag back on the counter. Taking out a parchment bakery bag, she filled it with a half-dozen of the frosted baseball cookies. She would give these to him as an apology for how she'd behaved earlier.

Wait a minute... why do you suddenly feel the need to apologize? Wasn't he the one who was in the wrong?

Maybe he was. But as much as she hated to admit this, he'd made a valid point. There was no reason why they shouldn't be friends.

Before she could change her mind, she tossed the cookies into the bag with the cat food and left the kitchen. The door shut behind her, she set off in a brisk trot to his condo.

She was half-way up his driveway when he came out the front door, slamming it behind him. He appeared to be in a hurry. She watched as he went striding towards his car before he glanced over and right at her.

He skidded to a stop and for a few seconds, he didn't move. Then a slow grin began to spread over his face.

And this, for some odd reason, had her almost giddy with happiness. But then he ruined it.

He opened his mouth.

"Red... what are you doing here?" He nodded towards the bag she was carrying, his grin growing even bigger. "You do realize Halloween is in October and not July, don't you?"

Even in the darkness, she could see the teasing glint in his eyes as he began patting the pockets of his shorts. He moved closer, shaking his head. "It seems like I don't have any sweets on me right now, so I can't add to the stash you already have in your bag. But how would it be if I give you a compliment instead?"

His gaze leisurely traveling over her, his eyes finally came to rest on her face. He cleared his throat. "Because I'd have to say, you are by far the most gorgeous witch I've ever laid eyes on."

Her mouth dropped open. "Witch?"

He slowly shook his head. "*Ah...* there you go, getting all riled up. Come on, Red... pay attention. If you notice, I didn't only say witch, I said the most gorgeous witch. There's a difference."

He nodded. "A big difference."

He sent her a lazy smile. "And somehow, it appears you've already begun to work your witch-like magic, casting some kind of spell over me." His eyes holding hers, then he waited...

And for what seemed like forever, she could only stare at him.

She knew she should say something. After all, he did just give her a compliment.

A frown flickered across her face. At least she was pretty sure it was a compliment. But she had nothing. Her mind was too busy running in circles, unable to let go of what he said.

Most gorgeous witch? Already casting a spell over him? What exactly did he mean? What kind of spell?

Kevin smiled at the bewildered expression on her face. He knew she was trying to figure out what he meant by his comment. Hell, he wasn't even sure what made him say what he had. She had a way of making the words come flying out of his mouth before he even had time to think if this was what he wanted to say.

But casting a spell? Yeah, crazy as it sounds, it's the only thing that makes sense to you right now.

He reached over to tuck a strand of her hair behind her ear. "What's wrong, Red? Cat got your tongue?"

This comment finally gave Abby something to focus on.

This was the third time he'd called her Red. If there was even the chance of a friendship between them, he needed to start taking her more seriously.

Her intention to remind him of this, she frowned over at him. "I believe I asked you not to call me Red. It brings back bad memories of grade school."

This was the absolute truth. She still wondered if Bobby Jansen had forgiven her for the black eye she gave him. But when he refused to stop calling her carrot top, let's just say it turned out not to be the best of moves for either of them.

Kevin's response was to move even closer, his eyes searching her face so intently she was beginning to wish he was still wearing those sunglasses of his.

This man was having a strange effect on her, sending all of these unfamiliar but extremely pleasurable sensations sweeping through her. She was finding it hard to breathe, her heart beating almost out of control.

And the closer he got?

The more she wanted to walk right into his arms.

Kevin wanted to touch her again.

How he wanted this.

He reached over, slowly winding a strand of her hair around his finger. When what he really wanted to do was bury his hands in the shining mass of curls. If only to see if they felt as soft and silky as they looked.

But he was pretty sure this would scare her away.

He smiled.

Or more likely, she'll haul off and smack you.

He cleared his throat, his voice so soft, she had no choice but to take a step closer to hear him. "But you haven't even told me your name. So, until you do, I'll just have to keep calling you Red."

"My name..." And this is as far as she got.

After staring wide-eyed at him, she finally got it together, mortified when it came out in a breathless whisper, almost as if she trying to sound sexy. "My name is Abigail. My friends call me Abby."

As she said this, she realized she was leaning towards him. In fact, the thought popped into her mind this would be the perfect opportunity for that kiss she couldn't stop thinking about. A faint smile on her lips, she closed her eyes.

He took a few steps, then stopped. With only inches now between them, he was aware of little else but how much he wanted to pull her into his arms and capture her mouth in a kiss. Then he would kiss her again... and again.

Yes, he knew this could change everything, but he didn't care.

He didn't need to know her name. Hell, he didn't even care if she had a temper. Or—this made him smile—she was a terrible driver. He only knew there was something about her that made him want her more than he'd ever wanted any woman.

He searched her face. Was she feeling the same? Her heart beating out of control? Her mind in a spin?

God, he hoped so. Because he was in a place he'd never been before.

And it's one you never want to leave.

It was Kevin's silence that had Abby opening her eyes. He was gazing down at her, a faint smile on his lips. Thinking this was because he knew she'd wanted him to kiss her, she became flustered.

Then she got mad. Why had she thought delivering this bag of cat food would be a good idea? Instead, she was setting herself up for disappointment.

Remember? This guy is trouble.

Shifting the bag to her other arm, she stared out at the street.

Kevin didn't know what happened, only that she was mad about something. And whatever it was, he needed to fix it.

He cleared his throat. "So, Abby.... since this middle of the night visit implies we're now friends and I can call you this, what brings you here? And what is in this bag of yours? A special treat?"

Abby blinked.

The middle of the night? Oh, no... why didn't you check to see what time it was? He probably thinks you were waiting up for him.

She glanced down at the bag, then back up at him. She would give him the bag and then she would turn and walk away.

Yes, this is exactly what she was going to do.

She held out the bag . But she didn't walk away. If anything, she moved closer. "It's not really that late. And I hate to disappoint you, but only a cat would appreciate what's inside this bag. While you were out, a woman stopped by and asked me to give this to you. I believe it's cat food."

Then, she couldn't help it... she grinned. "I'm sorry, but I just can't picture you as a cat lover."

A devilish smile tweaking the corner of his mouth, he crossed his arms over his chest. She could only wait, nervous and eager at the same time.

His response came in a slow drawl. "*Hmm...* so you've decided I'm not a cat lover. This has me wondering what kind of lover you think I might be? Passionate? Tender? *Ah...* or maybe the most important kind of all... a most satisfying one?"

He paused to give her a slow smile. "Of course, you do know there's always the option of choosing all three."

What? How in the world are you supposed to answer that?

Now beyond flustered, she shoved the bag right at him before she responded. "I assure you I have no idea what the answer would be to such a ridiculous question. Nor do I care. In fact, everything you just said makes me believe it might be in my best interest to leave."

Holding the bag, he knew he should try to wipe the grin off his face, but he couldn't. He loved teasing her. She looked so damn beautiful, her cheeks flushed and her eyes wide and bewildered.

But, what's this? She was planning to leave?

This had him moving a little closer, his goal to sound as desperate as he could. "Wait... do you know anything about cats? If you do, I could use your help. Because even though this is only temporary, I certainly don't want to be remembered as the guy who mistreated someone's pet while I was here."

What? He wasn't planning on staying? Why? And where was he going?

She opened her mouth to ask, but then shut it. As much as she'd like to know, it really wasn't any of her business.

She nodded towards the bag. "I believe, besides the cat food, there are also instructions from the owner. So, you should be just fine."

He looked into the bag and pulled out the parchment bag of cookies. After opening the bag and peering inside, he lifted his head, a strange expression on his face.

She felt obligated to explain. "Those are from me. Sort of like a peace offering because of how I acted this morning."

For a few moments, he was quiet. Then darn if he didn't aim that teasing smile at her again. "Baseball cookies for me? Did you make them?"

At her nod, his smile grew. In fact, he was now grinning from ear to ear. "*Hmm...* if I remember correctly, you informed me I'd never be so lucky to have any baked goods coming from you. It would never happen, you said." He laughed. "Well, what do you know, it looks like I just got lucky."

She closed her eyes.

Oh, no... you did say that, didn't you?

But wait a minute, why should this even matter? What was important was her attempt to be nice. And now he was throwing it back in her face?

She jammed her hands in her pockets. She couldn't win with this guy. How was it he could remember every single thing she said? This might be a big problem down the road.

Umm... there will be no down the road with this guy. Not a chance. So, don't even think about it.

She gave a huffy sigh. "I thought it was a nice gesture on my part. Weren't you the one who said we should try to be friends? Well, this was my try. It's not like I'm trying to impress you or something."

Chester's earlier comment about women coming out of the wood work on the hunt for their own personal sports star popped into his head.

He frowned. This couldn't be what was happening, was it? Had she somehow found out who he was?

He peered over at her. Her expression didn't come across as a woman who was trying to impress him.

No, if anything, she looked angry.

Suddenly, he was exhausted. Maybe it was the events of the last week catching up with him. Or his body's way of letting him know he needed to get some sleep, so he'd be sharp for tomorrow.

After all, it's going to be your major league debut.

He only knew he needed time to think. Before he said something he didn't mean. Or did something he had no business doing.

Abby was now halfway down the driveway. Her voice floating back to him was so soft, he almost couldn't hear her. "Good luck with your roommate. I'm sure the two of you will figure it out."

After a slight pause, she turned and began walking faster.

This is when he noticed she was limping, favoring her one ankle.

He groaned, closing his eyes.

You are such an idiot. You didn't even ask her about that. Thank God you didn't accuse her of trying to bribe you with cookies. Not good, not good at all...

He called out to her. "Hey..."

She came to a stop, but didn't turn around.

And he couldn't believe how much he wanted this. So he could explain.

Though he wasn't quite sure of how to go about this. He certainly couldn't ask her if she was only interested in him because of who he was.

Yeah, that wouldn't go over very well, would it? You can thank Chester for planting this doubt in your mind.

Searching his mind for something to say, he decided to begin by thanking her for bringing over the cat food. And the cookies.

He took a few steps closer.

"Thanks for the cookies. And for delivering the cat food."

She nodded. But she still didn't turn around.

Desperation grabbing hold of him, he spoke louder. "Maybe we'll see each other around?"

She gave a slight shrug.

Geeeez... this wasn't very promising, was it?

He took a few more steps "Goodnight Abby. And just so you know, I'm Kevin."

This was when she finally turned to face him, her eyes searching his face before she spoke. "Goodnight, Kevin. I hope you enjoy the cookies."

Then she smiled.

His world came to a standstill, the sound of his name on her lips and her smile hitting him hard and all at once. Almost as if the earth had shifted, settling more solidly under his feet.

Afraid to break the spell, he didn't move, watching in a trance as she turned and walk away.

He wasn't sure why, only that it was important he stay where he was until she reached her condo. But even when that happened, he stayed where he was.

Nor did he move after she closed her door or when he saw a light go on.

It was only when she appeared in the window, he knew this was why he had waited.

He smiled, and lifting his hand in a wave, he held his breath.

She waved back, and then she was gone.

A big grin on his face, he was whistling as he went inside to feed Bella.

Abby closed the door and, leaning against it, she gazed down at her hands. They were trembling.

Oh my, what have you done? Because look at what he's done to you.

She went into the kitchen and looked out the window.

Her breath caught in her throat.

Still holding the bag, and standing where she'd left him, he waved.

Her heart hammering in her chest, she waved back. Then she ducked away from the window.

In a daze, she bagged the finished baseball cookies and layered them in a bakery box. She was about to add another cookie to the box when she paused, staring off into space. She didn't understand Kevin's reaction to the cookies she gave him. It wasn't as if she gave him something personal.

Did he have something against baseball? Recalling all the sports gear in the trunk of his car, she could probably rule that out.

Or maybe he didn't like cookies?

She laughed. If this was true, she couldn't imagine him as a friend.

A horrified look came over her face. What if he was one of these crazy health fanatics who didn't believe in sugar?

She frowned, and picking up the last cookie, she shoved it in a bag so hard she almost broke it in half.

Then she smiled.

If he didn't like cookies? She was pretty confident she could change his mind. Wasn't she known for having the best cookies in this part of town? She'd be willing to bet, before he even knew what hit him, she'd have him begging for one of her cookies.

Even after she put the box of cookies in the pantry and cleaned up the kitchen, she was still smiling.

Yeah, you have nothing to worry about.

Abby's plan had been to read the book she had recently checked out from the library. There was nothing like a little dip into the world of romance to lift a girl's spirits.

But when she realized she was reading the same sentence over and over, she closed the book and turned out the light.

Settled under the blankets, she stared into the darkness. She couldn't stop thinking about the one nagging bit of information that overshadowed everything.

Kevin said he wasn't planning on sticking around.

CHAPTER 6

$\mathcal{A}$bby woke to a long line of messages on her cell phone. And all of them were from Sophie.

She groaned. She didn't want to talk to Sophie. No doubt she was calling to fill her in on Peter and Lucinda's wedding.

Sophie had been one of her closest friends since junior high. When the whole mess with Peter and Lucinda happened, Sophie had vowed she would never talk to Lucinda again. But seeing they were cousins, this proved to be impossible. And when Lucinda asked Sophie to be in her wedding, it was Abby who convinced her it was the right thing to do. She only had one request, and this was she didn't want to hear about a single detail.

Until now, Sophie had honored her request. But these seven messages were a sign she had finally cracked.

She went into the kitchen and turned on the coffeemaker. Only after she took Poppy out and had her breakfast would she read Sophie's messages.

Abby was sitting at the kitchen island, flipping through the pages of her order book. With only one big order at the end of July, she was worried. If she didn't get any last-minute orders by the end of the week, she would hardly have enough money to pay her expenses for the month. This included the extra money she made catering part time at The Regency.

Her monthly loan payment for her kitchen remodel was also due, a necessary undertaking when she expanded her business.

She needed a break.

A really big break.

Or better yet, a miracle.

She had just closed the order book when her doorbell rang. This brought Poppy out of her bed and in a barking frenzy as she went charging down the hall to the door. A hunch it was Sophie, Abby followed behind at a much slower pace.

She opened the door.

Madly typing on her phone, Sophie gave her a vague smile before she slipped past her and headed straight for the kitchen. After a searching glance around the room, she turned to Abby, a disappointed look on her face.

"What? No cookies? Oh Abby, I really need something sweet after all the excitement and drama that's been going on." Then she spotted the glass cake stand on the counter with a plate of cookies in full view. "*Ah ha*… are these for the taking?"

Abby took a coffee mug out of the cupboard and, filling it with coffee, she placed it on the island. "Go for it. And here's some coffee. Enjoy." She was smiling at Sophie's excitement.

See, this is proof you're on to something with your cookies. Take that, Mr. Sports Car. But wait, it's Kevin now, remember?

Sitting at the island, Sophie bit into a cookie, a look of complete bliss on her face. After Abby poured coffee for herself, they sat in silence as Sophie devoured the cookie. Then she went over to get another one, which she also finished.

After she licked her fingers and gave a satisfied sigh, she grinned over at Abby. "You make the best cookies. You really should be famous. The smartest thing you ever did was quit your management position at the party center and start up your own business."

She rested her arms on the counter and gazed over at Abby. "Okay, come on… spill. What part did you play in what happened?"

Abby shrugged. "I don't know what you're talking about. I haven't even read your messages yet. From the number you sent, I decided to fortify myself with coffee first."

Sophie's mouth dropped wide open. "You didn't read my messages? Are you serious? Abby, this is big news. Peter and Lucinda called off the wedding. It was the most bizarre thing ever! Even more than what happened with you and Peter. And now they can't find him. It's almost as though he disappeared off the face of the earth!"

Shocked, Abby stared at her.

Evidently, Peter hadn't been kidding when he told her he thought he was making a mistake?

Then she was hit with a horrible thought.

What if they try to put the blame on you? Everyone saw you talking to him yesterday.

She needed to act as far removed from this as possible, especially with Sophie. It was a well-known fact among their friends any information shared with Sophie was free game. She couldn't keep anything to herself for the life of her.

She felt like her words were coming from someone else. "I don't understand. What do you mean, he disappeared?"

Almost unable to sit still, Sophie was in her element. "Abby, I swear it was like we were all in a movie. There we were, minding our own business and waiting for someone to come and tell us it was time to line up to go down the aisle. Instead, Lucinda's dad walks into the room, his face all pale and sick looking. Holding an envelope in his fingers like it was poison, he drops it in her lap. She rips it open, reads it and Bam! She falls to the floor in a dead faint."

From this point on, Abby could only nod as Sophie's voice continued to drone on with each sordid detail.

She, of all people, knew how awful this must have been for Lucinda. After all, she had been there. At the time, she'd thought nothing could be worse than having your perfect wedding suddenly taken away from you. In the weeks that followed, she had walked around in a fog, wondering what she had done wrong. It was only a few months ago she'd finally accepted this had been a blessing in disguise.

And now this happens?

Sophie was shaking her arm. "Abby! Are you even listening to me? Because you should know the rumors going around have you and Peter running off together. Of course, I didn't believe this for a second. But when you didn't answer my texts, I'll admit I was a little worried."

Abby groaned, putting her head down in her hands. "For once and for all, Peter and I are done. Over. Finished. I have no desire to get back together with him. Never. Never. *Never.*"

She sighed. "The rumors probably started when everyone saw us talking to each other yesterday."

Sophie peered over at her. "I believe you. And even though there does seem to be a pattern going on with Peter, I find it hard to put all the blame on him." She shook her head. "Well, almost… because it was a terrible thing he did. But the last few weeks with Lucinda have been a nightmare. I could tell you stories…"

When Abby lifted her head, a warning expression on her face, Sophie held up her hands. "I get it. You don't want to hear it. And I don't blame you." Then she sighed, shaking her head. "What a mess."

Then she pushed away from the counter, loaded her cup into the dishwasher, and headed for the door. But this was typical Sophie. She did everything fast, always on the move to the next adventure, the next breaking story.

When she turned to find Abby right behind her, she gave her a big hug. "I need to go, since I promised Aunt Emily I would help her figure out what to do with all the wedding gifts. I can't even imagine how she must feel after watching her daughter get jilted."

She ran to her car, and after a beep of her horn, she drove away.

On her way back to the kitchen, Abby stopped to pick up Poppy, seeking her comforting warmth. As she gazed around the kitchen, filled with the morning sunshine, she was thankful for the life she had.

This latest development only enforced her belief she didn't need a man in her life.

She was more than fine on her own.

And the next time she ran into Kevin, she was going to tell him this.

On this sultry Sunday afternoon, the humidity hung over the stadium like a wet blanket. There wasn't even the hint of a breeze coming off the lake.

The crowd, who until now had bordered on the state of lethargy, had snapped to attention. This brought the noise level in the stadium to the loudest it had been during the entire game.

With one swing of the bat, everything could change.

It was the bottom of the ninth and Cleveland was trailing Boston by one run.

With already two outs in the inning, Alex had sent a bat-shattering ground ball out to center field. This went flying right past the diving center fielder, allowing Alex to slide in safe at second base.

Before the inning had started, Kevin received the sign he would be up after Alex, something he'd been waiting for throughout the game. Off to the side and taking practice swings during Alex's at bat, he kept reminding himself to stay as calm and focused as he could.

He didn't want to screw up his debut in his first major league game.

The first pitch he received almost hit him. Between this and the deafening noise of the crowd, it was taking every ounce of concentration he could muster. At the same time, he was filled with a thrill he had never felt before.

This is the real thing. They're cheering for you.

And he'd be damned if he let them down.

He swung at the next pitch, giving it all he had. The ball went sailing out into left field and hit the base of the wall before it careened back onto the field.

His adrenalin in high gear, he flew like a bat out of hell, rounding first base and sliding into second, just barely escaping the tag. Alex, who was known for his incredible speed, beat the throw to home plate with ease.

It was now a whole new ballgame.

Chester was up next. One swing of his bat turned out to be the game winning two-run home run, and the game was theirs.

The exuberant welcome he and Chester received at home plate was something he knew he would never forget. Only after his interview with the local news reporter and the bedlam that carried over into the locker room had settled down, he congratulated Chester, one on one.

The guy might be a little strange, but Kevin had to give him a lot of credit. He was as good of a clutch player as they come.

It was a good day at the ballpark.

Kevin had a plan.

He didn't know if he'd be able to carry it off, but he was going to give it his best shot.

After he called in an order for a pizza from a place Alex recommended, he left the clubhouse for his drive home. Once he'd picked up the pizza, he had one other stop to make. This was a little wine shop he'd recently noticed near his condo.

Mission accomplished, he was feeling pretty upbeat about how things were progressing when he drove past Abby's condo. He glanced over to see she was sitting out on the front steps, holding a little dog on her lap. It was the same dog he had seen her walking late last night.

Just thinking about this got him all riled up again. What was she thinking? He'd almost gone charging outside to ask her why the hell she was out walking alone and so late at night.

Instead, he had kept an eye on her until she was back in her condo, the door shut behind her.

You only hope she locked it.

It was becoming very clear she needed someone to look after her.

And with the way he'd over-reacted, he was seriously wondering if he was that someone.

Abby was taking a break, with Poppy asleep on her lap.

She had been baking and frosting cookies for the past five hours. In desperate need of some fresh air, she decided to sit on the front steps while she waited for the frosting to set on the cookies.

The humidity plaguing the city over the past few days had finally lifted, a welcome change on this warm summer evening. Raising her face up to the sky, she closed her eyes as a gentle breeze ruffled the damp tendrils of hair framing her face.

At the familiar rumble of a car engine, she lowered her head, watching through her lashes as Kevin drove by. She hoped he wasn't under the impression she'd been sitting here all day, hoping he'd drive by.

Yes, she'd admit she'd noticed his car had been gone all day. And yes, she was a little curious about where he was. Maybe he'd decided to do a little sightseeing? Or he had friends or family living in the area?

Then there was the cat. Was he taking good care of it? Had he remembered to feed it?

She closed her eyes, shaking her head.

She was in big trouble.

These excuses were her way of ignoring the obvious.

She was dreaming about a man that would never be hers.

She knew it was a long shot. He was the kind of man who could have any woman he wanted. A man, Sophie would be so quick to point out, he was just another player, enjoying the chase, but not ready to settle.

But for some reason, she couldn't shake the feeling the chemisty between them was real. He was as drawn to her as she was to him.

But right now, there were cookies to be finished. The frosting had surely set by now. Which meant she should be inside bagging them.

She sent a wistful glance over at Kevin's condo. He was out of his car, holding a pizza box in one hand and a bottle of wine in the other.

Then she watched as he went striding down his driveway and headed in her direction.

Oh, no... this can't be happening...

After her baking marathon, she couldn't even imagine what a mess she was. She looked down at her fingers, stained from the red and blue food coloring she'd used to tint the frosting for the flag cookies she'd made. She wouldn't be surprised if there were a few streaks of this on her face, and maybe even in her hair.

But none of this mattered as he was now standing right in front of her.

She glanced up at him. This is when she realized this was the first time she could see his eyes. A deep blue, they were studying her with an intensity that sent the blush rising in her cheeks. Suddenly shy, she looked away.

He smiled. He didn't know why, but her expression was like a little kid who had been caught raiding the cookie jar. Maybe it was the freckles, highlighted by her flushed cheeks. Or it could also be what looked like streaks of red and blue paint in the wispy curls framing her face.

He wasn't sure… he only knew she looked adorable.

He shifted the pizza box more comfortably on his arm.

"Hi."

Her blush deepened.

"Hi."

He smiled, taking a step closer. "I stopped on the way home and picked up this pizza and a bottle of wine. If you haven't had dinner yet, I wonder if you'd like to share it with me. It's been a great day, and I thought I'd ask you to celebrate with me."

He wasn't going to tell her, even with all the backslapping and high fives in celebration after the game, he couldn't stop thinking how nice it would have been to have her there to share his first major league game.

That he'd even thought this had blown his mind.

This was when he decided he had to see her. He needed to find out if there was something going on between them. Or instead, his imagination was working overtime. Because as it stood now, she was all he could think about.

And this would be almost all the time.

Last night, she'd even made an appearance in his dreams.

The memory of this had him sending her another smile. "So? Are you interested?"

Abby nodded. If he had been standing there with a box of animal crackers and a couple of juice boxes, she still would have nodded. She tilted her head, smiling up at him. "And what happened that made your day so great?"

He searched her face, trying to see if she was as clueless as she appeared and had no idea of who he was.

Hmmm.... If she wasn't, she's a damn good actress.

He grinned. "Let's just say my team won."

And just like that, her expression changed. Her eyes darkening with anger, she tightened her hold on Poppy as she scrambled to her feet.

You should have trusted your intuition with this guy. When are you going to learn?

She backed away, glaring at him. "I should've known you were too good to be true. But no, you're like every other guy out there. When are you going to realize it's all going to catch up to you in the end? Instead, you keep betting, raising the stakes even higher until someone gets hurt."

She hugged Poppy even closer, her voice choked with emotion. "And I refuse to ever be that person again."

Kevin was in shock.

Betting? Someone always get hurts? What is she talking about?

Mouth agape, he tried to think of what to say. At the same time, it popped into his mind this was proof she had no idea who he was. She wouldn't have thrown all this at him if she did.

As Abby waited for him to say something, she didn't even notice she had started to cry, a tear slipping down her cheek.

But Kevin did. He groaned. This was the second time he'd been the cause of her to tears and it was just about killing him.

He needed to figure out how to stop this.

His silence had her wildly searching for the doorknob. After she finally opened the door, she sent him a backward glance. "As you can see, you've picked the wrong person to celebrate with. So, if you'll excuse me…"

He was up the stairs in a second. "Hey, hold on there. You just can't leave like this."

When she went marching inside, he didn't even stop to think if it was okay to follow her, he just did. Down the hall and into the kitchen, he trailed right behind her. The whole time, he was searching his brain, trying to figure out what had set her off. And what he could do to make things right.

He only knew he wasn't going to let her go without giving him the chance to defend himself.

Abby dropped Poppy in her puppy bed, where she landed with a disgruntled yelp.

Then, ignoring Kevin, she went storming over to the counter and began gathering up bowls and utensils, tossing them around with a great deal of banging and clattering.

Kevin watched this for a few moments before he set the pizza and wine on the kitchen table.

Curious, he glanced around the room. When he saw the flag cookies Abby had finished, lined up on the island countertop, he moved closer to get a better look. Amazed at the detail she'd put in each cookie, he glanced over to where she was loading the dishwasher, throwing the dishes in at an almost frightening pace.

He cleared his throat. "I see you've made more cookies. A heck of a lot more. And each one looks perfect, almost like a miniature work of art. Not only that, I know how great they taste. I'm almost embarrassed at how I polished off those cookies you gave me in one sitting, they were that good."

He smiled. "Yes, I was a very happy man."

She glanced over at him, to then look away. But not before he saw a smile flicker across her face.

Encouraged, he pushed on. "Let me take a wild guess and assume this is a business you're running?"

She merely nodded, her attention now riveted on the counter she was scrubbing.

After he watched her for a few seconds, he moved until he was only inches away. Gently removing the sponge from her hand and tossing it into the sink, he leaned against the counter, gazing down at her. "Abby, what's going on here? What are you so mad about?"

When she didn't answer, he let out a long sigh. "I just want to share a bottle of wine and a pizza with you. In fact, this was about the only thing I've been able to think about over the past few hours."

Here he stopped to smile at her. "Spending time with you, that is, not the pizza and wine."

Encouraged when this brought on another smile, brief though it was, he continued. "But here we are, one of us very angry and one of us very confused. And hungry. Maybe more like starving."

Abby couldn't look at him. She was still upset, but now she was even more embarrassed. She honestly didn't know why she had reacted so strongly. She was surprised he hadn't left, while at the same time, she couldn't believe how relieved she was he hadn't.

It was what he said, his words reaching out to nudge her heart and giving her a reason to hope.

He wants to spend time with you. In fact, he said it was all he'd been able to think about.

She glanced up at him to see he was watching her. He raised an eyebrow, his smile hesitant.

Then make the effort. Meet him halfway.

Before she could change her mind, she opened a drawer and pulled out a corkscrew. She handed it to him. "Here, you're in charge of the wine. I'll get the glasses and napkins."

Her smile was shy. "I'm hungry, too."

CHAPTER 7

Kevin poured the wine remaining into their glasses.

After he threw out the empty wine bottle and pizza box, he returned to his seat at the table.

As Abby loaded their plates and silverware into the dishwasher, he studied her, a thoughtful expression on his face.

Until now, he'd kept their conversation casual. He could see she was trying so hard to avoid talking about what they really should be talking about.

But they needed to talk about it. Okay, maybe it was more like he needed to talk about it. It was suddenly very important to him she knew he was not a member of this group she disliked with such a passion.

He wanted her to see him for who he was. A nice guy and one who really liked her. In fact, with each passing minute, she was tugging at his heartstrings, pulling him in even further.

Yep, you're falling fast.

Yes, he had only just met her. And yes, it was bad timing, his career just starting to take off and all. But he was okay with this.

Even thinking about this made him smile.

She turned to see he was watching her, a smile on his face. She sent him a tentative smile in return. "A penny for your thoughts?"

Ah, here's your perfect opportunity. Don't blow it.

He slid her wine glass towards her. "Here, come sit with me."

An anxious look flitting across her face, instead she took a plate out of the cupboard. After filling it with cookies, she sat across from him and, avoiding his gaze, pushed the plate towards him.

"Cookie?"

It was killing him to see her like this, as if she was afraid of him. He needed to remedy this.

He gave her a warm smile. "*Ah*, Abby… I love your cookies. And I'll never turn down the chance to have one. But right now, we need to talk."

She closed her eyes, a soft sigh coming from her.

His voice was so soft. "Abby, look at me."

After she finally opened her eyes, he smiled at her again. "If we're going to be friends, we need to talk about what happened earlier, why you became so upset. And what made you feel this way."

She took a small sip of wine, her gaze focused on the glass as she spoke. "Everything is always about money, isn't it? Especially with professional sports. Look at how much baseball players make. It's a ridiculous amount. It makes you wonder if they even care about playing the game, or what the outcome is."

Lifting her head, her eyes met his. "And if the average person wants to get in on all of this money to be made, they can bet on the games. And with betting, most people lose more than they win… money, their job, self-respect and even the people who love you."

Her voice fell to a whisper. "And nothing is ever the same again."

She shrugged. "You said your team won. If that makes you happy, then so be it. But don't expect me to be happy for you." She shrugged her shoulders. "Because I can't."

In the silence that followed, he studied her. From what she told him, she was speaking from experience. And gambling was involved.

Was it a boyfriend? Someone in her family? Whoever it was and whatever happened, the experience had affected her deeply.

He chose his words carefully. "Ah, Abby… I don't think all professional athletes are as bad as you're making them out to be. For most, making it to the big leagues is like a dream come true. It's their passion for the game that drives them. Sure, the money is nice, but it's almost more of a bonus. And the betting?" He shook his head. "You're right, it can get out of hand. But I'm not sure how it can be stopped. The possibility of winning all that money is too tempting and easy. Of course, this is only when luck is on your side."

He shrugged. "I don't bet. I was taught if there's something I want, there is no shortcut. Instead, I put my mind to it and work hard. And if it's meant to be, I have the satisfaction of knowing I earned it, fair and square."

When this was greeted with silence, he slid his hand across the table until their fingertips touched. When she didn't move her hand, he reached to link their fingers together.

"Abby, tell me. What happened?"

When she shook her head, he got up and, coming around the table, took her hands to pull her up from her chair and into his arms.

As he held her, his hands moving in a gentle caress over her back, he couldn't help but notice how perfectly she fit in his arms, almost as if this was where she was meant to be. Impulsively pressing a kiss in her hair, he smiled when he felt her slowly relax against him.

Abby closed her eyes, everything in her craving the comfort he was offering. The luxury of being able to sink into his embrace felt so good, so right. And so, *so* much better than she'd imagined it would be.

He pulled back to look into her eyes. "You don't have to tell me now, but if you ever want to talk, I'm here for you. Okay?"

She nodded, lifting her face to kiss him on the cheek. When she thought about this later, she didn't know why she had acted so impulsively.

It just happened.

In one swift move, he turned his head, capturing her mouth in a slow, lingering kiss. When she leaned into him with a soft sigh, he pulled her even closer, lifting her higher against him.

And, as when he had first laid eyes on her and imagined a kiss such as this, he didn't want it to end

He wanted more.

Starting with her hair. He wanted to run his hands through her beautiful hair.

As he pulled at her hair tie, sending the soft curls cascading over her shoulders, something came flying at his legs. Almost thrown off balance, this abrupt move brought a startled gasp from Abby. Pushing away from him, she stumbled back into the table, a dazed expression on her face.

Their breath coming hard, they stared at each other.

The only thing Kevin could think about was how beautiful she looked. Her hair framing her face in a glorious riot of curls, her cheeks were flushed, bringing out those freckles he found so unbelievably sexy. While her eyes were deep pools of green, wide with what he sincerely hoped was desire.

While Abby was beside herself. Her intuition had been right. This man was dangerous. Why else would she be clutching the edge of the table to keep from throwing herself right back into his arms?

She pushed back the hair falling in her face, her intending to pull it back into a ponytail. But her hair tie was gone. After searching the floor around them, she sent a glance over at Kevin. Did he have it?

A bemused smile on his face, he held it out to her. That he could manage this with the way his mind was careening almost out of control, scrambling to come up with a way to get her back into his arms, was pretty close to a miracle.

The silence was broken by a sharp bark.

They both looked down to see Poppy sitting on the floor at their feet. Her tail wagging and her eyes darting back and forth between them, it was obvious she hadn't a clue of what she had interrupted.

There was only one thing she did know, and this was she needed to go out.

Now.

Abby was fumbling with the hair tie, but her hair wasn't co-operating. It also didn't help her hands were shaking. A smile tweaking the corner of his mouth, Kevin finally took the tie from her and stuffed it in his pocket.

He shook his head. "Leave it. I don't think you realize how beautiful you are when you let your hair go free. You should never pull it back."

Well… how could she even think of arguing with a comment like that?

She sent him a nervous smile before she darted over to get Poppy's leash from where it was hanging by the door. After she hooked it to the little dog's collar, she turned to see Kevin was still watching her.

He was still smiling, but there was something different in his gaze —an intensity that sent a shiver racing through her from her head to her toes.

She wanted to drop Poppy's leash, go right back into his arms and ask him to kiss her again. If only to find out if it felt the same the second time around. Or maybe even a third…

Instead, she opened her mouth, a sound coming out resembling a faint croak. Her face turning an even brighter shade of red, she cleared her throat and gave it a second shot. "Would you like to join us? It's not all that exciting, but it's a beautiful evening. After all, a little exercise never hurt anyone."

He grinned. It was the teasing grin she was beginning to know a little too well. Just thinking of what he might be planning to say, she braced herself.

One eyebrow raised, his expression was amused. "*Hmm…* you think we need exercise?"

He sauntered over to her, and cupping her chin in his hand, his eyes held hers. "In that case, I'd much rather continue where we left off only minutes ago. Because I'm pretty sure kissing is considered an excellent form of exercise. And a most pleasurable one, at that."

His gaze roamed over her face before stopping to linger on her mouth. "But I can wait. For now, I'll settle for this walk you're offering."

Gently releasing her chin, he stepped back and waved his hand towards the door. "After you..."

Her lips still parted in an invitation for another kiss, she couldn't seem to move.

"Abby?"

The amused tone of his voice finally snapped her out of her paralyzed state. After almost tripping over Poppy in her haste to get out the door, she took off in a brisk walk.

He was chuckling as he caught up to her and grabbed her hand. "Hey, hey... not so fast. It's not every night I get to take a romantic walk with a beautiful woman. So, I want to take my time to enjoy it. Especially when, for once, the woman in question isn't angry at me."

She sent him a sideways glance before she laughed. "I think the wine has addled your brain. Because taking a dog for a walk is not what I'd consider romantic. And I'm far from beautiful. Also, if I remember correctly, you're the one who determined the color of my hair gives me permission to occasionally be bad tempered."

He came to a halt, pulling her into his arms. "*Ah...* but you are beautiful. You're *so* beautiful. And let's forget about the bad temper bit for now. Instead, I think we should test out this other trait you've been rumored to possess."

His lips brushing over hers, his voice was a husky whisper. "You know, the passionate one."

When his mouth captured hers in another kiss, Abby fell right into it. In fact, the kiss was so spectacular, it was almost as though fireworks lit up the sky around them.

His mouth abruptly leaving hers, he pulled away, scanning the surrounding neighborhood.

Wow, did he feel it too?

But then he spoke, his voice incredulous. "What the hell? Did someone just take a photo of us?"

Abby was confused.

Who would do that? And why? She put her hand on his arm. "Kevin, what's going on? Why would someone take a picture of us?"

As if he suddenly remembered she was there, he glanced down at her, a preoccupied look on his face. Then he smiled. "Nah... it was probably some kids fooling around, trying to get a rise out of us. But, since Poppy accomplished what she came out here for, we might as well head back."

He took her arm and turned them back towards her condo.

So much for romance, it seems.

Kevin hoped the explanation he gave Abby was what happened. But he suspected it wasn't.

Damn...

If this is what it meant to be in the public eye, he wanted no part of it.

Then there was Abby... a photo of them in a passionate embrace on social media, or in some gossip magazine, was not how he wanted her to find out who he was.

He knew he should tell her this now, but after her emotional outburst earlier, he needed time to think about the best way to go about it.

He couldn't goof this up.

Because now, after having kissed her?

There was no doubt in his mind what they had was as real as you could get.

Abby was trying to figure out why Kevin was acting so strange. She also had the feeling he knew more than he was telling her.

Was he involved in something secretive? A government agent of some kind? Or heaven forbid, was he part of some illegal crime group?

She stole a quick glance at him.

He didn't look like a criminal. But then again, he did drive a very expensive car.

She sighed. Was it too much to ask for a man who was normal?

Even though she knew as well as anyone else, normal was over-rated.

After Abby unlocked her front door, she turned to find Kevin was again scanning the area around them. After one more searching glance, he leaned in to place a chaste kiss to her cheek.

Her reaction was not what he expected… she giggled.

He chuckled, pulling her against him. "*Ah…* I'm sorry. I guess I'm still kind of spooked from that flash." Gently brushing the hair back from her face, he hesitated a few moments before he spoke. "Can I ask you to do something for me?"

Tell him anything. Seriously, you know you'd do just about anything.

When she nodded, he smiled. "There's a Cleveland baseball game tomorrow. It's a home game. I want you to come to the game."

As he said this, he was slowly tracing her lips with his finger. This had her melting in his arms, her response a breathless whisper. "With you?"

His lips now taking the place of his finger, his answer against her mouth was also a whisper. "Yes, I'll be there. But since there's some-where I need to be before the game starts, I'll arrange for someone to come by and pick you up. Okay?"

When she nodded, his mouth took possession of hers. It was nothing at all like the kiss he'd just planted on her cheek.

No, this kiss was wonderful.

His hand resting below her ear, his thumb caressed her cheek as he leisurely explored her mouth before he deepened the kiss. She heard herself sigh into his mouth as he pulled her even closer, their hearts beating as one.

When he finally released her, almost reverently running his fingers through her hair, his voice was rough.

"On that note, I think it might be best if I left."

He slowly backed away, his eyes never leaving hers.

And even after he turned to start down the stairs, she continued to watch him, a dazed smile on her face.

He turned. "Do you have your phone? I'll need your number so I can let you know what time a car will come for you tomorrow."

She pulled her phone out of her pocket and held it out to him. After he entered his number in her phone, he headed back down the steps, only to turn back once more. "One more thing... I saw you out late last night walking Poppy. For the sake of my nerves, can you please not do this? Or at least call me before you do? Having just met you, I don't want to lose you."

This sent her heart almost leaping right out of her chest.

It's official. You don't have a chance.

She watched as he slowed his steps. It appeared he had something more to add.

"Sweet dreams, sugar."

With that, he turned to sprint the short distance to his condo, leaving her staring after him.

Sugar?

Kevin was leaning against the counter. Holding a can of cat food in his hand, Bella's mournful meows were coming at him, each one louder than the last. Planted at his feet, she wasn't the least bit shy in letting him know her irritation of being served at such a late hour.

Her cries disrupting his distracted state, he blinked. He glanced down at her. "Hey, give me a break. You're lucky I'm even here. God knows I don't want to be."

No... he wanted to be with Abby. His mind was flooded with everything about her... the heady scent of her perfume, the silkiness of her hair as it flowed through his fingers, and the softness of her under his hands as he held her against him.

Then there was the sweet, intoxicating taste of her kiss, her lips soft and eager against his.

He groaned.

A man could become addicted to her kiss alone.

He slapped the cat food into the dish and plunked it down on the floor. He watched as Bella strolled over to check it out. She gave one last meow, which he liked to think was her way of thanking him, and daintily began to eat.

After shaking his head at this dramatic display, he headed down the hall for the bedroom.

He threw himself down on the bed. Propped up against the pillows, he began scrolling through his phone messages. He was amazed at how many people had taken the time to congratulate him on his major league debut.

His favorite text was from Katy.

> You will always be my favorite All Star, Uncle Kevin! I can't wait to finally meet you!

Along with her message, she had sent a photo of her one-month old baby daughter Olivia, a tiny smile on her face as she slept.

He couldn't wait to meet her either. And who knew? Maybe one day she would be watching him play in an honest-to-goodness All Star Game.

An idea popped into his head. After scanning through his list of contacts, he typed out a message and sent it off. He also put in a call for Abby's ride to the game tomorrow. Now he only needed to text Abby.

A few minutes later, he was still staring down at his phone.

What's your problem? Just tell her the time. Isn't that enough?

No, for some reason, and he wasn't quite sure why, it wasn't.

He only knew he wanted the message to be perfect.

Finally, he typed it out.

> Pizza: Fifteen bucks. Wine: Twenty bucks. Kissing you: Priceless. The driver will pick you up at noon. I told him you would prefer he didn't drive too fast.

The message sent, he put his phone on the nightstand. After settling back against the pillows, he closed his eyes.

He was almost asleep when his phone beeped. Diving across the bed and grabbing it off the nightstand, he saw it was a text from Abby. Before he even started to read it, he was smiling.

> Definitely priceless. Thank you. You know how I feel about fast drivers. Until tomorrow.

The phone back on the nightstand and a smile still on his face, he fell right to sleep.

CHAPTER 8

They were shooting at her, the constant gunfire sending flashes of light everywhere. She was trying to get to Kevin, but when she came close, he disappeared into thin air. As the explosions intensified, she huddled even closer to the ground, her hands over her ears. This was then she realized she'd never survive without his help.

Abby shot straight up in bed, the quilt clutched to her face. Her skin was damp with perspiration, her heart pounding a mile a minute.

Her gaze darted around the bedroom. She was in her bedroom. She was fine. It was only another dream. Burrowing her face in the quilt, she let out a long, shaky sigh.

The moment her head hit the pillow last night, she'd gone from one dream to the next. With Kevin making an appearance in every single dream. To then disappear.

Dreams about criminals and guns going off. And running. She wasn't sure who or what she'd been running from, but this was probably for the best, since she never seemed to get anywhere.

She was exhausted.

And she wanted the noise to stop.

This was when she realized the noise she heard wasn't part of her dream. Someone was actually pounding on her front door. Her whole body protesting the move, she kicked her way out of the tangled sheets and, pushing her hair out of her face, she stumbled down the hall.

Squinting, she peered through the peephole in the front door.

She groaned.

Oh, Lord help you... it's Sophie.

Her eyes closed, she rested her forehead against the door. She considered not opening the door, but knew this wouldn't be a good idea. She wouldn't put it past Sophie to call the police. Or more likely, the fire department, considering her known fixation with these fire-fighting heroes.

She opened the door.

Her ear to the door, Sophie almost tumbled into the foyer. Once she regained her balance, she crossed her arms over her chest and gave Abby a long, hard look.

"It's a good thing you opened your door. I was going to give you five more minutes before I called the police. After I saw that photo online, I certainly wasn't going to take any chances."

She shook her head. "You have a heck of a lot of explaining to do."

With that being said, she went marching down the hall and into the kitchen. With Abby following more slowly behind her, still half asleep and totally confused.

What was posted on-line? Was this really happening, or was she caught back up in another dream? And if not, why did she have the feeling she was going to wish she had?

Sophie picked up the coffeepot. After she gave it a good shake to find it almost empty, she sighed. "No coffee? Abby, *come on...*" She pointed over to the island. "You sit right over there while I make a fresh pot. And while you're there, you can take a look at this and tell me what's going on."

After a frenzy of finger work on her phone, she handed it to Abby and started on the coffee.

Abby looked at the screen. Then she closed her eyes before she looked at it again.

This can't be... you must be seeing wrong.

But unfortunately, she wasn't. Staring back at her from an online Cleveland sports fan site was a photo of her and Kevin. Wrapped up in each other's arms, it was more than obvious she was totally caught up in his kiss.

But to be fair, he looks just as caught up in you.

She squinted at the photo to get a closer look... could she have been any closer? No, she didn't think this would be possible.

She read the post below the photo.

> *It looks like a certain little redhead has wasted no time in latching on to the newest addition of our one and only Cleveland baseball team. Yes, baseball fans, I'm referring to Kevin Kardell, major league baseball's newest rising star. From what we've been able to find out, living right down the street from each other makes this cozy tryst so very convenient for both of them. But, don't worry. We'll be sure to keep you updated on any new "hands on" developments that come our way. Until then, feel free to post your comments below.*

She scrolled down to find most of the comments gave Kevin high praise for a job well done. And this was not in reference to his baseball skills. There were also quite a few comments from adoring female fans, along with those that made her want to blush at their suggestive content.

She raised her head, staring into space.

He's a professional baseball player?

Why didn't he tell her this?

Um... maybe because you made it very clear you despise just about every athlete out there?

Putting her elbows on the table, she dropped her head in her hands.

What have you done? Will there ever come a time when you think before you open your mouth? Instead, you spouted off about how much you condemn people like him.

Sophie sat down next to her, bringing Abby to shake her head. "I had no idea who he was. The only thing I knew was his name. It's Kevin. Which I know sounds awful, but we just never..." She sighed. "Let's face it, no matter what I say, it's not going to sound good, is it?"

She shook her head again. "I can't believe this."

Sophie gave a rather unladylike snort. "Well, believe it. What I'd like to know, how long have you been keeping this guy a secret? By the photo, it appears you know each other pretty darn well." She shook her head. "You're the last person I would expect to see in a photo like this. And plastered all over social media to boot."

Abby shrugged. "I only met him a couple of days ago and until yesterday, I wanted nothing to do with him. At least I thought I didn't."

When Sophie raised her eyebrows, she groaned. "Honest, everything about him made me so mad. It all started out when he almost ran into me as I was backing out of my driveway. Then he called me Red. You know how much I hate that."

A startled look came over her face. "Wait a minute. You don't think he planned this, do you? Like a publicity stunt of some kind? Because there's a reference to my hair in the post."

Sophie gave another snort. "Abby, you've gotta be kidding. I went online to find a photo of him." At Abby's sharp look, she tried to justify this. "Can you blame me for wanting to see what he looks like? After all, you can't see much of him in that photo. Not with the way both of you are so wrapped up in each other."

Her face brightened. "I recognized you right away, though."

Abby dropped her head back in her hands.

This certainly isn't making you feel any better, is it?

Her head still in her hands, she waited for Sophie to continue. Which of course, she was quick to do. When Sophie was on a roll, there was no stopping her.

"Abby, I assure you, he doesn't need publicity stunts to get noticed. You hit the jackpot with this guy, that's for sure."

Finally gazing up at Sophie, Abby vigorously shook her head. "Believe me, I never... I mean, this came out of the blue." Feeling desperate, she stared at her. "Oh Sophie, what am I supposed to do now?"

Sophie was a little taken aback. Nobody ever asked for her advice. In fact, they tended to ignore most of what she had to say.

Her eyes wide, she shrugged. "*Uh...* I'm not sure. Maybe go talk to him? When do you have plans to see him again?"

Abby ran her hands through her hair. "Today. I'm supposed to meet him at the baseball game."

Her jaw dropped. "*My God...* what is he planning to do? Wave to me as he comes running out onto the field? Is this how he intends to tell me?"

Her eyes narrowing, she slapped her hands down on the counter and pushed away from the island. "You know what? I'm not giving him that option. I'm going to call him out on this. Right now."

She went stomping out of the kitchen, with Sophie running after her. She grabbed her arm. "Abby, no. You know what happens when you get all riled up. You say things you don't mean. And look at you. You can't go see him with the way you look right now. I don't want to sound mean, but you're looking pretty rough around the edges."

Abby wanted to scream.

Seriously? What was it with everyone and their constant remarks about her temper? She only wanted to talk to the guy, if only to let him know she was on to him. Make it clear there was no way she would be a pawn in his little plan.

She glanced down at her pajamas. Of course, she planned to change into something else. She would never think of going out dressed like this. Certainly not when it was to see him.

Again, she had her pride.

After she'd stormed into the bathroom. Sophie threw open her closet doors. Her eyes scanning the contents, she frowned. "*Hmm...* there's not much to work with, but don't worry, I'll find something. I think we should go with something sexy."

When Abby poked her head around the bathroom door, her toothbrush in her mouth and shaking her head, Sophie shrugged. "Hey, if you're going to break this guy's heart, you need to look as stunning as you can."

She grinned. "You want to leave him knowing exactly what he's going to be missing."

Twenty minutes later, after Abby had promised Sophie at least five times she would let her know what happened, she set off to confront Kevin.

The closer she got to his condo, the more she was convinced he had a part in what happened. It was all too much of a coincidence. Never mind, he'd seemed as confused as she was when that flash went off.

But this could have been an act on his part. To then use the excuse it was probably some kids fooling around, trying to get a rise out of them.

Really?

Because, come on... this was the kind of plan a man would come up with. Especially a man who needed all the publicity he could get to advance his career.

A certain little redhead, indeed.

So, it wasn't surprising by the time she marched up his driveway, her anger had just about reached its peak. And when she finally found herself standing at his front door, she was more than ready to give him a big piece of her mind.

She hit the doorbell. Twice. And just to show she was serious, she hit it one more time.

Hard.

After what seemed like an eternity, Kevin threw open the door, a towel flung around his neck and khaki shorts his only attire. Holding a razor in his hand, the remnants of shaving cream streaked his face.

"What the..." His annoyed expression turned into a lazy smile when he saw her. "Well, well, well... what do we have here? Couldn't wait until this afternoon to see me, sugar?"

She tried not to stare.

But how could she not?

He was perfect. And now, faced with this glorious display of masculinity so close and in full view, she wondered if she may have possibly over-reacted to the whole situation.

Oh, no you don't... put this right out of your mind and remember why you're here. The photo, remember the photo?

Her hands on her hips, she dove right in. "I bet you're very pleased with yourself right now, aren't you?"

Slowly pulling the towel from around his neck, he wiped the shaving cream off his face before he spoke. "*Um...* I don't know. Should I be?"

Briefly closing her eyes and fighting the urge to scream, she clenched her hands to her sides.

Men are just so infuriating sometimes.

She moved closer, glaring at him. "Come on, you know what I'm talking about. The photo. The one of you and your 'certain little redhead' now posted all over the internet." Then, even though this was the last thing she wanted to happen, her eyes began to tear up, her voice choked. "I can't believe you did this. And here I was starting to really like you. What was I thinking?"

Comprehension filling his face, he grabbed her arm and pulled her inside. After he slammed the door shut, he picked up his phone from the sofa and glanced over at her.

"Where?"

After she told him where to search for the post, she walked over and stared out the window. After what seemed like forever, she heard him chuckle.

She whirled around, sending him an icy stare. "I can't imagine what you could find so funny right now."

He tossed the phone back on the sofa and came to stand next to her. He was grinning. "Sorry, it was one of the comments." He chuckled again. "Let's just say I've never been referred to as a stud before."

With a sharp intake of breath, she turned and headed for the door. Just as she grasped the handle, his hands were on her, pulling her against him. She struggled to get away, horrified when she felt a tear roll down her cheek.

Oh, no. Don't you dare cry. You just can't.

She squeezed her eyes shut as she continued to struggle, her words coming out in a whisper. "*Please...* just let me go."

Kevin was having a really hard time.

As she continued to squirm against him, the only thing he could think about was how he wanted to pick her up and carry her right into his bedroom. Then he'd throw her on the bed and kiss away all this anger boiling over inside of her.

Or, what the hell... he'd kiss her until she kissed him back. Hopefully, this would be with a passion equal to what showed in the photo she was so upset about.

He wrapped his arms more tightly around her, his voice hoarse. "Abby, stop. Or I'm going to lose it here."

She stiffened against him, becoming completely still. After waiting a few seconds, he turned her to face him. The frightened expression on her face, all streaked with tears, cut him to the core.

Damn... what's going on here? You just keep pushing the wrong buttons with this woman.

He groaned. "Oh, sugar... I wasn't going to hurt you. I would never, *never... Oh,* Abby... come here." Gently enfolding her in his arms, he could feel her trembling against him. His mouth pressed to the top of her head, his words were a whisper in her hair. "Why is it I always end up making you cry?"

Pressed against the warmth of his bare skin, Abby was slowly becoming lost in the heat and feel of him. The intoxicating mix of soap, shaving lotion and just his scent alone were like the sweetest of aphrodisiacs, wiping any thoughts of anger right out of her head.

In fact, the only thing she could think about was how good he felt. If they somehow became frozen in the moment, she would want for nothing more.

She sighed, her voice muffled against his chest. "Why didn't you tell me who you are?"

His hands drifting across her back to pull her closer, he dropped a soft kiss in her hair. "You gave quite a speech about the depravity of the profession I had chosen. So, what was I supposed to do?"

She gazed up at him. "But why did you want me to come to the game today? What were you planning to do? Send me a wave as you came running out onto the field?"

Kevin was caught up in her eyes, shining back at him through her tears like the rarest and brightest of jewels. Unaware of what he was doing, he slid his hands under her shirt, his fingers drifting in a caress over her skin. This had him wanting more, pulling her even closer.

He smiled, pressing another kiss in her hair. "No, I'd never do that. I guess I hadn't really thought about what I was going to do, but it wouldn't have been that."

When he began pressing whisper-soft kisses over her face, she untangled herself from his hold. If there was one thing registering in this fog of desire she was swimming in, it was she needed to leave. If she didn't, there was no telling what she might do next.

She backed away from him. "Okay, I guess. Though I wish you had told me. But now I think it's best I leave."

She reached the door, a slow smile playing across her lips. "One more thing… last night and just now, you called me sugar."

"Yes, I did." He nodded. Seriously, he did this.

"Why?"

He took a step towards her. "It just came out. I don't know why. Maybe because you smell so sweet, like vanilla and fresh-baked cookies. Or because I find you so addicting? I don't know. I only know it felt right."

He shrugged his shoulders. "If you don't like it, tell me. I'll stop."

Her hand on the doorknob, she shook her head. "No, no, it's fine. I guess I like it."

She stared at him for a few seconds before she gave him a radiant smile. "Yes, I like it. A lot. So, until this afternoon, then?"

When she opened the door, he started towards her. "Abby…"

But she'd already slipped outside, closing the door behind her.

Leaving him with a faint smile on his face.

And not a clue of what just happened.

Abby had no recollection of her walk back to her condo.

It was only when, in a daze and standing in her kitchen, she realized she was smiling. As she wrapped her arms around herself in a hug, the smile grew even bigger.

Even when her phone chimed, alerting her of a call from Sophie, the smile refused to leave. She sent her a brief text.

> We're ok. I'm ok. It's all ok. We'll talk later, ok?
> (:

Yes, she'd promised to call her.

But she didn't want to talk to anyone right now. Instead, she poured out a glass of iced tea and sat down at the island, her chin resting in her hand.

She wondered… was this what it feels like to *really* be in love?

Because she had never felt like this before.

Never…

She shook her head.

No, she had no idea… no idea at all.

Kevin watched Abby walk back to her condo. When he was finally satisfied she was inside, safe and sound, he sank down onto the sofa and picked up his phone. He found the fan page and, after reading the post again, closely studied the photo.

He was grinning.

It certainly gave the impression they knew each well. More like very, *very* well. Which was kind of surprising, considering the short time they'd spent together.

Leaning back in the cushions, and staring down at the phone, he frowned. If only he could rid his mind of the nagging thought there was something she wasn't telling him, something in her past that had hurt her badly. Her passionate outburst yesterday, along with her reaction to him just a few minutes ago, was proof of this.

But it was the look of fear on her face after he let her go that was giving him such a hard time. An expression he never wanted to see on her face ever again.

And definitely not because of you. Dear God, no... you couldn't handle that.

He glanced down at Bella. She had jumped up on the sofa and was now sprawled out next to him. Regarding him through half hooded eyes, she stretched, pressing her paws against his leg.

As he began running his hand through her fur, he shook his head. "Ah Bella, you're of the female sex. From your perspective, can you tell me what's going on here? Am I falling in love with this woman?"

His hand stilled.

Falling in love?

You?

In love?

You think you actually might be in love with her?

How the hell did this happen?

He ran his hand down over his face, giving a short laugh. If there was any truth in this, he must be absolutely out of his mind.

Slowly pushing himself up from the sofa, he gazed down at Bella, who was regarding him with knowing eyes.

Could it be that Cupid's arrow had hit its mark?

CHAPTER 9

I want to be the guy
who makes your bad days better,
the one that makes you say
"My life has changed since I met him."
~ Anonymously Yours

The driver pulled up to the main gates of the stadium, jumped out of the car and came around to open Abby's door.

He smiled when she thanked him. "You're more than welcome. Come, let's find someone who can show you to your seat." He winked. "Your young man was very insistent I do this. He made it quite clear we were to take very good care of you."

Her young man?

The thought of this making her feel ridiculously happy, she gave the driver a brilliant smile before she followed him to one of the hospitality booths.

They were approached by a woman all decked out in a baseball jersey and hat with the team's logo. Nancy was the name on her name-tag.

She was smiling from ear to ear. "Abby? I'm Nancy and on behalf of everyone here at the park, I'd like to welcome you as Mr. Kardell's guest. Even though he only recently joined our organization, we already adore him." Here she actually giggled, a blush traveling across her face. "Come, I'll take you to where you'll be viewing the game."

She brought Abby to a loge and, after inspecting the area, she turned to her. "It looks like you're the first one here. Feel free to check everything out while you wait for the others to arrive. In the meantime, I will let Mr. Kardell know you've arrived."

After she left, Abby wandered over to the seats overlooking the field. Unable to find Kevin in the home dugout, she gazed out over the field.

Memories flooding her mind, she turned away.

Kevin was standing right in front of her.

In his uniform, he looked so unbelievably handsome it was hard not to stare. Filled with a strong urge to touch him, she ran her fingertips down over the buttons of his shirt. When she realized what she was doing, it took her a few seconds before she could finally meet his eyes.

He gave her a slow smile.

"Hey..."

She smiled shyly in return.

"Hey..."

Relieved to see their confrontation of earlier now seemed to have been forgotten, he pulled her into his arms. His hands spanning her back to hold her close, his lips traveled over her face in a trail of feathery kisses to end with a whisper at her mouth. "I'm glad you're here, sugar."

And this time, it was Abby who initiated the kiss. All her inhibitions flying right out the window, she reached up to tangle her fingers in his hair. Then she claimed his mouth with a kiss unlike any kiss she'd ever given to anyone.

A groan coming from deep in his throat, he pulled her even closer. He kissed her back, matching her passion and then some. He only knew he never wanted to let her go.

With a ragged breath, he buried his face in the curve of her neck, his voice unsteady. *"Damn... what are you trying to do to me, sugar? How will I be able to even think about playing ball after a kiss like that?"*

Embarrassed beyond words, her face turning a bright shade of crimson, she pulled away. What was she thinking? If she had kissed Peter in such a fashion, he would have been shocked. But if she stopped to think about it, she had never wanted to kiss him like that.

Kevin pulled her back, his lips brushing her hair. "No, no, no... I'm only kidding, sugar. You can give me a kiss like this whenever you want. In fact, from now on I'll be disappointed if you don't."

Casually leaning against the railing, he reached over to twirl a strand of her hair around his finger before he smiled at her. "I like that you left your hair down. You look beautiful." Then he waved his hand towards the field. "So, what do you think of all this?"

She glanced out at the field before she looked up at him, her smile wistful. "I haven't been to a baseball game for, well, for a long, long time. I used to go to games with my dad, but..." She hesitated, sounding lost.

As he watched the conflicting emotions flicker across her face, he decided to change the subject. Settling behind her, he pulled her back against him so they were both facing the field. His arms wrapped around her, he rested his cheek against hers.

His voice was soft, soothing. "Look at the field, sugar. Isn't it amazing? I've been dreaming about playing on a field like this ever since I was a kid."

He chuckled. "I played baseball every chance I got, even at night under the streetlights. I would pretend they were the lights at the ballpark. I'm sure I drove all of my friends crazy. After high school, I went on to play in college. And I can still remember every single detail, where I was and what was said, on the day I got picked by this team in the draft."

He placed a kiss in her hair. "I play because I love the game. Yeah, the money is nice, but I would be happy with whatever they gave me. So, please don't hate me for this obsession of mine, sugar."

She whirled around. Her hands clutching his shirt, she searched his face. "Oh, Kevin… no, *no*. I don't hate you. I could never hate you. I'm so sorry." She rested her head against his shoulder. "I'm so, so sorry."

The sound of voices coming from inside the loge, they turned to watch the two women making their way towards them.

Abby almost groaned aloud. They could pass as models, both blonde, tall and wearing itty-bitty little skirts that showed off legs that seemed to go on forever.

The kind of skirt she'd never think of wearing.

Not in a million years.

One of the women came sashaying over to Kevin, a tinkling little bell-like laugh escaping her before she gave him a hug. "Kevin, what a surprise to find you here. But it's a great surprise since we've both been dying to meet you. I'm Jordan's wife, Mia and this is my sister, Kelly. I believe you and Kelly are both the same age. So you should have a lot in common."

This was the cue for Kelly to do her slow, sexy walk over to Kevin. A heavy cloud of fragrance traveling with her, she leaned in to give him a slow, provocative kiss on the cheek. After a halfhearted attempt to wipe away the lipstick print she'd left behind, she greeted him with a husky drawl. "Hey, Kev… if you need someone to show you around, I promise one night out on the town with me, and you'll never want to leave."

Fascinated by this brazen display, Abby sent a glance up at Kevin.

He merely nodded. "Mia, Kelly, it's nice to meet you."

Then he smiled down at her, reaching for her hand. "And this is Abby, my favorite girl. Since I plan on having her with me for a long, long time, it would be great if you could take her under your wing, Mia. I know she'd like to get involved with the charity work you do here with the club."

He topped this off by bringing her hand to his mouth for a kiss.

Mia's and Kelly's expressions were priceless.—somewhere between disbelief and confusion.

While Abby was sure hers was one of shock. Did he really just say he planned on being with her for a long time?

Not just a long time, mind you, but a long, long time.

Filled with a sudden confidence, she sent both women a big smile. "Yes, it's so nice to meet you. Mia, if you ever need me to bake cookies for favors or whatever, please don't hesitate to ask."

There was another dainty little laugh from Mia. "Bake cookies? How quaint. I didn't think anyone did that kind of thing anymore."

Kevin squeezed her hand as he smiled over at Mia. "Abby's cookies have the reputation of being the best in town. So her business might be something for you to consider with any future events." He turned to Abby. "I need to go, sugar. Stay right here after the game and I'll come get you as soon as I can. Then we'll go out for dinner. Okay?"

She nodded, while at the same time, she reached up to swipe away the faint remains of Kelly's lipstick imprint. As much as she hated to admit this, it bothered her that it was there.

Kevin's eyes flashed with amusement as he leaned in to whisper in her ear. "Not fond of that shade, sugar?" He grinned. "Not to worry, Red. These women can't hold a candle to you."

After a quick kiss to her cheek, he left

Abby glanced over to see Mia was studying her, a calculating expression on her face.

Uh oh... here it comes.

Sure enough, Mia flashed her cover girl smile. "So, how long have you and Kevin been together? And how did you meet? Do tell."

Her face suddenly lit up in recognition. "Wait a minute... you're the redhead in the fan page photo, aren't you?"

She laughed, turning to Kelly. "Kell, you saw that, didn't you?"

Kelly was busy nibbling tiny bites from an olive she had taken from the cheese tray on the table. Glancing over at Mia, she shrugged before she broke off a small piece of breadstick and popped it into her mouth. She closed her eyes, her expression of someone savoring a delectable culinary delight.

Wondering if this could be her dinner, Abby shook her head.

Evidently, being beautiful had its price.

She turned back to Mia. "We haven't been together all that long." She shrugged. "But I guess you could say something just clicked. I guess we'll see what happens."

Four women came bursting into the loge, laughing and talking all at the same time. They came over to Abby, and surrounding her, their questions came all at once. But they were so sincere, Abby began to relax.

And before she knew it, the game was in play.

Kevin had never showered and dressed so fast in his life. Now striding towards the loge where he knew Abby was waiting, all he could think about was how much he wanted to see her.

He arrived to find she was the only one there, curled up in a seat by the railing. The breeze ruffling her hair, and her chin resting in her hand, she was watching the post-game activity on the field.

It came on him so suddenly he stopped dead in his tracks.

Damn… It's official. You're totally and madly in love with this woman. And you've only known her for what? Less than a week?

He wasn't sure how it happened. Nor did he care how it happened. Or even why it happened. He only knew this love for her had settled soul deep and was here for good. And wherever this crazy choice of a career took him? She was the only woman he wanted by his side.

Overcome with an unfamiliar shyness, this life-changing revelation so new, he didn't say a word as he took the seat next to her.

When he reached for her hand, Abby sensed right away there was something different about him. His gaze holding hers, she couldn't look away even if she wanted to. But it was his smile, so sure and filled with such tenderness, that had her falling into a place she'd never been before. And there was no way she could stop this from happening.

But this was okay. Because he'd be there to catch her. The message in his eyes was a promise of this.

All of this coming at her so soon and all at once, she turned her face away, taking in a long steadying breath.

After a brief silence, he cleared his throat. "So... what did you think?" He couldn't believe how anxious he was to hear her response.

"Oh Kevin, you were wonderful! I'm sure Mia thought I was crazy because I was cheering so loudly for you." She frowned. "She told me this will get old, but I can't imagine this happening."

She sighed. "You seemed so confident, yet at the same time, like you were enjoying every..."

She became silent. Looking down at their hands, her next words were almost a whisper. "I'm so sorry about what I said. I..."

He put a finger to her mouth. "Stop. It's not a big deal and already forgotten. I know someday you'll tell me what brought that on. But until then, everything is fine." He grinned. "I'm just glad I might be changing your way of thinking, if even just a little."

"Since you plan on being with me for a long time?" She laughed. "Thank you for that." She sighed. "I found Mia and Kelly so intimidating. You had to have noticed how perfect they are."

Who? Notice what?

He was having a hard time following what she was saying because, to be honest, the only thing he could think about was how much he wanted to kiss her.

Really kiss her...

He wanted to kiss her until she returned the favor, giving him a kiss just like she'd given him before the game.

But this was risky. They were in full view of anyone still hanging around the ballpark, which meant this would be a prime photo opportunity for the asking.

"Kevin?"

He blinked to find her face turned up to his. And suddenly he didn't care if they were being watched. Catching her by surprise, he swooped in, claiming her mouth in a kiss.

When they finally drew apart, he gave her a slow smile. "*Hmm...* now what was it you asked me? Ah yes, those two. Nope. Not my type at all. And I already have what I need. Why would I choose either of them when I already have 'a certain little redhead' of my own?"

Laughing, he grabbed at the hand she was about to swing at him, pulling her up with him as he stood. "Unlike you, I worked very hard over the past couple of hours. No appetizers or wine for me, which means I'm starving. So, come on. Let's go get something to eat."

He put his arm around her as they began walking out of the loge. He smiled down at her. "Is there any place special you'd like to go?"

She gazed up at him.

With him, she'd go anywhere.

CHAPTER 10

*A*bby watched Kevin pose for another photo, this time with an excited little boy all decked out in the team's apparel.

His parents had informed Kevin they'd come from the game and he was beside himself to see Kevin in the restaurant.

They had lucked out, catching a foul ball and he'd held on to it the rest of the game. When they stopped at the restaurant, he insisted on bringing it in with him.

And now they were so glad he did.

Abby smiled at the rapt expression on the boy's face as he nodded to everything Kevin said while he was signing the ball.

Finally handing him the autographed ball, Kevin smiled at the look of awe on the boy's face as he studied it. "There you go. And keep practicing those swings. I was just like you when I was your age. And look at me now."

With a big grin on his face and clutching the ball to his chest, the boy went running back to his parents.

Kevin reached for Abby's hand. "*Ah, sugar...* I'm sorry. But I remember how I was at that age. So I try to talk with as many fans as I can. And if you think about it, they're the reason I'm here today, able to do what I love."

After gazing down at their hands, wondering how a simple touch could make her feel so happy, Abby smiled. "I don't mind. You've definitely made his day, one I'm sure he'll always remember. It's moments like this that can forever change a person's life."

Forever... such a simple word, but one that means the promise of so much more.

This was when she realized more was what she wanted. The passionate kiss they'd shared earlier? This was no longer enough. Thinking of the possibilities, this sent the color rising in her cheeks. Flustered, she grabbed her napkin and began folding it back into its original state.

Kevin was intrigued.

What was she thinking about? Could it be you?

Determined to find out, he leaned in close. "Have I told you yet today how gorgeous you are? So much so, I'd like to kiss you. Right now, and right here. In this restaurant and in full view of every person here."

His voice flowing through her like honey, she wasn't aware she had leaned in to meet him, the words coming out of her mouth on their own accord. "Then do it... kiss me."

He studied her for a few moments, his eyes lingering on her mouth. Moving in even closer, his smile deepened as he reached over to frame the side of her face in the palm of his hand. Gently brushing his thumb across her bottom lip, his voice dipped to a husky whisper. "But what if someone takes our picture? Are you telling me you're willing to take this risk?"

A photo?

It took her less than a second to think about this. Because, who cared about a silly old photo? She knew she didn't. At least not right now, she didn't. Maybe if they showed up, plastered all over social media tomorrow, she might feel a little differently.

But right now? The only thing she could think about was how much she wanted him to kiss her.

Her voice coming out soft and throaty, surprising even herself with how sexy it sounded, she inched closer until her mouth was just a tantalizing whisper away from to his. "I don't care. Aren't you the one who told me no one even pays any attention to those silly old photos?"

When she felt him smile against her mouth, she brushed her lips lightly over his. "And if you don't make your move, I guess it will be up to me to kiss you first." Here she stilled. "And I mean, *really* kiss you..."

Oh boy, where is this coming from? Again, you don't say things like this.

These thoughts were completely forgotten when, with a soft groan only she could hear, his mouth claimed hers in a kiss. A kiss she wanted to go on forever.

And there's that word again. Forever... It keeps popping up, and you're really starting to like the sound of it.

But for now, forever would have to be on hold. They were now the center of attention, a silence falling over the room.

Abby was mortified. Her head down, she went back to folding the napkin.

And how was Kevin handling this?

He shrugged, and holding his glass up in a salute, he sent a big smile around the room. "What can I say? Everyone needs inspiration and she's mine."

Abby finally glanced up to see he was watching her. He chuckled, sending another teasing grin right at her. "So, did you want to order dessert? Since I've already had mine, I believe I'll pass."

He winked.

She answered with a brilliant smile.

And damn if he didn't want to kiss her all over again.

It was a beautiful summer evening, the moon high and full, the sky studded with stars.

Hand in hand, they strolled up to Abby's front door, where Kevin turned to her with a sigh. "It's been a perfect day and I wish it didn't have to end. But my flight to Boston takes off in less than five hours. But I won't leave until after you take Poppy out."

She unlocked the door, shaking her head. "You don't need to stay."

He shook his head right back at her. "Sorry, sugar, but I disagree. I'll wait here while you get her."

When she returned with an ecstatic Poppy dancing around at the end of her leash, she was also holding a parchment bag filled with cookies. She handed Kevin the bag. "For your trip."

He dropped a kiss to her cheek. "Perfect. Every time I have one, I'll think of you."

They trailed behind Poppy, sharing a companionable silence, until Kevin came to a sudden halt.

He pulled her against him, suddenly serious. "Abby, I want you to come to Chicago with me this weekend. I'm going home to visit with my sister and her new baby. With everything going on, this is the first chance I've had to make the trip. I also snagged two tickets for the All Star Game. We stay in the city, go to dinner and do it all."

The teasing glint was back in his eyes. "Or we could just hang out in the hotel room and keep each other company. It's your call. So, what do you think?"

She was thinking, by agreeing to this, she would be making a huge commitment. Something she was more than ready to take on. She wanted to be with him, no matter how or where it came about.

She reached up to catch the corner of his mouth with a kiss. "I'd like that very much. But are you sure your family won't mind me tagging along?"

"My family?"

He laughed. "They'll be fine with it. And I know you and my sister will hit it off. Katy is… well, she's Katy. You'll see."

He gave her a hug before they continued on their walk. "We'll make it a weekend to remember."

Once they were back at her condo, he took her into his arms. "I'll be back late Thursday night and we'll leave sometime Friday afternoon. Once I get all the travel arrangements set up, I'll text you. But until then…"

His mouth swooped in to cover hers in a kiss, a kiss so demanding it brought a passionate response from her beyond any she'd ever experienced.

She just held on tight.

Then his lips slowed, moving in a slow trail along her jaw before he sought her mouth again. But this kiss was softer, leaving her clinging to him and in a daze.

She opened her eyes to his grin. "Not so fired up now, are we Red? I hope I've given you a reason to keep me, and only me, on your mind until I see you on Friday."

He turned, and after running down the steps, he took off in a run to his condo. Once there, he turned to see she was still on the steps, watching him.

He waved.

After she waved back and was in her condo, she wandered over to sit on the sofa, with Poppy curled up beside her.

She couldn't stop smiling.

After sprinting through what he'd swear had to be the entire length of the airport, Kevin made it to his gate with only seconds to spare. Maneuvering his way down the aisle of the plane, he saw Alex sitting near the back, an empty seat beside him.

After he stuffed his bag into the overhead compartment, he sank down into the seat with an enormous sigh of relief.

Alex grinned. "Cutting it pretty close, aren't you? You look like you've just run a marathon. Or maybe this look is brought on by too many late nights with a certain little redhead?"

Kevin groaned. "I overslept. I never do that. Too much on my mind, I guess."

Alex chucked. "*Hmm...* again, let's reference back to what I just said. Pretty redhead... late nights... Trust me, we all know how well that's been going for you."

He held up his hands in defense at Kevin's glaring look. "Hey, I'm just calling it like it is. The evidence is out there for all to see."

After running his hand through his hair, Kevin leaned his head back against the seat and closed his eyes. "Yeah, okay. You're right. I'm guilty as charged. But the more I see of her…"

Alex nodded. "*Ah…* so I see. And what about her? Lisa really liked her, by the way. She said she seemed so genuine. She also loved how she didn't take any grief from Mia."

His eyes still closed, Kevin smiled, picturing the sparks flying from those green eyes.

How you would've loved to see that…

After several seconds, he broke the silence between them. "How did this happen? How is it possible to fall in love with someone in such a short time? And why now?"

Alex shrugged. "Beats me."

Then he laughed. "But wait a minute, you're serious about this falling in love? If so, you might as well just lie down and take it like a man. No pun intended."

He stopped to chuckle over this clever comment before he shook his head. "You can't fight it. This is one thing I do know. When I met Lisa, I swear it was like I got hit by a truck, I fell so hard."

Kevin turned to look at him, a bewildered expression on his face. "One minute I'm fine with it, the next minute it scares me to death. I feel like I've lost complete control of my life."

A resigned smile worked its way across his face. "She's all I can think about. I told her she's like sugar. *Addicting.*"

Alex nodded, his expression matching Kevin's. "Yep, that about sums it up."

The flight attendant, starting her spiel for take-off, put their conversation on hold. Once they were in the air, Alex peered out the window. "It looks like it's clear for miles. Hope it's the same in Boston."

After he unbuckled his seatbelt, settling more comfortably in his seat, he looked over at Kevin. "But back to your current situation, I assume you've come up a plan? Because, from what you've said so far, it sounds like this woman could very well be the one. With just any woman, you wouldn't be worried about the outcome."

He grinned. "And who says guys can't be sensitive?"

This brought a laugh from Kevin. "Yeah, since I had already made reservations to go home this weekend to see my sister's new baby girl, I made some calls. I was able to get tickets to the All Star Game and asked Abby to come with me. I told her we would stay in the city, go to the game and do the whole tourist thing. She agreed."

He shrugged. "This is what I've got so far." He frowned. "But now I'm wondering if it's enough."

Alex gave a huge yawn. "Sounds good. Just make sure you give it your all."

He leaned back in his seat and closed his eyes. "But for now, get some shut eye while you can. Boston is always a tough one with the crazy fan base they have."

But even after Kevin had settled more comfortably in his seat, and as exhausted as he was, sleep eluded him.

Instead, the dazed expression on Abby's face after that last kiss he gave her just wouldn't leave him. Not to pat himself on the back, but he was feeling pretty good about how that worked out. He'd put about everything he had into that kiss.

He smiled. Judging by her reaction, he'd been spot on.

After their game, and in his hotel room, Kevin sent Abby a text.

> Hey sugar, miss me? Did you watch the game? Because that home run was for you. I'll pick you up at one. I can't wait.

After he sent it off, he leaned back against the headboard, a smile on his face. He was still riding high from the game. With his contribution of a home run and a triple, the team had sailed to a well-earned victory.

His phone dinged. Abby had sent her reply.

> After your kiss, yes. You're my hero. I'll be waiting. Me neither.

Yep, it was another good day at the ballpark.

CHAPTER 11

*A*bby pulled her SUV into the garage. She had about fifteen minutes before Kevin would arrive for their drive to the airport.

She grabbed a large shopping bag from the back seat and hurried into her condo. Once she was in her bedroom, she removed a deep purple cocktail dress and a pair of wispy metallic high-heeled sandals from of the bag and added them to her suitcase.

She really couldn't afford either the dress or the shoes. But as soon as she saw the dress, she knew it was exactly what she was looking for. It was, beyond a doubt, the sexiest and most form fitting dress she had ever dared to try on.

And as any woman will tell you, when you finally find the perfect dress, it would be a crime to skimp on the accessories, a pair of sexy heels heading the top of the list.

She set the suitcase by the front door and went into the kitchen.

Over the past two days, she had worked non-stop to finish all her orders. She was leafing through her order book to make sure she hadn't forgotten anything when she heard the front door open.

"Hey, Abby… It's me, Kevin."

At the sound of his voice, she closed the order book. Sprinting out of the kitchen, she ran right into him.

He caught her, gazing down at her with a smile. "Whoa… I missed you, too. But never in a million years did I think you'd throw yourself into my arms like this."

He laughed. "I like it."

His hands drifting down over her back, his mouth hovered dangerously over hers. "*Mmm… I'm really looking forward to this weekend. How about you?*"

She nodded and closed her eyes, ready for his kiss. But after one quick brush of his lips over hers, he released her. After he glanced down at his watch, he reached for her suitcase. "Is this all you're bringing? If so, let's get going. I'm hoping we'll miss rush hour traffic. We don't want to miss our flight."

He turned back to her. "Ready?"

What?

No, she wasn't ready. She didn't understand. Hadn't he made it very obvious he was about to kiss her?

Yes, he did.

So, what happened?

Kevin was watching her, one eyebrow raised. "Well?"

She grabbed her purse, and pushing past him, she ran out the door. While Kevin followed behind, a faint smile on his face.

Yep, he had another plan up his sleeve. The last time he was at the dentist, he'd picked up one of the magazines in the waiting room. Leafing through it, he found this article about how to spice up your love life. It seems that anticipation was paramount in setting off that spark of desire between two people who were attracted to each other.

At the time, relationships were the last thing on his mind.

But now? He figured, why not give it a try?

And judging by Abby's reaction? Whoever wrote this article knew what they were talking about.

Don't think this little experiment was just about killing him. Because it was.

Big time.

It also had him feeling the tiniest bit guilty.

But he'd already decided, if there was even the slightest chance there was something more between him and Abby, he wanted her to want him with a passion like no other.

Like he wanted her.

During their drive to the airport, they chatted about ordinary things. His time in Boston, her cookie orders, and even Bella and Poppy.

But once they arrived at the airport, any further interaction between them was cut short by fans clamoring for Kevin's attention and the time they spent checking in for their flight.

The latter is what had Abby all worked up. As they made their way to their gate, she was still fuming about the woman who had checked in their bags.

Was it really necessary for her to be so overly friendly?

For heaven's sake, she'd practically thrown herself at Kevin in her eagerness to help him, while completely ignoring the fact he wasn't alone.

Abby doubted her suitcase would have made it on the plane if Kevin hadn't added it to the conveyor belt himself.

You could have fallen over in a dead faint at this woman's feet, and she would've just kicked you out of the way before turning back to Kevin.

What a surprise it was to learn this woman's favorite sport was, yes, you guessed it… baseball.

This was because baseball players were *so* smart. And so very strong. Why, Kevin must have to work out all the time to hit that little ball as far as he did.

And could she let him in on a little secret? Out of all the baseball players, she'd have to say he was her favorite. This wasn't only in

Cleveland. *Oh, no...* this was everywhere. The entire world, it seemed.

Seriously?

So, Abby was not happy.

When Kevin squeezed her hand, she glanced up to see he was grinning. A very satisfied and knowing kind of grin.

Great... you know darn well you're the reason for his smug look.

He cleared his throat. "So... the woman who checked us in... she was nice, wasn't she?"

Nice?

Refusing to look at him, she shrugged.

He came to an abrupt halt, and right in the middle of the crowded walkway, he pulled her into his arms. "Sugar, look at me..."

Her intention to hide she might be a little jealous—okay, maybe she was a lot more jealous than she should be—she sent him a bright smile. But judging by the gleam in his eye, he wasn't fooled.

He sighed, tightening his hold on her. "Abby, listen to me. The only woman I care about, the only woman who is always on my mind, is you. That woman checking us in could have paraded in front of me completely naked, and I still wouldn't have been the least bit attracted to her."

She raised an eyebrow. The woman had been very attractive. And so outgoing and eager to please. A man would have to be made of stone, not to be taken in by such a display.

He nodded, a very firm nod. "Cross my heart." Then his teasing grin made a repeat appearance. "Now if it was you who paraded..."

She clamped her hand over his mouth. "Stop it! I get it!"

They were both laughing when his expression turned serious. He framed her face in his hands, his words brushing over her mouth. "Sugar, trust me, you have nothing to worry about. Absolutely nothing."

After catching the corner of her mouth in a quick kiss, he rested his forehead against hers, oblivious of the people that had to skirt around them.

But, remember, they were in an airport terminal.

Where emotions run high. And spontaneous greetings are common, some more demonstrative than others.

Again, this is what love can do to a person.

Settled in their seats, the plane on the runway and waiting its turn for take-off, Kevin reached over to frame the side of Abby's face in his hand. "Ah sugar… have I told you yet how much I'm looking forward to spending this weekend with you?"

Caught up in the warmth of his gaze, she smiled. "You might have mentioned this earlier. I'm looking forward to the weekend, too. Very much so."

He reached for her hand and, leaning his head against the back of his seat, he closed his eyes.

Abby wasn't sure what was going on in Kevin's mind right now. She glanced over at him.

He appeared to be totally relaxed, his eyes closed and a faint smile on his face.

She rested her head on his shoulder.

She had a feeling everything was going to be just fine.

Kevin would be the first to tell you he was having a hard time. He couldn't even trust himself to look into Abby's eyes. Every time he did, he could feel himself falling deeper and deeper in love with her.

And this is scaring the hell out of you, isn't it? One wrong move and you could goof it up. Just like that.

So, this was why he was pretending to be asleep. Otherwise, there was a pretty good chance some insane nonsense about love and what he was thinking could fly right out of his mouth.

He wanted this weekend to be perfect.

And, *God help him…* he didn't want to see any tears.

When Abby rested her head on his shoulder, a smile tweaked the corner of his mouth. Bringing her hand to his lips, he brushed his mouth over her fingers in a kiss.

He'd say they were off to a pretty good start.

While Kevin was on the phone with Katy confirming their dinner plans, Abby wandered around their hotel room, checking it out. They had arrived only about ten minutes ago, and she was still in awe of the luxurious decor.

The suite was huge.

She peeked into the bathroom. This space alone was the size of her kitchen and living room combined. A designer's dream, the room was all black and white marble, accented with polished brass fixtures. Two oversized and plush white cotton bathrobes were draped over a padded white leather bench. Next to this was an ornate glass table piled high with fluffy white towels and an assortment of bath soaps and lotions. Candles were arranged throughout the space, ready to provide a romantic glow.

An ornate crystal chandelier hung from the center of the twelve-foot ceiling of the main room of the suite. The floors were a rich, dark mahogany, the walls covered in a gold, silver and black metallic paisley patterned wallpaper. These same colors were carried over into the striped silk window treatments.

A king-sized bed, centered on a plush and hand carved black area rug, was the focal point of the room. The luxurious and oversized white down comforter was piled high with a collection of white, fluffy down pillows of all different sizes. The hand cut crystal lamps on the bedside tables sent a soft glow throughout the room.

A small sitting area was located at the far end of the room, with a plush black and gold striped velvet sofa and a matching armchair arranged in front of a gas-burning fireplace. A painting of the Chicago nightlife hung above the mantle. There was also a well-stocked wet bar.

She wandered over to the large window that provided a panoramic view of Michigan Avenue in all its glory. She was taking in the view when Kevin came up behind her. He wrapped his arms around her and dropped a kiss to the top of her head.

She leaned back against him, and gazing up into his face, she smiled. "Why, hello there… do I know you?"

His head tilted, he appeared to think about this. "*Hmm…* might you be confusing me with that crazy guy who moved in down the street from you? The one who keeps doing stupid things when he's around you."

Now that they were finally alone, and he had her in his arms, any restraint he had been holding on to, had all but disappeared. He turned her to face him, his voice dropping to a husky whisper. "I think it's only because you've turned his world upside down and he doesn't know what hit him."

When she reached up to link her fingers behind his neck, he smiled, pulling her even closer. "So, maybe you should put him out of his misery? Give him a kiss every so often. You know, sort of like…"

He captured her mouth in a kiss. A kiss that made up for all the kisses he'd wanted to give her ever since he picked her up earlier.

A kiss long overdue.

He finally lifted his head. "If you need me to show you that again, sugar, you just let me know. I'll be more than happy to oblige."

He ran his fingers through her hair, smoothing it back from her face. "So, what would you like to do? We're meeting my family for dinner in about four hours. So until then, the time is all ours. We can go out and explore the city. Or…" Here his expression changed. The smile was still there, but it was now laced with a hint of desire. "Or we could stay here."

She hesitated, a sudden shyness coming over her. "I've never been to Chicago. I've heard it's a fun city to visit."

A look of understanding crossed his face. He could wait. He wasn't going to push it. No, believe it or not, more than anything, he wanted a sign from her when the time was right.

He placed a quick kiss to the tip of her nose. "You've never experienced the magic of the great city of Chicago? It's settled then. I'm going to give you the grand tour."

Striding over to grab his sports coat, he slipped it on. "If you brought a sweater, bring it along. There's a reason they call Chicago the windy city. Since we're so close to the lake, even though it's summer, it can turn cold very quickly."

Patiently watching as she rummaged through her suitcase looking for a sweater, he was hit by a feeling close to one of almost awe. How was it he felt like he had known her forever? As though she'd already become a part of him, the connection between them so right.

Caught up in this thought, he wasn't aware she had turned to him, holding up the elusive sweater. She tilted her head. "It's all good, isn't it?"

And this is when it hit him.

She feels it, too.

"You know what? It is. The best."

He held out his hand.

"Come on, If I'm to show you what the city of Chicago is all about, we have a lot of ground to cover in the time we have."

CHAPTER 12

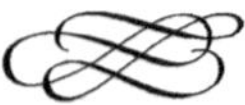

The Chicago wind had whipped Abby's hair into a mass of unruly curls, and her attempt to arrange them into a sleeker look was proving to be impossible.

Accepting she had done the best she could, she took a step back from the bathroom mirror to get a better look.

Even she'd admit she looked good.

She felt so sexy in this dress.

It hugged her curves in all the right places, and the deep shade of purple made her eyes appear an even more brilliant green. Going for a simple, yet sophisticated look, the only jewelry she wore was a delicate gold chain with a small diamond pendant and matching earrings, both once belonging to her mother.

When she walked out of the bathroom, she saw Kevin was standing by the window. A preoccupied look on his face, he didn't notice she'd entered the room.

She smiled. He was wearing the tie she'd convinced him to buy earlier.. The dark red background, scattered with a random design of baseballs and bats, was a tie every professional baseball player should own, she'd informed him. And though she had wanted to buy it for him as a gift, he'd refused to let her do this.

His reasoning?

She had already given him the best gift of all by agreeing to spend this weekend with him.

How can you not love a guy who says things like this?

She sighed, thinking how nice it would be if they could have the night to themselves. Not that she didn't want to go out to dinner with his family…

She'd just rather be with Kevin.

While he was waiting for Abby to get ready, Kevin had a lot of time to think. This probably wasn't to his advantage.

Dinner with his family? This no longer seemed like such a good idea. He'd much rather spend the time with Abby.

Alone.

This had him sending a quick glance over at the bed.

Remember? You can wait. Isn't this what you've already decided?

He wandered over to the window, his thoughts drifting to the afternoon they'd spent together.

He'd taken her to all of his favorite places, ending with a leisurely stroll along the Navy Pier boardwalk. After they browsed through a few of the shops, he'd insisted they share a huge chocolate chip cookie and a cup of hot chocolate at Ghirardelli's.

It was there he'd managed to embarrass Abby when he told everyone in the little shop that, even though Ghirardelli's cookies were good, they couldn't hold a candle to the cookies she made. He grinned, recalling how flustered this had her.

He should have known she'd find a way to get back at him. After shrugging off his compliment, she'd informed everyone he couldn't possibly be qualified to make such a claim.

After all, he was a professional baseball player. So what did he know about cookies?

When this brought on a flurry of requests for autographs and photos, she had been content to watch as he chatted and joked around with the fans clustered around him.

They had lost all track of time, making it back to the hotel with hardly enough time to get ready for dinner. And now, in the short time he'd been waiting for her, he couldn't believe how much he already craved her company.

"Kevin?"

He turned from the window.

Abby was standing only a few feet away.

Mesmerized, he could only stare. Every emotion he could possibly feel—longing, desire, tenderness, and so much more—had come at him in a rush and all at once.

She took his breath away.

It was when she sent him a tentative smile, he came to life. In less than five-seconds flat, he was at her side. His eyes locked with hers, he reached out to run his fingers through the soft curls framing her face. "*Ah...* Sugar, you look amazing. There's only one thing. May I?"

She nodded, moving closer.

If he keeps looking at you the way he is right now, he can do anything he wants. Anything.

Gently pulling the clips from her hair, a smile spread across his lips as it tumbled in soft waves around her face. Tossing the clips on the nearby table, he gathered her in his arms. "There... now you're absolutely breathtaking."

His hands sliding in her hair to bring her closer, he claimed her mouth in a kiss. Slowly, tenderly, he did this. It was a beautiful kiss. Lost in the sweetness of the moment, everything they felt for each other came through in this kiss.

Kevin only knew he didn't want to let her go.

His breathing no steadier than hers, he rested his forehead against hers, his sigh brushing over her cheeks. "Oh sugar, promise me you'll never change."

The kiss she gave him was better than any promise. And now, he definitely didn't want to let go.

A wistful smile on his face, he glanced around the room. "Suddenly, dinner with my family doesn't sound like all that much fun. I'd much rather stay here with you. But I know they'd never forgive us if we didn't show up. I've already been reminded far too many times how long it's been since I've been home."

He slipped into his sports coat. When Abby picked up her evening wrap, he moved to take it from her, gently draping it over her shoulders. His hands drifting to her waist, he smiled down at her. "I believe I need one more kiss to hold me over…"

She was more than happy to comply.

Seated next to Abby in the taxi, Kevin gazed down at their hands, almost hypnotized by the movement of his thumb, drawing lazy circles over the inside of her wrist.

He wanted to laugh aloud.

Shout out to the world.

Along with all the other silly things people did when they realized they were in love. He had turned into someone he didn't even know anymore.

You're crazy. You do realize this, don't you?

She had bewitched him. This had to be what it was.

What else would explain why he was acting like he was on a first date, afraid he'd make the wrong move? Or blurt out something stupid? And even though he knew he should try to start up a conversation, he just couldn't seem to find the words.

But talking wasn't what he wanted right now. No, he wanted to take Abby into his arms. Then he would kiss her. Everywhere… her lips, her eyes, the tender spot behind her ear. Or where he could see the faint beat of her pulse at the base of her neck.

A soft groan escaping him, he brought her hand to his lips and placed a soft kiss to her wrist.

This would have to do for now.

Abby wasn't the least bit uncomfortable with the silence between them.

In fact, she wished she was brave enough to catch the driver's attention and tell him there had been a change of plans. He should keep driving. It didn't matter where or when their journey ended.

All that mattered was she and Kevin were together.

When Kevin pressed a kiss to her wrist, she glanced over to see he was watching her, the intensity of his gaze sending her heart beat up more than a few notches. Gently pulling her hand from his, she traced the line of his jaw with her fingertips before she leaned in to brush her lips over his.

Her words were a whisper against his mouth. "Thank you."

Surprise showing on his face, he captured her hand back in his. "Sugar, whatever for?"

She moved closer to give him another glancing kiss. "For everything. This weekend. For putting up with my tears and making me laugh. For making me feel like the most beautiful woman in the world. And, even more so, for just being you."

She paused, her voice coming at him even more softly. "But most of all, for coming into my life."

His gaze holding hers, for a moment he was silent. Then he pulled her into his arms, the huskiness of his voice revealing his emotional response to her words. "You just keep surprising me. Over and over and over again. I can only hope you'll feel the same when we're old and gray."

Just when she was so sure he was planning to follow this with a kiss, the taxi pulled up in front of the restaurant. His lips nuzzling her ear, his next words sent a shiver racing through her. "Right now, I can think of so many ways to show you how I feel about you in return. But it looks like we'll have to continue this conversation later." His voice deepened, becoming so, *so* seductive. "And I, for one, can't wait."

With a teasing brush of his lips against hers, he slipped out of the taxi. Unable to meet his gaze, she took the hand he extended.

He grinned at the blush staining her cheeks.

How he loved it when he was able to bring her to this state.

CHAPTER 13

Sometimes you need to distance yourself
to see things clearly.
~ Anonymous

As the hostess escorted them to their table, Abby could feel the eyes of the other diners follow them as they passed by. Their furtive glances turned into excited whispers when Kevin was recognized.

Holding onto his hand, and caught up in trying to act as indifferent as she could about this sudden attention, when he came to an abrupt stop, she ran right into him.

Good job... so much for making a good impression. You can only pray this won't turn into a future fan photo.

Kevin turned to her. "*Whoa...* are you okay?" When she nodded, a serious look on his face, he leaned in to whisper in her ear. "Don't let my mother get to you. She means well most of the times."

What? Wait a minute... what does he mean?

But before she could ask, something she definitely would have liked to do, they'd arrived at their table.

"*Kevin...*" With a loud shriek, a willowy and gorgeous model-perfect brunette jumped up from her chair. Wearing an incredibly tight fitting and low-cut ivory silk dress, leaving Abby feeling like she'd purchased her dress from an online discount site, she ran around the table and launched herself at Kevin.

This was followed by a long and dramatic sigh as she gazed up into his face. "Darling, I can't believe you've finally made it home to me."

Clutching the lapels of his sports jacket, she sent a brilliant smile around the table. "Is he not just the perfect man alive? I love him to pieces."

This is when she noticed Abby.

Moving even closer to Kevin, she gave her a glaring once over. Her inspection was so thorough it was as if not only did she know the brand and the cost of the dress Abby was wearing, she also had a pretty good idea how much she weighed and what size bra she wore.

She looked up at Kevin. Her eyes narrowed, her voice was dangerously smooth. "And who, may I ask, is this? Your assistant?" She frowned. "She looks awfully young for the job. Are you sure she's capable?"

Then, with a toss of her head, she gave a throaty laugh. "And, darling… seriously? Wouldn't a man be a better fit? You know, with all of those locker room interviews and all."

Kevin felt Abby stiffen beside him.

Yes, Abby was fuming all right. This Melissa, or whatever her name was, needed some lessons in manners. Starting with talking over her head like she wasn't even here.

She didn't understand. What was with this—*Darling? How I love this man*—bit? What was she implying?

And finally, she was confused. Is this what Kevin had told his family? He was bringing along one of his crew?

So, even though she knew she should keep her mouth shut and wait to hear Kevin's take on this, she decided to fight back.

She gave Melissa her best smile. "My goodness, you do realize this is the twenty-first century, don't you? A time when women have made great strides in the world of sports broadcasting."

She shrugged. "And just between you and me? The locker room is actually one of my favorite places to be. With all those athletic and toned bodies on display?" She raised her eyes to the ceiling, fanning her face with her hand. "Why, it can make a woman's imagination run wild."

When her comment was met with silence, Abby glanced over at Kevin. His eyes closed, a look of total disbelief on his face.

And Melissa? Still hanging on to Kevin as if she had no plans to let go, it was obvious she hadn't heard a word Abby said.

Abby gave a frustrated sigh.

Well, that didn't go well, did it? You should've stayed in the taxi.

Kevin couldn't believe what was happening. He wanted to grab Abby, whisk her right out of the restaurant, and back into another taxi.

Or the train.

Or even a bus.

He didn't care what the hell they wound up using. He only wanted to get back to where they were before they walked into the restaurant.

Dragging his hand through his hair, he groaned. This was not how he'd envisioned the evening would go. No, he'd foolishly thought his family would welcome Abby with open arms. Instead, they were now in the middle of what could very well turn into a catfight.

He, for one, knew how nasty Melissa could be when someone crossed her.

Abby wouldn't have a chance.

He frowned. But why was Melissa even here? This was supposed to be a family dinner.

A glance over at his mother and he had his answer. The critical once-over she was giving Abby told him she had already made up her mind.

She didn't approve.

He wouldn't be surprised if she had come to this decision before she even walked into the restaurant. And, from experience, he knew her opinion wasn't going to change.

He caught her eye, she frowned, shaking his head. In return, she gave him the I-know-what's-best-for-you look he knew so well.

Damn...

It appeared Melissa still topped her list as his potential wife. He didn't understand this and until now, had chosen to shrug it off.

Well, it looks like you can't ignore it any longer.

He moved closer to Abby, reaching for her hand. In response, she clasped her hands together behind her back. Her expression was furious.

And this is when everything got even more crazy. A camera flashed, so close it was almost blinding.

Kevin glanced over at Abby. The expression flashing through his mind of someone looking like a deer caught in the headlights.

But change this to a *very angry* deer, because this was exactly how he would describe her.

Where Melissa took full advantage of the situation. Throwing her arms around his neck, she claimed his mouth in what could only be described as the kiss of the century.

As luck would have it, this happened as another camera flash went off.

After Kevin untangled himself from Melissa's grip, he sent a quick glance around the restaurant, hoping to find the source responsible for the flash. But in the crowded room, this proved to be impossible.

He gave a frustrated sigh. This 'in the public eye' status wasn't working out in his favor. Massaging his forehead with his fingers, he tried to think. There had to be something he could do to fix this.

A thoughtful look on his face, he glanced over at Abby. Catching her completely by surprise, he pulled her against him. When she sagged against him, he pressed a quick kiss right below her ear. "Bear with me, sugar. *Please...*"

For a few seconds, she didn't move. Then, to his relief, she slowly straightened against him and gave a slight nod.

His arm around her, he motioned for silence. "Hey, can I have your attention, please? I'd like you to meet Abby, a woman who has become a very important part of my life." Here he stopped to smile down at Abby. "In fact, only a short time ago, she made me the happiest man alive when she agreed to become my wife. We hope we can count on your total love and support as we move on to this new chapter of our lives."

During the collective gasp that echoed around the table, he glanced down at Abby. Her eyes were wide, her mouth was open in shock. Deciding he might as well take advantage of this, he framed her face in his hands.

"Again, back me on this. I'll explain later." He whispered this against her lips right before he gave her a kiss. A kiss you'd expect from a man who had just received a yes from the woman he loved.

To say Abby was in shock would be an understatement. But as she glanced around the table, it appeared she wasn't the only one who was having a hard time dealing with Kevin's announcement.

The woman she'd already assumed was Kevin's mother looked like she was about to pass out. Her eyes closed, she was gripping the stem of her wine glass as though she wanted to hurl it across the room.

Not a promising sign.

And Melissa? It was obvious this news was the absolute last thing she had expected to hear tonight. Slumped down in her chair, she looked deflated, her hopes and dreams of becoming the future Mrs. Kevin Kardell, now gone up in smoke.

The only person at the table who seemed to be happy about the news was a young woman with such a strong resemblance to Kevin, Abby knew at once she was his sister, Katy. Leaping up out of her chair, she ran around the table and wrapped Abby in a big hug.

She was almost jumping up and down with excitement. "*Ooooooh!* I finally have a sister! I can't wait until we get to know each other better." She leaned in closer to whisper in Abby's ear. "And don't worry, I'll fill you in on all the little secrets you need to know about my brother."

Then she turned to Kevin, flinging her arms around him. "Kevin! I'm so happy for you!"

Then she turned back to Abby and grabbed her left hand, zeroing right in on her ring finger. Her face scrunched up in confusion. "What, no ring?"

Her hands going to her hips, she turned to glare at Kevin. "Kevin! How could you?"

Abby was pleased to see he actually looked embarrassed. At least for a second, he did. Then, in his usual don't-worry-I've-got-this fashion, he drew Abby close, flashing that winning smile of his.

"Let's just say this was a spur-of-the-moment thing. Trust me, the ring is coming." He then put his finger under Abby's chin, lifting her face to his. "Even though no ring or jewel could ever match this beauty."

As he leaned in to give her a kiss, she heard Katy give a long sigh.

She, on the other hand, wanted to scream.

Instead, she was wrapped in a big hug from Katy's husband, Stephen, as he came over to offer his congratulations.

This was followed by a kiss to her cheek from Kevin's father. "Congratulations, my dear. I can't even begin to tell you how happy both Kevin's mother and I are to hear this news. If you make our son happy, there's nothing more we could ask for."

Abby shot a glance over at the women in question. A furious look on her face and her wine glass still clutched in her hand, made it hard for Abby to believe she shared his opinion.

Still holding her hand, he nodded. "I take that back. There is something else we'd like, and this would be more grandchildren."

He nodded towards Katy. "Now that we've been blessed with our first from Katy and Stephen, we wouldn't mind a houseful of little ones."

Again, Abby glanced over at Kevin's mother. She certainly wasn't giving off a grandmotherly vibe. No, she definitely didn't come across as someone who would enjoy spending her time with "a houseful" of little ones.

Once everyone had returned to their seats, Kevin gave her hand a gentle squeeze. "So, is there something you'd like to add?"

For a moment, she stared at him. Was there something she wanted to add? Yes, there was plenty she'd like to say. But the anxious look on his face had her falling right into the part of the ecstatic fiancée.

She sent a big smile around the table. "It's so nice to meet all of you. And to be honest, I'm just as surprised by this announcement as all of you are."

When Kevin tightened his grip, she added. "What I meant, I didn't think it would be tonight... and so, uh... so soon." She glanced up at Kevin, one eyebrow raised. "I guess with Kevin, life is bound to be full of surprises."

Then her next words came out not at all like she intended. "I'm sure he'll be very happy."

When everyone laughed, she shrugged. What could she say? She did the best she could.

Kevin was right there to save the day. He chuckled, shaking his head. "*Ah...* it appears she's already making decisions for me, and we're not even married yet."

He pulled her close to whisper. "Thanks, sugar. It looks like the tables have turned. I'm the one that owes you... big time."

She was going to hold him to this. She wasn't sure how, but she'd think of something.

And it would definitely be something big.

While Kevin's father went about ordering champagne for the table, Kevin settled right into his role as the adoring fiancé. He pulled out a chair for her and, once they were seated, draped his arm along the back of her chair. Running his fingers through her hair, he smiled over at her as though nothing unusual had just taken place.

In fact, he looked totally at ease.

She didn't know whether she wanted to kiss him...

Or kill him.

CHAPTER 14

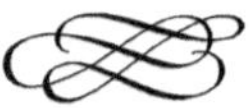

*I*f you were to ask her, Abby wouldn't be able to tell you what she had for dinner.

She only knew she ate everything that was put in front of her, her only goal to get through dinner as quickly as possible.

This all took place while Katy, who had claimed the seat next to her, kept up a continuous chatter. That Abby had little to say didn't seem to bother her.

But Abby welcomed the distraction. This made it easier to avoid the angry glances coming from both Kevin's mother and Melissa.

After asking Abby a few basic questions about her life in general, his mother had gone on to completely ignore her. She'd also refused to join in when Kevin's father raised his glass of champagne in a toast to their engagement.

Instead, she had pushed her glass away, a disgusted look on her face.

Not an encouraging sign.

And Melissa?

A bright smile pasted on her face, she'd downed her champagne in almost one gulp. Then, reaching for Kevin's mother's glass, she'd inhaled the contents of that as well.

After that, everything had gone downhill at an alarming rate.

Melissa had hardly touched her meal and was now on her third martini, having downed the first two in an unbelievably short time. Her eyes narrowed, she'd watched Abby and Kevin throughout dinner, her expression more calculating by the minute.

It looks like you'll need to be very careful with this one. Because it sure looks like she's putting some kind of curse on you.

And Kevin... how was he handling all of this?

He was his usual charming, cheerful self, chatting with everyone around him. Completely at ease in his new role as a pretend fiancé, he couldn't resist leaning over to kiss her every so often.

This was a move that had Katy clasping her hands to her heart and giving a rapturous sigh.

Every. Single. Time.

And Abby? She was trying, she really was.

But she still just wanted the evening to be over with.

After dessert and coffee had been served, Melissa unexpectedly came to her feet and weaved her way over to where the band had just finished setting up.

Watching this with a sense of foreboding, Abby saw her point over to their table, her arms flailing around as she attempted to make her point to one of the band members.

When the band began playing their opening number, I Will Always Love You—the lead singer belting out her best Whitney Houston imitation—Melissa stumbled back to their table.

After she gulped down what was left of her martini, she weaved her way around the table to stand next to Kevin. Grabbing his hand in a feeble attempt to pull him up out of his chair, slurring her words. "Kevin, this is our song. Dance with me."

He looked surprised... very surprised. After shaking his head, he gave her a rather regretful smile. *"Ah, Melissa... I don't think this is a good idea. Why, I haven't even danced with Abby yet."*

His mother immediately chimed in. "Kevin, be the gentleman that you are and dance with Melissa. I've always enjoyed watching the two of you dance. You move so well together."

He looked at her like she was joking.

They did?

He didn't remember this.

In a panic, he glanced over at Abby.

His please-you've-got-to-help-me expression almost did Abby in. And for a moment, she almost caved. Should she go to his rescue? After what he had put her through this evening?

Nah, she didn't think so. And with the condition Melissa was in, it might be better if Kevin went along with her request.

She gave him a brilliant smile. "Go ahead, sweetheart. I don't mind. We have the rest of our lives to dance together."

Reluctantly hauling himself out of his chair, he followed Melissa out onto the dance floor, stopping halfway to shoot a puzzled glance back at Abby.

Sweetheart?

Why did he have the feeling this endearment hadn't been given from her heart?

This was when Abby realized she was now alone with Kevin's mother. Katy had left to check in with the babysitter, and Stephen and Kevin were talking with friends at another table.

She smiled tentatively over at his mother. She responded with a long, hard stare. Then, with no warning, she threw out a zinger. "Is it the money that attracted you to my son?"

Unable to understand why she'd even ask this, Abby's only response was to shake her head.

His mother gave a sarcastic laugh. "Oh, come on… you must know if he does well at this baseball thing, as far as salaries go, the sky's the limit. You'd be set for life, a huge step up from what you must make selling your cookies. Or whatever it is you do."

She gave a brief wave of her hand in Abby's direction, as though she was dismissing what she did as of no importance.

Now Abby was beginning to get angry. But the last thing she wanted was to say something she'd later regret. So, she decided it would still be best to say nothing at all.

After all, this woman *was* Kevin's mother.

Taking Abby's silence as an agreement to her comment, his mother nodded. Then, leaning forward in her chair, she spoke slowly, as though she was addressing a child. "A career as a professional baseball player is not what I'd envisioned for my son. How he could waste his intelligence on such a frivolous choice of career is beyond me."

She frowned. "Then there's the matter of our family business. My great grandfather spent his entire life building it into the success it is today. And, it has always been my plan, and I'm sure my husband would back me up on this, Kevin would step in and take over. The possibility that it could fall into the hands of an outsider?"

She shuddered. "Well, this is just unthinkable."

She reached into her purse and pulled out a lace-trimmed hand-kerchief. After dabbing at her eyes, she sent a furtive glance in Abby's direction.

This dramatic display had Abby wondering if she'd been involved in theater at one time in her life. When a smile flitted across her face at the thought, his mother shoved the handkerchief back into her purse and closed it with a loud snap.

She glared at Abby. "I assure this is nothing to laugh about. We can only hope Kevin will eventually get this baseball thing out of his system. Then he can return home and he and Melissa can settle in and raise a family."

Abby finally spoke. "But I don't understand. He's mentioned nothing about Melissa to me. So, why are you so sure of this?"

His mother leaned forward in her seat, her next words delivered in a furious and barely controlled whisper. "The plan has always been for Melissa and Kevin to marry. And I will do everything in my power to make sure this happens. Which means it would be in your best interest to remove yourself from the picture. And the sooner you do this, the better it will be for all of us."

Now that she'd had her say, she stood, the regal nod of her head a sign their conversation was over. "Now if you'll excuse me, there are friends here I need to talk with."

She turned and walked away.

Abby watched her leave, her mind stuck on one thing.

Friends? How could this woman have any friends?

Then the threatening nature of her warning sank in, sending a chill running through her.

She glanced over to where Kevin was still on the dance floor with Melissa. Her arms wrapped around him, it didn't look like she had any intention of letting go.

It was suddenly too much. She looked up at the ceiling, blinking to keep the tears from spilling over.

Don't you dare cry. Because this is what she wants. You need to get your-self together before Kevin and Melissa come back to the table.

Or maybe... she should just leave?

While this drama was playing out with Abby and his mother, Kevin was having problems of his own.

Since he and Melissa had stepped onto the dance floor, they had barely moved. But this was probably for the best since he was having a devil of a time trying to keep her on her feet. The only way he could accomplish this was by keeping her in a tight hold. Other-wise, it was a safe bet she'd slide right down against him onto the floor.

She wasn't making any sense, rambling on about soul mates and the names of people he didn't even know. From what he could make out, these were the people who would be devastated if he married someone else instead of her.

In return, he didn't say a word. From experience, he knew she couldn't be reasoned with when she was in this state.

He gave a frustrated sigh. This was why he'd kept his distance.

He didn't understand. Why couldn't his mother see this?

He glanced over to their table to see his mother lean in towards Abby as if to confide in her.

Thank God... this had to be a sign they were getting along.

Melissa had now gone completely silent, a very disturbing development. Worried she was on the verge of passing out, he began to half lead, half drag her back to their table.

A table that was now deserted.

Abby was gone.

Almost throwing Melissa down into her chair, where she dropped her head down on the table in a stupor, he searched the room for Abby. He finally caught sight of her, making her way to the main entrance of the restaurant. Once he informed his father he was leaving, he went sprinting after her.

After he searched the crowded entrance, he pushed his way outside. This is where he found her, huddled near the far corner of the building.

Her eyes closed, she looked lost.

And so alone.

Now standing outside in front of the restaurant, Abby was wondering if she'd been a little hasty with her decision to leave.

She was trying not to panic, but how could she not? She'd left her phone back in the hotel room.

Not that she knew anyone in Chicago to call

She had her purse, but the only items it held were a lipstick, a comb, two free parking passes from the last time she used this purse and a slightly used and wadded up tissue. No money. No credit cards. Nothing of any help to her right now.

She also didn't have a key to the room.

To top it off, she'd left her evening wrap in the restaurant, and she could really use it right now. Not only had the notorious Chicago wind made an appearance, the distant rumble of thunder and lightning strikes flashing across the sky were a sign a storm was soon to follow.

All things considered, it wasn't looking good for her right now.

She shivered as another gust of wind came whistling through the covered entrance. Seeking shelter, she leaned against one of the tall planters lining the front of the building, where she tried to appear as inconspicuous as possible.

A huge flash of lightning lit up the sky. When this was followed by a long rumble of thunder, she sent a glance over at the entrance to the restaurant.

Maybe she should go back inside and act as if nothing happened?

Her expression hardened.

No. Absolutely not. You'll do no such thing.

She'd rather freeze to death.

Yes, she knew she was being dramatic, but there was no way she would go crawling back into the restaurant and give his mother the satisfaction of knowing her comments had hit their mark.

She also knew it would only take one look at Kevin and she would break down completely.

Wrapping her arms around herself, she closed her eyes.

Think... there has to be something you can do.

Abby was enveloped in a familiar pair of arms.

And she fell apart... every emotion she'd been holding inside, erupting in a flood of tears.

Holding her against him, Kevin's lips moved in her hair. "Oh sugar, you scared me. Why did you leave?"

She shook her head. She wasn't ready to tell him about her conversation with his mother.

In fact, she was beginning to think she wasn't ready for any of this.

She looked up at him, her response coming out in a shaky sob. "Please... I just want to go home."

He closed his eyes. He couldn't believe it.

Again?

He'd made her cry again?

This wasn't supposed to happen. Not tonight.

Without a word, he removed his jacket and wrapped it around her. Holding her close, he moved them to the curb and hailed a taxi.

From the back seat of the taxi, Kevin watched the driver navigate through the congested night traffic. Holding Abby close, he was relieved to feel she had stopped shivering.

They hadn't spoken since they got in the taxi. But this was okay. He wanted to wait until they were in their hotel room before they talked about what happened.

He closed his eyes, resting his cheek against the top of her head.

She said she wanted to go home.

You can only hope she meant your hotel room.

With an enormous boom ending in a long rumbling of thunder, the heavens released a torrent of rain down on the city. Sweeping across the street in waves, it slowed the taxi's progress to a crawl, blurring everything from view. The thunder shook the ground beneath them, while lightning strikes lit up the sky, one after another.

Kevin pulled Abby even closer, wrapping his arms around her. Listening to the rain drumming on the roof of the taxi, he hoped the storm wasn't an omen of what was to come.

He closed his eyes and said a little prayer everything was going to be okay.

He figured this couldn't hurt.

Abby wasn't sure what to do.

After the bizarre series of events during dinner, followed by the stormy drive back to the hotel, the silence of the room was almost overwhelming.

She removed Kevin's jacket and draped it over the back of the chair. She turned to find he was watching her, an apprehensive expression on his face.

He started towards her.

"Abby…"

When she took a step back, holding out her hands in a warning, the look of pain that flashed across his face was almost her undoing. But if he came any closer, she was afraid he'd try to take her into his arms.

And she didn't want him to do this. Nor did she want him to kiss her.

Oh, come on… whom are you kidding? Of course, you want him to kiss you. You want him to kiss you until you can't even think anymore.

But before this happened, she needed answers.

Her arms wrapped around herself, she searched his face. "Kevin, what happened back there in the restaurant? Why did you tell everyone we're engaged? And…"

She hesitated, the image of his mother's angry face still so clear in her mind. Did she really want to know his answer to this next question?

She closed her eyes. Yes… she did.

She took a deep breath. "And Melissa… who is she? And what does she mean to you?"

He shoved his hand through his hair. "Oh sugar, I panicked. I don't know why, but my mother has been pushing Melissa at me ever since we were kids. Something I've ignored. At least until tonight, I have."

He shook his head. "Melissa has so many problems, she always has. She's like a walking time bomb, ready to go off at any moment. You saw how much she drank tonight. And her temper is one you don't want to mess with."

Here he stopped to smile at her. "You're like a kitten compared to her, sugar."

When he saw a brief smile flit across her face, hope filling him, he tentatively moved closer. "I haven't seen her for months. But she must have asked my mother if she could come to dinner with us tonight, leading her to believe we had made some kind of commitment to each other. Which I assure you, we never, ever did. And we never, ever will."

He ran his hand through his hair again. "When she came at me tonight, I knew I had to do something. And this is when I came up with the idea to tell them you and I were engaged." His eyes pleaded with her. "I'm sorry. I shouldn't have done that. Obviously, I wasn't thinking clearly and put you on the spot. Again, I'm so sorry about that."

He was right next to her now, close enough to take her into his arms. And he couldn't believe how much he wanted to do this.

So damn much…

He sounded so sincere, Abby had to believe him. And now that he was so close? Honestly? The only thing she could think about was how much she wanted to sink into the safe shelter of his arms and forget everything that happened. But first, she needed to know how they were going to handle this pretend engagement. She swallowed. And this time, she was the one to move closer. "But what's going to happen when everyone finds out there is no engagement?"

"*Ah*, sugar… it will all work out. I know it will." In one swift move, he had her in his arms.

She relaxed against him, and resting her head on his shoulder, she gave a long, trembling sigh.

He sighed in response. "But right now? I want this weekend to be about us. No one else matters. Nothing else is important." He cupped her chin in his hand, his eyes searching her face. "Okay?"

She nodded. She needed to trust him on this.

He quickly sensed her change of mood. As he was about to remind her of the promise he'd made to her in the taxi, she framed his face with her hands.

And before the words could leave his mouth, they were swallowed up in her kiss.

"Mr. Kardell, complimentary room service." This loud announcement was followed by a knock on the door to their rooom.

Kevin dragged his mouth from Abby's, and lifting his head, he groaned. "*Damn*… I should probably answer that. Don't move, sugar."

When he opened the door, a hotel attendant wheeled in a cart holding an assortment of silver serving dishes and a champagne bottle nestled in a silver ice bucket.

He smiled, and with a slight bow, waved his hand towards the cart. "Mr. Kardell, ma'am, on behalf of both our management and staff, we'd like to offer you this complimentary midnight feast our hotel is famous for. This is just our way of thanking you for choosing us for your stay here in Chicago."

He turned to grin at Kevin. "I wonder if you can do me a favor. My son is an avid baseball fan and I know he'd be thrilled to have something autographed by you." Whipping a baseball out of his pocket, he tossed it over to Kevin.

After the ball had been signed and the attendant had left with a generous tip, Kevin grinned over at Abby. He undid his tie and threw it on top of his suitcase. Then, after he unbuttoned the top buttons of his shirt and rolled up his sleeves, he walked over to the cart.

He pulled the champagne bottle from the ice bucket to read the label before he turned to her. "Would you like some champagne?" He smiled. "It appears to be a good year."

Shaking her head, she began walking over to him.

He gave her a surprised look and, after he's settled the bottle back into the ice bucket, he removed a cover from one of the dishes.

"*Hmm*... no? Then how about strawberries?" He lifted another cover. "Or what's this? A cheese tray? Does any of this look good to you, sugar?"

She was now standing next to him. She shook her head again.

He tilted his head, a look of concern on his face. "Are you sure? Maybe there's something else you'd like instead?"

Her eyes never leaving his face, she nodded.

The message in her eyes filling him with a sudden sense of anticipation, he went to replace the cover, dropping it in his haste. They both watched as it slid off the cart and went crashing to the floor, where it rolled across the room in an almost drunken fashion and hit the wall.

It was only after it had stilled, they turned to gaze at each other.

With every ounce of control he possessed, he waited. It was when she reached for his hands, he whispered her name.

"Abby?"

She gazed up at him, her voice soft, but sure.

"Yes, you. The only thing I want is you."

CHAPTER 15

The first time you touched me,
I knew I was born to be yours.
~ Anonymous

With a gentleness Kevin didn't even know he possessed, he framed Abby's face in his hands, his eyes searching hers.

"Abby, I..."

Then an incredulous expression filling his face, he slid his hands into her hair and tilted her chin up to his. What he saw in her eyes was more than he could have ever hoped for.

She wants you... just as much as you want her...

His mouth crashing down on hers, he kissed her like there was no tomorrow.

He knew he should slow down. But after the past few hours, fraught with such tension and uncertainty, the relief that flowed through him at this sudden move of hers exploded into a frenzy of need.

His mouth never leaving hers, he reached to the back of her dress, pulling down the zipper as he moved them across the room.

After he pushed the dress down over her shoulders, to drift in a cloud of fabric at their feet, he toppled her back with him onto the bed.

His hands were everywhere, his lips right behind, leaving a trail of heat across her skin. Clutching his shirt in her hands, Abby kept trying to pull him closer, meeting him kiss for kiss.

He pulled back to watch, almost hypnotized by the movement of her hands down the front of his shirt as she undid each button. After she yanked the shirt from his trousers and pushed it off his shoulders, her fingers traveled over him, exploring every muscle, every angle, everywhere she could.

She was taking him to the brink… and far beyond. And he seriously didn't know if he had the strength to stop her. It was when she began fumbling with his belt buckle, he finally got a grip on the small bit of sanity he still possessed.

He gathered her hair in his hands, and his lips traveling in a trail of kisses up her neck, he whispered in her ear. "Abby, we need to slow down. I don't want to rush this. I want to remember every minute, every single second we have together."

Her hands stilled. Then she reached up to run them through his hair before she linked her fingers behind his neck. Closing her eyes, she lifted her face to his, giving him a slow, languid kiss.

She couldn't believe how much she wanted this man. And she wanted him anyway she could get him. Fast or slow, it didn't matter.

Ever since he'd picked her up earlier in the day, his subtle hints and chaste kisses had driven her crazy, bringing her to an almost feverish state of anticipation. And if he didn't make love to her soon, she was pretty sure she would go insane.

She opened her eyes, a delicious shiver running through her at the heated look in his. After pressing a trail of kisses along the line of his jaw, she whispered against his mouth. "It doesn't matter. Whatever happens, I know we'll never, ever forget this night."

And now, for Kevin, there was no longer any thought of taking it slow. His mouth never leaving hers, together they removed the rest of their clothing. And once the barriers were gone, he moved so that he was over her, surrounding her. With every inch of him pressing against her, it was as though he'd already become a part of her.

But it wasn't enough. She wanted him to ease this desperate ache building inside of her. She gripped his arms with her hands, trying to pull him closer.

Tenderly brushing the hair back from her face, he gazed down at her. His lips just grazing hers, he whispered against her mouth. "I want you, sugar. I want all of you. Tell me you want this, too."

She was going to try, but honestly? It was taking everything she had to even breathe. But it really didn't matter, because her heart had already decided for her. She belonged to him, no matter what happened.

Tonight, tomorrow and all the days to come.

Her answer finally came in a long sigh.

"Oh, God... yes, I want all of you."

With one last look into her eyes, he murmured her name right before he claimed her mouth in another kiss.

Then he went on to do exactly what she'd asked of him.

Besides the muffled voices of hotel guests as they passed by in the hallway outside Abby and Kevin's room, there was only silence.

Sprawled beside Kevin, her head resting on his chest, Abby was held spellbound by the steady beating of his heart. The memory of how furiously it had been beating only minutes before, a faint smile drifted across her face.

Or had it been hours? She wasn't sure. Nor did she care. All she wanted was to hang onto this warm lethargy filling her, to soak up the feeling of being loved by Kevin, to remember every kiss, every touch.

His eyes closed, and in the same dream-like state, Kevin lazily ran his fingers through her hair. He had known to be with her would be amazing, but never had he thought it would be as mind shattering as this. Responding to him with a passion beyond his wildest dreams, she took his body and heart by storm, leaving him feeling like he was on top of the world.

He pressed a kiss in her hair. "You okay, sugar?"

She lifted her head to give him a kiss. "Yes, being with you… I've never…" She sighed, shaking her head.

"I know, sugar, I know. I feel it too." And even though he could see she was on the verge of tears, he was smiling. These tears he could handle… happy tears.

He gathered her hair in his hands, and burying his face in the soft curls, he sighed against her neck. "From the very first moment I saw you, even though you were yelling at me, all I wanted was to run my hands through your hair. Your glorious hair. And, though you won't admit to this, we both know it's red. And now my favorite color."

She snuggled closer. He could hear the smile in her voice. "I don't believe I was yelling at you. I was merely trying to make a point."

"*Mmm…*" When this was his only response, she sighed. "Ok, so maybe I got a little carried away. But you made me so mad."

In the midst of pressing a trail of kisses up her neck, his voice was teasing. "That's because you didn't want to admit you liked me. Or how much you wanted me to kiss you."

He began to chuckle. She searched his face, her expression now suspicious. And though he tried to be serious, the smile tweaking the corner of his mouth gave him away. "I was just thinking about the one trait we discussed. You know… how redheads are known to be…"

She pressed her hand to his mouth, struggling not to laugh. "Don't! I can't believe you're bringing…" This was as far as she got before she found herself on her back with him gazing down at her.

He couldn't keep the boyish grin off his face. After dropping a quick kiss to the tip of her nose, his lips traveled down to brush over her mouth.

"*Ah…* but it looks like it's true, sugar. And I'm never going tire of testing it out." He shook his head. "Nope, never."

His head tilted, he gazed down at her. Again, his attempt to remain serious fell flat. "*Hmm…* correct me if I'm wrong, but I also remember you so adamantly insisting proof of this so-called trait would never come from you. I'd have to find the answer elsewhere, you said."

He chuckled. "Yes, I do believe that's exactly what you said. So high and mighty you were back then. And now look at you, already with two strikes against you. The 'you'll never bake for me' threat being the first, this the second."

His lips brushing over hers, his voice grew husky. "One more strike, sugar, and you'll belong to me. Yep, you'll be all mine."

She laughed. "I don't think that's the way it's supposed to go."

He smiled. "In this game, it is."

His very convincing kiss was a confirmation of this.

His eyes adjusting to the darkness, Kevin leaned over to look at the clock on the nightstand.

Four-sixteen glowed in red.

He turned to search for Abby, to find she had strayed to the far side of the bed. She had left the covers behind and was now curled up into herself to keep warm.

Moving next to her, he drew her under the comforter with him. After he adjusted the pillow more comfortably beneath his head, he closed his eyes, his intention to go back to sleep.

But she gave this soft little sigh, her arm drifting down over him as she snuggled against him. His eyes going wide, he knew there was no chance of falling back to sleep now.

Lifting his head, he watched her lashes flutter open, only to close again. Then she turned to him with a sigh. *"Umm... nice."* She reached over to link her hands behind his neck and, lifting her face to his, gave him a lazy kiss.

Peering more closely at her, he was almost more intrigued than aroused.

Well, maybe, but not quite. Was she doing this in her sleep? Because even though his first impulse was to go along with what she was offering, he'd rather she be awake for this.

He also wanted to be able to look into her eyes.

He couldn't even begin to explain what it did to him when they turned dark with passion at his touch, becoming an even deeper shade of green.

Her lashes fluttered open again. But this time they remained open, her mouth curving into a smile when she saw him gazing down at her.

He smoothed her hair back from her face, the deep timbre of his voice sending a shiver through her. "Hey, you kicked the blanket off and I thought you might be cold."

She gave him another kiss, her voice drowsy with sleep. "You're really here." Her eyes slowly searching his face, she sighed. "It wasn't a dream…"

His hand stilled in her hair. In a way, it was a dream, he thought. But it was their dream. The perfect dream.

He smiled at her. "What we have is so much better than a dream, sugar. It's the real thing. And yes, I'm right here. I'm not planning on going anywhere."

Not now, not forever.

His lips moved in a slow trail over the curve of her jaw before his mouth came down on hers, claiming it in a kiss. When she reached up to tangle her hands in his hair, what had started out so slow and easy, now became more demanding, more urgent.

His whispers became promises, his touch more daring. Caught up in the passion they had now discovered as their own, they became lost in each other once again.

But this time, it was different.

This time they took it slow.

CHAPTER 16

Giving the salad one last toss, Abby set it next to the basket of rolls on the kitchen island of Katy and Stephen's Lincoln Park brownstone.

She took a sip of her Mimosa, watching as Katy added more salt and pepper to the potatoes she was sautéing. This was all happening as she kept up a constant chatter.

When Katy went to the refrigerator to take out a carton of eggs, Abby glanced over at Kevin. Walking around the room, he had one-month old Olivia Rose tucked against his shoulder.

Whatever magical words he whispered to her were working. Her eyes closed and a tiny smile on her face, she hadn't uttered a single peep since Katy had placed her in his arms.

Abby smiled. She knew all too well what it was like to be in his arms. So she could understand the spell Olivia was under right now.

He came to stand next to her. "Would you like to hold her?"

She peered up at him. She wasn't sure.

Did she?

Children were a mystery to her. Since she had been an only child, her time growing up had been spent almost entirely with adults.

And babies?

Well, they seemed so fragile.

What if you drop her?

Her brow creased in concern. "I don't know. I've had little experience with babies. What if I do something wrong?"

He chuckled as he gently lowered Olivia into her arms. "Aw, Abby, she won't break. Just look at her. She's such an amazing little miracle."

Once Olivia had settled in her arms, gazing down at her perfect little face, a feeling of peace flowed through her. And love… suddenly she was filled with such a fierce tenderness for this tiny little person.

Almost in awe, she glanced up at Kevin to find he was watching her, a strange expression on his face. Gently tucking a straying strand of her hair behind her ear, he cleared his throat. "Holding her in your arms, you look like an angel. I bet you'll be an amazing mother."

Then, in an attempt to lighten the moment, he grinned. "I can see it now… you with a houseful of kids, all with red, curly hair and your spirited disposition."

He winked at her. "Paybacks. Because I'm sure you were a handful when you were little."

A flash of uncertainty crossed her face. Then she smiled. "I'll have you know I was a model child. And please, tell me what's up with you and your father and this 'household of kids' comment? Seriously, Kevin, I don't know if I'll ever be ready for that."

Katy had been whisking eggs while listening to their conversation. She laughed. "*Ha,* I don't think anyone is ever ready for kids. Stephen and I still wonder what we got ourselves into."

Scrunching up her face, her hand stilled. "I still can't believe last night was the first time we've gone out since Olivia was born. Just the two of us. I almost forgot how to put on my makeup."

She set the bowl of eggs on the island. "It was so nice. We actually talked about adult things. Not our usual conversations involving diapers or bottles."

After a long sigh, she picked up the bowl and went back to whisking the eggs.

Kevin had leaned against the counter, watching Abby and Olivia. He shot a glance over at Katy. "I have an idea. Why don't you and

Stephen go to the game tonight while Abby and I stay here with Olivia?"

When Katy began shaking her head, Stephen turned to her, a pleading expression on his face. "Oh, Kat… come on. How can we turn down an offer like this? It's the All Star Game."

He sent a guiltily glance over at Abby. "Unless you were looking forward to going to the game, Abby."

Abby tore her gaze away from Olivia to smile at him. "I don't mind. If I had a choice, I'd rather go to a game Kevin was in."

Kevin smiled, rubbing his hands together. "It's settled then. You'll go to the game and Abby and I will stay with Olivia." When Abby nodded, he leaned over to give her a kiss. "Thanks, sugar."

This instantly brought a dramatic sigh from Katy. "You two are so perfect together. I'm so glad you're getting married. Have you set a date yet?"

Abby fixed her gaze on Olivia, rearranging her blanket. She was going to let Kevin handle this one.

Kevin shrugged. "Well, if it was up to me, we'd find a courthouse and get married." His grin was teasing. "Or maybe make a quick trip to Vegas."

At Katy's horrified look, he laughed. "Just kidding, just kidding. Come on… you know me better than that."

His eyes went to Abby. "But I have a feeling Abby would much rather wait until the season is over so we can do it up in style. After all, you only get married once."

Abby glanced up at him to see he was gazing down at her, an almost challenging look on his face. It took all the control she had not to blurt out, if he was serious, she'd be perfectly happy with a courthouse wedding. Or a trip to Vegas. She wouldn't care.

But why say anything at all?

Because they both knew none of this was going to happen.

But let's say they did decide to get married. That there was even the slightest chance this could happen. With Kevin standing at the altar, waiting for her to walk down the aisle?

Then, yes. You'd definitely entertain the possibility of a big wedding. Because you're pretty sure you'd want to invite the entire world.

She smiled, just thinking about this.

"Abby? Are you still with us?" Katy was grinning at her. "My, my, judging by the dreamy look on your face, whatever you're thinking about must be pretty wonderful."

When Abby only responded with a smile, Katy took off her apron and, tossing it on the counter, gestured for Abby to follow her. "Come on, let's go upstairs so you can see Olivia's room. After we put her in her crib, I'll show you where everything is for tonight. Then we'll enjoy a peaceful and baby free brunch."

Stephen gave a short laugh. "*Ha...* don't get your hopes up. It seems our little angel has some kind of alert button that goes off when we even think about sitting down to eat."

Katy smiled over at him, shaking head. "Maybe if you'd stop picking her up every time she even makes a peep, this would change,"

He shrugged. "*Aw, Kat...* I can't help it. She's so little. And so dependent on us."

Kevin laughed, shaking his head. "It looks like she's going to be spoiled, just like her mom."

Still holding Olivia, Abby put her finger to her lips. "Shush, all of you. Or you'll wake her. I don't know about you, but I'm really hungry after watching Katy prepare all this food. So, Katy, lead the way."

Katy pointed her finger at Stephen. "You're in charge of scrambling those eggs while we're gone."

After Kevin watched Abby and Katy walk out of the room, he turned to Stephen. A huge grin on his face, he was shaking his head.

Kevin groaned, holding up his hand in protest. "*Damn...* don't even start."

Stephen shrugged. "Sorry, but this is too big. Never did I think I'd see you this crazy about a woman. I thought for sure you'd be playing the field now that you're this hot shot baseball sensation."

He poured more wine into their glasses, still grinning. "Correct me if I'm wrong, but weren't you the one who gave that stirring speech at our wedding about how your career took precedence over everything? With women being at the top of the list to avoid?"

Kevin had the grace to look embarrassed. "I believe a lot of that was due to the top shelf liqueur Nicholas had on hand. And his second cousin, or whatever she was, who wouldn't leave me alone."

He shook his head at the memory. "I couldn't shake that woman for the life of me." Then he grinned. "And hey, there's no law against changing your mind, you know."

Stephen chuckled. "*Uh huh...* it all flies out the window when love comes knocking on your door."

He turned on the stove before he glanced over at Kevin. "So, exactly how long have you and Abby been together? Katy and I were floored when you made the announcement at dinner last night. We weren't even aware you were dating anyone, let alone about to get engaged."

He placed a pan on the burner, dumping in a huge chunk of butter. Noting Kevin's raised eyebrow, he shrugged. "Hey, she put me in charge." Then he grinned. "And you just wait. After she tastes them, she'll say they're the best scrambled eggs she's ever had."

He raised his glass in a toast. "I guarantee this."

He poured the egg mixture into the now sizzling pan before shooting another glance at Kevin. "So? You and Abby? How long?"

Kevin cleared his throat. "*Umm...* believe it or not, I've only known her for not even two weeks."

Stephen let out a big laugh. "That long? I think I asked Katy to marry me after only a couple of days, blurting it out while I watched her make dinner, right in this very kitchen. I had worked out this elaborate plan to lure her here, using this gourmet kitchen as bait. Along with the promise we would make dinner together. Unfortunately, cooking was not my forte."

He waved the spatula in the air. "I didn't know a knife from one of these things. But look at me now!" He grinned. "Let's just say it all went as planned, turning out to be a night I'll never forget."

He shook his head. "I'm pretty sure I shocked the hell out of her when I threw out the idea of marriage so quickly. She retaliated by making me wait for almost three months before she finally said yes."

Kevin leaned against the counter, and crossing his arms, he chuckled. "From the day she was born, Katy has never been one to make a quick decision. Except when it came to you. I remember the text she sent the night of your first date, that you were the one. When that happened, I figured it was a done deal."

He studied the wine in his glass, a goofy smile on his face. "I feel the same about Abby. I can't even remember what my life was like before I met her. And I don't even want to think how it would be without her."

He held his wine glass up to Kevin in a toast. "She's definitely the one. Wish me luck."

Kevin tipped his glass against Stephen's. "I never thought I'd say this, but let's hear it for love."

They both grinned.

Who says men aren't sentimental?

Abby gazed around Olivia's room before she smiled, turning to Katy. "Oh Katy, how precious! I would have given anything to have a room like this when I was growing up."

Olivia's room was the perfect little girl's room, all done up in white and different shades of pink. Three of the walls were covered with a pink and white striped wallpaper, the fourth featured a mural of a mystical fairy tale land, complete with a castle.

The furniture and wood trim were a soft white, a pink and white shag area rug a soft contrast against the gleaming oak floors. While the window treatments, window seat, rocking chair cushions and bedding for the crib were done in a pink and white plaid fabric.

A collection of dolls and teddy bears, along with an impressive display of books in the built-in bookshelf on one wall, added the finishing touch.

While Katy put Olivia in her crib, Abby studied the mural. "Did someone paint this for you?"

Katy nodded. "My friend Anna. Isn't it wonderful? She's such a talented artist. She recently got married and is now living in London with her new husband, Nicholas. They are expecting a baby in September."

She sighed. "I miss her. I wish she lived closer so our children could be friends. Best friends like we have always been."

Abby reached over to give her a hug. "I am sure she misses you even more, since she's the one who had to move away."

Then, her thoughts going to Kevin's mother and her obsession with him and Melissa, she felt she had to say something. "If two people are meant to be together, as friends, or maybe more, it will happen. But you can't force it."

Katy glanced over at her. Then she laughed. "Why do I feel you're telling me this for a reason? Maybe because of Melissa?"

She enveloped Abby in a hug. "Oh Abby, trust me... you have no reason to worry. Melissa and Kevin are only friends, if even that. You're the one he loves. This is obvious by the way he looks at you."

She shrugged. "And Melissa? Since she's been around forever, I think my mother always assumed she and Kevin would marry. But once she sees more of you and Kevin together, she'll realize this will never happen."

She frowned. "I wish she and my father hadn't cancelled out on us today. This would've given you the chance to get to know each other better. But my father called earlier to say there was a change of plans and they'd have to pass. I'm sure Kevin is disappointed."

She shrugged. "Oh well, there will be other times."

Abby had her doubts about this. She could only hope Katy knew what she was talking about.

This was all forgotten when Katy began showing her what was needed to take care of Olivia, along with a long list of detailed instructions.

After she checked to see Olivia was still sleeping, Katy motioned for Abby to follow her out of the room. She was all smiles. "Come on. I'm starving! I hope Kevin didn't make a mess of things. Between him and Kevin, who knows what kind of trouble they got into?"

She laughed. "When I first saw the gourmet kitchen Stephen had, I thought I'd struck gold. I'd found a man who could cook. But no such luck." She grinned. "But there are so many other things I love about him. And now, with Olivia? I have to pinch myself to prove it's all real. I love being married and I know you will, too."

She gave Abby another hug. "I'm so excited for both of you."

Abby smiled, wishing she had a reason to feel the same.

The sound of Abby and Katy's voices floated into the kitchen.

Stephan tore his gaze away from the All Star Pre-Game coverage he and Kevin were watching on the big screen. Then he took a big gulp of his wine.

He shot a guilty look over at Kevin. "I better concentrate on these eggs. If I mess up, Katy will never let me hear the end of it. One job, she'll say... I gave you one job and you couldn't even handle that."

Waving the spatula to emphasize his point, he sent a chunk of egg flying. When it landed on the counter right in front of Kevin, he scooped it up in his hand and tossed it into his mouth.

After he swallowed, he sent Stephen a big grin. "There you go... the evidence has been destroyed. With no one to witness your blunder but me."

Laughing, Stephan grabbed the bottle and topped the wine in their glasses.

This called for another toast.

Abby and Katy came into the kitchen to find both men still laughing, their wine glasses raised in a toast.

Katy took the spatula from Stephen, giving him a curious glance. "What's so funny that has the two of you laughing like this? And what are you celebrating?"

When Stephen only smiled, shaking his head, she pointed him towards the island. "Okay, at least it looks like you did a good job with the eggs. So, go ahead, sit down."

After she motioned for Kevin and Abby to join him, she spooned the eggs into a serving dish. Scooping up the last bit of eggs left in the pan, she popped it in her mouth.

She smiled at Stephen. "I have to hand it to you, you make the best scrambled eggs."

Their eyes meeting, both he and Kevin burst out laughing. Puzzled, Katy glanced at the eggs and then over at Abby, who shrugged.

Still laughing, Kevin held up his hand, his palm facing Kevin. "What did I tell you? Man, why didn't I make that bet with you? I would've won big."

He held out his hand. "Come on, give me five!"

Abby had intended to stay awake to watch the World Series Game on TV with Kevin. But snuggled up against him, the comforting sound of his heartbeat next to her ear, she drifted off to sleep.

But now her sleep had been interrupted. Someone was talking. Very loudly, they were doing this. Burrowing further into the shelter of Kevin's arms, she tried to block it all out.

Then she remembered where she was.

In a panic, she tried to push her way out of Kevin's arms. But he pulled her back, holding her against him. "Hey, hey... calm down, sugar. Everything's fine. I changed Olivia, she had her bottle, and she's sound asleep in her crib. Katie and Stephen just got back from the game and Katy just went up to check on her."

He chuckled. "It seems I'm very good at putting people to sleep tonight."

Abby relaxed back against him with a huge sigh of relief.

Thank God. But what kind of baby sitter are you?

Kevin smiled when he saw the frown on her face. "I know what you're thinking and you're wrong. You're a great baby sitter." He caught the corner of her mouth in a kiss. "*Hmm... could it be you didn't get enough sleep last night?*"

Before she could respond, Katy came bouncing back into the

room, a big smile on her face. "She's sound asleep. So, it's settled. You two can watch her for us anytime."

She sighed. "This has been such a wonderful day. We can't thank you enough."

Kevin stood and after he gave a long stretch, he reached for Abby's hand, pulling her up from the sofa. "Next time we're in town, we will be more than glad to do that. But now, we're going to take off. I called for a taxi and it should be here any minute."

He reached over to give Katy a big hug. "Since we have an early flight tomorrow, we won't see you again before we leave. Thanks for brunch and for letting us watch Olivia. It was great spending time with you."

He turned to Stephen. "And you better send lots of photos and updates of my new favorite niece. I'm so proud of the both of you. She's beautiful."

After Abby had also said her goodbyes, she and Kevin ran down the front steps to their waiting taxi. Just as Kevin was about to shut the door, Katy called out. "Don't forget, as soon as you two decide on a date for the wedding, let us know. We can't wait!"

Kevin sent her a thumbs up. It was only after he gave the driver the name of their hotel and they'd pulled away from the curb, he glanced over at Abby.

She was frowning.

He put his arm around her. "*Aw, sugar...* trust me. It's going to be fine."

"But..."

He pressed a kiss to her mouth. "Don't worry, we'll figure it out. But right now? I want to enjoy this time we have, maybe even open that bottle of champagne they gave us."

He smiled. "We have one more night here and I don't want to waste a single moment."

CHAPTER 17

I can't promise I'll fix all your problems.
But I can promise I'll never let you face them alone.
~ Unknown

*A*bby was finding it hard to get back to her usual routine.

Ever since Kevin had dropped her off at her condo after their weekend in Chicago, she'd been moping around, not accomplishing much of anything.

She felt unsettled.

As if something wasn't right.

Of course it wasn't.

How could it be, when you're here and Kevin isn't?

She missed him more than she thought she could miss anyone.

Come on, he only lives down the street. You'll see him before you know it. Tonight, as a matter of fact.

She signed into her computer, and scrolling through her emails, she was surprised to see one had just popped up from Mia. The same Mia she met when she went to Kevin's game.

The email was regarding a benefit for The Children's Hospital on the last Monday of July. Yes, she knew this was only a little over two weeks away, but they were in a bind. If Abby could donate cookies for favors, this would be fantastic. Three hundred and fifty cookies should do it, Mia wrote.

The theme was Baseballs, Babies and Teddy Bears.

Oh… and if this was possible? The more colorful and unique the cookies, the better.

Abby groaned, dragging her hands through her hair.

Was she serious?

Three hundred and fifty cookies? The more colorful and unique the better?

Mia threw this out like it was no big deal. It was obvious she had no clue how much work this would involve, having never made cookies in her life. If anything, both she and her sister Kelly probably avoided cookies like the plague.

Stop it. They both could be very nice. You can't hate them just because they're beautiful.

She sighed. It wasn't like she had a lot of orders to fill. And it was for a good cause. It could also bring in new customers, something she would welcome right now.

So, before she could change her mind, she sent back the response she would be more than happy to make the cookies.

She picked up her phone to see if she had any calls, hoping for one from Kevin. Disappointed there wasn't, she saw someone had left a voicemail.

She checked the name.

Ann Kardell?

Kevin's mother?

She almost dropped the phone, her stomach muscles clenching in fear.

Yes, fear… because whatever this woman had to say, she knew it wouldn't be good.

After setting the phone on the counter, when she'd rather throw it in the trash instead, she tried to ignore it was there.

But it's Kevin's mother. So, it could be important.

She picked up the phone and holding her breath, she hit accept.

His mother's voice resonated in the silent kitchen, not a hint of friendliness in her message.

> *"This is Ann Kardell. I will be in*
> *Cleveland this Wednesday for a*
> *meeting. While I'm in the area,*
> *I'd like to meet with you at Café*
> *Latte on Cedar Road at noon.*
> *Respond only if you're unable*
> *to come."*

Abby felt like she was back in the restaurant, her stomach in knots, her hands shaking. His mother's tone of voice was so formal and demanding, her message an order on her terms, and her terms only.

But why are you surprised?

Abby's first impulse was to reply with a definite no. But since his mother had already made it clear she didn't approve of her as Kevin's choice of fiancé, she certainly didn't want to give her even more of a reason to dislike her.

But maybe she should give her the benefit of the doubt, find out what she has to say? And was it possible Katy may have been right? This was her way of reaching out?

If so, she had a strange way of going about it.

She realized she was pacing back and forth. With a frustrated sigh, she found a pen and notepad and sat down at the island. After she made a list of the ingredients she would need for the benefit cookies, she grabbed her car keys and credit card.

Then after giving Poppy a treat, she ran out to her SUV.

She needed to keep busy, to stop thinking about this meeting with Kevin's mother.

Otherwise, she would surely lose her mind before Wednesday rolled around.

The game had gone into extra innings, ending in a loss.

This meant the atmosphere of the locker room was subdued, only a few of the guys still hanging around.

After closing the door to his locker, Kevin turned, almost running into Chester. The mocking expression on his face was a warning he was ready to fire off a new round of insults.

He groaned.

Geeez... now what?

He tried to sidestep him, but Chester was not so easily put off. His arms crossed over his chest, he grinned. "Hey, I see you and your hot little redhead are in the news again. But it looks like things aren't going so well, huh?"

Kevin came to an abrupt halt, every muscle in his body tensing.

What the hell? What was with this guy? But, wait... what does he mean?

The memory of flashes going off in the Chicago restaurant, he almost groaned. Then he caught himself, giving a short laugh instead.

He'd be damned if he let Chester get the better of him.

His expression unreadable, he jerked his head over at Chester. "Come on, are you telling me you believe everything you read in those social media posts?"

He laughed. "I thought you were smarter than that."

The locker room became deathly silent, everyone's attention shifting to Chester, who looked like he was ready to explode.

Alex jumped off the bench, and stepping between the two men, he laughed. "Hey, you two... come on, cool it."

He shook his head over at Kevin. "Of course, he doesn't. He just likes to razz people. This is what he does."

His glance shifted over to Chester. "Right, Chez?"

When Chester appeared to have nothing to say, Kevin sent him a curt nod. "Since you seem so interested, I can assure you everything is fine between me and Abby. In fact, it couldn't be better. So, thanks for asking."

After a quick salute and a smile, he left.

Once he was in his car, he leaned his head back against the seat and closed his eyes.

What is it about Chester that bugs you so much? And why do you let him get to you?

Whatever it was, the feeling seemed to be mutual.

He shook his head.

He didn't have time for this.

And now? With the news of this recent photo, Chester was the least of his worries.

Damn...

He wondered if Abby had seen it yet. And if she was okay with it.

He sighed…

There was no way it would be this simple.

Abby had returned home with her baking supplies, and now she was taking a break.

Leaning against the kitchen counter, she was reading a text from Sophie.

She wanted to know if Abby had seen the latest post about her and Kevin on the Cleveland sports fan page.

Sophie was curious, who was the other woman in the photo?

A famous model?

Or maybe an actress?

And how did she know Kevin?

Looking up from her phone, Abby groaned.

Oh, no... was this in Chicago?

She had the sudden urge to toss her phone into the garbage. Or hide it somewhere. Because it certainly hadn't brought her any good news today, had it?

But a sign she had lost her mind, she logged onto the fan page. She scrolled down through the posts until she found the one she was looking for.

> *So, it now looks like it's not all love and*
> *kisses between Kevin Kardell and his little*
> *redhead. Take a look at this photo taken*

*in a Chicago restaurant last weekend. She
certainly doesn't look very happy with the
attention Kevin is receiving from another
woman - with the whole Kardell family as
witnesses. Does this mean Kevin has struck
out? Or will he be able to make a comeback?
It will be interesting to see how he handles
this. As always, we'll keep you posted.*

The photo showed her scowling face as she watched what appeared to be a very passionate kiss shared between Melissa and Kevin.

Could you look any worse?

She groaned, dragging her hands through her hair. No, she didn't think this would be possible.

Was it just her imagination or did it seem like there was something bigger than the both of them, trying to tear them apart?

First his mother?

And now this?

Parked in his driveway, Kevin took out his phone. Finding the fan page, he scrolled down until he found the photo.

Damn...

Abby was not going to be happy when she saw this, not with the angry look the photographer had captured on her face.

He read the comment, shaking his head.

Nope, this wasn't going to go over well at all.

He studied the photo more closely. He smiled. With her face all scrunched up, Abby looked like a little girl, all ready for a fight.

Unfortunately, he knew she wouldn't be of the same opinion.

On a more positive note, the photographer must have run off before he'd shouted out, not only to his family, but almost the entire restaurant, he and Abby were engaged. Had the photographer captured this? They'd have a much bigger problem on their hands.

He shook his head. He didn't understand.

Why wouldn't everyone just leave them alone?

The ingredients assembled in front of her, Abby was ready to mix up her first batch of cookie dough.

She measured out the dry ingredients, but couldn't remember if she'd added the baking powder. So she had to start all over again.

Then the butter hadn't softened enough, taking forever to mix in. After the mixture of butter and sugar had finally reached the right consistency, she reached for the vanilla. Her hand hit the bottle, sending it crashing to the floor.

She was seriously beginning to doubt herself.

Why did you even think this would be a good idea? Especially, in the mood you're in?

Well, she was better than this. It was time to concentrate on this cookie dough in front of her. Forget about everything else, starting with Kevin's mother and the photo.

She cleaned up the spill, brought out a new bottle of vanilla, and got to work.

With the mixer running at high speed and her music as loud as it could go, Abby didn't hear Kevin knock on the front door.

Nor did she hear when he let himself in.

She also didn't notice when he turned off the music.

So, she had no idea he was watching her as she began adding the flour to the other ingredients in the mixing bowl.

And this was when everything went so horribly out of control.

As she began scraping the sides of the bowl, her spatula got tangled in the beaters. Jerked out of her hand, it hit the measuring cup of flour she was holding in her other hand and flipped it, sending a shower of flour right at her.

And suddenly, it was all too much.

Is anything going to go right for you today?

She turned off the mixer and after she yanked the spatula out of the bowl, she flung it into the sink. Then she grabbed a dish towel, scrubbing it over her face and through her hair.

"Damn... damn... damn..."

She suddenly lifted her head, confused.

What happened to the music?

She whirled around, her mouth dropping open in shock.

Kevin was standing a few feet away, a concerned expression on his face.

"Abby, are you okay?" He kept his eyes on her as he inched closer. "What's going on here?"

At first, she only shook her head. Then, with a hysterical sob-like-laugh, she launched herself into his arms and wrapped her arms around his neck. The kiss she gave him was as passionate, if not even more so, than the kiss she gave him that day at the ballpark.

He was thrilled to get such a kiss.

But at the same time, he was very worried. There was a sense of desperation about her. And even though he knew this frantic greeting of hers was most likely brought on by what just went wrong in her kitchen, or because of the latest fan photo, he had the distinct feeling there was something deeper going on.

And it was time he found out what it was.

Tonight.

And you aren't leaving until you do.

When she slipped her hands under his shirt and began running them over his skin in an almost frenzied motion, he scooped her up and carried her into the bedroom. Once he was settled next to her on the bed, he smoothed the hair back from her face. "Tell me what's wrong, sugar."

She closed her eyes, shaking her head. "I don't think I can do this, Kevin. I can't. Everyone seems to be against us. Maybe it's all because of me. Or maybe we aren't meant to be together. I don't know."

Now becoming even more concerned, he continued to run his fingers through her hair, his voice soft and soothing. "Who's all against us? If you're talking about the new photo posted today, you can't let it get to you. You need to ignore it. That's what I'm going to do."

She searched his face. "But then there's…" She pressed her lips together, shaking her head.

She certainly couldn't tell him about the message from his mother.

He sighed. "Sugar, just tell me."

She kept shaking her head. Now that he was with her, she only wanted him to hold her, nothing more.

She took a deep breath and reaching up to clasp her hands behind his neck, she smiled up at him. "I missed you. How was your game?"

He leaned in to place a kiss to her mouth, smiling when she responded by closing her eyes and giving a little sigh. "I missed you, too. And we lost."

Her lashes flying open, she frowned. "Oh Kevin, I'm so sorry."

He placed another kiss to her mouth. "It's okay. There are a lot of games still to be played. What's more important right now is you. And that you're okay."

His lips had now traveled along her jaw and up to her ear, his mouth curving into a smile against her skin. "I've never kissed anyone covered in flour before. It's an… *umm*… unique experience."

Flour? Oh no, the cookie dough. If you leave it out, it will be ruined. And you can't afford to let that happen.

She tried to scramble out of his arms, not quite making it to the edge of the bed before he pulled her back. "Hey, where are you going?"

After she managed to escape his grasp, her response came over her shoulder as she hurried down the hall. "My cookie dough. It won't be any good if I don't finish it."

Falling back on the bed, he groaned. *So, so close, yet still so far…*

With a long sigh, he hauled himself off the bed and set off for the kitchen, his voice resigned.

"Tell me what you want me to do."

The cookie dough had been mixed, divided, wrapped, and placed in the freezer. The dishwasher was running, counters had been cleared and the floor swept.

And now, Abby was showing Kevin the three different cookie designs she'd chosen for the benefit. A baseball with the team logo, a teddy bear with a bow in the team colors, and a baby's face with a baseball hat sporting the logo of the Children's Hospital.

Leaning against the counter, Kevin was trying to concentrate on what she was telling him.

He wanted to, he really did.

But he couldn't stop thinking about how much he'd missed her. And how he wanted to take her into his arms and love her.

This was when he realized she had become silent. Gazing up at him, the tentative smile on her face had him snapping back to attention.

He smiled. "Sugar, you'll wow everyone with these. But can you afford the time away from your business to do this?"

Tracing the marble pattern of the counter with her fingertip, she shrugged, a wry smile on her face. "My business isn't exactly booming right now. So, I'm hoping this might be the big break I've been looking for."

She shot him a guilty look. "Not that I don't care about helping the children's hospital. Because I do."

He reached out to stroke her cheek. "I know you do. And if you need help, I'm here for you."

A stubborn look came over her face and her hands clenched to her sides, she backed away from him. "No, I can do this on my own. I'm not one of those girls. You know, the kind that only wants to be with someone like you because of what they can get. Somehow, I'll make it work." She turned away and began loading the dishwasher.

And as strange as this might seem, all he could think about was Chester.

And why the hell was he thinking of Chester at a moment like this?

Maybe it was because he couldn't wait until he had the chance to tell him he was wrong about Abby?

Yeah, Chester... you are so wrong.

Abby was not even close to being one of those women looking for their own personal sports star. Chester could only dream of finding a woman like he'd found in Abby.

But right now? He had been patient long enough. Moving behind her, he wrapped his arms around her.

Her head falling back against his shoulder, she relaxed against him as he kissed his way up her neck. His lips brushing over hers, once, twice, she sighed, closing her eyes.

This had him smiling as he whispered in her ear. "How about we clean this up later? Because right now, all I can think about is how much I want your undivided attention, flour covered and all." He stepped back, and taking her hand, he began leading her out of the kitchen.

She could hear the smile in his voice.

"And the first thing I want from you is another one of those kisses of yours."

Abby trailed her fingertips down the side of Kevin's face, her whisper coming against his shoulder. "When we're together like this, I feel like nothing matters but us. I wish we could stay like this forever."

"You'd probably get tired of me." She could hear the smile in his voice. "Too much of a good thing."

"*Umm… you're very confident. Aren't you?*"

He gazed down at her, a deep sigh coming from him. As much as he wanted to stay in each other's arms, sated from the love they'd shared, he knew they couldn't. He needed to find out what burden she was carrying, unable to let go. His mind wouldn't rest until he did.

His hand traveled down her arm in a gentle caress. "Abby, we need to talk."

When she looked up at him, an anxious expression on her face, he pressed a kiss to her forehead. "It's nothing bad, sugar. I just want you to be open with me. I sense something hurt you in your past and whatever it is, you need to let it go. And whatever it is, I will be right here for you."

Lowering her head to his chest, she was silent.

He shifted, moving to face her. "Sugar, look at me. Trust me. Nothing you could tell me would change the way I feel about you."

Her eyes beginning to fill, she shook her head, burying her face deeper into his shoulder.

His hand trailing through her hair, he waited.

She finally let out a long, shaky sigh. And once she began to speak, she didn't stop.

"You would've liked my dad. He had the same dream you have, to be a professional baseball player. But, unlike you, he didn't have what it took to make the team."

She smiled. "But I thought he was the best baseball player in the whole world. One of my fondest memories was playing catch with him in the backyard. He also coached my softball team one summer."

When he smiled, a look of surprise on his face, she shook her head. "Oh no, I wasn't very good. I can still remember him telling me I didn't pay attention, and I talked too much. That's how he came up with his nickname for me, Gabby Abby."

He chuckled, envisioning this younger Abby. Her hair in a tangle, freckles scattered across her cheeks and her green eyes challenging her father's request to stop talking and listen.

She sighed. "He got a job in the team's office. According to what little my mom told me, he didn't think he was making enough money. So, he started betting on the games. And whenever he could, he would take me to a game. I knew nothing about the gambling, only that he claimed I brought him good luck."

Her smile was wistful. "We had so much fun. He introduced me to everyone he worked with. I even got to meet some of the players. And during the games, he would always explain what was going on, never tiring of my questions. I loved going with him. But then he started losing, and he was no longer the dad I knew. He became moody. And he would get so mad, blowing up at even the littlest thing."

Her voice began to shake. "One day, when he was getting ready to go to a game, he told me I couldn't go with him. He said… he said it just wasn't working out. And then he left. I can still remember sitting on the front steps, watching as he drove away. And he never took me again."

This is when she began to cry, each breath she took, coming out in a sob.

She cried as though her heart was breaking.

Unable to swallow past the sudden lump in his throat, Kevin pulled her even closer. And even though he knew it wasn't enough, he tried to comfort her with the kisses he pressed in her hair.

She took a shaky breath. "I was so scared. I didn't know what was happening, only that my world was falling apart. He and my mom started fighting, their arguments sometimes so violent, I'd hold a pillow over my head to block out their voices. It got to the point I was almost relieved to hear the door slam, because this meant he was gone and the yelling would stop. But this also meant he could be gone for days."

His heart aching for her, Kevin closed his eyes. If there was some way he could bear the pain for her, he would do this in an instant. He wanted to tell her to stop, that she didn't need to tell him all of this. But deep inside, he knew he had to let her go on.

She was now crying in earnest. "I think he was in charge of the money they took in from the games, I don't know. And I'm not sure how, but they discovered money was missing. When they questioned my dad, he broke down and confessed he'd used it for gambling."

She sighed. "It must have been a lot of money because the next thing I knew, he was gone. Everyone around me was talking about how he had to go to jail, but they weren't telling me anything. So, I pretended I didn't care. My mom and I moved out of our house into this tiny apartment. We even had to move to a hotel for a short time where my mom did the cleaning in return for a room for us. I almost never saw her because she was always working. I just tried to be good, waiting for the day he would come back…"

Her voice trailed off and, closing her eyes, she was silent. When she spoke, the tone of her voice was weary. "But he never did. And to this day, I don't know what happened to him."

She searched his face. "I don't understand. Why didn't he come back? I didn't care what he did. The last time I saw him, he told me he would always love me, I was not to worry, and he would be back as soon as he could. He promised me this. So, I waited. And I waited. But he never came back."

Her hands clenched against him, her words ended in an anguished cry. "How could he just write me off? After he promised?"

Her eyes were pleading with him for an answer he didn't have. He could only shake his head as he held her against him, his fingers still running through her hair.

He finally found his voice. "Oh Abby, no child should have to go through what you did." He sighed. "I don't want you to think I'm taking your father's side, but I find it hard to believe it was his choice to cut you out of his life."

He wiped away the tears still slipping down her face. "Maybe something prevented him from coming home, something beyond his control. Or he was too ashamed of what he'd done and was afraid you wouldn't want to see him. Who knows what goes on in a person's mind in a situation like this?"

He brushed the hair back from her face, his heart aching at the pain he saw there. His voice was hesitant. "And your mother?"

She shook her head. "She never forgave him. Even though she kept us together, it was almost as if she lost her will to live. Eight years ago, she passed away. Her heart just gave up." Her smile was faint. "I like to think she died of a broken heart. That she really loved my dad, after all."

Then she gave a long, exhausted sigh. "It's okay. I've accepted I'll never see him again. And even if I did, I don't know if I could forgive him. It's been so long, I don't know if care anymore."

But as he watched the tears continue to slip down her face, he knew this wasn't true. She did care. And it was eating her up. She needed closure, one way or the other. Only then would she be able to move on with her life.

The sound of her voice, soft and anxious, interrupted his thoughts. "My parents must have been in love in the beginning, and look at what happened to them. What if the same happens to us?"

Desperately seeking an answer, her eyes searched his face. "What if what we feel for each other doesn't last? You'll change your mind... or you'll leave and never come back."

Speechless, he could only stare at her, thinking he must have heard wrong. How could she think he would change his mind? Or the unthinkable... he'd leave her?

But then again, he had never been in her shoes. His ability to trust hadn't been so brutally tested, only to be broken.

He cupped her chin in his hand, tilted her face up to his. "Abby, look at me. I'm never going to leave you. I'm not like your dad. And we'll never be like your parents. You will always, always come first in my life."

He rested his forehead against hers, his words brushing over her mouth.

"You will come before everything."

She began to relax in his arms, her next words coming from her heart.

"Oh Kevin, how I love... " Her eyes going wide, her mouth snapped shut before she turned her face away.

If she hadn't, she would've seen he was smiling. In fact, he was grinning like a kid on Christmas morning.

Propped up on his elbow, he tucked her hair behind her ear as he gazed down at her. "Abby..."

Drawn by the tenderness in his voice, she turned to face him, her eyes wide and trusting.

He pressed a kiss to her forehead, a hint of unsteadiness coming through in his voice.

"I want you to repeat after me. I..."

"I..." Her eyes searched his.

He nodded, his voice becoming softer. "Love..."

"Love..." This was barely a whisper.

He leaned in closer. "You."

"You." He could see the beginning of a smile on her lips.

He whispered. "Now say them together."

She squeezed her eyes shut. "You say it first."

His fingers caressing her cheek, his eyes held hers. "Ah, Abby… I love you. I don't know how it happened so fast. Nor did I know what I was missing before you came barreling into my life, flashing those gorgeous eyes and tossing your glorious hair around until I couldn't even think straight. I was lost from the very start. You've taken hold of my heart, and it will be yours for as long as you want it."

His voice deepened. "Now that I know what it feels like to be in love with you, I never, ever want it to end."

Her eyes were shining back at him. Lifting her mouth to his, she gave him the gentlest of kisses.

"I love you, too."

"Abby… wake up, sugar."

With a soft moan, Abby turned her face into her pillow. When he said her name a second time, she opened her eyes just enough to see he was sitting on the edge of the bed, dressed and ready to leave. He smiled as he brushed the hair from her face.

"I have to leave. God knows I'd rather stay with you, but I have to get all my stuff together before my ride gets here. I'm cutting it close as it is."

He leaned in to place a quick kiss to her mouth, but she wasn't going to let him get away with this. Oh, no, there was no chance of this happening.

Not after he had told her he loved her.

She wrapped her arms around him, pulling him down for a kiss, leaving no doubt how she felt about him. After he reluctantly pulled away, he stood, holding out his hand. "Come, walk me to the door. Then you can lock it after I leave. This will give me peace of mind, knowing you'll be safe while I'm gone."

With the quilt wrapped around her, she stumbled with him to the door. He took her into his arms. "I'll be back late Wednesday night. And before I forget, I don't think I formally asked you to be my date for the Children's Hospital benefit. I think I might've taken it for granted you'd go with me. I hope you will."

She nodded, following with an enormous yawn.

He smiled. "Good, because I can't wait to show you off. Both you and your cookies. I know you'll wow everyone, sugar."

Giving her one more kiss, he started down the steps, stopping midway. Satisfied at the click of the lock, he broke into a run.

He was singing under his breath.

> *"Take my hand,*
> *take my whole life too,*
> *For I can't help*
> *falling in love with you."*

He was smiling.

All those love songs on the radio? They're all starting to make sense to you, aren't they?

CHAPTER 18

*A*bby had been sitting in the parking lot of the Café Latte for what now felt like hours, or maybe even days. When in reality, it had only been about twenty-five minutes.

She should have known the one time she allowed for extra time, she wouldn't need it. The traffic had been lighter than usual and not once did she hear the dreaded 're-calculate' coming from her GPS.

Any other time, she would be happy.

But not today…

At least Kevin's mother wouldn't have another reason to find fault with her. Abby had a feeling punctuality would be pretty high on her list and a late arrival wouldn't be easily forgiven.

Even more so, if Abby was the one guilty of this.

She was about to venture out of her SUV when a taxi pulled up to the entrance. She watched as Kevin's mother stepped out, brushing off the skirt and jacket of her pale pink suit as if she'd just escaped from a trash bin. Observing her regal stance, Abby decided she'd fit right in as a member of any royal family.

The only thing missing was a matching pink hat.

She looked down at her simple gingham sundress, feeling almost indecent. But there was nothing she could do about it.

So, after one last check in the rearview mirror, and satisfied with what she saw, she went marching across the parking lot.

Everyone in the room glanced over in her direction when Abby entered the café.

Except for Kevin's mother. Tapping her nails on the table in front of her, she was talking on her phone.

Abby glanced around the room, tentatively smiling at anyone who met her gaze. She would venture to say the café was a neighborhood kind of place. A place where, even if you were alone, you could count on finding a kindred soul to share a conversation and a cup of coffee.

You can only *hope you won't be the topic of conversation in the coming months.*

She walked over to where Kevin's mother was seated and sat across from her.

Not even looking up from her phone, his mother ignored her. There was no wave, no smile... not even a brief one.

This certainly wasn't a good sign.

Abby watched as his mother glanced down at her watch before she spoke into the phone. "I assure you, I will not be long. I just want to get this over with. Count on my arrival in about 15 minutes at the latest. I will see you then."

She dropped her phone in her purse and, looking over at Abby, she gave her a haughty nod.

Any confidence Abby had brought with her had disappeared after she heard the end of his mother's phone conversation. In fact, she was beginning to feel a little scared.

What did his mother wanted to get over with as soon as possible?

Determined to start the conversation out on a positive note, she smiled, her voice coming out extremely loud in the now eerily silent room. "I'm so glad you wanted to meet, Mrs. Kardell. This will give us a chance to get to know each other better."

His mother gave her an icy look. "That will never happen. Because after today, we will never see each other again. This is why I called this meeting… to make my wishes perfectly clear."

Called this meeting? What kind of wishes?

Abby was confused. This was a business meeting? Weren't they both here because of their love for Kevin? At least she hoped his mother loved him, something she was now finding hard to believe.

His mother reached into her purse, pulling out a checkbook and a pen.

Abby's hands started to shake.

Oh, my God… why would she be writing a check? She's not planning to bribe you, is she?

It appeared this was exactly what she planned to do. She opened the checkbook and, after uncapping the pen, glanced up at Abby.

"How much do you want?"

Abby froze. She honestly couldn't move.

His mother frowned. "If you don't come up with an amount, I will. So, what will it be?" She started tapping her nails on the table, obviously irritated at Abby's lack of response.

Filled with the sudden urge to break into hysterical laughter, Abby pressed her lips together. Then, with a straight face, she threw out what she knew was an outrageous amount.

"A million dollars."

Hey, why not? The way she saw it, a ridiculous request deserved an even more absurd answer.

After a sharp intake of breath, his mother began filling out the check, pressing the pen down with such force it almost tore through the paper. When she was finished, she ripped the check out of the checkbook and shoved it across the table to Abby. Her face livid with anger, she stuffed the pen and checkbook back into her purse.

She came to her feet. "You must take me for a fool. Of course, I'd never give you that much. But what I've given you should be more than enough to satisfy you. And it fulfills my reason for coming here today. Because once you cash this check, Kevin will no longer be available to you."

On her way out of the café, she stopped to address Abby one more time, her words resonating throughout the hushed room. "If you go back on this deal, Kevin will be cut off… from his family, his inheritance, and his place in the family business. And don't underestimate me. If I have to, I can, and will, do all of these things."

She swept out of the restaurant, her head held high.

The silence in the room was almost overwhelming. No one spoke, no one even seemed to move.

In a state of shock, Abby glanced over at the woman who was seated at the next table. She had a look of complete horror on her face. In fact, everyone in the room seemed to be in the same state. It was obvious something like this just didn't happen in this friendly little neighborhood gathering place.

Abby wanted to slide right down her chair and under the table.

But you can't. No. You need to convince everyone in this room you're not a bad person. So, say something. Now.

She gripped the edge of the table and gazed around the room, shaking her head. "I didn't mean it, you know. About the million dollars. She wanted to meet me and I thought she wanted to be friends. I never thought… I only want Kevin. I love him. Honest…" Her words trailed off into silence.

The woman at the next table jumped up from her chair and put her hand on Abby's shoulder. "Oh, honey, we can see that. What a terrible, *terrible* woman. Are you going to be okay?"

At the sympathy in her eyes, Abby nodded. Then her anger kicked in.

Big time.

And she lost it.

A sob rising in her throat, she came to her feet and grabbed her keys and the check from the table. Tearing the check into pieces as she went running out of the café, she reached his mother just as she was about to get into her taxi.

"Wait!"

When his mother turned to face her, Abby threw the torn pieces of check right at her. She knew this was childish, but she couldn't help it. And it was a much better alternative to what she really wanted to do.

And this would be to reach out and slap her… hard. If only to knock the vile look off her face.

After taking a deep breath to ward off the anger waiting to erupt inside of her, she spoke. "I want nothing from you. Nothing. And just so you know, I've made no promise to you."

She fought off another sob. "I don't understand… is this how you show your love for your son? You can't control his life. And if you think being his mother entitles you to this kind of behavior? You're wrong. So, *so* wrong."

She was now shaking so hard, she could hardly get out her next words. "I should hate you, but I refuse to do this. This would mean I've stooped to your level." Wiping away her tears, she shook her head. "If anything, the only thing I feel for you right now is pity."

Almost running over to her SUV, she somehow managed to start it up and drive out of the parking lot. Keeping a tight grip on the steering wheel, she kept her eyes on the road.

She was going to pretend this meeting with Kevin's mother had never happened.

Yes, everything was good.

She knew this was the only way she'd make it home without breaking down completely.

CHAPTER 19

*K*evin shook his head at the bartender's questioning look. He didn't need another beer.

He turned his attention back to the big screen TV behind the bar and tried to focus on the scores running along the bottom of the screen. But he couldn't seem to concentrate.

There was only one thing on his mind right now, and this was Abby. He couldn't stop thinking about everything she'd told him. No matter how hard he tried.

Even during the game, she had been on his mind.

And the home run he hit in today's game? This could be credited to her dad. What he did to Abby popping into his mind when he was up at the plate, he'd swung at each pitch like a madman.

Thank God, his bat finally connected with the ball, sending it flying out of the park.

You were lucky, that's for sure. You would have looked like a fool had you struck out.

Tossing aside the coaster he was tapping against the bar, he picked up his beer and drained what was left in the bottle. Then, holding up the bottle, he studied it. As though it could give him the answers he needed.

Umm... come on, are you crazy or what?

He groaned, setting the bottle down hard on the bar. He just wanted to make all her hurt go away.

If you can't do this, what kind of man are you?

He picked up the coaster again, and turning it in his hands, he tried to remember back to his childhood. If he'd ever experienced anything close to what Abby had.

He came up empty.

Granted, his childhood wasn't perfect. Not with his mother, who, to this day, still thought she knew what was best for him. But he'd always shrugged her off, knowing whatever decision he made, both she and his father would be there to support him. Never had he experienced the feeling of abandonment Abby had.

A hand coming down on his shoulder, Alex slid onto the stool next to him. He grinned. "Hey, great game today. If you had hit that ball any harder, it would've sailed all the way back to Cleveland. One would think you were trying to fulfill a personal vendetta of some kind."

Kevin nodded. "Maybe I was, maybe I was." Then he smiled over at him. "You have a daughter, right?"

His eyes lighting up, Alex smiled. "Yes, I do. Chloe, who would be quick to tell you in ten days she'll be seven years old." He laughed. "I got a package deal when I married Lisa. We heard only yesterday the request I put in to adopt Chloe is close to being finalized. It will be nice to finally be able to call her my daughter."

He grinned. "I can't tell you how much I hate the word stepdaughter."

Kevin grinned back at him. "Congratulations."

Alex nodded. "Thanks. So, why did you want to know if I had a daughter?"

Relieved to share what was so heavy on his mind, Kevin told him about Abby and her father. When he finished, Alex shook his head. "Man, I don't know about you, but this makes me realize how lucky I was to have a pretty normal childhood. Poor Abby. Something like this must always be lurking in the back of her mind."

After motioning to the bartender for another round, Alex smiled over at Kevin. "But why do I feel like you're already working on a plan to fix this? Even after Abby told you it doesn't matter."

Kevin grabbed the coaster, shoving it hard enough to send it flying over the edge of the bar. "But it does matter, she cares a lot. Whatever the outcome, good or bad, she needs answers." Then he shrugged. "I guess you know me pretty well. I've asked Jake for help. He's going to check the archives to see what he can find on the guy."

Alex took another swig of his beer. "You didn't waste any time, did you? But it's good to know you're still together."

He shook his head. "After that last fan photo of the two of you, wait… let's make that the three of you, I've been wondering if you were still on. Again, this proves you can't trust social media."

Kevin laughed. "Yeah, that was unfortunate. But it turned out well." A faint smile on his lips, he nodded. "It was a good night. Yeah, it turned out to be a great weekend."

And now he wanted to call Abby, if only to hear her voice.

He pulled out his wallet, threw a twenty on the bar, and patted Alex on the shoulder. "I'm going to turn in. I think that home run took everything out of me. See you in the morning."

As he walked away, Alex called out. "Yeah, sure. And Kev? When you call Abby? Make sure you tell her I said hi."

He was grinning.

It looked like his friend had it bad… *real* bad.

Abby didn't answer her phone.

Or respond to his text.

And even though Kevin knew he had no reason to worry, for some reason, he was. He just couldn't shake the feeling something was wrong.

He turned on the TV, only to doze off. The phone in his hand, and the TV still on.

Abby couldn't find her phone. She'd looked everywhere.

Her biggest fear was she'd left it in the coffee shop. If she had, it was going to stay there. There is no way she could show her face there again.

Now sitting at the kitchen island, her head resting on her arms, she was waiting for her last tray of cookies to finish baking.

She couldn't get the horrible encounter with Kevin's mother out of her mind. When she'd first arrived home, after what his mother had alleged would be the last and only "meeting" between them, she had still been in a state of shock.

She hadn't known whether to laugh or cry.

And now, after going over everything that had happened, she still didn't know what to make of it all.

What was she supposed to do now? She certainly couldn't drop the news to Kevin, his mother had tried to bribe her. He'd think she was crazy.

She groaned, dragging her hands through her hair.

Why didn't you keep the check?

How ironic she hadn't taken the time to see what amount his mother had decided on. Instead, she'd let her anger get the best of her, tearing the check into pieces and throwing them at her. Something she wasn't feeling very good about right now.

You can't even imagine what she thinks after that little act you put on.

There was one thing she did know. The check wasn't for a million dollars. Hadn't his mother been quick to let her know she wasn't foolish enough to do this?

But she was foolish. Enough to jeopardize the relationship she had with her son. Or even with the rest of her family, if they were to find out what she did.

If there was anyone who knew how fragile families were, and how quickly they could be torn apart, it was Abby.

Burrowing her face in the crook of her arm, she closed her eyes.

It's going to take you a long time to get over this...

Something was burning.

Lifting her head, Abby peered over at the timer to see she'd forgotten to set it. She ran over to the oven, and yanking open the door, she was met with a cloud of smoke. This meant she would have to make another batch.

But not tonight. She needed to go to bed. The cookies could wait.

After she tossed out the burnt cookies, she went over to wake Poppy for her nightly walk. This was where she found her phone, tucked behind the cushion of the dog bed. She must have dropped it there when she came home from her meeting with Kevin's mother. In need of comfort, she'd picked up Poppy for a hug.

She scanned through her messages.

Kevin had called. He'd also sent a text message.

> Hey sugar, missing you. Call me.

Holding the phone in her hand, she wasn't sure how to respond. She knew what she wanted to say, but after what happened with his mother, nothing sounded right.

She typed out her response.

It wasn't what he'd want to see.

Then again, it isn't what you wanted to send.

Kevin woke to a late night TV infomercial for the Ultimate Indoor Exercise Machine. In the middle of his sales pitch, the host was pointing his finger right at Kevin.

After he shut off the TV, he checked his phone to see it was a little after two in the morning. There was a message from Abby, sent about fifteen minutes ago.

Not even stopping to think, he hit her number.

She answered on the second ring, the sound of her voice easing his anxiety.

He sighed her name. "Abby… did I wake you? If I did, I'm sorry. I called because I needed to hear your voice."

As soon as he spoke, every emotion Abby had been fighting since she left the coffee shop came at her in a rush. Her hand over her mouth to muffle her sobs, she couldn't answer him.

Her silence worried him. "Hey, sugar, what's going on? Are you still there?"

She took a deep breath, pressing the phone even more firmly to her ear as though this would somehow bring him closer. "Yes, I'm here. You didn't wake me. I was baking cookies for the benefit, and I guess I lost track of time."

She leaned back against the kitchen counter. "I watched the game and I am so proud of you. When you hit that home run, I picked up Poppy and danced around the room with her. I think I scared her."

He chuckled. "I do it all for you, sugar."

He'd swear she was crying. "Are you sure you're okay? Because your voice sounds different. Like you've been crying."

She clutched the phone even tighter.

No, she wasn't okay. And yes, she was crying.

But she couldn't tell him this. Because how would she explain?

Wiping the tears from her face with the back of her hand, she could only think about how much she wanted to be with him.

"I miss you."

"I miss you, too."

He did. He missed everything about her. Closing his eyes, his smile came through in his next words. "I'd give anything for one of your kisses right now."

She smiled through her tears. "I'll save one for you."

"I'm counting on that, sugar. But now that I've heard your voice, I need to go to sleep. And you do, too."

His next words came through like a caress. "I love you. And I always will."

The tears came in a flood, her response barely a whisper. "I will. Good luck tomorrow."

I will? Good luck tomorrow?

In disbelief, Kevin stared at his phone, willing it to ring.

When it did, it would be Abby. Calling to say she'd been cut off.

Yeah, this had to be what happened.

He'd settle for any explanation right now, as long as it ended with her telling him that, yes, she loved him, too.

But this didn't happen.

You never read the message she sent. Maybe she said it then?

He found the message.

Hi, see you soon.

That's it?

"Hi, see you soon?"

What the hell?

He tossed the phone on the nightstand.

He couldn't do this right now. It was late and he needed to go to bed.

Turning out the light, he closed his eyes.

But sleep was a long time coming.

Abby couldn't sleep either, haunted by dreams, all with the same theme—searching for something out of her reach, only to be left in the dark.

So she got out of bed and headed for the kitchen.

Her plan was to bake enough cookies to replace the batch she'd burned. Oven on, she got to work.

Since Kevin had rolled out of bed, he'd done a lot of thinking.

This had turned out to be a bad move, because he was now in a nasty mood.

So much so, everyone tried to stay out of his way.

During batting practice, each ball he hit went sailing through the air like it had been shot out of a cannon.

Alex was worried.

When Kevin finally threw down his bat and went over to sit on the bench, he meandered over to sit next to him. After he watched him wipe the sweat from his face and guzzle down a bottle of water, he cleared his throat. "I don't know what's hotter, this humid Cincinnati weather, or you and the way you've been hitting the ball lately."

Kevin gave a sharp laugh, crushing the empty water bottle in his hand.

"Yeah, I'm hot, all right."

They both watched the action on the field for a few minutes before Alex shot a sharp glance over at Kevin. He gave a long sigh.

"You need to get a handle on this situation with Abby. At least I assume this is what brought on this foul mood of yours. Because as it stands right now, you've got everyone in this ballpark scared to death of you, even the guys who are on your side." He jerked his head towards Chester, who was eyeing them from a good fifteen feet away. "Including that guy. Something you don't see all too often."

Kevin was saved from having to answer him when his phone rang. After he checked to see who was calling, he turned to Alex. "I have to answer this. Give me a couple of minutes."

In no time at all, he came back to sit next to Alex. "That was Jake. He's sending me the info he has for Abby's father. It seems he lives right outside of Toledo, wherever the hell that is. So as soon as I find out the details, I'm going to pay him a visit. Maybe this will be a start at getting them together again."

He picked up the empty water bottle, twisting it in his hands. "I guess even if things don't work out for me and Abby, I'll have done some good."

Alex patted him on the back. "I have a feeling everything is going to turn out just fine."

CHAPTER 20

$\mathcal{K}$evin parked his rental car in front of a small blue bungalow. It was almost identical to the rest of the houses lined up on the quiet, tree-lined street.

After he'd read the information Jake had sent in his email, he decided to skip the team flight back to Cleveland. Instead, he'd rented a car and headed for Toledo. And now, according to his GPS, after three hours on the road, he had reached his destination.

He found it hard to believe he could soon be face to face with Abby's father. He'd considered calling before he made the drive, but then decided the element of surprise might be the better way to go.

Once he was out of the car, he turned to check out the neighborhood. The small single-story houses, boxy, brick and ordinary, were reminiscent of the architectural style so popular in the fifties. They gave the neighborhood an almost cookie-cutter feeling.

But what the hell was he doing? It didn't matter what the neighborhood looked like. Or what kind of houses there were.

You're stalling. Come on, do what you have to do.

He ran up the steps to the porch and hit the doorbell.

When the door opened, Kevin's first thought was he'd made a mistake. That he had the wrong address. Because the man standing in

172

front of him looked much older than his alleged sixty years. But upon closer inspection, the reddish blond streaks in his gray hair were enough to convince him this was Abby's father.

He cleared his throat. "Hello, are you Matt Evans?" When the man nodded, a suspicious look on his face, Kevin smiled. "Great. I wonder if I could talk to you for a few moments, Mr. Evans. I'm Kevin Kardell, a very good friend of your daughter, Abigail."

As soon as these words left his mouth, Abby's father clutched the door frame for support, his expression bordering between disbelief and hope.

"Abigail? You know Abigail? Where is she? Have you seen her? Is she okay?" He put his hand to his chest. "She's not hurt or in some kind of trouble, is she?"

Kevin smiled, shaking his head. "Nothing has happened, Mr. Evans. She's fine."

Well, yeah. She's fine. Except for the fact you've cut her out of your life.

Her father waved him inside. "Come in. So, you can tell me what brings you here."

Once they were inside, he gestured for Kevin to follow him into the kitchen, where he brought out a pitcher of iced tea and two glasses. It was only when he was seated across the table from Kevin, his eyes lit up in recognition. "Kevin Kardell... I knew the name sounded familiar. You just recently got called up. Congratulations on making the roster."

"Thanks. It's been an amazing experience so far."

Nodding, her father leaned back in his chair, a puzzled expression on his face. "How do you know my daughter?"

Kevin grinned. "I was given the temporary use of a condo in Abby's neighborhood, just down the street from her. We met when she marched up my driveway and accused me of driving too fast. She flashed those gorgeous green eyes of hers at me and she had me." He snapped his fingers. "Just like that."

His expression became serious. "Before we say more, I want you to know I would do anything for your daughter, Mr. Evans." He leaned forward and rested his arms on the table. "I don't know the circumstances surrounding your disappearance. So, I have no reason to judge you. But Abby won't be able to move on with her life until she knows why you never came home."

After a long sigh, her father slowly rose from his chair. He nodded over at Kevin. "Wait here. I'll be right back."

After he walked out of the kitchen, Kevin gazed around the room, a silver picture frame perched on top of the refrigerator catching his eye. He took it down to see it held a photo of Abby and her father, taken when she was about seven or eight years old. They were at a baseball game, the field in clear view behind them. Sitting on her father's lap, Abby's arms were wrapped around him in a hug.

They were both laughing.

He stared down at the photo. And this is when he made a promise to himself. No matter what it took, he would find a way to bring them back together again. He wanted to see a new photo take the place of this one. A photo taken now, with them as happy as they once were.

After he put the photo back on top of the refrigerator, he turned to see Abby's father had returned and was watching him. He set a stack of letters, bound with a rubber band, on the table.

He nodded towards the photo. "This is the only photo I have of us. To this day, I still imagine her as that spunky little girl." Sinking down into his chair, his shoulders sagged. "I think I've been trying to hang on to the belief she's always been better off without me. But in my heart, I know this isn't true."

His smile was bittersweet. "There isn't a day that goes by I don't think about her. Wondering what she's doing, praying she's okay."

Kevin met his gaze. "It's not too late, you know. It's never too late to make amends with someone you love."

After studying Kevin for a few moments, he pushed the bundle of letters towards Kevin. "These are all the letters I sent to Abby over the years. I stopped sending them when I got the news Rose, Abby's mother, passed away. After that, whenever I tried to find out what happened to Abby, I hit a dead end, getting the same answer. The information was confidential and not available."

He nodded towards the letters. "As you can see by the markings on the envelopes, I only had a post office address. And every letter I sent came back marked return to sender."

Kevin flipped through the letters before he looked up, a puzzled expression on his face. "These are still sealed. You're telling me your wife gave none of these to Abby?"

Her father shrugged. "It sure looks that way, doesn't it?"

Kevin glanced down at the letters, then back at him. "But why? Why would she do that when she must have known how much Abby missed you? Abby told me she didn't care what you did. She only wanted you to come back. To this day, she thinks you abandoned her. And I'm pretty sure she believes she was partly responsible for this."

Her father's chin trembling in his effort to keep from breaking down, he shook his head. "It's a long story…"

Taking a long drink of his iced tea, Kevin leaned back in his chair, stretching out his legs. "If you don't mind, I'd like to hear it. Like I said before, I'm here because of Abby." He smiled. "For her, I have all the time in the world."

At first, her father was silent. Then, after exhaling a long breath, he began to speak.

"The moment I laid eyes on Rose, I knew she was the woman for me. When we met, I was in the minors and trying to work my way up into the big leagues. This didn't stop us from making plans to marry. But her parents, both from long-standing families with big money, were appalled. This wasn't what they wanted for their daughter. So, they tried to keep us apart. But growing up as an only child, Rose wasn't used to being denied what she wanted."

A smile flashed across his face. "And believe it or not, she wanted me. When we got married, her parents disowned her on the spot. But we didn't care. We were in love and ready to take on anything. And when we found out we were going to have a child, we were thrilled."

A wistful expression settling on his face, he took a few moments to relive that time. Then he shook his head. "After Abby was born, Rose's parents came around a little, but the tables had turned. Rose couldn't forgive them. Because as far as they were concerned, I still wasn't good enough. I didn't exist."

When he ran his hand over his chin, Kevin saw it was shaking. So, he poured more iced tea into his glass and pushed it towards him.

After he took a drink, he continued. "Her parents were both killed in an auto accident right before Abby's first birthday. When Rose learned they'd left all their money to charity, she was furious. Not because she wanted the money. She just couldn't believe they'd made no provisions for Abby. I tried to tell her they probably didn't have a chance to change their will, but she wouldn't listen."

He glanced over at Kevin, his expression bleak. "And this is when everything spiraled out of control. I was plagued with injuries and any chance of making the team was over. I took the office job they offered me in Cleveland and, unhappy with the move, Rose sank even further into depression." He frowned. "This was also when I started betting on the games. I'm not making excuses for what I did, but it all started when I thought if we had more money, Rose would be happy. And at first, she was. But then my luck turned sour and the extra money stopped coming in. We started fighting, and sometimes I'd leave and not come back for days."

He shrugged. "With my job, I had easy access to all this cash. This made it easy for me to take what I needed, a little here and there. I kept telling myself, once I started winning again, I'd pay it all back. But we all know how that goes. Instead, it all snowballed on me. The money was discovered missing, and I confessed. But by then, I was in so deep, it was almost a relief to be caught."

For a few moments, he was silent. Then, after a long sigh, he continued. "Suddenly I was serving time in jail. I only received one letter from Rose, and this was to inform me she never wanted to see me again. She also told me she was going out of state to stay with friends and she was taking Abby with her. She relented, giving me a post office box address."

He nodded towards the letters on the table. "But as you can see, things changed. But I continued to send the letters, hoping one would make it to Abby."

"After I was released from jail, I tried to find Rose. But it was as though they'd disappeared off the face of the earth. So, I did what I had to do. I took any job I could get, slowly digging out of the mess I'd made. I paid back all the money I took, down to the penny." He smiled. "I may not be rich, but I'm holding my own. I've even put money aside for Abby. It's not much, but I wanted to have something to give her, in case I ever found her. And now..."

He grew silent, staring down at his hands.

Kevin was the first to move. He bundled the letters back together and looked directly at Abby's father. "Mr. Evans, I'm in love with your daughter and this is never going to change. I want to marry her and grow old with her. And like I said before, I'll do anything for her."

Unsure if he should tell him Abby had claimed she never wanted to see him again, he hesitated. But then he knew it would be unfair to him if he didn't. "Abby said she's fine. She also told me that it doesn't matter if she never sees you again. But I know this isn't true. So, what do you think we should do?"

There was another long silence before her father shook his head. "I don't think I could take it if she turned me away. Even though I know this is what I deserve."

Kevin studied him. "But after what I just told you, how could you live with yourself if you never took the chance to find out?"

He smiled. "I'm confident this will end well. All you have to do is tell me when and how you want to go about making it happen."

He gave a nod towards the photo on the refrigerator. "Then you'll have more in your life than just a photo."

He smiled. "You'll have the real thing."

It was already past eight when Kevin left Abby's father.

But everything was set. They'd decided on a plan.

After that, they'd talked about everything baseball, with Abby's father firing questions at him. He wanted to know how Kevin got interested in the sport, what he'd learned during his time in the minors, and what his thoughts were about this year's play-off chances. Then there were the stories he had to share from his time in the minors.

So, after what had been such a long day, there was only one thing Kevin wanted.

And this was Abby. He needed the reassurance he had her love. He wanted to hear her say the words, letting him know she loved him as much as he loved her.

Even though she didn't say this to you on the phone.

Yeah… but things were fine. He had no reason to worry.

Right?

Abby had been decorating cookies all day, every inch of counter space now covered with rows of finished cookies. Once they were sealed in their own individual cellophane bags, she would pack them away in boxes. Only then would she have room to get started on the next batch.

She gazed around the kitchen. She was going to need a larger working space if she planned on filling big orders like this in the future. Leaning against the counter, she spent a few minutes thinking about this.

You can dream, can't you?

But she didn't have time for dreaming right now.

She had cookies to bag.

The cookies bagged and packed away, she took a shower and washed her hair. After she dried her hair, she glanced over at the clock.

Kevin's flight hadn't even landed yet. This meant she still had time for a quick nap.

Yeah, just for a few minutes. This is all you need.

As soon as her head hit the pillow, she was out.

Her doorbell was ringing. For a few seconds, she stared up at the ceiling, trying to gather her thoughts.

Then she remembered.

Kevin.

She dove out of bed. Pulling on her robe and tying the sash as she ran to the front door, she yanked it open.

But it wasn't Kevin who was standing in front of her.

No, t was the last person she wanted to see.

Tonight, tomorrow, and maybe even never.

It was Peter.

CHAPTER 21

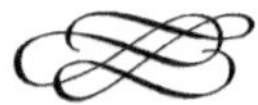

You're nothing short of my everything.
~ Anonymous

Peter pushed his way past Abby and right into her living room.

He turned, and throwing his hands up in the air, his voice was loud enough to send Poppy shooting out of her dog bed with a yelp.

"I can't do this anymore, Abigail. I can't."

Abby closed the door and, without a word, walked past him into the kitchen. Her mind still blurred from sleep, she was trying to figure out why he was in her condo.

She certainly didn't want him here. And she didn't have a clue what he was talking about.

What was it he couldn't do?

She frowned. If he had come to let her know he wasn't the marrying kind of guy, he needn't have bothered. This was old news.

There's also the fact you just don't care.

After he followed her into the kitchen, he sank down into a chair at the kitchen table. Staring down at his hands, he sighed. "Don't get me wrong, I'm not trying to implicate we share equal blame for what happened. But I think we can both admit we should have put forth more effort into making our relationship work. And yes, I'll be the first to admit I may have acted like a jerk, but believe me, I've changed."

Here he looked up at her, a mournful look on his face. "What I'm trying to say is I finally know what I want."

He shrugged. "I want you."

Abby stared at him in disbelief.

Share the blame? Put forth more effort?

Why did he always have to use his lawyer tone of voice with her? She always felt like she was on trial when he came at her like this.

And wait a minute here, he was the one who broke off the engagement, not you. So, there will be no blame put on you for this. Absolutely not.

When she remained silent, he rested his elbows on his knees, dragging his hands back through his hair, "My life is a mess. All I can think about is you. How much I love you, and how much I want you back."

She leaned back against the counter, shaking her head.

Now a little mad he wasn't getting the reaction he wanted, he stood and began pacing back and forth. "Abigail, come on. Surely you remember how good it was between us? I'm sure we can get that back. I know I'm more than willing to try."

This was when something snapped inside of her. And she became angry.

Very angry.

He was more than willing to try, was he? And he thought she'd be just as willing to go along with this?

Had he lost his mind?

She glared at him. "Peter, no. I don't feel that way about you anymore. And even if I did, it would never happen. Because I know I could never trust you again."

"Abigail, come on..." This coming from him in a groan, in what seemed like one stride, he was next to her, and planting his hands on the edge of the counter, he effectively locked her in place.

She didn't understand.

This wasn't the Peter she knew.

But, wait a minute… was that alcohol she smelled? She sniffed the air between them. Yes, it was definitely alcohol. But Peter didn't drink. Never.

Maybe this could explain his behavior?

She peered more closely at him. "Have you been drinking?"

He laughed. "I planned on getting drunk out of my mind. But after two shots of whiskey, I realized alcohol wasn't the answer." He shuddered. "Plus, I can't stand the stuff. Instead, I came to see you."

Wow… lucky, lucky you.

He lifted his face to the ceiling, letting out a loud groan. "See what you've done to me?"

She sighed. "Peter, I've done nothing. You and me? It just wasn't meant to be. I've already moved on. I have a whole new life now."

The smile he gave her was bitter, his words sarcastic. "So, I've heard. *My God,* Abigail… it's all over town you're linked with this… this Kevin Kardell guy, the new baseball player everyone is carrying on about."

His laugh was sharp. "Can't you see he's using you? A guy like him has a girl in every city. He'll drop you in an instant to marry some hot supermodel or famous actress. That's what those guys do. A small-town girl like you, awed by his status? You don't have a chance."

How could he say this? He didn't even know Kevin. If he did, he'd realize Kevin would never do this. She glared at him. "That's not true. Kevin's not like that. He loves me and he's not going to leave me."

And who was he to talk? He had been far from faithful. Granted, Lucinda wasn't a supermodel or a famous actress. But the bottom line was he chose her over the small-town girl he just said you are.

Doubt kicking its way in, she closed her eyes. Peter took this as a sign his words had hit their mark. He tightened his hold on her, pressing her even further back against the counter.

Her eyes flew open just in time to see the determined look on his face as he swooped in, his mouth searching for hers. He was caught up in the moment, his voice all business-like. This was the no frills Peter she remembered.

"Kiss me now, Abigail."

In a panic, she tried to pull her hands from his. When this didn't work, she pleaded with him. "Peter, no... I don't want to do this. Please, just let me go."

But he was already too far gone.

Ignoring her cries, he tightened his hold on her. "Come on, I know you don't mean this."

"I'm pretty sure she means exactly what she just said. So why don't you let her go like she asked?"

Abby felt Peter stiffen before he whirled around, dropping his hands from hers. After she scooted over to the other side of the island, she glanced over to where Kevin was now miraculously standing in her kitchen.

His arms crossed and a dangerous expression on his face, he was leaning against the doorjamb. After he studied Peter for a long and tense filled moment, he gave him a curt nod. "I don't know who you are or why the hell you're here, but I have to tell you I'm not very happy with what I just saw. Or with what I heard."

His gaze shifted over to Abby. "Are you okay, sugar?"

She nodded, sending him a nervous smile. Once he was assured she meant what she said, he smiled back at her.

Only then did he return his attention back to Peter, who hadn't moved, his fists clenched at his sides, and his expression just as fierce. The two men remained motionless, staring each other down. Almost as if they were biding their time, waiting to go in for the kill. It was like tuning into one of those wild animal documentaries on TV.

Abby didn't get it... they were fighting over her?

But men don't fight over you. They fight over women like Mia. Or Megan. The beauty-queen-model-types.

Kevin pushed away from the doorjamb, and sauntering into the kitchen, he opened a cupboard and took out a cup. He picked up the coffeepot and after he shook it, he glanced over at her. *"Hmm... it's almost empty. We'll need to make more, so we'll have some for tomorrow morning, sugar."*

He sent her a wink. "Just one of the many things you've taught me."

He poured what was left of the coffee into the cup.

As if he suddenly remembered his manners, he nodded over at her and Peter. "Any coffee for either of you? We can easily make more."

When they both shook their heads, he strolled over to where there was a plate of cookies on the counter, glancing once more over at Abby. "Is it okay if I have one of these?" When she nodded, he winked at her.

Having never seen him act like this before, Abby was puzzled by his behavior. As she watched him take his time selecting a cookie, she finally realized what he was doing.

He was marking his territory. A territory that no longer in any way, shape, or form included Peter.

Peter had also caught on to this. He nodded towards a cupboard, his comment directed to Kevin. "If you need artificial sweetener, you'll find it there." He followed this with a smug smile.

The corner of his mouth turning up at this, Kevin leaned back against the counter. "Nah, we don't use that stuff. There's nothing artificial about our relationship, is there sugar?" He sent her another wink.

Abby glanced over at Peter.

A bewildered look on his face, it was clear he was frustrated with the way things were going. She was almost tempted to tell him he might as well give up while he still had the chance.

Because it was obvious Kevin was on a roll. And he had no intention of backing down until he won this battle between them.

Something she was fine with.

He appeared completely at ease, as if they had all the time in the world. Leaning against the counter, one hand holding a cookie, the other holding his cup of coffee, he sent Peter a casual nod. "So, tell me... exactly who are you?"

He took a big bite out of the cookie

Peter bristled at his question, clearly insulted it even needed to be asked. An arrogant expression settling on his face, he tried, but couldn't quite match Kevin's casual tone.

"I'm Abby's ex-fiancé. I came here tonight planning to win her back."

Kevin merely nodded before he took another bite of the cookie. Abby had told him she'd been engaged. She had also told him how it ended, something he had a hard time trying to understand.

Because what the hell had this guy been thinking? Was he nuts? This had to be the only explanation for why he'd broke it off with Abby.

But this was probably for the best, as he really didn't seem to be her type.

Nah, he was too pompous. And *way* too uptight.

He also couldn't be the smartest guy on the block, since he hadn't recognized what he had in Abby. If he had, they'd be married right now.

But lucky for him, in the end, it had worked out in his favor. And now Abby was his.

And, seriously? There's no way she ever kissed this guy like she kisses you. He wouldn't known what to do if she had.

He gave a short laugh, shaking his head at the thought. When this brought a worried glance from both Peter and Abby, he smiled back, with a much more reassuring smile directed at Abby.

He nodded. *"Ah,* yes... Abby told me all about your engagement. So, about this plan you had for tonight? How did that work out? Not all that great, huh?"

Peter actually began sputtering. "Well, no. But I may have taken her by surprise. I just need a little more time."

He shot Kevin a pointed look. "Time with no interruptions."

Then, in an effort to appear more intimidating, he drew himself up to his full height. Crossing his arms over his chest, he narrowed his eyes. "At least I'm sincere."

Kevin didn't seem the least bit fazed by Peter's show of bravado. Popping the last bite of cookie into his mouth and washing it down with a gulp of coffee, he set the cup on the counter.

Then he nodded. *"Hmm...* I guess it all depends on how you define sincere."

Leaning back against the counter, he also crossed his arms over his chest. His face was void of expression. "Now call me old-fashioned, but I believe sincere means once you get engaged to a girl, you follow up with the whole deal, wedding and all. Then you go on to honor that 'until death do us part' promise that marriage is all about."

He shrugged. "But then again, what do I know? It seems I'm too busy taking advantage of every small-town girl I can get my hands on right now. Of course, this is only until some famous-model-actress-type comes into my life. All of which would make me quite the man about town, wouldn't it?"

He shook his head. "Then again, this is all hearsay."

He turned to rinse his cup out in the sink before he put it in the dishwasher.

When he turned back to them, Abby saw he'd reached his limit, his anger clear in how tightly he was gripping the edge of the counter.

He jerked his head towards Peter. "Yeah, that's right. I heard you. And let me assure you, you couldn't be more wrong about what you said."

The silence in the kitchen was so heavy, Abby could hear her heart racing in her chest. Her gaze darting back and forth between the two men, she wanted to say something.

But she knew she needed to let them battle this out between themselves.

So she waited, her eyes riveted on Kevin.

Any pleasantness he had shown toward Peter had disappeared. His eyes narrowed, he didn't even bother to hide the contempt in his voice. "I'm finding it very hard to like you right now. So, maybe it would be best if you left."

Peter took a step towards Abby.

But when he saw she was gazing over at Kevin, a rapt expression on her face, he turned and stormed out of the kitchen.

This was followed by the slam of the front door.

For a few seconds, Abby and Kevin stared at each other.

Then, a slow smile curving his mouth, he made his way over to her. Wrapping his arms around her, he rested his cheek in her hair.

With her pressed against him, everything that had just took place was now a distant memory.

Her scent surrounded him. Burying his face in her hair, he breathed in the intoxicating combination of freshly baked cookies, shampoo, and the subtle musky scent of her perfume.

She smelled like home…

She was home… the only place you'll ever want to call home from now on.

He pulled her closer, pressing a kiss in her hair. "You okay, sugar?"

She was clinging to him, her words muffled against his chest. "I didn't know he was coming here. I didn't. The only reason I opened the door was because I thought it was you."

When he pulled back, shaking his head, she tightened her hold. "I know, I know. I shouldn't have opened the door. But when the doorbell rang, it woke me out of a sound sleep. So I wasn't thinking clearly. I was waiting for you. I only wanted it to be you."

She sighed, rubbing her face against him. "He came storming in here, claiming he'd made a mistake and he wanted us to get back together. But the only thing I could think about was how much I wanted him to leave." She shook her head against him. "And even though I know he'd never hurt me, he scared me."

He leaned back, his finger tipping her face to his. "I figured as much. So, I'm glad I got here when I did. I hope I didn't scare you. But I wanted to send him the message he was no longer welcome here. I don't want to share you with anyone."

His gaze traveling over her, he drank in every detail.

She looked beautiful. Her eyes were wide, searching his, her lips parted, anticipating his kiss. Her cheeks were flushed, and her hair was in complete disarray, framing her face in a lustrous tangle of curls.

After only being able to imagine being with her like this over the past few days, it was taking everything he had to keep a gentle hold on her. He wanted to whisk her off to the bedroom, where he would make mad, passionate love to her until… well… forever.

You want to lose yourself in her...

He placed a soft kiss to her mouth, her name coming from him in a deep sigh.

"Abby… how I missed you, sugar."

Her cheek resting against his chest, she was lulled by the beat of his heart. And as with every other time she'd been in his arms, the only thing she wanted was to stay there forever.

Forever… there's that word again... it keeps popping up.

She smiled up at him. "I'm so glad you're back. Please don't let me go. Let's just stay here like this forever."

He chuckled. "As much as I'd love that, can we at least get out of the kitchen? I'm afraid you might set me to work and right now there are other things I'd much rather be doing with you."

His hands had drifted down her back, where he could feel her soft curves beneath the silk robe she was wearing. This was when it dawned on him, and he was pretty sure about this, she was wearing nothing underneath.

His eyes holding hers and a smile on his lips, he pulled at the sash until it unraveled. When she reached up to put her arms around his neck, he slid his hands under the robe to come in contact with the heat of her bare skin. She pressed even closer, her mouth moving up his neck in a trail of urgent kisses.

Her words were a soft purr in his ear.

"I missed you… so, *so* much."

And he became completely undone.

He captured her mouth in a deep, scorching kiss before he scooped her up into his arms and carried her down the hall to the bedroom.

When he went to lower her to the bed, she tightened her hold on him, bringing him down with her. Pulling at his shirt, she didn't even wait until he had yanked it off over his head before she feverishly began working at his belt.

Hoping to slow her almost frenzied movements, he grabbed her hands. His voice was deep with concern. "Abby… sugar, what's…"

Untangling her hands from his, she reached up to wrap her arms around him. Her eyes searching hers were filled with desire. Yet at the same time, this was overshadowed by a hopelessness he didn't understand.

She shook her head. "Don't talk. I don't want to talk. Just make love to me. Please?"

Then she pulled his head down, kissing him with a passion he couldn't fight even if he'd tried.

Though he gave in, loving her with everything he had, it was bittersweet. This frantic behavior of hers could only mean something was still very wrong. The desperation was still there. And now it was even stronger.

And he was at a complete loss to know why.

The moonlight coming in through the window made a trail over the bed, falling across Kevin's face.

Abby had awoken, finding she'd again drifted away from him in her sleep. Since then, she had remained where she was, so as not to disturb him. Hardly daring to breathe, she studied him in the darkness.

She watched the rise and fall of his chest, mesmerized by the ripple of his muscles with each breath he took. Then there was the curve of his mouth, with the hint of a smile, leaving her to wonder what he was dreaming about. That it might be about her brought on a deep longing to lean over and press her lips against his.

Until he woke up and kissed her back.

He was just so incredibly handsome.

And so absolutely perfect.

And to think he could be yours.

Each night he spent with her, and in her bed, had her sinking deeper and deeper into a place she'd never been before. As though she'd fallen into the perfect dream. How was it, only a fortnight ago, she had known nothing about him? Yet now she felt as if she'd loved him for a lifetime?

That this was soon to become only a memory was something she didn't want to think about.

This will break your heart.

Filled with a sudden sense of urgency, she scooted across the bed and settled next to him under the quilt. Resting her hand on his chest, she gave a contented sigh.

He stirred, muttering incoherently, before he turned his face to hers. His eyes opened, and for a few moments, they studied each other. Then, brushing her hair back from her face, he gave her a soft kiss.

His voice was blurred with sleep. "What's going on, sugar? Can't sleep?"

She snuggled closer. "I was cold, but I'm okay now that I'm back in your arms." She sighed. "I think you've worked some kind of magic on me, because this is the only place I want to be."

He tucked the quilt around them. "I know. I feel the same way. It's overwhelming at times, isn't it?" Then he yawned, closing his eyes. "I love you."

She pressed a kiss to his shoulder. "I love you, too."

Wide eyed and staring into the darkness, she fought the sudden threat of tears. If she let them begin, she knew they would never end.

She wanted to remember this… every single moment.

Every kiss... every touch... every whisper...

She wanted to hold on to what it felt like to have his arms around her. With his hands drawing her closer, until they fit together, as though they were one. Then she'd be able to look back and remember how amazing their love had been.

She lifted her face to place the softest of kisses to his mouth. His even breathing told her he'd already drifted back to sleep.

And even though she knew she should do the same, her eyes remained open and staring into the darkness.

CHAPTER 22

*K*evin woke to what sounded like an entire flock of birds perched in the tree outside of Abby's bedroom window.

Eager to share the arrival of morning, they were chirping in unison in the silvery predawn light. This was along with what he was pretty sure sounded like someone singing.

Gradually becoming aware of his surroundings, a warm body curled up next to him, he smiled.

Abby...

He turned.

It wasn't Abby.

Instead, it was Poppy, who gave him a big, wet, sloppy kiss to his face.

"What the...?"

When the little dog began showering him with even more kisses, he gave her a few pats on the head. Then he propped himself up on his elbows, his eyes searching the bed.

No Abby.

Then he heard it again. Someone *was* singing, he hadn't imagined it.

He decided to investigate. Searching the floor for his clothes, he found his shorts and pulled them on. Poppy, who had already taken over his place on the bed, gave an enormous yawn, her eyes already closing as he left the room.

Kevin came to a stop at the entrance of the in the kitchen.

He smiled.

Her hair tied up in a loose ponytail, and wearing only his shirt under her apron, Abby was holding a pan of cookies in one hand and a spatula in the other. Swaying to the music playing in her earphones, she was singing.

> *"There is no mountain too high,*
> *No river too wide.*
> *Sing out this song and*
> *I'll be there by your side."*
>
> *"Storm clouds may gather,*
> *Stars may collide.*
> *But I'll love you,*
> *Till the end of time"*

He watched as she danced her way over to the island to set the pan on the countertop. Waving the spatula about with a flourish, she sang along with the last words of the song.

> *"Come what may*
> *Come what may.*
> *I will love you,*
> *Until my dying day."*

After staring down at the cookies, she gave a dramatic sigh before she began transferring them to the cooling rack on the counter. This was when she also glanced over and saw Kevin watching her.

Her cheeks flushing with embarrassment, she ripped the earphones from her ears. After she stuffed them in her apron pocket, she began removing the rest of the cookies from the tray, sending some of them shooting across the counter and even a few to the floor.

As Kevin made his way around the island, she ducked out of sight to pick up the cookies from the floor.

He couldn't stop smiling.

How he loved when she became so flustered. It made him want to take her into his arms and, well, let's face it, you already know there were about a million things he could think of.

He was casually leaning against the counter when she finally came back up to face him. He reached over to cup her chin in his hand. "Hey beautiful, what were you singing?"

At the huskiness of his voice, the cookies she held in her hands went sailing right back to the floor. Trying to avoid his gaze, she lowered her eyes, only to find she was now looking right at his chest. Which turned out to be not the best of alternatives. All that bare skin, so muscular, so close and so tantalizing real, was now right at her fingertips, just waiting to be touched.

She swallowed.

You don't have a chance here, do you? He's just getting started and you're already lost.

In an attempt to act as casual as she could under the circumstances, she squeaked out an answer. "The name of the song is Come What May. It's from the movie Moulin Rouge."

She shrugged, giving him a shy smile. "It's my favorite song."

Pushing the tray of cookies across the counter and away from them, he moved in even closer. His eyes holding hers, he slowly pulled the tie from her hair, sending it cascading to her shoulders.

He gathered her hair in his hands and, tipping her head back, he leaned in to kiss the pulse that was now rapidly beating at the base of her neck.

His lips moved up to whisper in her ear. "It's a nice song. I like the words. Sort of says it all about being in love, doesn't it?"

As with every other time he came at her like this, his intentions so clear and the deep sexiness of his voice traveling through her like fire, she was pretty much of a goner. So, she did the best she could. She nodded.

When his lips came back to hover over hers, teasing them with feathery kisses, she moved closer, her hands drifting up his arms.

She could hear the smile in his voice as he whispered against her lips. "Isn't this the love everyone wants? Until the end of time?"

He placed a kiss to the corner of her mouth. "I know this is what I want."

Then he pressed a kiss to the other corner of her mouth. "What about you, Abby? What do you want?"

She reached up to wind her arms around his neck, running her fingers through his hair. As she rested her head against his shoulder, her answer was so clear in her mind.

You... only you... I want you today, tomorrow and every day after. Just like in the song, I want you until the end of time.

Instead, her eyes bright, she gave him a tremulous smile. "I think everyone wants the same thing, no?"

For a few moments, he studied her. Then he groaned, pulling her against him. "Ah sugar, what am I going to do with you? I wish you'd just let go." He pressed another kiss to her mouth. "But do you know what? It doesn't matter. Because I'm not going anywhere. So, remember that."

Eyes closed, she nodded against his chest.

If only you could make the same promise.

He glanced over at the clock before he gazed down at her. "I have about an hour and a half before I leave. Do you have any suggestions of what we could do with this time?"

Unable to hide her smile, she glanced around the room. "Well, we could finish up the rest of these cookies."

He gave a slow nod, while at the same time he reached around to undo the ties of her apron. After he removed it, he smiled down at her, his eyes caressing hers.

"*Hmm...* we could very well do that. Any other suggestions?"

It was official. She was now completely under his spell. And with his hands now slipping under her shirt, his thumbs tracing lazy circles over her skin, she was more than ready to go along with whatever he had in mind.

A shiver of desperate longing surged through her. She reached up to trail her fingers through his hair again. "I don't care what we do. Honestly, I don't. As long as I'm with you."

"I like that answer." He placed a soft kiss to her mouth. "I like it a lot."

She let him lead her to the bedroom, where he reached for the hem of the shirt and in one quick tug, pulled it up and over her head. After he lowered her onto the bed, and his eyes never leaving hers, he removed his shorts and settled next to her, pulling her against him.

She closed her eyes, her words a soft murmur in his ear. "I missed you. I missed being with you like this…"

He was busy pressing kisses along her jaw and up to her mouth. "Mmm… I'll never tire of hearing that." His eyes holding hers, he placed a soft kiss to her mouth before he whispered against her lips. "I missed you, too. And I missed this. But I especially missed being able to look into your eyes while I tell you how much I love you." Then his mouth claimed hers in a deep kiss.

He didn't need to hear her say the words.

No, for now?

He only wanted to claim her as his own.

When Kevin had walked into her condo to find her ex-fiancé holding her trapped against the counter, he'd seriously almost lost his mind.

My God, it had taken every ounce of control he possessed to keep from punching the guy out.

That you remained as calm as you did is a miracle in itself.

He had never been the type of guy to come out with his fists up and ready to fight. No, he'd rather win his battles using words, convinced this was a more civilized way to deal with a problem.

The one and only fist fight he'd ever been involved in, taking place when he was in his teens and over a petty remark he now couldn't even remember, had taught him this. The talk from his father after that altercation also played a big part in his decision.

A man of few words, when his father did lecture, it always stuck.

> *Men that bear the last name of Kardell*
> *don't resort to fighting with their fists.*
> *Their good breeding doesn't allow this.*
> *Always remember to remain civil, and*
> *you will come out the winner every*
> *time. Guaranteed.*

At his first sight of Peter, Kevin knew he wasn't worth the effort of a fight. And once he saw the expression on Abby's face when he took charge of the whole ridiculous situation, he knew he had no reason to worry about whose side she was on.

When Peter had gone storming out of Abby's condo, slamming the door behind him, Kevin knew he'd never be back.

That chapter of Abby's life was now over and done with.

And now he wanted her to stop thinking… about Peter and whatever else was clouding her mind.

His plan was to love her with a passion deep enough to show her that this love they shared was stronger than anything they would ever have to face. Enough to drive away all the tension and uncertainty he knew she was still holding inside. Where it would shatter to pieces, never to come between them again.

You want it all.

At first, Kevin's kisses were slow and gentle. Then his mouth became more passionate, more demanding. His hands tangling in her hair, he claimed Abby's mouth in another deep kiss as he moved over her, easing himself inside of her.

He stilled.His face pressed his face in the curve of her neck, he tried to acclimate himself again to this intimacy they shared, a union that felt almost sacred.

How was it each time was better than the last?

Each time a gift?

Abby tangled her hands in Kevin's hair to pull him closer... then even closer still.

She wanted him to remember how, when she kissed him, she never held back, kissing him with a passion only he could bring from her.

But most of all, she wanted him to never forget this moment and this time with her, just as she would always remember being with him.

Like him, she wanted it all.

In tune with Kevin's every move, Abby let him take her beyond where he had taken her before. Swept by the passion that raced through her, she cried out his name, coming apart in his arms.

With a gentleness he would always reserve only for her, he cradled her against him, his whispers soft and soothing against the curve of her neck.

His lips brushed over hers. "Look at me. I want to see your eyes." He wanted to see the love there... a love shining for only him.

Her lashes fluttering open, his words were a whisper against her lips. "I'll love you until the end of time..."

Her eyes still hazy with desire, she gazed up at him. She responded with barely a whisper, but he knew what she was trying to say.

"As I will always love you..."

With this promise, he let go, surrendering to her completely.

And this time, it was he who shattered into pieces.

Abby woke to the late morning sun peeking its way through the slats of the window blinds.

She was alone in the bed.

Unless you counted Poppy. Jumping up from where she had been sleeping at the foot of the bed, she hovered over Abby, her nose nudging her for attention.

She was running her hand through the little dog's fur when she saw the note propped up on the pillow.

Sugar, I had to leave. But I'll stop by later this afternoon, and I might bring someone with me. I'll love you until the end of time. Always, Kevin.

She held the note in her hand, smiling each time she read the last sentence.

She got out of bed and slipped into a pair of shorts and a tank top. With Poppy right beside her, she wandered down the hall and into the kitchen.

She slipped on Poppy's leash and took her outside. As she followed behind the little dog, she wondered who Kevin was planning to bring with him.

Maybe it was Alex? He was the one guy on the team Kevin seemed to talk about the most. And she did like his wife, Lisa.

She smiled.

I guess you'll just have to wait and see.

Back in her kitchen, she began filling the coffee maker. This was when she realized the mess they'd left in the kitchen last night had disappeared.

The counters were all cleared, and the cookies were wrapped and stacked in the freezer.

She checked the dishwasher. It was full of clean dishes, still hot from the dry cycle.

Wrapping her arms around herself in a hug, she gazed around the room. This was when she saw a second note, this one propped up on the island.

Sugar, You owe me. And I already have a pretty

good idea of how I want to be paid. Again, I will always love you. And this would be, of course, until the end of time. Always, Kevin

She closed her eyes, pressing the piece of paper to her lips. And, with no warning, she began to cry.

CHAPTER 23

I'm pretty sure I didn't meet you just for nothing.
~ Anonymous

hester Mazzori wasn't in the best of moods.

He'd just left his Aunt Evelyn's house. Where he'd been forced to listen to her ongoing lecture about the fact he wasn't getting any younger.

Like you need to hear this?

It was time he found a wife, he was told. His mother, God rest her soul, was probably rolling in her grave at this very moment, wondering if this was ever going to happen.

Yes, you know this. But what the hell are you supposed to do? It's not like women are fighting over you.

At least, not the kind of women he wanted to spend the rest of his life with.

He made it a point to visit his aunt at least twice a month. Besides his youngest sister, Carrie, who lived about five minutes away, his aunt was the only other family member living nearby. His one sister, Livy, lived in Manhattan. His other sister, Carolyn, along with the remaining handful of relatives still around, had moved as far west as they could get. He hadn't seen them in such a long time, he wouldn't recognize them if they got right in his face.

Though he did get to see his sisters if he had a game close by to where they lived.

The one big plus of visiting his aunt was the dinners she made for him. She never failed to disappoint, setting the table with enough food to feed an army. And, even better, -it was all homemade.

So, since he lacked even the most basic of kitchen skills, the lectures she gave were a small price to pay for one of her home-cooked meals.

He sighed. Almost, but maybe not quite. At least not today. Nope, today she'd been on a roll. She hadn't let up once the whole time he was there.

To make this day even better, this intended to be sarcastic, he had no sooner left his aunt's house when he got a call from Carrie. So, for the past fifteen minutes, he'd been listening to a very long and dramatic narrative of her latest failed relationship.

He gave a short laugh. Why she came to him for advice was beyond him. He was far from an expert on relationships. Or anything to do with love.

The only thing positive about these conversations with his aunt or sister? He didn't have to do much talking. Nope, they both took care of this.

His sister's mournful goodbye still lingering in his ears, he now intended to enjoy the rest of his drive in silence... sweet, uninterrupted, silence.

Don't get the wrong idea. He liked women. He liked them a lot. But they confused the hell out of him.

He just didn't understand why they needed to discuss everything in such detail. Or the ultimate worst, they wanted you to share your feelings.

At the thought of this, he nervously ran his hand through his hair.

This is when the car in front of him came to a screeching halt. He jammed on the brakes, just managing to avoid a collision, and sending his car swerving to the side of the road.

Muttering a few curses, most unrepeatable, he waited for the stopped car to start up again. He didn't know what happened. Nor did he care.

He only wanted to be on his way.

He didn't like getting to the ballpark late.

But the car didn't move. Instead, the door on the driver's side come flying open. This was followed by a teenage girl who almost tumbled to the ground in her haste to get out of the car. He watched in horror as she ran out in front of the oncoming traffic, sending cars veering in all directions. After scooping up something from the road, she miraculously made it back to her car.

Then, as though nothing out of the ordinary had happened, she turned to him and waved.

But, from what he could see, she was crying.

Damn... you can't leave her like this.

Letting loose another string of curses, louder this time, he put his car in park and flipped on the hazard lights. With a long and very exaggerated sigh, he hauled himself out of the car and began making his way over to her.

This was then he saw she wasn't a teenager. His guess would be she was in her mid-twenties. It was hard to tell, because everything about her was small, almost tiny. She reminded him of one of those little angels on the front of the Christmas cards his aunt always sent out, her hair a halo of wispy blond curls.

But it was obvious this woman was no angel. An angel would never have behaved so irresponsibly, almost causing a major accident. Now even more determined to call her out just thinking about this, he quickened his pace.

He took her arm, leading her over to the sidewalk. His arms crossed over his chest, his words were harsh. "What the hell were you thinking, running out into traffic? Do you realize you could have been killed?"

She drew herself up to her full height, which he would guess to be about five-foot-four, if even that. Holding up the shaking bundle of fur she was holding, shoving it almost right in his face, she glared up at him through her tears.

"Are you telling me you would have stood aside and let this poor defensive animal get run over by some crazy driver? If your answer is a yes, then I am very disappointed in you as a human being. You should be ashamed of yourself! How can you be so cruel?"

He stepped back, almost tripping over his own feet.

What the hell? How could someone so small be so threatening? And why are you the one at fault?

She was still talking. In fact, the words were coming from her so fast, he wanted to press his fingers to her mouth and tell her to please, *please…* slow down.

A look of indignation in her eyes, her voice was trembling with anger. "Someone probably decided they didn't want this little guy anymore, so they just let him go. And if I find out who this person is, I'm going after him. And yes, I meant to say him. There's no doubt in my mind it was a man. A woman would never do such a thing."

Even with the big frown that followed this passionate speech, it was hard for him to take her threat seriously. How could he when it was delivered from such an innocent and delicate heart-shaped face?

But underneath it all, it seems she's a little spitfire. Something you're beginning to find very intriguing.

He knew this wasn't going to be the reaction she expected, but he couldn't help it.

He smiled.

His arms still crossed over his chest, he took in her enormous blue eyes, eyelashes that seemed to go on forever, and her pert little nose.

Then there was her mouth. Perfectly shaped, it was a mouth that begged to be kissed.

What was standing before him was damn well close to perfection.

He looked down at his hands. Then he glanced over at her.

Damn, you could frame her entire face in the palm of your hand if you wanted to.

Now feeling big and clumsy, he jammed his hands in the pockets of his shorts, shaking his head. This was crazy. He needed to get his mind back to the situation at hand. Starting by defending not only himself, but every other man out there.

He cleared his throat. "I'll have you know not all men are animal haters. Some of us even have one as a pet."

Here he stopped to think about his three-year-old miniature greyhound, Mr. Pickles. And no, he did not give the dog this name. Rescued by Carrie, she'd chosen the name.

A cute little dog, always happy to see him.

But enough of that. He needed to get back to his lecture.

"No matter how much you want to help, you need to think of your own safety first. This means not running out into traffic and taking the chance of getting run over. Because this certainly won't help the cause, will it?"

It was then he noticed she wasn't listening to a word he said. Instead, she was staring at him with an intensity that made him feel very uncomfortable. Just as he was about to ask her what she found so interesting, a big smile lit up her face.

"You're Chester Mazzori, aren't you?"

He couldn't answer. This was because he was having a hard time trying to get past her smile. It had come at him like a bolt of lightning, and now he wasn't sure who he was. Or what his name was.

"*Uh... yeah. I think so.*"

Jesus, what kind of answer is that? Is that the best you can come up with?

She tilted her face up to his and, *God help him*, he'd swear her smile became even brighter. Accompanied by that breathless voice of hers, he could only watch, mesmerized, as her lips formed each word. "You think so? You don't know what your own name is?"

A spark of understanding lit up her eyes, and she nodded. "Oh, I get it. Athletes always change their names to something fancy or sporty like, don't they? So, is it a secret? Or can you tell me what your real name is?"

He shook his head... he shook it hard.

He felt like a fool.

The knowledge this might be his only hope of hanging on to what shred of dignity he still had left, he mumbled out his answer. "No, that's my real name. No fancy or sporty like name for me. Named after my late grandfather, who would have been a lot happier if I'd become a shoe salesman to carry on his family owned shoe store. Instead of pursuing the frivolous career of a baseball player."

She continued to study him, making him feel extremely nervous. Then damn if she didn't do it again.

She smiled.

Right before she shook her head. "Oh, I find that hard to believe. I bet he's looking down on you right now, so proud of how your life has turned out. How could he not?"

He could only stare at her. Her words had slammed into him, shattering all the self-doubt he'd been carrying around for so long. A rush of emotion filling him, he closed his eyes.

Go. Get away from this woman. Now... before it's too late.

She was an enchantress. Granted, she was a cute little enchantress, but one who was also clever enough to have sprinkled some kind of fairy dust over him when he hadn't been paying attention. Or whatever the hell it was they used to cast their spells.

And for you, a very powerful dose of it.

"Hello?"

He blinked. She was gazing up at him, a hesitant smile on her face as she cuddled the little dog next to her heart.

And now all he could think about was how he wanted to trade places with the little mutt. He wanted to be the one in her arms.

He shook his head again. But more vigorously this time, trying like mad to shake this nonsense from his mind.

You need to get away from here.

But he couldn't seem to move. And now she was off and talking about something else. A trait he was beginning to find very charming. This had something to do with her voice. Soft and breathy, it was a voice that stirred a man's senses.

Her head tilted, her eyelashes fluttered up at him. "Are you friends with Kevin Kardell? He's dating my friend Abby. I'm sure you saw those steamy photos of them posted all over the internet. Which is such a joke, because Abby's not like that at all."

She shook her head. "She was actually engaged about a year ago. But Peter, the guy she was engaged to, broke it off only a month before the wedding because he said was in love with the maid of honor. Then he decided he wanted to marry the maid of honor. But he called that wedding off, too. Everyone thinks it's because he's still in love with Abby. But I know she's not in love with him."

She stopped to take a break, another one of those little frowns flashing across her face before she was off and running again.

"Don't tell Kevin this, but I think... wait, let me change that. I know for a fact, Abby is madly in love with him. But, and again, this is just between you and me, this is the best thing that could ever happen to him. Because Abby is the nicest, sweetest and kindest person you'll ever meet. And she is so talented, too. She really is. Her cookies are to die for. If you had one, I know you'd agree."

He was having trouble keeping up. Did she always talk so much? Was it because she was nervous?

He wondered what she would do if he just leaned in and kissed her? Would this slow her down?

Okay, now this is really getting weird. You want to kiss her?

He ran his hand down over his beard. Yes, it was obvious he needed to leave. Before he did exactly that.

Kiss her, that is.

At the beep of a horn, followed by another, he saw they had created quite a traffic jam.

This meant it was time for him to shake this fairy dust out of his system and take off. Before people got really irritated. Or the police showed up.

He groaned, dragging his hand through his hair. This was the absolute last thing he wanted to happen. The media would have a field day with this.

He could see the headlines now.

BASEBALL PLAYER STOPS
LOCAL WOMAN FROM SAVING INNOCENT
PUPPY FROM IMPENDING DEATH!

Yep. You can bet it wouldn't be good, with your reputation as, what was it they said? A little rough around the edges?

Then there were the guys on the team.

Hell, you'd never hear the end of it.

But she was already on the same page. Giving him one last breathtaking smile, she began moving towards her car. "It looks like we're holding up traffic. And I imagine you need to get going. Do you have a game today? I haven't been to one in such a long time, I'm embarrassed to say I don't even know when they are anymore."

The words came out of his mouth before he could stop them. "You should come to a game. I could get you a ticket."

Now he wanted to kick himself. What was he doing? She didn't want to come to a game. Certainly not because of him.

But she gave him another smile. A bigger one, if this was even possible. "Really? You want me to come to one of your games?"

When he nodded, she laughed. It was a laugh that reminded him of the wind chimes his aunt had on her back porch.

He liked it.

Yeah, he liked it a lot.

It made him feel happy.

She hugged the little dog even closer as she gazed up at him again through her lashes. A move that had him holding his breath.

"I would like that."

He was speechless, his mind flooded with all kinds of possibilities. With all of them involving her.

He began searching his mind for a clever response, something she wouldn't be able to forget, but she was already walking away.

He watched as she got into her car.

Then he watched as she got back out of her car.

After a wave, she called out to him. "Chester… I never gave you my name. It's Sophie. And I know I probably shouldn't say this, but you should think about shaving off that beard and doing something with your hair. You would be so handsome if you did."

Her eyes going wide, her hand flew to her mouth. "Not that you aren't already handsome. Of course, you are." Then she shook her head. "Oh my, I'm sorry. I'm so, so sorry. I always say what I'm thinking. Yes, I'll admit it's not one of my better traits, but I can't help it."

He returned her wave, surprised he wasn't the least bit upset at what she said. In fact, once he was back in his car, the first thing he did was check his profile in the rearview mirror.

Hmm... maybe she's right. It can't hurt.

Filled with a sudden sense of loss when he saw she'd already driven away, he started up his car and pulled out into traffic.

He said her name... softly.

Sophie.

Yeah, *Sophie.* He liked it.

He turned on his favorite sound track. But he didn't even hear it, his mind already plotting a way to get Sophie to a game.

Kevin. He would talk to Kevin. After all, she said she was a friend of Abby's.

He'd take the casual approach, ask Kevin if he could get her number from Abby so he could contact her about the tickets he'd promised her. No other explanation needed.

Yeah, this is what he was going to do.

And, hey... maybe you could even take her out to dinner afterwards?

Yeah, that would be nice. *Really* nice.

He was suddenly in a much better mood.

A great mood, in fact.

He didn't even notice his hazard lights were still blinking.

CHAPTER 24

*K*evin glanced down at his watch. He groaned when he saw not even five minutes had passed since he last checked.

He couldn't believe how nervous he was. He was usually a pretty low key kind of guy. But not this time.

He sank down on the sofa, drumming his fingers on his knee.

He was late.

But, more importantly, why was he late? He hoped this didn't mean he'd changed his mind.

Thank God you mentioned nothing about this to Abby.

He sighed, dropping his head back against the sofa cushions. He just wanted to get this over with so he wouldn't have to think about it anymore.

The longer they waited, the more he wondered if they were doing the right thing.

But this was going to make Abby happy, right?

Yes, it was. And yes, it should.

But you know how you're always wrong. Especially when a woman is involved. Even more so if the woman is Abby.

The sound of a car door closing brought him almost shooting off the sofa. He opened the front door and watched Abby's father make his way up the walk.

He sent Kevin a nervous smile. "You were about to give up on me, weren't you? I confess, I had second thoughts. Then I decided I've been a coward for too long."

Holding his hands up, he shrugged. "So here I am."

Kevin was so relieved to see him, he gave him a quick hug. Then he waved him inside.

"Have a seat. And when you're ready, let me know."

Abby's doorbell rang.

Talk about perfect timing.

She had just finished filling her last pastry bags with frosting. The bags lined up on the counter in every color of the rainbow, she was feeling quite proud of herself.

She glanced out the window. There was an unfamiliar car parked over in Kevin's driveway. As she hurried to the front door, she wondered if this was Kevin's mystery person.

She opened the door, confronted by an ecstatic Sophie. With a big smile on her face, she wrapped Abby in a hug, almost knocking them to the floor in her excitement.

"Abby, I've found him! The man of my dreams. I think I'm in love." She followed this with a wild dance around the living room before she came back to give Abby another hug. With Abby following right behind, she continued to dance her way down the hall and into the kitchen.

She sat at the island and rested her chin in her hands. A dreamy smile on her face, she gazed over at Abby. "Oh Abby, I've never believed in love at first sight, but now I do. You'll never believe what just happened to me."

In her typical dramatic fashion, Sophie gave Abby the scoop on how she met this new love interest. Except for his identity, she made sure not to leave out a single detail.

Then, after a dramatic pause, her voice sank to an exaggerated whisper. "Abby, this is the best part. He's a baseball player. And he's on the same team as Kevin. Wouldn't it be something if they were friends? Just like us?"

Dropping her chin back in her hand, she smiled. "He said he's going to get me a ticket to a game. Do you think this is the same as asking me out on a date? It has to be, don't you think?"

Her forehead creased with worry. "Though I'm afraid I may have insulted him by suggesting he should shave off his beard and get a haircut. But this is only because I know he would be so handsome if he did."

She nodded. "I can't even tell you the amazing transformations I witnessed when I took those hair and make-up classes at the fashion institute. Trust me on this, the right grooming can change a person's life."

She gave a firm shake of her head. "No that I want to change him. Or he's not handsome now. Because he is. He's so darn attractive. So tall and so strong." Her eyes lit up. "Like a medieval warrior. Or a super hero." This was followed by a long sigh.

Abby, who until now had been patiently waiting to have her say, looked over at Sophie and grinned. "Wow… I can see this guy hit all the right buttons with you. But you still haven't told me his name." A concerned look on her face, she peered over at her. "You got his name, I hope?"

Sophie stared at her for a few seconds before she spoke, her voice hushed. "It's Chester… Chester Mazzori."

This brought on another dreamy sigh. "It's such a nice name, don't you think? Did I tell you he has beautiful eyes? They're brown, but not an ordinary brown. No, they're a rich, coppery brown."

Her eyes lit up. "Like an expensive chocolate. I swear, I seriously thought I was going to drown in them."

She tilted her head, a thoughtful look on her face. "I think he must be shy, because he didn't talk much, just kept watching me with this little smile on his face. When I asked him what his name was, he got all nervous and said he wasn't sure. This is a good sign, isn't it?"

Then she sent Abby an anxious look. "You don't think he has some kind of head injury from playing baseball, do you? Like getting hit in the head with the ball? I looked him up, and he seems to have pretty good stats." She grinned. "That's baseball lingo, in case you didn't know. It means…"

Abby laughed. "I know what it means. And could it also be he was so overcome by your beauty, maybe he couldn't think straight?"

After she watched Sophie blush at her comment, she shook her head. "I hope this is what happened, because I've never seen you like this before. Aren't you the one who said you'd take your four-legged friends over a man any day? *Hmm…* how quickly things change."

She sat next to Sophie. "When Kevin gets here, I'll try to get as much information about Chester as I can."

Sophie wasn't even listening. Back to dreaming about Chester, she sighed. "Chester… don't you just love the sound of that name? It sounds so royal, almost commanding, doesn't it?"

Then she changed course, sending Abby a big grin. "So, what cookies do you have today? Any that need to be sampled? Please say you do."

Abby pointed over to the glass covered cake dish filled with cookies. "Go ahead, help yourself. And while you do, I'm going to seal up the rest of these pastry bags. It's too late to decorate the cookies now. And, to be honest, I feel like I've already done enough for today."

Again, Sophie wasn't listening.

But this was because she was busy searching for the best cookie. This would be the one with the most frosting.

When Kevin opened Abby's front door, he could hear her talking to someone in the kitchen. He smiled reassuringly at Abby's father, motioning for him to come inside. "Wait right here, I'll go get Abby."

He walked into the kitchen, and coming up behind Abby, put his arms around her. He pressed a kiss right below her ear.

"*Hey…*"

She smiled.

"*Hey…*"

After she lifted her face to his for a kiss, she glanced behind him. "I thought you were bringing someone with you?"

"I have." He smiled before he nodded over at Sophie. "Sophie, I hope you don't mind if I steal Abby from you for a bit. Someone is waiting to see her in the living room."

Pointing to her mouth, which was now occupied by a big bite of one of Abby's cookies, Sophie nodded.

He laughed. "I understand. Enjoy!" He took Abby's hand to lead her into the living room.

CHAPTER 25

You cannot change
what you refuse to confront.
~ Unknown

When Abby saw her father, she froze, struggling to comprehend.

After what seemed like forever, her voice came out in a choked whisper.

"Daddy?"

He cleared his throat. "Abby, I…"

It was when he took a step closer, she snapped, a strangled cry escaping her.

"No!"

He quickly stepped back, his expression of hope giving way to concern.

Abby turned to Kevin.

After searching his face, but not finding the explanation she was looking for, she shook her head. "What is he doing here? Did you bring him here?"

Before he could answer, she looked back at her father, a look of anguish on her face. "Oh no, this is all you, isn't it? You're here because of Kevin, aren't you? How did you find out? Was it the photos?"

He remained silent, shaking his head.

Her words were harsh. "This has to be the only reason you're here. Because you've never tried to get in touch with me before."

Her hands had started to shake. In fact, she was trembling all over. This carried over in the unsteadiness of her voice. "Do you know how long I waited for you to come home? I didn't care what you did. I loved you. And I waited. For what seemed like forever. All because you promised. And that's what was the worst. You promised."

Closing her eyes, her next words were barely audible. "I only wanted to be a family again."

His hat clutched in his hand, his head was bowed, her father had now become completely still.

Cautiously making a move towards her, it was Kevin who finally broke the silence.

"Abby, you…"

She whirled around to face him, her eyes wide with anger. "No, don't touch me. And don't talk to me. I don't want to hear it."

This is when she broke down. The sobs rising one after another in her throat, she almost couldn't get out the words. "I can't believe you went along with this. Can't you see what's happening here? He doesn't care about me."

After she sent an angry glance over at her father, she turned back to Kevin. Her words were bitter. "He only cares about you and baseball. He wants to be a part of what he missed out on… the fame, the glory, and everything else that comes with being a professional baseball player." Her voice rose in a sob. "Why can't you see this?"

Kevin grabbed her arm, pulling her against him. "Abby stop. You need to calm down. You don't want to say what you'll later regret."

She pushed away from him, her voice vibrating with anger. "Don't you dare tell me to calm down. I know what I'm talking about."

She glared over at her father, almost spitting out the words. "The truth."

Huddled at Abby's feet, Poppy let out a whimper. When Abby saw she was shaking, she scooped up the little dog, burying her face in her soft fur.

Kevin was at a loss. Never had he thought Abby would react in this way. He took a deep breath. "Abby, please talk to me. "

She lifted her head. Her face void of emotion, her words were unbelievably calm.

"I want you and my father to leave. Now. And I never want to see either of you ever again. I did fine without you before, and I'll be fine without you now."

Kevin stepped back, his face registering his shock. "Sugar, you can't mean this."

Closing her eyes, she choked out her next words. "I do. I have never meant anything more in my life. And don't call me sugar. You no longer have that right."

Another sob tearing through her, she clutched Poppy even more tightly against her. "It's better this way. Then everything will be the way it should be." Her voice dropped to a whisper. "She got her wish."

Kevin was frantic. This couldn't be happening. What was she talking about? Who got their wish? What wish?

He tried to match the calmness of her voice in his. "Abby, who are you talking about? Who got their wish?"

She closed her eyes, shaking her head. "I'm sorry. I'm so, so sorry. Please, I can't do this. You need to leave."

She turned to Kevin, her mouth working as though she wanted to say something. Then, after shaking her head one more time, she turned and left the room.

This was followed by the sound of a door closing.

What the hell happened? How did it all go so wrong?

Kevin felt like he'd been thrown into someone else's nightmare. And now, his mind was running all over the place, he was trying to make sense of everything.

He sent a glance over at the closed bedroom door.

Go… open the door and demand to know what's going on.

He groaned. He couldn't do that. Not after the mess he already made. He'd only make things worse.

He glanced over at Abby's father. His head bowed and his shoulders hunched, he looked like he'd aged ten years.

Sensing Kevin's gaze, he lifted his head, his voice cracking with each word. "This is all my fault. I don't blame her for not wanting me here. But now it seems I've only made things worse. Especially for you."

His shoulders sagged. "I've let you down, both of you. I'm sorry. So sorry…" His voice trailing off, he stared down at the floor.

Kevin shook his head, and crossing the room, he placed his hand on his shoulder. His voice was thick with emotion. "No. It's not your fault. I'm the one who is to blame. I never should have sprung this on her. It was too much of a shock."

He shook his head. "And I don't think her reaction was brought on only because of you. There's something else going on, something she isn't telling us. And somehow I'm going to find out what it is."

This was then he noticed Sophie standing by the entrance to the living room. Her arms wrapped around herself, there was a concerned look on her face.

She sent them a timid smile. "Don't worry, she'll come around. She always does. Abby tends to over-react when her emotions are involved. But after she takes the time to think things through, she calms down. And like you said, she's in shock."

Then, with a sigh, she turned to Kevin. "But Kevin… seriously? What were you thinking, surprising her with something like this?"

When he closed his eyes, a look of such misery on his face, she took pity on him. "It's okay. I know you meant well. And please, *please* don't worry. Abby didn't mean it when she said she never wants to see you again. Trust me, she's crazy about you."

She turned to smile at Abby's father. "She'll come around to you, too. I know she will."

When she saw Kevin glance once again at Abby's closed bedroom door, she walked over and put her hand on his arm. "You should leave like she asked. But don't worry, I'll stay here to make sure she's all right."

So, even though it was the last thing they wanted to do, they didn't have a choice.

So they left.

Curled up on the sofa with Poppy, flipping through the TV channels, Sophie's plan was to stay awake in case Abby needed her for anything.

And, hey… she was more than happy to oblige. This gave her time to think about a certain baseball player…

His only flaw that she knew of so far was he had a hard time remembering his name.

CHAPTER 26

*K*evin watched Abby's father back his car down the driveway and drive slowly down the street.

The memory of when he first met Abby and watched her drive this same route, and at almost the same rate of speed, brought on his faint smile.

Abby...

He closed his eyes, massaging the back of his neck.

What the hell are you going to do?

He was sick with worry.

Never had he imagined Abby would react as she had. He'd been so sure once she saw her father, they would fall back into a relationship close to what they shared before. Of course, he hadn't expected this to happen right off the bat. He knew it would take time. But after a little time, it would be all good.

But this didn't happen, did it? You goofed up again. What a surprise...

He glanced over at Abby's condo. He couldn't believe how much he wanted to go to her, take her into his arms, and kiss away her pain. A pain she was refusing to share.

Even with you.

He didn't understand.

What wasn't she telling him?

He went inside his condo, met by a starving and vocal Bella, meowing as if she was on the brink of starvation.

After he set her bowl of food on the floor, which she greeted with her usual cautiousness, as though he was trying to trick her, he gazed around the kitchen. He should eat, too. Then he would watch some TV and make it an early night. With a three-game series starting tomorrow against Detroit, he needed to be on his game.

There was also the benefit on Sunday night.

Which it now appears you'll be attending alone.

Suddenly, he wasn't hungry.

Sinking down onto the sofa, he turned on the TV, catching the weather segment of the local news. He watched as the forecaster droned on about fronts and averages before getting down to what really mattered, the forecast.

It looked like they were in for lots of sunshine, blue skies and low humidity. Perfect weather if you were planning on catching a game this weekend.

He should be happy, right?

No, this wasn't doing a thing for him.

He turned off the TV.

He didn't give a damn about the weather. In all honesty, he didn't care about anything right now.

All that mattered, all he cared about, was Abby.

Her pillow clutched to her chest, Abby stared wide-eyed into the darkness.

She couldn't close her eyes. When she did, an image of Kevin played in front of her. The pain and disbelief on his face when she told him she never wanted to see him again had the tears starting up all over again.

Her head ached, her eyes felt like they were all swollen, and her nose was so stuffed up she could hardly breathe. Then there was the deep, almost crushing ache in her chest.

She'd swear this was the result of a broken heart.

After all, her heart had been broken today.

Not once, but twice.

And now she was a mess. Her whole life was a mess. A big miserable mess.

What have you done?

She shoved the pillow aside and stared up at the ceiling. She needed to accept what had happened, convince herself it was for the best. The unexpected arrival of her father, and everything that followed, was part of a grand plan and out of her control.

She didn't know where the bitter words came from, only that she'd become so angry. Filled with an uncontrollable urge to lash out, it was as though she'd wanted to punish her father for all the hurt he had given her. After that, everything had spiraled out of control and, not only did she wind up losing her father for a second time, she lost Kevin, too.

There was only winner in all of this.

This would be Kevin's mother.

She dragged herself to a sitting position on the bed, staring at the moonlight coming in through the window. The memory of this same light falling across Kevin's face as he lay beside her, came to her so vividly, she almost couldn't breathe.

How could you have ever thought holding on to the memory of that would be enough?

Because it wasn't.

And it never would be.

Sophie opened Abby's bedroom door and peeked inside.

When she saw she was awake, she sat next to her on the bed and put her arm around her.

She didn't say a word. This was unusual for Sophie. But to be honest? This was one of the few times she didn't know what to say.

It was Abby who finally broke the silence, her voice thick from crying. "I'm such a fool."

With a sigh, Sophie rested her head on her shoulder. "Oh, Abby… no you're not. You are the least foolish person I know. You're just so passionate about everything. I don't think anyone would have reacted differently, given the situation. And though I don't know the whole story, I'm sure you have your reason for doing what you did."

Which was a lie.

She didn't understand.

If she could, she'd try to shake some sense into Abby. Then, after lecturing her on the importance of forgiveness in a relationship, this based on an article she'd read in a fashion magazine she'd found in her aunt's boutique, she'd make her march right over to Kevin to tell him how much she loved him.

And this would be now.

But this wasn't what friends do. No, friends were supposed to stand by and support each other's decisions. No matter what they thought.

Well, there was no way she was going to sit back and watch Abby screw this up. If she did, she knew she'd never forgive herself.

She would start by putting a hint of doubt in Abby's mind.

She patted her hand. "Do you realize how lucky you were to have someone love you as much as Kevin did? Most people would kill for what you two had. And to think I once thought you and Peter were the perfect couple. Boy, was I wrong about that."

She sighed. "And now this happened. But I'm sure Kevin will be fine. Once it becomes public knowledge he's available, every single woman in the city will be after him. After all, he's quite a catch."

She nudged Abby with her elbow. "But I'm sure you can vouch for that."

After a short laugh, Sophie forged on. "Speaking of Peter, did I tell you someone saw his car parked at Lucinda's condo this morning? The rumor going around is it was there all night."

Unable to let go of Sophie's comment about all the single women waiting to make their claim on Kevin, Lucinda and Peter's latest rendezvous was the least of her worries. She shrugged. "Good for them. They deserve each other."

"Yeah, you're right. Maybe they really are suited for each other. I can't see my aunt and uncle footing the bill for a second wedding, though. Not after the way my uncle carried on about how much money they 'wasted' on the first wedding."

She turned to Abby, taking her hand. "But, back to Kevin… don't make the mistake of pushing him away. The same goes for your father. Don't let your anger keep you from doing what's right. If you do, you'll regret it for the rest of your life."

Abby's sigh was frustrated. "Sophie, you don't understand. It's not only about my father. There's so much more going on, so much at stake. It's to the point I'm wondering if Kevin and I aren't meant to be. Especially when there's so little hope things will change."

Sophie studied her for a few seconds, a confused look on her face. Then she shook her head. "You might as well be speaking a foreign language, because I have no idea what you're talking about. But whatever it is, I'm sure it can't be all that bad. If you and Kevin really want to be together, you'll work it out."

She stood, extending her arms up above her head in a long stretch. "I need to get home. I have a hungry brood waiting for me. And with this new puppy, who knows what's been going on while I've been gone."

She nodded over at Poppy, who was curled up and watching them from the end of the bed. "She's been fed, and I took her for a walk, so she's all set."

Abby followed her outside, watching as she ran to her car. She was careful not to look over at Kevin's condo. She didn't want to know what he was doing. Or if he was even home.

Well, she did. But she'd given up that right, hadn't she?

Blinking away the start of new tears, she gazed up at the sky. How badly she wanted to make a wish on every single star. With every wish the same… to be safe in Kevin's arms, so she could tell him how much she loved him.

Over and over and over you would wish this. Until you ran out of stars. Then somehow, you'd find more stars.

After the lights of Sophie's car disappeared from view, she went back inside. She curled up on the sofa with Poppy and turned on the TV, scrolling through the channels.

Then she turned off the TV.

She knew she should go to bed, but she couldn't bring herself to do this.

Not without Kevin.

Holding Poppy, she fell into a fitful sleep.

CHAPTER 27

*A*bby was sitting at the kitchen island, her head resting on her arms.

From this angle, she had a good view of the trays on the counter, stacked high with cookies. These were located right next to the pastry bags, filled with frosting.

Yep, they were all ready and waiting. Just for her.

She. Just. Didn't. Care.

She lifted her head as if she planned to make a move towards the apron in arms reach on the counter. Instead, she dropped her chin in her hand and stared into space.

She couldn't seem to get moving. It didn't help the night she spent on the sofa with Poppy had resulted in very little sleep for either of them.

But she couldn't sleep in her bed.

She sighed. It really didn't matter, did it? Where she slept, where she went or how hard she tried to forget.

No, it didn't. Not as long as your heart refuses to let go.

She picked up her phone to see if she had any messages. There were two cookie orders. One for a September baby shower, the other asking for back-to- school themed cookies for a school fundraiser at the end of August. She stared down at the phone, too exhausted to even care.

There was nothing from Kevin.

No text.

No message.

But then why should there be?

Frustrated, she pushed at the phone, sending it sliding across the counter. Of course, it rang. Almost crawling across the counter to grab it, she groaned when she saw the screen.

It was a text from Sophie.

> Hey, do you still want me to bring over the dress I told you was perfect for the benefit? If I don't hear from you, I'll bring it by this afternoon. xoxo

She stared down at the phone, shaking her head.

You don't need a dress. Because you won't be going.

She had already decided she would deliver the cookies tomorrow afternoon. The sooner they were out of her kitchen, the better. Then she would put these past weeks behind her and move on.

She got over Peter, didn't she? So, there was no reason she couldn't do the same with Kevin.

But she didn't want to even think about this right now.

She picked up her phone, amazed to see it was almost four o'clock. Time for her to stop feeling sorry for herself and get to work.

She put on her apron and pulled her hair back into a ponytail. After she lined up the cookies on the parchment paper lined counter-top, she picked up a pastry bag of frosting and got to work.

But this proved to be much harder than it should be. She couldn't concentrate, her mind refusing to forget what she didn't want to remember.

Tears pooling in her eyes, the cookies in front of her began to blur.

You're fooling yourself if you think you'll be able to move on. You've already given Kevin your heart. And even if you were to get it back, it will have been broken beyond repair.

She set the pastry bag on the countertop and, dropping her head back down on her arms, she closed her eyes.

"Come on, Abby. I know you're home. Answer the door."

Shifting her hold on the garment bag draped over her one arm, Sophie knocked again. Harder this time.

There was still nothing.

She set the heavy shopping bag she'd been holding in her other hand on the steps. She glared down at it, shaking her head. Why had she felt the need to bring so many accessories? One or two pairs of shoes and a few pieces of jewelry would have been more than enough.

She tried the door handle, to find the door was unlocked. Muttering to herself about the stupidity of not checking this in the first place, she maneuvered herself and the bags inside. Once the door was closed behind her, she leaned against it with a big sigh of relief.

"Hello? Abby, are you here?"

Except for Poppy, who came stretching and yawning over to meet her, there was only silence.

After she draped the garment bag over the sofa and set the shopping bag next to it, she peeked into Abby's bedroom. Relieved to find the room was empty, she made her way to the kitchen.

She found Abby seated at the island. Her head resting on one arm, her other arm was flung across the counter.

Not wanting to scare her, she spoke in a loud whisper. "Hey, Abby? Are you okay?"

Abby lifted her head. In a daze, she pushed her hair back from her face before she gave Sophie a guilty smile.

Then she glanced over at the clock. "Oh, no... it's already after six? I must have fallen asleep." She dragged her hands through her hair. "I didn't get much sleep last night and I..."

Sophie interrupted her. "And I bet you've also had nothing to eat, have you? Because, well… I'm not trying to be critical here, but you look like you've been run over by a truck."

"Thanks." This was delivered sarcastically. Even with her brain still foggy from sleep, the comment still registered.

Sophie leaned against the counter. "I'm sorry. So, I take it nothing has changed?"

Abby shook her head. Her eyes tearing up, she turned her head, refusing to meet Sophie's gaze.

Not knowing what to say, or what to do, Sophie was silent. Then, after a resigned sigh, she opened the refrigerator and took out a carton of eggs and a container of butter.

She set them on the counter and looked over at Abby, who gave her a blank look. She snapped her fingers. "Hey, work with me here. Do you still keep your frying pan in the same place? I'm going to make you some scrambled eggs and if you point to where you keep your bread, I'll make toast, too."

She shrugged. "Unfortunately, that's the extent of my culinary talents. But you need to eat something. It will make you feel better." After glancing over at Abby's forlorn expression, she sighed. "Well, at least it'll be a start."

Sophie kept up a constant chatter about anything she could think of as she went about preparing the food. It was only after Abby had barely eaten any of what she'd made, listlessly staring off into space, she brought up the reason for her visit.

"I brought a dress to wear for the benefit. Along with a few pairs of shoes and jewelry you might like. The dress is an emerald green. So, with your eyes and hair color, you'll be a knockout. It's one of the most elegant dresses we've ever carried in the boutique. At least since I've been working there."

Abby precisely placed her fork next to her plate, arranging it just so.

She avoided Sophie's gaze. "I'm not going."

Sophie studied her, a troubled look on her face. "Abby, you can't mean this. You have to go, if only to promote your cookies. Aren't you the one who keeps saying you only need one big break to get the business to take off? Well, isn't this that big break?"

When Abby remained silent, she sighed. "Abby, you're one of the smartest people I know. At least until now, I believed this."

Abby sent her a quick glance, an offended expression on her face.

Sophie shrugged. "I'm sorry, but I just don't get it. What's going on? I thought by now you would've come to your senses..." Here she paused, giving Abby a sharp look. "Unless you're having second thoughts about Kevin?"

Shaking her head, Abby picked up her fork, only to put it down again. When what she wanted to do was take the fork and her plate, along with anything else she could get her hands on, and fling them across the room. Maybe even scream as loud as she could.

She would scream and scream and scream. If only to let go of all the pain and anger she was holding inside.

Maybe then Sophie would leave her alone?

She sighed. She couldn't do this. Not only would she scare Sophie to death, she didn't think she had the strength to carry it off. And not to be melodramatic or anything, but she felt like she was weighed down by grief. So much so, she found it almost impossible to even move.

She was tired of talking about this. In fact, she was tired of just about everything right now. The one thing she wanted was no longer hers to have. And now she only wanted to be left alone to mourn her loss.

She gave a frustrated sigh, throwing her napkin down on her plate. "I can't go, I just can't. Not when Kevin... well, I just can't see him. And is it really necessary for me to be there? If people like my cookies, they'll come to that decision whether or not I'm there. So, it doesn't matter."

As far as she was concerned, it was this simple.

It was all settled... she wasn't going.

But Sophie wasn't of the same opinion. A look of determination on her face, she held Abby's gaze. "I disagree. And you know what? It doesn't matter anymore what you think. Because you're going. And

I'm going to make sure of this. I refuse to stand by and let you pass up a chance like this. Or turn your back on what you have with Kevin."

Pushing away from the counter, she grabbed Abby's arm, almost dragging her into the living room.

After she picked up the garment bag and shoved it into Abby's arms, she pointed towards the bedroom.

The commanding tone of her voice brooked no argument. "Now go… try on this dress so we can make sure it fits. No excuses, just do it."

Abby did as she was told.

Sprawled out on the sofa and reading her phone messages, it was the rustle of the taffeta underskirt of the dress that finally caught Sophie's attention.

She jumped up off the sofa, a big smile spreading across her face. "Abby, I was right. It's perfect. If Kevin doesn't fall in love with you all over again when he sees you in this dress, there's something wrong with him!"

She pulled Abby over to the foyer and positioned her in front of the mirror.

For a few moments, they were both silent.

The dress was everything Sophie had claimed it would be, and more. It was stunning. A deep emerald green, the silk fabric gave off an almost opalescent glow with every move Abby made. Even though it was form fitting, at the same time the fabric flowed freely, giving the illusion of softness. A gathered chiffon scarf, in the same shade of emerald green, bordered the sweetheart neckline. Hanging in two panels down the back of the dress, these reached all the way to the floor.

And yes, it brought out the color of Abby's eyes, making them an even deeper shade of green.

Sophie sighed. "Look at you. You would swear this dress had been designed just for you. And once you add the shoes and jewelry?" She shook her head, a mischievous grin on her face. "Let me just say, you're going to be so hot, every woman there will be 'green' with envy."

They laughed before Abby threw her arms around Sophie in a big hug. "Oh Sophie, what would I do without you?"

Sophie grinned. "Does this mean you've changed your mind about not going to the ball?"

Abby was silent as she stared back at her reflection in the mirror. Then she smoothed her hands down over the silky fabric, a sad smile on her face. She shrugged. "I can't go by myself."

Busy rummaging through her shopping bag, Sophie pulled out a pair of burnished gold high-heeled sandals.

She rolled her eyes. "Oh Abby, come on… we both know that's not going to happen."

She handed her the shoes.

"Now here, try these on."

CHAPTER 28

Kevin sank down on the bench in front of his locker. His head down, he avoided eye contact with the rest of the guys as they filed into the room.

He groaned... a long and frustrated groan.

Yanking off his hat and tossing it on the bench, he dragged his hands through his hair. He should be furious with his poor performance during the game. But to be honest? He was so damn tired, he was finding it hard to even care.

You should be thankful you didn't lose the game. Luck was on your side with this win, that's for sure.

After massaging his forehead with his fingers, he looked down at his hands as if they might give him a clue of what happened out there on the field. It just didn't make sense. How could he have bobbled that ground ball? In what should have been a routine play?

You almost let the damn ball go right through your legs.

Then, to make things even worse, when he finally got his hands on the ball, he made a wild throw. This sent the ball careening about three feet left and out of the reach of Alex, who was covering second base.

He could still see the shocked look on Alex's face. He was no lip

232

reader, but he was pretty damn sure whatever Alex had to say about his throw, it was far from complimentary.

Whatever made you think you would be good enough to be a part of all this?

He leaned back against his locker and closed his eyes.

Welcome to the big leagues…

He jerked, catching himself before he almost slid sideways off the bench.

In a daze, and rubbing the back of his neck, he glanced around the room. It looked like he was the only one left.

How long had he been sitting here? Did he doze off?

He sighed, massaging the back of his neck. He needed to take a shower. His uniform looked like he'd slid down the entire length of the baseline, his skin was covered with a layer of grit and sweat.

Then he needed to stop somewhere and get something to eat.

Staring off into space, he tried to remember the last time he ate. Was it breakfast? It had to be.

He groaned. He didn't want to take a shower. And he didn't need food.

You want Abby…

He wanted to feel the softness of her fitting against him as he held her in his arms.

He wanted to tangle his hands in her hair, the silky strands gliding through his fingers.

He wanted to get lost in her eyes. And drink in the sweetness of her kisses.

Then maybe he'd be able to forget about how everything in his world had fallen all apart.

Wearily getting up off the bench, he opened his locker.

After he combed his fingers through his hair, still damp from the shower, Kevin shoved his wallet into the back pocket of his jeans.

It was when he went to pick up his keys from the bench, he sensed someone was behind him.

He turned. It was Chester, an uneasy expression on his face, somewhere between a smile and a grimace. But then he could be wrong. Maybe this was the best Chester could offer when it came to a smile?

He almost groaned aloud.

Please God, no. He's the last person you want to deal with right now.

Whatever Chester had to say, he didn't want to hear it. No sarcastic remarks. No lecture on his disastrous performance on the field. And most of all, he wanted no snide remarks about him and Abby.

Please, please... you wouldn't be able to handle this right now. So, say something. Fast...

He shut his locker door with a decisive bang, and after grabbing his keys from the bench, he turned, his voice coming out sharper than he intended.

"Before you say anything, I'll admit I'm guilty. I goofed up big today. Something I'm sure, with your perfect defensive record, you find hard to fathom. But it's done and over with and I want to move on. So, whatever smart remark you've got waiting to come out, I'm not interested in hearing it. Save it for the next time."

His laugh was sharp. "I'm sure there will be many opportunities for this."

He gave a curt nod as he moved to get past him. "Have a great night."

Chester grabbed his arm. "Hold on. I have no intention of giving you a lecture on what was, yes, a disastrous display on your part. Hell, we've all been there. I've had quite a few mess ups of my own, some a lot worse than yours. None of us are perfect."

At Kevin's skeptic look, he nodded.

"Yeah, as you'd say, 'fathom' that. But I've learned, you get up, brush yourself off, and get right back into the game. It also doesn't hurt to send up a little prayer your good moments will eventually outweigh the bad."

He smiled. "I'm probably only going to say this once, so you better enjoy it while you can, but you've got a lot of talent. Stupid mistakes and all."

They eyed each other before Kevin finally grinned back at him. Running his hand through his hair, he shook his head. "Thanks, and sorry about the rant. It's only that I feel so damn stupid. A ten-year-old could have made that play. I'm just glad it didn't turn into something worse and we still got the win." A wry smile twisted his lips. "I'm sure I'll never hear the end of it."

Chester grinned. "No, I can guarantee you won't. The guys on this team don't forget a thing, bad or good."

Then his smile disappeared, his expression hesitant. His hands shoved in his pockets, he rocked back and forth on his heels.

"It seems you and I have started off on the wrong foot. I'm sure you've noticed I get carried away sometimes, shooting my mouth off before I think. Then there's my warped sense of humor."

When Kevin only nodded, Chester continued. "But I have a hard time with some of you younger guys who come in here, acting like some kind of celebrity instead of a baseball player. And I guess I automatically put you in that category. But now I see you don't belong there." Another grin crossed his face. "Even with your all-American good looks."

He held out his hand. "So, how about it? Can we call a truce?"

After giving his hand a firm shake, Kevin grinned back at him. "Yeah, sure. I'd like that."

Chester cleared his throat, an indication he had more to say. The fact he seemed nervous made Kevin want to help him out.

He raised an eyebrow. "I take it there's something else?"

A redness began to spread across Chester's face and down his neck before he jammed his hands in his pockets.

He finally just blurted it out. "Sophie… do you know Sophie?"

At first, Kevin was too dumbfounded to reply. Was Chester actually blushing? Because of a woman?

And, Sophie? Who the hell was Sophie?

Then it clicked. Sophie… he was talking about Abby's friend, Sophie.

Or was he?

But who else could it be? He couldn't imagine there were a lot of women running around this part of town with the name Sophie.

He peered over at Chester. "Sophie? Are you talking about Abby's friend, Sophie?"

Chester was now beet red. Looking anywhere except at Kevin, he sputtered out the words. "Yeah. She told me she was Abby's friend. I met her when she was trying to rescue a puppy who got caught up in a busy intersection. I almost ran right into the back of her car when she braked to a dead stop in front of me.

His expression was indignant. "She jumped out of her car and ran out into the middle of traffic to save the damn dog. Granted, it was just a puppy. But I about had a heart attack. When I confronted her, she lectured me, accusing me of being unsympathetic to the plight of abandoned animals. Hey, I like dogs. I always have."

He smiled, an almost goofy smile. "But she was so damn cute. And so little, so fragile looking. I just wanted to..."

He shook his head, staring down at his feet.

Kevin was almost in shock.

Did Chester know what a chatterbox Sophie was? Once she got started, there was no stopping her? He obviously hadn't spent enough time with her to pick up on this.

He must be crazy.

But then, who was he to talk?

His mind taking him back to when he met Abby, he remembered that sudden need to be close to her, to find out everything about her. This had hit him so hard, he knew right then and there, he'd never be able to let her go.

He smiled. Even if she started talking a mile a minute like Sophie, his feelings for her wouldn't change. He'd only take her in his arms and listen.

So again, who are you to judge?

A deep sadness consuming him, he shook his head at what a mess everything had become. He glanced over at Chester to see he was watching him, a curious expression on his face.

He ran his hand through his hair, letting out a slow breath. "So… you and Sophie. I take it you want me to talk to Abby about this. So, she and Sophie can discuss all the likely reasons she might be interested in hearing from you. And if this is your time to get lucky, Sophie's phone number will be yours."

When Chester started to smile at the ridiculousness of this process that seemed so crucial in getting two people together, he grinned back at him. "Yep, it all seems so exhausting, doesn't it? And so damn unnecessary. But it's the rig-a-ma-roll all women go through when they're interested in someone. How much easier it would be if they just came out and let us poor guys know how they really feel."

Chester laughed. "So, you'll do it?"

After studying him for a few seconds, Kevin sank down on the bench. He shook his head. "I don't know if I can."

Staring straight ahead, he hesitated. He wasn't sure if he wanted to acknowledge the one thing he'd been trying so hard to forget.

He sighed. "As of last night, it looks like Abby and I are finished. According to her, she no longer wants to see me. Not ever again, she said."

This was the first time he'd admitted this out loud. And to someone else.

And it hurt like hell.

Damn, how it hurt…

He looked down at his hands, her words like an echo in his mind.

And don't call me sugar. You no longer have that right.

He glanced up at Chester, shrugging his shoulders. "What I thought was a good idea wasn't one at all. I messed up. Big time."

Abruptly coming to his feet, he glanced over at Chester, who suddenly had nothing to say.

Well, this wasn't helping matters.

Couldn't he at least come up with something to make you feel better? Like don't worry… or you guys will work it out… or she'll come around. Just about anything would do. You're not picky at this point.

Suddenly, he was exhausted. And frustrated. This had his words coming out more sharply than he intended. "So, it looks like you've picked the wrong guy for…"

Chester cut him off.

"Don't be an idiot. We've all seen how you've been since you met her. Confident, Mr. King of the World. You're hitting home runs like you own the field. If you want her that much, then you need to go about it the same as when you're up at the plate and down to your last strike. You give it all you've got. And if you play it just right, you'll hit it out of the park. And damn if it isn't all yours."

Kevin stared at him, his mouth agape. Never would he have expected such words of wisdom and encouragement coming from Chester, of all people.

"And from what Sophie told me?" Chester was on a roll, a grin on his face at Kevin's reaction. "You've got nothing to worry about. Your 'certain little redhead' wouldn't be able to walk away from you even if she tried. I don't know what you did, or how you did it, but it seems you've convinced her you're her knight in shining armor and Prince Charming, all rolled into one."

He dug his keys out of his pocket, nodding over at Kevin. "I don't know about you, but I'm starving. I could also use a beer right now. So I'm heading over to The Home Plate. It's a little bar where no one cares who you are, and even if they do, they still leave you alone."

He grinned. "And the best part? They have the best hamburgers in town. So, come on, join me."

As he began walking out of the room, he had one more thing to add, his words thrown over his shoulder.

"Just follow me. Unless you don't think you can keep up."

Kevin grinned.

He was never one to pass up a challenge.

CHAPTER 29

bby found the unopened bottle of wine in her pantry. She couldn't remember where it came from, but knew it had been there for a while, waiting for the right occasion to be opened.

She wondered if maybe that time was now.

She wasn't a wine drinker. Oh no, far from it.

Two glasses were the most she could handle, if even that. But the way her life had gone the past few days, she decided a few glasses of wine could be exactly what she needed.

Never mind that, except for the few bites of scrambled eggs and toast Sophie made for her earlier, she had eaten nothing else all day.

She also had slept very little in the past twenty-four hours.

Oh, well...

She opened the bottle and, pouring a generous amount of wine into a glass, she took a drink. Followed by another.

Then she put on her apron.

She was ready.

Her plan was to frost half of the cookies. And she wasn't going to stop until she did.

Pastry bag in hand, she started on the first cookie.

Abby carried another tray of finished cookies into the pantry. She glanced over at the clock. Where had the time gone? She'd been at it for almost four hours.

She reached for her wineglass, nearly knocking it over.

No worries. It was almost empty.

She picked up the wine bottle and held it up to the light. For a moment, and we're talking a very brief moment here, she was a little concerned. How could the bottle be almost empty? This wasn't what she'd intended to happen.

She glanced over at the counter. There was only one more tray of cookies to go. This was about two or three dozen, give or take a few.

Maybe she should celebrate this milestone by finishing off the rest of the wine?

Again, she momentarily stopped to think about the logic of this, but for some reason, her mind refused to cooperate.

So, she poured what was left of the wine into her glass.

She picked up a bag of frosting, only to set it back down.

Music.

It was too quiet. She needed music.

She signed into the music app on her phone and turned up the volume. Then she opened all the windows. This would speed up the drying time of the finished cookies.

She celebrated both moves with another large gulp of wine and danced her way back to the island, singing along with the music.

She was ignoring the letter she'd left on the counter. The bank's official logo jumping out from the top of the page, it was a grim reminder the monthly payment for her kitchen makeover was due.

Even in her befuddled state, she knew this was a problem. She wasn't sure if she would have enough money to cover the loan on top of her other monthly expenses.

A very depressing situation, indeed.

But also the perfect reason to finish off the wine remaining in her glass.

Yep, you might as well live it up while you can.

Pastry bag in hand, and a song on her lips, she began piping frosting on the cookie in front of her.

She was a disaster waiting to happen.

After he and Chester left the bar, Kevin swore his drive home was taking twice as long as it normally did. But this was because he couldn't bring himself to drive anything but the legal speed limit.

Hell, he hadn't even come close to reaching it yet.

You're driving like an old man.

No, it wasn't that. He was stalling. This was exactly what he was doing. Because he knew, once he finally arrived home, he'd be alone. In the past, this wouldn't have been a problem. He might have even enjoyed it.

But Abby has changed all of this.

He drove down their street. And even though he tried to fight it, his gaze was drawn to her condo. Puzzled, he slowed the car to get a better look. There were lights shining from every window, and the kitchen windows were wide open.

He pulled into his driveway. After he turned off the ignition, he stayed in the car.Should he be concerned?

He groaned, dropping his head down on the steering wheel.

Did you forget? You're not a part of her life anymore. So, it's really none of your business.

Wondering how he could feel so miserable, yet at the same time so angry, he slid out of the driver's seat and slammed the door.

This was when he heard music.

He peered over at Abby's condo. Was it coming from there?

He weighed his options. Then he dropped his keys in his pocket. Bella would have to wait a little longer for her dinner. There was no way around it. He needed to check it out. If he didn't, he'd drive himself crazy with worry.

He arrived at Abby's front door to find that the music was definitely coming from her condo.

And it was loud.

Very loud.

He knocked. Then he knocked again. After no response, he turned the handle to find the door was unlocked. He stared down at his hand holding the handle.

Is she ever going to take your advice and lock her doors?

He shook his head. From what he had seen so far, this could be the least of his worries.

As soon as he pushed open the door, Poppy came flying across the room, leaping and running circles around him. After he managed to calm her down, he headed for the kitchen with her scampering at his heels.

He came to an abrupt stop. His hand slowly going up to run through his hair, he gazed around the kitchen in disbelief.

What the hell went on in this kitchen tonight?

The room looked like a major hurricane had passed through, almost every cupboard door and drawer standing wide open. Every inch of counter space was covered with boxes of bagged cookies, bowls, pastry bags and every kind of kitchen utensil imaginable. There was also what looked like a trail of flour across the floor, disappearing around the other side of the island.

And the music he'd heard when he was outside? It was ten times louder in the kitchen.

After he turned off the music, he noticed a wine bottle, along with an empty wineglass on the island countertop. Gingerly picking up the bottle, he found it suspiciously light.

This was because it was empty.

Again, he glanced around the room. Then, dragging his hand down over his face, he groaned.

Did she drink all of this by herself? And where is she now?

Afraid of what he might find on the other side, he cautiously made his way around the island. After uttering a sigh of relief at finding nothing more than an empty pastry bag on the floor, he heard a sound behind him.

It was Abby.

Coming out of the pantry, and holding a large tray, piled with cookies, she was humming what sounded to him like... Silent Night? Tilting his head, he listened more closely.

It was definitely Silent Night.

He chuckled.

Startled, Abby glanced over at him. Their eyes meeting, everything came to a standstill in the now eerily silent kitchen.

Then she smiled

"Kevin..."

And almost as if it was happening in slow motion, the tray slipped from her fingers.

Frozen in place, they could only watch as it went crashing to the floor, cookies flying everywhere, hitting the floor in an explosion of crumbs.

"Oh no, no, no, no, no..." Her hands going to her mouth, she sank down onto the floor and began to cry.

At least he thought she was crying. It was only when he squatted next to her, brushing away the broken pieces of cookies littering the floor around them, he realized she was actually hysterically laughing and crying at the same time.

This immediately confirmed his fear the empty wine bottle was all her doing.

He reached for her hands, patiently waiting for her to calm down. It was only when her outburst finally dwindled down to only a few erratic hiccup-like-gasps, he spoke.

"Abby, look at me."

Squeezing her eyes shut, she shook her head.

No.

She didn't want to look at him.

She couldn't look at him.

If she did, she knew she'd want to go right into his arms. And for some reason, and she couldn't quite remember why, she was no longer allowed to do this.

In fact, he wasn't even supposed to be in her kitchen. Or even in her condo. At least not with her.

His voice tugged at her like an invisible thread. "Sugar, come on... look at me. *Please?*"

Slowly opening her eyes, his expression one of such genuine concern, she had this sudden need to reassure him. Pulling her hand free to press her index finger to his lips, she spoke in an exaggerated whisper.

"*Shhhh...* It's okay. It's all okey-dokey." This was followed by a very loud hiccup. Her hand going to her mouth, she giggled.

Sinking down onto the floor so that he was facing her, Kevin shook his head. "Oh, Abby... what have you done? If you drank that entire bottle of wine, I'm afraid you won't be this happy when you wake up tomorrow. I hope you didn't do this on an empty stomach."

She glanced over at the bottle, then back at him before she scooted between his legs until she was almost leaning against him. She clasped her hands behind his neck, and tilting her head, she gave him a huge smile.

"You're just so, so, so cute." Holding her finger to his lips, her whisper was exaggerated. "*Shhhh...* it's okay. 'Member I said so?" Then she buried her head against his shoulder, and closing her eyes, her words came in a slurred sing-song voice,

"*I-love-you-Kevin-Kardell... I-do. I-love-you-so-much... I-do, I-do... And I'll-always-love-you... until-the-end-of-time...*"

He held her against him, his eyes closed as he pressed soft kisses in her hair. He knew she was a little drunk. Okay, maybe she was more than a little. All right, he'd admit it. She was very drunk. But the words she sang were by far the sweetest he'd ever heard.

And after the events of the last two days, he needed this moment with her more than he'd ever needed anything in his life.

He pulled her close, wanting to get lost in the familiar feeling of having her in his arms. But he needed to get her up off the floor and away from the disaster so plainly on display around them.

As if she sensed what he was thinking, she pushed away from him, her gaze going to the floor. She turned back to him, her expression one of complete horror. "Did I do this?"

Before he could answer, she scrambled out of his arms and began crawling around the floor. After she had gathered up some of the broken cookies, she tried to piece them together on the tray.

She abruptly sat back on her heels. After staring down at the broken cookie pieces in her hands, she turned to him with an agonized cry. "What am I going to do? Everything's ruined..."

She threw the pieces on the floor and burst into tears.

He scrambled to his feet, pulling her up with him. Swaying unsteadily against him, she continued to cry as he brushed the hair back from her face, his thumbs swiping away her tears.

His voice came at her softly, tenderly. "We'll figure it all out somehow. But for right now, we need to sit you down and get some coffee into you."

Seated at the island and her chin resting in her hand, Abby was totally drained. She couldn't take her eyes off Kevin, her mind desperately trying to believe he was real. She searched his face, drinking in every detail as if she hadn't seen him in days.

Maybe you're dreaming?

In a daze, she watched as he took a cup out of the cupboard to fill it with coffee. When he set the cup in front of her, she frowned down at it, shaking her head.

She didn't need coffee.

No. The only thing you need, the only thing you want, is him.

She wanted to crawl into his lap so she could curl up in his arms and rest her head against his chest. Where she could get lost in the warmth of his embrace and the soothing sound of his heartbeat.

The thought of this made her smile

Encouraged by this, he smiled back. "Drink your coffee, sugar. But be careful, it's pretty hot." Then he stood, brushing his knuckles down the side of her face in a soft caress. "I'll be right back."

Anxiously watching as he left the room, she sighed with relief when he returned. She studied the two aspirins he placed in her hand, unsure of what he wanted her to do with them. He smiled, pushing the cup of coffee closer to her. "Take them with your coffee. It can't hurt."

She did as he asked, her eyes again drawn to him. She wondered, did he have any idea how much she'd missed him?

Maybe you should tell him this?

But to do this, she would need to get closer. So, she leaned towards him, almost sliding off the stool before he reached over to steady her. Wrapping her arms around his neck, she whispered in his ear. "I missed you."

She followed this with a big kiss to his mouth before she rested her head on his shoulder.

He chuckled. Pulling the hair tie from her disheveled ponytail, he ran his fingers through the tangled curls before he placed a soft kiss to her forehead. "Oh sugar, I missed you, too. I don't think you could know how much."

She sighed against him as she reached for his hand. Her fingers linked with his, she settled even more closely against him.

She was going to hold on and never let go.

They remained like this, leaning on each other for support.

Well, Abby was doing most of the leaning, but Kevin didn't seem to mind.

The only sound in the room was the hum of the refrigerator and an occasional sigh from Poppy. She'd settled herself in her dog bed and was watching them through hooded eyes. If either of them was to make a move, she wanted to know about it.

Abby was fighting the overwhelming urge to close her eyes. She was afraid if she fell asleep, Kevin would leave. And she couldn't let him do this because there was so much she wanted to say to him.

But she didn't have the strength. In fact, she couldn't even drum up the energy to open her mouth. Certainly not enough to put together the words she needed to make him understand how she felt.

She wanted to tell him she was sorry. She knew he'd only been trying to help. And she had made a terrible, *terrible* mistake when she told him she never wanted to see him again. She didn't mean this. No, she didn't want this at all. She wanted to spend the rest of her life with him.

You want a forever with him.

If only she could somehow block out the awful memory of what had brought them to this point. Lurking in the back of her mind, it was a reminder nothing had been resolved.

But unable to fight it any longer, she gave in, closing her eyes.

And what about Kevin?

He had no intention of going anywhere. He would be happy to stay right where he was and hold her for as long as she'd let him.

Like Abby, there was so much he wanted to say. He wanted to tell her how bad he felt about what happened with her father. He'd meant well, his only intent to make things right between them.

Like Chester had bluntly put it, he was an idiot. He'd tried to be some kind of super hero, bursting in on the scene to fix things, when he had no business even getting involved.

Yep, he'd screwed up. Something he just kept doing, over and over again.

Now watching Addy struggle to stay awake, he brought her hand to his mouth, placing a soft kiss to her wrist. Her head jerked up. Her lashes flying open, she tried to focus on him.

He smoothed the hair back from her face. "Sugar, let's get you to bed. I think this is the best place for you right now."

When her only response was to settle back against his shoulder and close her eyes, he gathered her in his arms and carried her down the hall to the bedroom. He gently lowered her onto the bed and pulled the quilt over her. When he brushed the hair from her face and saw her eyes were still closed, he placed a soft kiss to her cheek.

Her voice came at him, soft and uncertain.

"Don't go. Stay with me. Please?"

Without a moment's hesitation, he kicked off his shoes and emptied his pockets of his phone, keys, and wallet. Sliding under the quilt and settling next to her, he pulled her against him.

She sighed, her words so faint, he almost missed them.

"I love you."

He was smiling as he pulled her close, pressing a kiss right below her ear.

"I love you, too."

They were both sound asleep within seconds.

CHAPTER 30

Kevin opened his eyes.

A slow smile spread across his face when he realized Abby was curled up beside him, her arm flung across his chest.

Moving slowly so he wouldn't wake her, he reached over to get his phone off the nightstand to check the time. It was a little after seven.

He glanced down at Abby, a long sigh escaping him.

He'd give anything to stay right here in this bed with her, all day, if he could. But he'd promised Alex he'd go with him to a dedication for a community ballpark he'd helped sponsor. It was on the east side of town and Alex asked him to be there by nine.

Surely a few more minutes with Abby couldn't hurt. Nestling back beside her, he closed his eyes.

His hand going to his head, he groaned.

Her kitchen… it was a complete disaster.

Damn...

Planting a soft kiss to her shoulder and sliding his arm out from under her, he inched his way off the bed. When he tucked the quilt around her, she gave a soft moan before she mumbled something, his name the only word he could make out.

He smiled, recalling her rambling declaration of love last night while they sat on the kitchen floor, surrounded by broken cookie crumbs. An experience he knew he'd never forget.

Hey, he'd take whatever he could get. Wasn't it a well-known fact, most people were apt to say what they really thought after a few drinks.?

Yeah, he remembered hearing this from somewhere.

But he knew Abby's memory of last night would be nowhere as sweet as his. She was sure to be hurting when she finally woke. Drinking an entire bottle of wine could do that to a person.

Giving her one more kiss, he stuffed his wallet and keys in his pockets and slipped into his shoes. After he picked up his phone, he crept out of the room. Poppy hopped out of her bed and came trotting over to join him.

After he took the little dog for a short walk, he cleaned the kitchen as best he could, sweeping up the cookie crumbs, cleaning off the countertops and loading the dishwasher.

He gave one last swipe over everything, his gaze going to the letter he'd found when he'd first began clearing the cluttered counter. He picked it up and read it a second time before he set it back on the counter.

Before he could change his mind, he picked it up and stuffed it in his pocket.

Feeling pretty proud of what he had accomplished, he glanced once more around the room. There was one last tray of cookies on the counter, still waiting to be finished.

This is when it occurred to him Abby could probably use some help. He took out his phone and hit Alex's number. After about four rings, Alex's cheerful voice came at him.

"Hey, you aren't bailing out on me, are you?"

Kevin chuckled.

"Nope, I'll meet you as planned. I'm actually calling to talk to Lisa. Is she there?"

He grinned.

"I have a favor to ask of her."

CHAPTER 31

If you're lucky enough to get a second chance, try not to waste it.
~ Anonymous

Her arm thrown across her eyes to block the early morning light, Abby was afraid to move. If she did, she was pretty sure her head would explode.

It didn't help that every bird in the neighborhood must have gathered outside her window, each chirp enough to wake the dead.

She'd already made one attempt to open her eyes, only to close them again. The light streaming through the window blinds was much brighter than she remembered.

And her mouth… it felt like it was stuffed with cotton balls.

Dirty cotton balls.

Exactly how much wine did you drink?

Judging by how horrible she felt, it must have been a lot more than she should have.

A lot more...

She didn't know how she'd ended up in her bed—everything that happened after she opened that bottle of wine had settled into a complete blur.

The one thing she did remember was bringing a tray of cookies out of the pantry so she could bag them.

She frowned. Did she ever actually do that? Because she couldn't recall if she had.

Her arm still thrown across her eyes, she desperately tried to unscramble everything swirling around in her mind, hoping something would come to her.

Please... anything.

Her lashes flying open, her hand went to her mouth.

Kevin...

He was in her kitchen when she dropped the tray. She cringed, remembering how it crashed to the floor, cookies flying everywhere.

And after that?

She was pretty sure he'd also been in this bed with her.

She sat on the edge of the bed, the terrible pounding in her head intensifying with the move. After a few minutes, or maybe longer, she wouldn't be able to tell you for sure, only that it seemed to be an agonizingly long time, she slid out of bed and stumbled into the bathroom.

She took one look in the mirror and wished she hadn't. If possible, she looked worse than she felt. Sinking down to the floor, she rested her head back against the wall and closed her eyes.

She wanted to just die.

Her head jerking up, Abby dragged her hand through her hair.

What was that noise?

Was there someone in her condo?

She heard it again. It was the sound of someone laughing. It was a child's laughter. This was followed by an excited bark from Poppy.

She splashed her face with cold water. After she brushed her teeth to get rid of the awful cotton ball taste, she gathered her hair up in a ponytail.

Cautiously making her way down the hall, she came upon a little girl sitting next to Poppy's dog bed. All curly blonde hair and big, blue eyes, she was brushing the little dog's fur. She was using one of Abby's large pastry brushes as her brush.

She looked up and saw Abby. With a little shriek, she flung the pastry brush down on the floor, scrambled to her feet and went flying into the kitchen. Her loud whisper carried back to Abby. "Momma... she's up. She looks sad, just like you said she would. And she has red hair."

She peeked around the corner.

Abby sent her a little wave. "Hi..."

After a shy smile, she ducked back into the kitchen.

Not sure what to expect, Abby entered the room. Alex's wife Lisa was seated at the island, a pastry bag in her hand, and a row of cookies lined up on the counter in front of her. She smiled, waving the pastry bag. "*Ah...* good morning, sleepyhead. Or should I say good afternoon?" She peered over at Abby. "How are you feeling?"

How was she feeling? Abby wished she could say she felt better than she looked, but this would probably be stretching things a bit.

She pushed the hair back from her face and gave Lisa a weak smile. "So-so? Not the best, but probably much better than I should." She looked inquiringly at Lisa. "I didn't expect to find anyone here."

Lisa laughed. "Yes, I'm sure the last thing you wanted this morning was to find us in your kitchen. Let's just say someone who cares about you very, *very* much convinced me you could use some help." She shook her head. "How are you able to refuse Kevin anything? Why, just the sound of his voice alone makes a girl want to melt."

She nodded over at the little girl who'd now climbed up to sit on one of the stools by the island and was curiously studying Abby. "We got here about fifteen minutes ago. And by we, I mean me and my favorite little helper. Abby, meet my daughter, Chloe.

She gestured for Abby to sit down next to Chloe before she poured her a cup of coffee. "Now, you sit there and relax while I make you some toast. In the meantime, drink this coffee."

As she went about preparing the toast, she gave Abby a curious glance. "So, tell me, what happened here last night? From what Kevin told me, it sounds like quite a few cookies were ruined and you might've had a few too many glasses of wine. This was the most I could get out of him. He also seemed to think everything that happened was his fault."

Abby slowly set her coffee cup down on the counter. And darn if she didn't look over at Lisa and start to cry.

Quickly coming to her side, Lisa wrapped her in a big hug.

She sighed. "Isn't love wonderful? Even more so when it's all so new. You just cry it out." She sat down next to Abby and gave her a warm smile. "If you want to talk about it, I'm here to listen."

One look into Lisa's eyes, filled with such kindness and concern, and Abby told her everything.

She started out by telling her all about her father. How she turned him away. Something she now realized wasn't what she'd wanted to do at all.

She went on to tell her about Kevin's mother and how she'd offered her money, threatening to disown Kevin if Abby continued to see him. This was why Abby told Kevin the same thing she told her father... that she didn't want him in her life anymore.

But at the time, she'd thought this was the only thing to do. She'd never be able to live with herself if she came between Kevin and his family.

And even though Kevin had showed up in her condo last night, she wasn't sure how things stood between them, the whole evening pretty much of a blur.

So, in the last few hours, she'd managed to lose the two people she loved the most. And now she didn't know what to do or where to even start at making things right.

Everything having been said she wanted to say, she stared down at the coffee cup she was cradling in her hands. She felt completely drained. But at the same time, she was relieved to have finally shared what she'd been keeping bottled up inside over the past few days.

For a long moment, there was only silence. Then a small voice piped up. "I like Kevin. He's nice, even when he teases me. Daddy really likes him, too. I don't want you to be mad at him."

Lisa and Abby glanced over at Chloe with surprise. She shrugged, giving them a big smile.

Lisa began to laugh. "Well, there you have it. The highest praise a person could ask for. If daddy likes him, he's got to be a good guy."

Reaching over to give Chloe a hug, Abby smiled at her. "Oh, Chloe, I know. He is nice, isn't he? I know he would be so happy to know both you and your daddy like him. And just between you and me, even when I get mad at him, I really can't be mad at him at all."

At Chloe's puzzled look, Abby smiled. "Oh dear, that didn't make much sense, did it?"

She looked over at Lisa, grinning shyly, before she turned back to Chloe. "What I mean is… I guess I'm just too head over heels in love with him to ever stay mad at him."

"Head over heels?" After she repeated this, Chloe laughed. "Like when I do a somersault? I'm dizzy, but happy?"

Abby laughed. "Yes, that's exactly what Kevin does. He makes me both dizzy and happy, all at the same time."

Lisa smiled at this exchange between the two of them before she gave Abby a thoughtful look.

"So, it sounds like he's the one for you."

Her eyes meeting Lisa's, Abby sighed. "He's like a dream come true. Even though I've known him for such a short time, I don't even want to think about how my life would be without him."

She looked down, her voice barely audible. "Sometimes it scares me how much I love him. I've never experienced this kind of love before. It's taken me to a place I've never been before, a place I never, ever want to leave."

She shrugged. "This must be why I'm not good at it. Look how badly I went and made a mess out of everything."

"Oh, Abby, no one is either good or bad at loving another person. Not if it's really true love." Lisa shook her head. "But I think being able to trust each other is the most important part of a relationship. Because if you don't trust someone, how can you ever completely give yourself to that person? And from what you've just told me, you aren't trusting Kevin at all, are you?"

When Abby slowly shook her head, Lisa reached over to place her hand over hers. "Abby, you need to tell him what his mother did. Let him be the one to decide what should be done. And your father … you have to let him tell his side of the story. Otherwise, you're not being at all fair to him. You two need each other. You're family. You *always* need family."

She sighed. "I believe this awful confrontation with Kevin's mother and then seeing your father after so long, well, both of these things coming at you almost at once, was too much. So, you did what any normal person would do. You cracked."

She smiled. "And from what Alex has told me, Kevin is just as 'head over heels' about you as you are with him. Which leads me to believe this is just a big bump in your relationship. So, let him be the one to take over from here."

Picking up the pastry bag she had been using before their conversation began, she waved it at Abby. "But it seems I'm lecturing you and telling you what to do. When you should be making all of these decisions yourself. So, let's get to work and finish decorating these cookies. Then we can get them packed up and out of your kitchen."

She made a face over at her phone. "Then maybe Mia will stop pestering me with all of these messages, asking when they'll be delivered."

She smiled over at Abby before she began piping frosting on another cookie. "Think of this as your first lesson about what it means to be involved with a baseball player. You'll find out it's always all for the love of baseball. In July, or whatever month of the year it is."

She stopped to admire her work before she moved on to the next cookie. "And, contrary to what you may think, there is no off-season in baseball. Or in love, for that matter."

When she saw Abby was intently watching her progress, she laughed, waving the pastry bag at her. "Don't worry. I took some cake decorating classes. So, I sort of know what I'm doing, even though I'm sure your end results are much better. You can take over when you finish drinking your coffee."

Chloe pulled on Abby's arm. "Abby, if you aren't going to eat your toast, can I have it?"

Lisa's head shot up. "Chloe!"

Chloe looked over at her, a guilty look on her face. "I can't help it. I'm hungry."

Abby glanced over at the clock. "I see it's around lunchtime. Would you like a grilled cheese sandwich? I'll make one for your mom, too."

Chloe kept up a constant chatter as she watched Abby make the sandwiches. She then went on to talk the entire time she was eating her sandwich and even while she helped Abby and Lisa finish the remaining cookies. It was her job to place them in the bakery boxes, a job she took very seriously.

She couldn't help it. She just really liked to talk. But not so much she couldn't take a break to eat two of Abby's cookies, announcing they were the best cookies she'd had in her whole life.

Which, she was quick to inform Abby, would soon be all of seven years since her birthday was only seven days away.

The mid-afternoon sun was shining through the kitchen window when they finished.

Lisa picked up her phone. "I'm going to call Alex to see if he can get someone to deliver these cookies." She glanced over at Abby while she waited for him to answer. "Will you talk to Kevin again? Has he told you what time he's picking you up tomorrow night?"

Since she didn't have an answer to either of those questions, Abby was relieved when Alex answered his phone, occupying Lisa's attention.

After she ended the call, Lisa turned to Abby. "Well it looks like both Alex and Kevin will be delivering the cookies. They stopped to get a late lunch after the dedication ceremony and aren't far from here. They'll be here in a few minutes. I hope this is okay?"

Abby continued to load the dishwasher, her mind in a whirl. Was it okay? She didn't know. Her headache was just about gone and she was feeling almost normal. And she did want to see Kevin. But at the same time, she was afraid of what might happen when she did. There was too much from last night she didn't remember and even more from the day before she wanted to forget.

She turned to give Lisa a faint smile. "Sure, that's fine."

She took off her apron, glancing down at her wrinkled clothing. She was still wearing the same shorts and tee shirt she'd worn yesterday. And her hair? She couldn't even imagine the condition it was in.

She ran her hands down over her shorts. "I need to take a shower. Look at me, I'm a mess."

Lisa nodded, an amused expression on her face. "*Ah...* I think you're stalling, but go ahead. Even though I have the feeling Kevin will want to see you no matter how much of a 'mess' you are."

She smiled. "Again, I'm sure the two of you will be just fine."

Alex laid his phone back down on the bar. He glanced over at Kevin. Perched on the edge of the stool, his eyes were fixed on the big screen TV over the bar. He looked like a panther, ready to pounce and Alex knew this was in no way related to the sports commentator's take on last night's games.

He had no idea what happened between him and Abby last night. There was only Kevin's claim he'd made a complete mess of things. After that single revelation, he'd gone on to refer to himself as a damn idiot before he changed the subject.

But Alex wasn't worried. He knew he'd get the low down from Lisa. She'd find out what was going on, she always did.

He smiled. Lisa had a way of getting people to pour out their most innermost feelings without even realizing they were doing so. Whatever the situation, she made everyone feel good in the end.

Suddenly eager to see both her and Chloe, he looked over at Kevin. "I just told Lisa we'd deliver the cookies for Abby. We can leave whenever you're ready."

When Kevin didn't answer, completely engrossed in whatever he had going on in his mind, Alex threw a pretzel at him.

Startled, Kevin turned to him. "What the hell? What was that for?"

Alex laughed. "Hey, trying to get through to you is not easy. We need to make a stop at Abby's. The cookies are all packed up and ready to go and I just volunteered you and me as the official delivery-men. We'll drop them off on the way to the ballpark."

When Kevin only gave him a blank stare, Alex gave him a curious look. "Are you up to this?"

Sliding off the stool and taking out his wallet, Kevin pulled out what looked like way too many bills and threw them on the bar. "Ok, let's go. I've got this."

He turned and began walking out of the room, leaving Alex to grab his glass and quickly drain the last of his beer. Glancing over at the bartender who was watching all of this, he shrugged before he went after Kevin.

It was a good thing they had driven separately. If they hadn't, there was no doubt in his mind, Kevin would've driven off without him, given the state he was in. He shook his head.

Love… it sure had a way of messing with people's minds.

CHAPTER 32

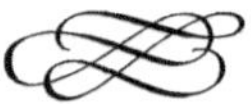

*L*isa and Chloe were in the middle of a rousing game of I Spy when Kevin and Alex walked into Abby's kitchen.

As soon as Chloe saw Alex, she went diving off her chair to run right into his waiting arms.

"Daddy!"

He picked her up and swung her up high in the air before he set her back down, both of them laughing. Then he walked over to Lisa and, pulling her up out of her chair and into his arms, captured her mouth in a sweet, lingering kiss.

She pulled away from him, breathless. "Oh my, what was that for?"

She narrowed her eyes. "*Uh oh*, what did you do?"

He merely smiled as he put his arm around her. "Nothing. I did nothing. I just want to make sure you know how much I love you."

He turned to Chloe. "So, did you help mommy and Abby finish the cookies?"

Chloe grabbed his hand and pulled him over to where the boxes were lined up, waiting to be delivered.

After Kevin set what looked like a stack of mail on the counter, he turned to smile at Lisa "Thanks for helping out. I'm sure Abby appreciated your help. By the way, where is she? And, how is she?"

Lisa had noticed how he'd scanned the room when he walked in, his disappointment obvious when he saw Abby wasn't there.

"She's taking a shower." She shrugged. "And she seems to be okay. A little off, but I don't know if this is from the wine, or what's going on between the two of you."

At Kevin's stricken look, she put her hand on his arm, her smile meant to reassure him. "Once you sit down and talk it out, everything will be okay."

Kevins smile was brief, his attention now drawn to Chloe, who had come to stand next to him. Pulling at his hand, she had a serious expression on her face.

He smiled. "Hey, Peanut. What's up?"

"Will you be my BFF?"

After he lifted her up to sit on the counter, he tilted his head, studying her. "BFF? What's this? Some king of secret friend?"

She giggled, looking over at Lisa. "Momma, can you believe it? He doesn't know what it means." She pointed her finger at his chest. "It means Best Friends Forever." Then the corners of her mouth turned down. "Betsy was my BFF. But after I told her you and daddy are friends, she told me I had to find a new BFF because her daddy doesn't like you."

Taken aback, a concerned look came over Kevin's face.

She chattered on. "She said her daddy thinks you like to play too much. But you should be playing with baseballs instead of girls. That's what you get paid to do." She scrunched up her face. "I thought that's what you did? Played baseball like daddy."

Now Kevin was speechless. *What?* This Betsy's father didn't even know him.

Why is your personal life of such interest to everyone? Don't these people have better things to do than criticize your every move?

But Chloe wasn't finished. No, she had even more to say. "Is this why your mom is so mad at Abby?"

"Chloe ..." Lisa made a move towards them.

Kevin held up his hand. "No, wait. Something tells me I need to hear what Chloe has to say." His hands resting on the counter and on each side of her, his look was serious. "Chloe, what do you mean? What's this about my mom and Abby?"

After Chloe glanced nervously over at Lisa, getting a nod, she looked back at Kevin. "She was mean to Abby. She tried to give her bunches of money so she would go away. But Abby tore it up and threw it at her."

A stunned look on his face, Kevin glanced over at Lisa. She nodded before mouthing the words, I'm sorry.

Chloe was pulling on his sleeve. "Abby was scared." Then she grinned. "But she's heels over heads..."

Her face scrunched up in confusion. "No, that's not it." This was followed by a big smile. "I remember, she said she's head over heels in love with you. So that's good, right?"

His head bowed, Kevin was speechless. He honestly had no idea how to respond to what she told him. It was almost too bizarre to comprehend.

Your mother offered Abby money? And Abby is scared?

He stared down at the floor, trying to calm the different emotions coming at him. Shock, disbelief, rage, and almost more than anything, a sense of relief he might now have the answer to what was going on with Abby.

What the hell had his mother been thinking?

He finally glanced up to see Chloe was watching him, her eyes wide and anxious. After he took a deep breath, he smiled. "Sweetheart, thank you for telling me about my mom. I'll talk to her and find out what's going on. I'm sure it will turn out okay."

Then he winked. "And this BFF thing? I can't think of any other person I'd want as my BFF except you."

Chloe threw her arms around him, planting a big kiss to his cheek. "You're the best!"

Kevin grinned, returning her hug . "And when you see Betsy, I want you to let her know her dad is wrong. I'm all about playing baseball."

Tilting her head, Chloe studied him. "But what about Abby?"

Lightly tapping her nose with his finger, he spoke in an exaggerated whisper. "Just between you and me, Abby will always be my girl. I guess you might even say she and I are in the same boat. Since I'm just as much, if not even more, head over heels in love with her, as you say she is with me."

He suddenly knew what to say to Chloe to bring it all home.

"She will always be my princess. As I will always want to be her prince."

Chloe's big smile told him she understood completely.

Alex cleared his throat, indicating with a nod, Kevin should look behind him.

When he turned, he saw Abby was standing by the entrance to the kitchen. A hesitant smile on her face, she gave a slight shrug.

For a few seconds, Kevin could only stare. She, in turn, remained completely still. Her eyes searching his, she was looking for some kind of sign.

Any kind of sign, she didn't care. She wanted to know what he was thinking, hoping his thoughts were filled as much with her, as hers were with him.

He abruptly turned away, sending her heart dropping to her toes. Only to then let out a sigh of relief as she watched him lift Chloe off the counter and set her, feet first, on the floor.

After Chloe ran over to Lisa, he turned to Abby with a shrug. He moved closer. "Sorry, I didn't want her to try getting down on her own. She could have hurt herself."

As he continued to gaze at her, such naked emotion in his eyes, Abby's bottom lip begin to tremble in an effort not to cry. She wrapped her arms around herself, wishing it was his arms holding her instead.

Lisa jumped into action in the now silent kitchen. She began giving orders, starting with Kevin and Abby. "Okay, you two have to talk. And while you do that, we'll load up the cars. Though I have a feeling we're not going to fit much in that thing you drive, Kevin."

She sent him a stern look. "Could this be what's fueling this 'playboy' reputation you've been labeled with? *Hmm...* I think so." She turned to give Alex a warning look. "Don't think we don't notice how you guys eat up all the attention you get from your adoring fans."

He grinned, his hand held up in protest. "Hey, wait a minute here... in case you've forgotten, I now drive a minivan. A mode of transportation certainly not what one would consider a chick magnet, babe."

Chloe looked up at him, a puzzled look on her face. He laughed, ruffling her hair with his hand. "Don't worry, sweetheart. You and mommy are the only chicks I want in my life."

"And don't you forget it." After reaching up to press a kiss to his cheek, Lisa handed him a stack of boxes. "Here ya go."

With Chloe scampering beside them, they left the kitchen.

Kevin had moved even closer to Abby. Filled with an overwhelming urge to touch her, he ran the back of his hand down her cheek in a soft caress. When she trembled at his touch, he had to close his eyes.

There was a huskiness in his voice.

"Hey..."

What I mean is... I've missed you.

She closed her eyes.

"Hey...

I missed you, too... so much.

They both started to speak at the same time, only to stop and smile at each other.

He spoke first. "So, how do you feel?"

Suddenly unable to meet his eyes, she shrugged. "Okay, I guess. I've definitely felt better." She shuddered. "I only know I never want to drink another glass of wine. At least not for a long, long time."

He chuckled. "This seems to be the overwhelming consensus when a person drinks more than they should. After all, a bottle of wine is meant to be shared." He smiled at her. "But we've all been there. I, for one, can attest to this, sugar."

He was suddenly reminded of what she'd said, the words cutting almost as deep as when he first heard them.

And don't call me sugar. You don't have that right any more.

A stricken look crossed his face. "I'm sorry, I didn't mean…"

Her hands fluttered towards him. But, unsure, she pressed them to her sides, shaking her head instead. "No, no. It's okay. It is. I never meant it, I didn't."

He could call her whatever he wanted to. She didn't care. She only wanted him with her.

He smiled, the relief so transparent in his eyes she almost had to look away, wishing there was some way to make those words disappear forever.

Nervously tucking her hair behind her ears, she searched his face. "Since I don't remember a lot about last night, I'm afraid I may have said or done something I shouldn't have."

The color rising in her cheeks, she looked down at her hands. "So, whatever happened, whatever I said, I'm sorry. I didn't mean any of it."

When he lifted her chin with his finger, bringing her face to his, she was surprised to see he was smiling. "Well… I must say I'm a little disappointed to hear this since I rather enjoyed what you had to say. In fact, it gave me hope. Something I was so desperately looking for."

When he saw her eyes begin to fill, he had to close his. He didn't think he could handle her tears right now.

No, if she starts crying, you're going to start bawling right along with her.

At the sound of voices, he was almost relieved to see Alex, Lisa and Chloe come back into the kitchen.

Chloe came running over to them and grinned up at Kevin. "We put one box in your car. Daddy said we had to so you don't look bad." Then, her hands going to her hips, shaking her head hard enough to send her curls flying around her face, she frowned. "Boy, you're having your problems, aren't you? It looks like you need to suck it up, baby!"

Everyone looked over at her in surprise. Then they began to laugh. After Lisa reached over to wrap her arms around her in a big hug, still laughing, she shrugged "I'm afraid she got that from me. Sometimes, but not that often, we have a bad day and this is our battle cry."

She picked up her keys from the counter before she smiled over at Kevin and Abby. "I'm glad we were able to help. But now we have errands to run, birthday presents to buy." She rolled her eyes, nodding towards Chloe "The one drawback of having too many friends who are always having birthdays."

Abby hugged her and Chloe before she smiled over at Alex. "Thank you for helping with the cookies. Finishing them, delivering them, just everything. And for making me forget about how awful I felt when I first woke up this morning. I would have been scrambling right now if I had to do this by myself."

When Chloe came running back into the kitchen after saying goodbye to Poppy, she took a box off o the counter and handed it to her. "These cookies are for you. I hope you come back to visit Poppy and me again. I won't even make you work."

This earned Abby a big hug before Chloe went flying past Alex and out the door after Lisa, her excited cry floating back to them.

"Momma! Abby gave me a whole box of cookies!"

As Alex began to follow her, he stopped at the door to look back at Kevin, one eyebrow raised.

"Chester?"

For a second, Kevin appeared confused. Then he turned to Abby with a grin. "Oh yeah… it seems Chester ran into Sophie. Almost crashing into the back of her car, in fact. He said she was trying to save a puppy. I guess they hit it off and now he wants her number. His story is he promised to get her tickets to a game."

Abby laughed. "Thank goodness, because I've never seen her like this. She was over the moon after she met him."

Kevin smiled as he reached over to tuck her hair behind her ear. Such a simple touch, but one that had her almost forgetting what they were talking about. Then she saw the familiar teasing glint in his eyes.

Uh oh, here it comes.

"Hmm… over the moon? I've never heard that one before. But I like it. Funny, I don't remember you being 'over the moon' the first time we met." He grinned. "I guess it's a good thing my charming personality kicked in and won you over."

This brought a groan from Alex. He rolled his eyes. "Oh geeez… with that, I'm outta here."

He went out the door. Then he walked right back in, grinning over at Kevin. "Ill be out here waiting, Since I know you'll never find the place on your own. Even with the fancy GPS system you've got in that car of yours."

With a wave, he was gone.

Kevin and Abby studied each other, unsure of what to say.

Again, they both started to speak at the same time.

Kevin smiled, reaching over to take her hand. When what he really wanted, was to take her into his arms. Then he would never let her go. But with the way things stood right now, he felt he didn't have the right.

You need to get this thing with your mother straightened out.

He owed Abby this more than anything else right now.

He looked up at the ceiling, giving a frustrated sigh. He was still finding it hard to imagine what had been going on in his mother's mind. It just didn't make sense. Sure, some of the things she had done over the years were a little questionable.

But never to this extreme.

"Kevin?"

He blinked. Abby was gazing up at him, a worried look on her face.

He cleared his throat. "I need to go. Even though I'd give anything to be able to take you with me. Because right now, I don't want to let you out of my sight. But there's something I need to do before I see you again. Tomorrow night? I'll pick you up around six-thirty. Okay?"

But he couldn't leave her like this. Bringing her hand up to his mouth, he pressed a slow kiss to her fingers, his heated gaze almost making her almost dizzy with longing.

Drawn in by the fire in his eyes, she swayed towards him. But after he pressed a soft kiss to her forehead, he turned and walked out of the kitchen.

Abby leaned against the counter and watched him leave. Everything inside of her was screaming at her, urging her to run after him. If only to keep him with her a little longer.

Instead, she closed her eyes, remembering what he said to Chloe when he hadn't known she was behind him.

> *Abby will always be the girl for me.*
> *I guess you might say she and I are*
> *in the same boat. Since I'm just as*
> *much, if not even more, head over*
> *heels in love with her, as you say*
> *she is with me. She will always be*
> *my princess. As I will always want*
> *to be her prince."*

She was going cherish these words forever. Her lips curving into a faint smile, she clasped her hands over her heart, knowing this was where they'd already gone to stay.

At the sound of someone entering the kitchen, she opened her eyes. She watched as Kevin swiftly covered the space between them to pull her roughly into his arms.

Their eyes locking, his lips parted as if he was going to speak. Then, he groaned her name before his mouth covered hers in a demanding, hungry kiss. She wrapped her arms around his neck and hung on, her feet barely touching the floor as his hands pressed her even more closely against him. She struggled to keep up, giving back all she could.

It was a kiss filled with everything they wanted to say, but hadn't. It was an unspoken apology with the promise of total forgiveness. And it was a vow of their complete trust in each other.

But most of all, it was a pledge of their love.

Forever...

When the kiss finally ended, they clung to each other, almost as if they'd weathered a raging storm. Which, if you were to stop to think about it, was exactly what they had done.

Her face pressed against his shoulder, Abby tried to catch her breath. A faint smile on her face, she gazed up at him to find he was looking down at her, a smile also lurking at the corners of his mouth.

Despite this, his voice was rough as he brushed his mouth over hers. "We've still got it, Red. And we always will. Until tomorrow then."

He winked at her before he turned and left the kitchen. Seconds later, she heard the front door close.

Her hand gripping the edge of the countertop, she slowly sank down onto one of the stools. Putting her fingers up to her lips, she saw her hand was shaking.

Well... that was certainly unexpected.

But nice... very, very nice.

In fact, it was more than that.

It was absolutely amazing.

In a daze, she gazed around the kitchen, taking in the discarded pastry bags, dishes and other utensils cluttering the counters. It looked like she had a lot of work to do. And she should probably start on it right now.

Yes, you should.

But she had more important things to think about. Like, how was she going to be able to wait until tomorrow night to see Kevin again? Or at least talk to him?

Sophie... she'd text him Sophie's phone number. He did ask for it.

She picked up her phone to type out her message and sent it off.

It was when she set her phone down on the countertop, she noticed the stack of letters lying there. Intrigued, she reached for them and pulled off the rubber band holding them together.

On top of the stack was a note. It was in Kevin's handwriting and addressed to her.

Abby,

Your father wanted you to have these. They are letters he sent to you after he left. As you can see, your mother had them all returned, unopened. Maybe after you read them, you'll have a better understanding of what happened. But whatever you decide, I want you to know that I'll be here for you. I'll always be on your side. Just like the words to your favorite song, I will always love you, until the end of time.

Kevin

She eyed the letters warily, a sick feeling beginning to churn in her stomach, her heart thumping wildly in her chest. She was almost afraid to touch them. She finally took a deep breath and picked up the letter on top of the pile. She saw it was postmarked shortly after her father had left.

She opened it.

She let out a soft cry when she saw the greeting, her father's nickname for her. And as she began to read, tears slowly began to slip down her face.

> *Gabby Abby,*
> *I hope this letter finds you well and happy. It's not so bad here. They keep us busy. The food isn't as good as your mom makes, but it's okay. I wish I could've had more time before I left to explain what was going to happen, but that didn't work out. But please know that I think of you all the time and can't wait to come back home to see you again. Until then, be good for your mom, do all your homework*

and write to me as often as you can.
I promise I'll answer you right away.
Maybe your mom will bring you here
to visit me sometime soon
Love you always, Daddy

She looked over at the stack of letters. The realization her father had never given up hope, continuing to send them, even though they were returned unopened, brought on such an overwhelming rush of grief, she put her head down on her arms and wept.

She cried for all of them. For her dad, her mom and herself, and how the life they should've shared as a family had fallen apart, going so terribly wrong.

When she was finally drained of tears, she pulled the stack of letters in front of her. Messy kitchen completely forgotten, she began to read the letters, one by one. It was the least she could do.

She owed her father this.

It was early evening when she finally put down the last letter. Bundling the letters back together with the rubber band, she put them in the keepsake box in her bedroom closet.

She was exhausted. But it was a good and cleansing kind of exhaustion. Gone was all of the anger and self-doubt she'd been holding on to for so long. Instead she was filled with a feeling of peace.

And now she knew what she had to do.

But right this very moment? She needed to eat something.

She was suddenly very, very hungry.

CHAPTER 33

Fate decides who comes into your life,
your heart decide who stays.
~ Anonymous

*K*evin pulled up behind Alex at the entrance to the Cleveland Auto Museum where the event was going to be held.

Only after he put the car in park and turned off the ignition, did he reach for his phone.

When his phone had rung earlier and he saw it was a text from Abby, he almost ran the car right off the road. This explained his now more cautious approach.

Yeah, almost killing yourself tends to make you think twice about taking your eyes off the road, doesn't it?

He scrolled down to find her message.

> You asked me for Sophie's number, so here it
> is. I would also like to thank you for the kiss. It
> was totally unexpected, but quite enjoyable. I
> believe I owe you.

He sent off his response.

> You are more than welcome. And let me assure you, the kiss was unexpected for me, too. But as you said, very enjoyable. And yes, I agree. You do owe me. P. S. You failed to send Sophie's number. Got something on your mind, sugar?

A shadow falling over him, he glanced up to see Alex standing next to the car, shaking his head.

"Man, what am I going to do with you? Not only did you almost drive off the road back there, now I catch you texting love messages? Do I need to take your phone away?"

He ran his hand through his hair. "*Geesh,* I feel like I'm dealing with someone Chloe's age here."

He reached down to pull the car door open. "Now get out of the car so you can help me carry in these boxes. Because I'm certainly not going to face all those women alone. I want to get in there and get out. We have tonight's game as an excuse to leave."

Once Kevin was out of the car and had taken the one lone box of cookies out of the trunk of his car, he grinned. "Hey, I only checked to see if Abby sent me Sophie's number. Weren't you the one who brought that to my attention?"

Alex snorted. "I don't think Sophie's number is what brought that goofy smile to your face. Remember, I've been there. I know the signs." He gave a wry grin. "In fact, I'm still there. I don't think it ever ends."

Waiting as Alex dropped another box on top of the box he was holding, Kevin laughed. "To tell you the truth, I'm just so relieved she's talking to me, I couldn't care less what anyone has to say. Including you."

As he leaned back against the door so Kevin could enter the building, Alex rolled his eyes. "Welcome to the club. Believe me, there's going to be a lot of 'no-talking' in your future. And a good number of these times, you won't have a clue what you did to bring them on.

And, just so you know, you'll always be the one at fault. This is a given."

He shook his head. "I don't understand a woman's way of thinking, and I'm willing to bet you won't either. If you do, you're a genius."

They walked into the room where the event was to be held. Mia glanced up from the flowers she was arranging and let out a loud shriek. "Girls, look! The cookies are here!"

She made a beeline right for them, the other women following right behind.

It was like a stampede.

Alex and Kevin looked at each other, groaning almost in unison.

If they could, they'd drop the cookies and run.

Kevin was buttoning up his uniform shirt when Alex went sprinting past him to his locker.

He sauntered over to him, a grin on his face. "Well, what do we have here? You've finally decided to join us?"

Randomly throwing things left and right out of his locker, Alex sent him a dirty look.

This only made Kevin grin even more. "So, it turns out you were dead wrong about that minivan of yours, huh? It seems it's more of a chick magnet that you thought it was." He shook his head, a glint of amusement in his eyes. "Yep, it looks like I'm up against some mighty stiff competition here."

Alex was hopping around on one foot, trying to pull on his uniform pants. Having accomplished this, he slipped into his shirt, his fingers fumbling in his haste to get it buttoned.

He was grumbling under his breath. "I hate being late. It throws me off." He glared over at Kevin. "I don't know why the hell they waited until now to pick up those damn trees and why I was the one to do it. When Mia started dragging in all these big boxes filled with lights, I put my foot down."

Then he grinned, typical of Alex. Nothing ever made him angry for very long. "Trust me, I was cursing you the whole time for leaving me like you did."

Kevin burst out laughing. "Wait a minute, did I just hear right? You put your foot down? *Hmm...* I'll have to ask Lisa about the validity of this claim."

Reaching over to pick up Alex's hat from where it had landed on the floor, he tossed it to him before he began walking out of the room.

Unable to resist, he threw one more parting remark. "And, of course, I left. Why wouldn't I? They didn't want me. They wanted the big, strong guy with the minivan."

After he ducked to avoid the hat Alex sent flying in his direction, he turned, almost running into Chester.

One eyebrow raise, Chester sent a pointed glance at his phone.

Still laughing, Kevin remembered Chester's request for Sophie's number. He pulled out his phone to check if Abby had sent it.

She had. In fact, there were two messages. One with Sophie's number, the other a message exclusively for him.

He read the message.

A silly grin on his face, he read it again.

> This is what you do to me... EVERY. SINGLE.
> TIME. And my answer would be, Yes, you.

Chester cleared his throat. "Well?"

Kevin lifted his head, the grin still there. After he scrolled back to the message with Sophie's number, he handed the phone to Chester. "From what I've been told, the feeling is mutual. So, go for it."

The number added to his contact list, Chester grinned. "Thanks." Then he stared down at his phone, a big smile on his face.

Kevin shook his head... he still didn't get it. Chester and Sophie?

But look how you've been grinning like a fool ever since Abby sent you that last text...

He needed to send her a response, but he planned to do this when he was alone. He didn't need any input from the guys in the locker room.

Proof of this was when Alex walked over to Chester, playfully punching him in the arm. "So, when are you going to ask this Sophie out?"

Of course, everyone within hearing range had something to say about this.

"Sophie? Who's Sophie?"

"You've gotta be kidding. Chez with a girl?"

"Is the woman desperate?"

"Or more like crazy. What other explanation could there be?"

"She can't possibly know what he's like."

"Wait a minute, is he going to ask a girl out?"

"Come on, Chez, give us the details."

"Are you planning to ask her to the benefit tomorrow night?"

Chester groaned, stuffing his phone in his pocket. "Come on, knock it. And no, I can't ask her to be my date for the benefit. Talk about short notice."

Casually crossing his arms over his chest, Kevin sent a nod in his direction. "What's wrong? Chicken?"

This brought a roar from everyone in the room, along with a loud chorus of clucking sounds.

Almost in shock, they watched as Chester yanked his phone out of his pocket and hit Sophie's number. He sent a threatening glance around the room, his warning coming in a growl. "Make a sound, any sound, and you're dead."

Then, with a look of pure panic on his face, he made a hasty retreat, speaking into his phone.

After a few minutes, Chester walked back into the room, slipping the phone back into his pocket.

Dragging his hand through his hair, he had a stunned look on his face.

"She said yes. She said there was nothing she would love more."

He broke out into a huge grin. "I can't believe it."

You know that feeling you get when you hit a home run?

Well, this was even better.

For Chester, this was like a walk-off-grand-slam kind of feeling.

CHAPTER 34

$\mathcal{C}$urled up on the sofa, Abby was waiting for the game to start on TV. Poppy was sprawled out beside her, sound asleep and still holding her favorite chew toy in her paws,

She glanced down at her phone. It couldn't hurt to read his text one more time. Could it?

Come on, how many times have you already read it? A dozen?

She'd read it just one more time. Then she'd put her phone out of reach.

Yeah, like you'll be able to do this. Remember what just happened?

Only minutes before, she'd nearly wiped out, tripping over Poppy when she went flying down the hall to grab her phone off the kitchen counter. Anxiously waiting for Kevin to respond, well… let's just say she overreacted when she heard it ring. This explained why her phone was now right next to her on the sofa and in reaching distance.

Oh, what the heck… she was going to read it again. She tapped the screen, his text jumping out at her.

> I know the feeling well, sugar. Until tomorrow
> night. And remember, I will always love you.
> This, of course, will be until the end of time.

A dreamy smile on her face, she set the phone back in her lap just as the doorbell rang.

This sent Poppy in a frenzy, leaping off the sofa and over to the door.

When Abby opened the door, without a single word, Sophie walked right past her and over to the sofa. When Poppy jumped up to settle next to her, she began running her fingers through her fur, a preoccupied look on her face.

She finally glanced over at Abby, sending her a tentative smile. It was obvious she had something on her mind and was about ready to burst.

Her head tilted, Abby smiled at her. "So, what's up? Are you okay?"

Sophie took a deep breath. "I… um, no. Wait, I mean yes. I just closed the boutique and thought I'd come over to see how you're doing." She peered over at Abby. "So, is there anything new? Have you heard from Kevin?"

Abby nodded. "He was here, and we got to talk a little. It looks like I'll be wearing the dress after all." She hugged herself, smiling. "He's picking me up tomorrow at six-thirty."

This sent Sophie flying off the sofa, almost knocking Abby to the floor in her excitement. "*Yes, yes, yes…*"

She twirled around before diving back on the sofa to give Abby a big hug. Then she gathered Poppy in her arms and, leaning back in the cushions, she gazed over at Abby. There was a huge grin on her face.

"Even though I knew everything would work out, I was so worried. And even though I said yes, I was planning to cancel if things didn't turn out for you."

She jumped up from the sofa to twirl around again. Her hands going to her face, they were trembling. "Oh, Abby… I'm so excited!"

Abby laughed. "Sophie, take a deep breath. Who did you say yes to? And why?"

Sophie fell back onto the sofa. She was grinning from ear to ear. "Chester. He called to ask me to be his date for the benefit. We're going to have so much fun!"

She picked up Poppy again before she glanced over at the TV.

"Oh… the game is on. Has it started yet?" Then she sank back down on the sofa. "Look! They're interviewing Kevin."

Riveted to the screen, they watched as the announcer began asking Kevin questions. Beginning with his impression of Cleveland, what he thought about his team mates, the fans, and finally, what his prediction was on the team's chances of getting into the play-offs.

Before giving his answer to this last question, Kevin grinned, shaking his head. "If we keep playing the way we are now, we have an excellent shot at playing October baseball. But we still have a lot of games to play, so we know not to get too comfortable. Not with the stiff competition we're up against. Our goal as a team will always be the same, to keep winning, one game at a time."

Here he stopped to smile into the camera, the teasing smile Abby knew so well. "It's addicting. Sort of like sugar. You know, once you've had a taste of something so sweet, you vow to never give it up." Then he winked.

The broadcast moving on to a commercial break, Sophie started talking a mile a minute. About what she was going to wear and was Abby going to get her nails done? Because if she did, could they do it together? Maybe even get a pedicure, too? And her hair, she had no idea what to do about that. What was Abby going to do with her hair? Wear it up? Or leave it down? There was so much to think about, but so little time. Why, she was actually starting to feel dizzy with it all.

Abby wasn't really listening. She was too busy thinking about what Kevin said in his interview. She was pretty sure that last answer of his?

With his reference to sugar?

It could only be meant for her.

CHAPTER 35

It's better to know and be disappointed
than to never know and always wonder.
~ Anonymous

Kevin settled more comfortably in his seat as the rest of the passengers filed onto the plane, their weary expressions reflecting the lateness of the hour. After he watched a man struggle to fit his bag into the overhead compartment, this had him a little more thankful for his lack of luggage.

This hadn't been his intention, but when the game had gone into extra innings, with only the clothes on his back, he'd left straight from the ballpark.

He'd made it to the airport only minutes before his flight was scheduled to depart. Only to find his flight to Chicago was delayed because of a band of severe thunderstorms moving across the Midwest.

But now, after an almost two-hour delay, he was in his seat, his seatbelt fastened and the plane was only minutes from taking off.

He pulled out his phone. Curious as to whether Abby had seen his interview before the game, he wanted to send her a text before they took off. Deep in thought, he stared down at the phone.

He finally typed out his message, smiling as he hit send.

A woman about to take the seat in front of him caught his smile. After she smiled back at him, she peered at him more closely, recognition registering in her eyes.

He groaned.

Please, no... not now. You're not in the mood to talk baseball right now.

Grabbing the safety manual from the back pocket of the seat in front of him, he began studying it as though his life depended on it.

The elderly lady sitting next to him leaned over to pat his hand. "Don't worry. I've been flying for a long time. It's very safe. In fact, it's safer than driving." She frowned. "At least this is what they claim."

"I'm sure you're right." He gave her a reassuring nod before going right back to studying the manual.

He wasn't trying to be mean. It was only that he was too keyed up to talk to anyone. About baseball, or whatever. His mind was racing a mile a minute, nothing making sense.

When the plane finally began its journey down the runway, he leaned his head back and closed his eyes. He wanted to be refreshed and ready for what was to come.

Yep... you might say he was on a mission.

One that could very well change everything.

The taxi pulled up in front of his parent's house. Before he opened the passenger door, with the promise of a large tip, Kevin convinced the driver to wait.

He sprinted down the sidewalk and up the front steps. After he punched in the security code, he opened the door and stepped into the foyer. He flipped the switch to turn on the chandelier and waited.

Within seconds, his father came striding across the landing of the second floor to peer down over the railing,

"Kevin, what are you doing here? It's almost two o'clock in the morning!"

His mother appeared behind him. She cried out his name and ran down the steps, zipping up her robe as she came. When she wrapped her arms around him in a hug, he didn't move. He couldn't, instead remaining stiff in her embrace.

She sensed this, taking a step back. "Kevin, what's wrong?"

He wanted to confront her outright. Ask her what she'd been thinking. He searched her face for some kind of sign, remorse, or maybe even guilt. But he saw nothing.

And this is when it occurred to him, no matter what the outcome of this visit, there was only one thing that mattered.

And this was Abby

His father, ever the diplomat, ushered them to the kitchen, gesturing for them to sit.

Only then did he turn to Kevin. "Son, tell us why you're here."

His gaze returning to his mother for a few moments, he finally turned to his father.

"I recently found out mother tried to bribe Abby with a large sum of money to stay away from me. I'm not sure how this came about, but Abby turned her down. And no, she didn't tell me this. I found out from someone else."

He turned to address his mother. "Why would you do such a thing? You don't even know Abby. If you had a problem with her, you should've come to me. This has been devastating for her."

After a long silence, his mother finally spoke. "Melissa is the woman you should marry. She's always been in love with you. She is the right choice for you."

Briefly closing his eyes, Kevin shook his head. "Mother, I love Abby, I don't love Melissa, I never have. I don't know what she told you, but I've never considered her as anything but a friend. And I've never led her to believe this would change. I don't understand. Why are you so insistent about this?"

She came to her feet, almost knocking over her chair as she pushed away from the table. She began to cry. "This is the only way I know how to make it up to her. And from what she told me, I assumed the two of you had an understanding." Her voice shaking, she began wringing her hands. "She told me you made it very clear once your career took off, the two of you would marry."

He ran his hand through his hair, a frustrated sigh coming from him. "I don't know what to say, except she lied to you. That will never, ever happen." He was puzzled. "And what do you mean... you have to make it up to her?"

"If it wasn't for me, Karen would still be here. I'm the one who was responsible for what happened." Her mouth working, she shook her head. "I'm sorry... I'm so, so sorry."

She turned and ran out of the room. When Kevin jumped up to go after her, his father grabbed his arm. "No. Let her go."

Slowly sinking back into his chair, he looked over at his father. "Who the hell is Karen?"

His father stared at him for a few moments, a resigned expression slowly coming over his face. "Melissa's mother."

Kevin glanced over to where his mother had gone, then back at his father. "But, I don't understand... what happened?"

Wearily running his hand over his jaw, his father exhaled a long sigh. "Karen and your mother grew up together, went to the same college and were in each other's wedding. So, it wasn't even a surprise when they both became pregnant at the same time and you and Melissa were born only days apart.

"One night when I was out of town and you were just a few months old, you started running a high fever. Your mother panicked and called Karen, who insisted on coming over. No one was ever able to figure out what happened, but on her drive to our house, she ran a stop sign and collided with another car. She was killed instantly. Your mother was inconsolable.

"Melissa's father eventually remarried, but his new wife didn't get alond with Melissa, they argued about everything. Your mother felt sorry for her, so this is why she was always with us. She and Katy hung around together, but it was you Melissa idolized.

"I let it slide, thinking there was some truth to what Melissa implied about the two of you. After all, you never showed an interest in any other girls. When you announced your engagement at dinner, your mother's reaction worried me. But when she refused to go to brunch at Katy and Stephen's, I became concerned. But never did I think she'd resort to something like this…"

His voice trailing off, he put his hand on Kevin's shoulder. "I can't tell you how sorry I am, son. I will talk to your mother. And we'll both talk to Melissa. But most importantly, I'll make sure she rights things with Abby."

He shook his head. "This may be a wake-up call for your mother and me. Maybe this wouldn't have happened if I hadn't been so caught up with the business. I would have been more sensitive to what she was thinking and she might have confided in me."

His eyes pleaded with Kevin to understand. "Just give us time, okay?"

At a loss of what to say, Kevin stood, giving his father a hug.

After his father responded with a pat on his back, a move his version of a hug for as long as Kevin could remember, he cleared his throat. "What are you going to do now? You're more than welcome to stay here."

Kevin shook his head. "No. I have an early morning flight back to Cleveland. For now, I think I'll go to Katy's." He smiled. " I could use some cuddle time with my favorite niece right now."

He walked over to open the door. There he turned to look back at his father. "Thanks, Dad. I love you. And tell mom I love her, too."

At his father's nod, he closed the door and ran to the waiting taxi. He gave the driver Katy's address, and leaning his head back against the seat, he closed his eyes.

Why did you think you'd be feeling better than you are right now?

Katy was about to give Olivia her bottle, having refused Stephen's sleepy offer to take on the job.

The hushed silence and peacefulness of the night had become one of her favorite times to spend with Olivia.

Her phone flashed in the darkness, she saw it was a message from Kevin.

> Hey, are you up? I'm about five minutes away.
> Can I come see you?

She swiftly typed out a response.

> Yes, I just started giving Olivia her bottlHow?
> Why?

He answered just as quickly.

> I'll explain when I get there. Tell Olivia to slow down with that bottle so that her Uncle Kevin can give it to her.

With Olivia in her arms, Katy made her way downstairs at the light knock on the door. His finger to his lips, Kevin reached out to take Olivia and the bottle from her before he settled on the sofa, Olivia in his arms.

Katy sat next to him. When she opened her mouth, about to say something to say something, he shook his head. "*Shhh...* when she's done, I'll explain. Right now, let me enjoy this."

She smiled at his occasional whispered comments to Olivia. Her eyes wide open, she watched him as she drank her bottle, almost as if she understood every word he said.

She hoped Olivia knew how lucky she was to have an uncle like Kevin.

Olivia had finished her bottle and, after giving the required burp, was now sleeping like an angel in Kevin's arms.

Leaning his head back against the cushions of the sofa, he closed his eyes. And he told Katy everything.

He told her about the meeting he'd arranged between Abby and her father and how it had gone all wrong—with Abby informing both him and her father she didn't want them in her life.

He told her about the events leading up to the shock of finding out their mother had tried to bribe Abby. How this had left him no other option but to book the spur-of-the-moment flight to Chicago so he could confront her in person.

Then he shared everything he'd learned from his conversation with their father.

Completely spent, his mind still struggling to come to terms with what happened, he let out a ragged breath. "So, that's a summary of my life right now. And thank goodness—through it all—Abby and I are okay. I'm just glad I found out all of this now, before it all spiraled out of control."

"If I'd lost Abby because of this…" He closed his eyes, a pained expression on his face.

Then he glanced over at Katy. Shaking her head, tears streamed down her face."Oh, Kevin… I don't even know what to say. What a terrible mess. I thought mom seemed nervous and distracted lately, but never in a million years would I've envisioned her doing something like this. Poor Abby. I can't even imagine what she's been going through."

As she wiped away the tears with her fingers, her voice grew angry. "I blame most of this on Melissa. I never did like her. To tell you the truth, I've always been more than a little afraid of her."

Then she glared at him. "But you… how could you do that to Abby? Showing up with her father, with no warning? What were you thinking? This reminds me of our wedding when you told Anna about Marc's accident. You certainly aren't very good with your timing."

Kevin groaned. "I've already been told I'm pretty much an idiot. But I was only trying to help. Honest."

He shot her a guilty look. It was an expression she remembered so well from their childhood when he'd been caught in one of his many boyish pranks. It appeared some things were never going to change.

She sighed, patting his arm. "I know, I know."

He yawned before he squinted over at the clock on the fireplace mantle. "My flight leaves around ten thirty. Which means I have to head back to the airport in about six hours. I'm cutting it pretty close since our game starts at one. But I couldn't do this over the phone. I had to do it in person and I had to do it now."

Katy glanced over at him. "Have you set a date for the wedding?"

Uh, oh... it looks like you neglected to tell her everything, doesn't it?

He cleared his throat. "You're probably going to be very unhappy when I tell you this, but we aren't actually engaged. I just threw that out in a panic when Melissa put on that dramatic show at dinner. I don't know how, but somehow I managed to persuade Abby to go along with me."

The expression on Katy's face was one of absolute horror. "Kevin! How could you? *Oh my God...* poor, poor Abby. You've got to do something and you have to do it quick."

For the second time, she glared at him. "I swear, if you weren't holding Olivia right now, I'd smack you."

His expression wary, he moved a little away from her. "Don't worry. I'm already on it. Geesh... get that mean look off your face."

Still glaring, Katy gave an angry huff. "Well, whatever you do, it better be good. Really good."

She shook her head. "I can't even imagine what Abby must think about our family at this point."But Kevin wasn't listening. He'd already dozed off.

Hmph... Men.

She couldn't believe it. Here he was, almost asleep, no doubt confident everything was under control. While she was headed for a sleepless night, worrying about what he'd told her.

It just wasn't fair

She took Olivia from his arms and settled her into the portable baby bed next to the sofa. Then she covered Kevin with the blanket draped over the back of the sofa. She gazed down at him.

Her little brother was in love. And the fact he'd made this trip was proof of how deeply he'd fallen.

But now he needed to take the next step and ask Abby to marry him. And this better be a real, honest-to-goodness proposal.

With a ring and everything.

She frowned.

Seriously? What had he been thinking?

Stephen was looking for Katy.

Half asleep, he'd wandered downstairs, the tantalizing aroma and sound of bacon frying luring him into the kitchen.

This was where he found Katy, taking a coffee cake out of the oven.

After she set it on the counter, he came up behind her. He wrapped his arms around her and kissed the sensitive place he knew so well below her ear.

He smiled as he felt a shiver go through her at his touch.

"*Hmm...* this is a pleasant surprise."

She gave him a quick glance. "It's not for you."

He drew back, chuckling at her seriousness. "It's not? Well, I know it can't be for Olivia. So, tell me... who is this mystery person that rates this fabulous breakfast you're making?"

She nodded towards the sofa. "Kevin."

He glanced over to see Kevin's sleeping form on the sofa. "Kevin? What the. Heck? What happened?"

"I'll tell you later." Then she suddenly turned to wind her arms around his neck, giving him an almost desperate kiss. Resting her forehead against his, she sighed. "We're so lucky to have each other. Promise me you'll always tell me if something is bothering you. Or if I do something terribly wrong."

He pulled her close. "Oh honey, I promise... though I can't imagine you ever doing anything wrong, let alone terribly wrong."

When she just continued to gaze back at him, the worried look still in her eyes, he reached over to shut off the burner. After pulling her up against him, he placed a trail of soft kisses across her face.

His voice was deep, filled with a sudden passion. "Come... let me take you back to bed."

When she hesitated, her gaze going to the stove, he stopped to give her another kiss before he pulled her with him out of the kitchen.

"Kevin's breakfast can wait."

Kevin was smiling.

Having been awakened by Katy and Stephen's conversation, he waited until they left the room before he reached for his phone to check the time.

He still had about two more hours to sleep.

The smile still on his face, he closed his eyes as he burrowed deeper under the blanket.

Tonight couldn't come soon enough.

CHAPTER 36

*A*bby woke to seven text messages on her phone.

One was from Kevin.

The rest were from Sophie.

She'd already gone to bed before Kevin had sent his text around midnight. Done in after the events of the past twenty-four hours, she'd also been more than ready to escape Sophie's non-stop chatter.

She read Kevin's text.

> Did you catch the interview before the game? It was all for you, Sugar. Can't wait until tomorrow night. And as always, I will love you, until the end of time.

She sent back her answer.

> I fell asleep before you sent this. The interview? I loved it. But not as much as I love you. I miss you, so, so much.

Only then did she read Sophie's messages. She had less than a half hour before Sophie would pick her up. It appeared she was destined for what could be a complete makeover this morning.

She could only blame herself. She should've paid more attention to the plans Sophie had been making last night.

But it was okay. She didn't care what she did.

She only wanted tonight to come so she could be with Kevin.

Kevin was in a great mood. He'd made it from the airport to the ballpark with forty-five minutes to spare before game time. He'd also read Abby's text at least ten times, smiling like a crazy person every time.

On his way to the locker room, he passed a guy on the team, giving him a casual nod. It was only after he had gone a few more steps, he whirled around.

"What the hell? Chester, is that you?"

Chester, and yes, it really was Chester, turned, a quirky smile on his face. Twisting his cap in his hands, he shrugged.

Gone was the beard and the unruly mop of hair. The Chester standing in front of him was a different man.

Kevin moved closer. If he had to describe Chester's new look, he would say he could pass as one of those male models you find in a magazine ad. Their rugged handsomeness making you want to run right out to buy the same designer underwear or cologne they were promoting. So, you too, could lead the charmed life they did with the use of these products.

He shook his head. *"Damn...* who'd have thought?" Then he grinned. "Man, I don't know what Sophie did to you, but she's in for a surprise when she opens the door and finds this new and improved Chester in front of her."

Chester, who until now had been trying to carry off an act of indifference regarding his new look, finally cracked.

He grinned. "Well, since it was Sophie's suggestion, I guess I'll have to wait to see how it goes, won't I?"

He nodded towards the locker room. "Enough gawking. You better get a move on and get suited up for the game. You're cutting it close."

Kevin laughed, getting in the last word. "Tonight is going to be a night of surprises, that's for sure."

Their game was not only the shortest game they'd played so far this season, it was also the highest scoring, with Cleveland coming out on top in the winning column. Their pitchers hit the strike zone with an accuracy that had the Detroit players swinging at empty air.

And Cleveland's offense? With each hitter picking up from where the last left off, the runs lit up the scoreboard, one after another.

So, it was a high-spirited group celebrating in the locker room after the game. This "after party" of sorts was made even sweeter with the promise of a fun night ahead, followed by an off day tomorrow.

After the game, and in his car, Kevin reached over to open the glove compartment. It was still there, right where he put it.

Tonight was going to be a great night.

CHAPTER 37

I don't open up to many people.
So, if I like you enough to show you the real me,
you must be pretty special
~Unknown

Sophie was a nervous wreck.

She grabbed her phone from the counter and checked the time. This sent her into even more of a panic. Chester would be picking her up in fifteen minutes.

This meant she needed to kick into high gear.

Not only was her townhouse a complete disaster, she'd also jammed the zipper on the back of her dress. And now she couldn't move it up or down.

But before she dealt with that, she had to clear up some of the clutter. As she began tidying up the living room, she heard a series of growls and barks coming from the laundry room.

There she found Snowball, the puppy she'd rescued, and her toy poodle, Tinker Bell, playing tug of war with one of her high-heeled sandals.

She separated the dogs and rescued the sandal. After she herded both dogs into their crates, with the bribe of an extra treat, she made her way to the bathroom, slipping into the sandals as she went.

She gave one last check in the mirror. Even with the dress not completely zipped up, she was confident she'd chosen the perfect dress. New to the boutique, it was by one of her favorite designers.

A deep royal blue, it was simple, yet elegant. The fabric was an almost metallic hued satin with just a hint of spandex. Hugging her body before it flared out at her knees, the back of the dress swept the floor in a slight train. The deep V-necked bodice was anchored at the empire waist by a wide beaded band. The dress had a vintage look, Sophie's favorite design style. It was a dress she'd imagine Jean Harlow might have worn.

A pair of dangling rhinestone earrings and a trio of thin rhinestone banded bracelets were her only jewelry. Add the silver sandals and the result was exactly what she'd been going for.

She applied one more coat of lipstick and slipped her phone into her clutch.

She was as ready as she'd ever be.

Chester pulled up in front of the townhouse with the address Sophie had given him. He shut off the ignition and checked his phone for the time.

He was early. But this was okay. He could use this extra time to calm his nerves.

After nervously drumming his fingers on the steering wheel, he checked his appearance in the rearview mirror. The clean-shaven Chester staring back at him had him wondering if he might have gone a little overboard with this new look?

He felt so exposed… with nowhere to hide.

Well, it's done now. Learn to live with it.

A determined look on his face, he was out of the car and striding to Sophie's front door. Running his hands down over his jacket, he reached up to straighten his tie.

He shook his head.

You're ready as you'll ever be. Come on. Make your move.

He took a deep breath and knocked on the door.

Sophie opened the door.

She took one look at Chester and took a step back. Her hand going to her mouth, her words came out in a strangled whisper. "No, no, no... I can't. I mean... you can't. Oh, no, this isn't going to work."

Chester didn't know what to think. What wouldn't work? Was there something wrong with his tuxedo?

And here you thought you were looking pretty well put together.

Then he was hit with a horrible thought. Was his zipper open? Shooting a glance down in that direction, he was relieved to see everything seemed to be under control in that department.

Then what the hell is going on here?

His mind had gone into overdrive. He needed to figure out what he had to do to make things right. Because if there was one thing he did know, there was no way in hell he was going to walk away from this vision of pure loveliness now standing in front of him.

She took his breath away.

He took a step closer, a tentative smile on his face. "Hey, is something wrong?"

To say Sophie was in shock would be putting it mildly. She took a half step back.

Was something wrong?

Yes, everything was wrong. Beginning with him, standing in front of her and looking like he did.

It was crazy wrong.

There was no doubt about it, hands down, this was by far the most amazing transformation she'd ever witnessed in her life. He was just too handsome, too suave. Add to that, the hint of his well-toned and athletic build, hidden beneath the perfect cut of his tuxedo... well, it was almost too much to take.

He was the perfect embodiment of everything a woman could want in a man.

How could she possibly go with him tonight? She couldn't even look him in the eye, afraid if she did, she'd hurl herself right into his arms. Or worse yet, come out and say something incredibly stupid.

Somehow she had to make him understand. "I just can't. I never thought. You..."

She shrugged, gazing up at him.

For a few moments, they stood in silence, staring at each other.

Then, for Chester, everything clicked. A quirky smile tugging at the corner of his mouth, he reached over to brush his knuckles lightly over the curve of her cheek.

"Hey, I only took your suggestion, angel. That's all. I'm still the same guy you met the other day, now just a little easier on the eye."

She closed her eyes at the soothing tone of his voice. She wondered, was it possible she might melt? Right here and at his feet?

At the dreamy expression on her face, Chester felt encouraged. But even though he was pretty sure he was on the right track, it would help if he could at least get her to look at him.

He cleared his throat. "But now you've got me thinking. You may be right. Maybe we shouldn't go tonight."

He watched her lashes fly open.

Ah hah... this is a good start.

He smiled, waiting.

Her lips anxiously parted. "No?"

He tilted his head, his eyes holding hers. "No. But only because I know every man at this event will be insanely jealous when I walk in with you on my arm. I'll be fighting them off all night."

He didn't know where he was getting all this from, because he sure as hell had never spoken to a woman like this before. Never in his entire life. Certainly not that he could remember, that's for sure.

But somehow, one look into her big blue eyes, and everything he was thinking, came shooting right out of his mouth.

She definitely must have sprinkled more of that fairy dust over you. What else could it be?

His confidence rising, he smiled at the blush filling her cheeks. "But I'm willing to chance it. I would hate to think we both got dressed up for nothing. What do you think?"

She studied him for a few moments.

You think you want to marry this man. This is what you're thinking.

Then she smiled.

Right before she nodded.

Thank God...

Chester couldn't believe how relieved he was. Feeling like he'd just scored a major victory, he held his arm out to her. "So, are you ready for what should be a wonderful evening?"

It was when she turned to get her clutch and her wrap, she remembered the state of her zipper. In a panic, she went to whirl back around, but he put his hands on her shoulders to stop her. She could hear the smile in his voice.

"Hmm... what have we here? Hold still while I try to fix this for you." And as if it were the most natural thing in the world, he began working at the jammed zipper.

Who would've thought the simple act of fixing a zipper would bring on such a whirlwind of feelings inside of her?

As his fingers brushed against her skin, Sophie was gripped by an almost overwhelming feeling of lightheadedness, a shiver running through her. She had to fight the urge to lean back against him.

She wondered what would happen if she actually did this? Would he put his arms around her? Maybe even press a trail of kisses up her neck? Possibly even moving on up to her mouth?

She closed her eyes, a faint moan escaping her.

Oh, dear God... you're in big trouble

Sophie wasn't the only one who was having a hard time.

The shiver he felt go through her at his touch, the smoothness of her skin, so soft and warm beneath his fingertips, and the intoxicating scent of her perfume? These things were completely messing with him.

Big time.

He couldn't believe how hard it was for him to concentrate on such a simple task, his mind careening off on what he would much rather be doing with her zipper.

And it sure as hell wouldn't be zipping it up...

This showed in the strained tone of his voice when he finally stepped back from her.

"There, you're all zipped up and ready to go."

When she turned around, so obviously embarrassed, he shrugged. "Having grown up with three sisters, I'm used to these fashion mishaps."

Again, he held his out his arm to her. "Shall we try one more time?"

And Sophie, the same Sophie known for her nonstop chatter and never-ending opinions? It appeared this Sophie had disappeared.

In her place was a whole new Sophie.

A Sophie that was completely smitten.

After she applied her lipstick and threw it into her purse, Abby took one last look in the bathroom mirror.

She felt beautiful.

Her eyes sparkled back at her, filled with excitement. The dress was perfect. For once, her hair had cooperated, falling in shining waves over her shoulders.

At the soft knock at the door, she grabbed her purse and her shoes. As she came into the living room, she saw Kevin had let himself in. Squatted down next to Poppy, he was talking softly to her.

When he glanced up to see she was watching him, he slowly stood. His eyes meeting hers, she could feel the heat of his gaze all the way across the room. And if this wasn't enough to deal with, he looked so incredibly, amazingly handsome in his tuxedo.

Now she finally understood what Cinderella must have felt like the night of the ball.

Was he her prince?

Yes. A billion times yes. Everything you've ever dreamed about is standing right here in front of you. So maybe you should say something?

She swallowed, her voice coming out in a whisper. "You… you look so good. You look so, so…" Then she was suddenly babbling, with not a clue of what she was saying. "But you're early. And I still don't have my shoes on. I didn't expect you to…" Her voice trailed off as he came closer.

He hesitated, almost as if he wasn't sure how to answer her. Then he smiled. "I guess I'm sort of early, aren't I? But this is only because I couldn't wait to see you."

The roughness of his voice set her heart pounding. But it was the look in his eyes that did her in. Sending a message filled with so much love, she felt it settle inside of her, deep within her soul.

And in that instant she knew, no matter what happened, she would never be able to let him go. She loved him too much to let this happen.

He was now next to her, close enough to touch her if he wanted. Which, thank goodness, he did. When he rested his hands on her hips, she swayed towards him, every inch of her reacting to his touch.

He pressed a soft kiss to her forehead, his voice a husky whisper. "You look beautiful, sugar."

He felt like he should say more, but for the life of him, the words wouldn't come. But she seemed to understand. After a slight shake of her head, she reached up to brush her fingertips over his lips. Her hands drifting under his jacket, she rested her head on his shoulder and gave a long, contented sigh.

It was enough for him to know everything between them was the way it should be. He leaned into the curve of her neck to whisper in her ear. "Promise me…

She gazed up at him, her answer leaving her lips before she even had time to think about it. "Anything."

He smiled. "You always have the answer I want, sugar." This was replaced with a sudden seriousness. "Promise me you'll never again tell me to leave. I never want to feel like that again."

Her arms crept up to go around his neck, her voice choked with emotion. "Oh, Kevin… I promise. I didn't mean it. I didn't. I never wanted you to leave." Gazing up at him, her eyes desperately pleaded with him to believe her.

He pulled her closer. "*Shh…* it's okay, it's okay."

She rested her head back on his shoulder, but not before she saw the beginning of a teasing smile.

"It's all settled then. You don't want me to go and I'll never want to leave. And in just a few minutes, we'll leave here together and have a wonderful time."

He tightened his hold on her. "Even though I'd rather stay here, just the two of us. So we could show each other how much we never want to leave each other ever again."

He groaned, burying his face back into the curve of her neck. "Silly as that sounded, how I want this."

She was smiling as she sighed against him. "I have a feeling there would be a lot of disappointed fans if you didn't show up tonight. I will be more than happy to spend the night tagging along with you, my only consolation knowing at the end of the evening, you will be mine." Here she reached up to brush her lips over his. "All mine."

The intensity of his gaze just about took her breath away. "Always, sugar, always…"

He pressed a soft kiss to her forehead. "And on this note, I think we better get out of here."

As they began walking towards the door, he grinned, giving a pointed look at her shoes. Which she was holding, along with her purse, in her hands.

He chuckled. "It might help if you put them on. I believe this is how it's done."

A puzzled look coming over her face, she looked down to see her bare feet peeking out from under the hem of her dress.

She laughed. "Oh Kevin, see what you do to me? My mind is so caught up with you, I can't even think straight."

He took the shoes from her and getting down on one knee, he slipped them on her feet.

He grinned up at her. "Well, look at this. They're a perfect fit."

Still gazing up at her, his expression was thoughtful. "Does this mean I've found my princess? When we haven't even yet made it to the ball?"

He smiled. "*Hmm...* I guess this means there's only one more thing left to do."

As he stood, she smiled at him.

"And what would that be?"

He winked.

"*Ah...* I guess you'll just have to wait and see."

CHAPTER 38

The Auto Museum was a hub of activity. With one car after another pulling up to the main entrance to unload their passengers, the valet service was in constant demand.

Servers, with trays balanced high on their shoulders, wove their way through the packed lobby, tempting the crowd with one display after another of tantalizing appetizers, along with flutes of sparkling champagne.

As the newest member on the team, Kevin drew a lot of attention when he and Abby entered the lobby. Through all of this, he kept her close to his side, making it a point to include her in every conversation and in every photo.

After another round of photos, he put his arm around her, his lips close to her ear. "Sugar, we need to get out of here. I'm afraid I'm going to lose you in this crowd, and I don't think I can smile for one more photo right now. Let's go check out the other room to see what they did with your cookies."

Taking her hand and responding to any requests with a shake of his head and a promise of later, he guided them through the crowd.

The main room, where the dinner and dancing portion of the evening would be held, was known as the Sterling Room. It was a room of majestic proportions, the hand carved cedar beams and leaded glass skylights of the domed ceiling, dated back to when the building had been built.

For this event, the room had been transformed into a fantasy garden of flowers and lights. The trees Alex had grudgingly helped set up were scattered all throughout the room, twinkling with miniature lights. The gauze draped tables, sparkling with a sprinkling of glitter, were the perfect setting for the elegant fine china and hand cut crystal glassware.

In the center of every table was a towering, clear glass cylindrical vase. These were filled with miniature lights and crystal beads, each one topped off with a riot of red roses, white carnations, blue hydrangeas and cascading ivy.

At each place setting, propped up against a baseball cap with the team logo, was one of Abby's cookies.

Kevin put his arm around her, dropping a kiss in her hair.

"Sugar, I am so proud of you. Look at how great they look. Now I want one. In fact, I'm going to go check the seating chart in the lobby to find out what table we're at. I'm starving and I want to eat my cookie right now."

He gave her a quick kiss on her cheek. "I'll be right back. I promise."

He was gone, leaving her staring after him, a puzzled expression on her face.

"Oh Chester, you're just too cute!"

This gushing comment came from Mia's sister, Kelly. Even after Chester's many attempts to discourage her, she would not let go of his arm. This was all happening while another woman, one of the five gathered around him, was chattering non-stop, trying to impress him with her knowledge of baseball.

Ironically, this was her favorite sport. She didn't miss a game. Or so she said.

He gave her a skeptical look, wondering how often this ranking of hers changed. He had a feeling it all depended on the company she was in. In fact, he'd be willing to bet in a few months, football would become her new favorite sport.

He gave a frustrated sigh, gazing around the room. This was not what he wanted to be doing right now.

What the hell happened to Sophie? Where did she go?

So, to say he was relieved when he saw Kevin heading in his direction would be an understatement.

The desperation in Chester's eyes was enough to convince Kevin he needed rescuing, Casually strolling over to him, he took hold of his arm and began pulling him away from the group.

He smiled. "Sorry girls, but it seems someone is looking for him in the other room. You'll have to catch up with him later."

After he pointed Chester in the direction Sophie had gone, watching him almost break into a sprint in his haste to get away, Kevin continued his search through the crowded room. This had nothing to do with seating arrangements. Nor did it have anything to do with cookies.

No, he was looking for Amelia and Victor Porchini. A husband and wife team who were well known vocalists affiliated with the Cleveland theatre district, they were also staunch supporters of the Children's Hospital. He had been told they would be here tonight, having never missed an event.

Finally, he spotted them.

He had a big favor to ask of them.

Abby wandered through the maze of tables, admiring the decorations. She glanced over at the entrance to the room, hoping to see Kevin. Instead she saw Sophie.

Moving remarkably fast, considering the stiletto heels she was wearing. Sophie grabbed her arm for support "Thank goodness I found you. I'll probably kill myself in these shoes, but I had to wear them because Chester is so tall. And do you know what? He's still so tall."

She gave an enormous sigh. "I think I created a monster. Have you seen him yet?" Before Abby could even answer, Sophie chattered on.

"Oh Abby, he's drop-dead gorgeous. All that hair was hiding one amazing man. The problem is, one look at him and my mind goes completely blank. It's a struggle for me to even get out a single word. And we all know I never have that problem."

She frowned. "Unfortunately, it seems I'm not the only one who feels like this. When I just left him, he was surrounded by women. Beautiful women, who were not only hanging on to his every word, but to every inch of him they could get their hands on. I couldn't take it anymore. I had to leave."

She became silent. She couldn't bring herself to tell Abby what the real problem was. And this was how she wanted him to kiss her. To the point, it was all she could think about. There was something in the way he looked at her that made her think it would be a kiss, until now, she'd only dared to dream about.

She sighed. "I don't know… I'm beginning to think I don't belong here. At least, not with him. I bet he probably hasn't even noticed I left."

Abby laughed. "*Umm…* it appears you're wrong about that. Because, guess who's coming our way?"

Sophie didn't have to guess.

"*Oh, my… Lord help me.*"

Chester had also embarked on a mission of sorts, and this was to find Sophie. He wanted to ask her why the hell she ran off and left him with all those crazy women.

Again, this proved what he'd believed all along.

Women were too damn confusing.

He scanned the room, relieved to see her talking with Abby. He made his way over to them, his gaze going directly to Sophie. "Why did you leave like that?"

Sophie gazed up at him, confused. His behavior wasn't what she expected. He looked totally bewildered.

This is when it dawned on her. He really didn't get it. He had absolutely no idea how attractive he was. And even if he did, he probably didn't have a clue of how to handle all this attention coming at him.

Which meant it was up to her to help him out. After all, it was because of her influence he was now in such demand.

Filled with a newfound confidence, she smiled up at him. "I'm sorry. I promise not to leave you again. In fact, from now on, you won't be able to get rid of me. No matter how hard you try."

He studied her for a moment before he reached over to take her hand. And then… there it was again. The look she had such a hard time dealing with. As though his eyes were sending a message, one only she could see.

Do something. Or say something. Otherwise, you're going to lose your mind.

Going up on her toes, she placed a soft kiss to his cheek. As she watched the blush creep over his face, she felt her heart give a little leap.

Yep. This is definitely the man you're going to marry.

A few minutes later, Kevin came up behind Abby, wrapping his arms around her. His voice was like a caress in her ear. "Hey beautiful, I'm back."

She smiled up at him. "So, I see. did you find out which table is ours? Are Sophie and Chester at the same table?"

He stared at her, momentarily at a loss for words.

Damn. You were so bent on pleading your case with the Porchinis, you completely forgot to check that out.

He cleared his throat. "Umm… I guess I sort of forgot to do that?"

She stared at him in disbelief before she laughed. "Seriously? But, I thought you…"

He interrupted her. "Look, it appears Lisa is trying to get our attention. I bet she found our table."

Abby's expression was even more puzzled. This was a sign he needed to keep talking. "And I see she and Alex brought Chloe, who I've learned is an excellent example of why we're here tonight. I guess she had a rough start when she was born and spent her first few months in the Children's Hospital. Alex told me Lisa claims Chloe wouldn't be here today if it weren't for the wonderful care she received."

He smiled down at her. "Come on, let's go join them."

Taking her hand, he began making his way over to where Lisa was waving at them, leaving her no choice but to go with him.

He suddenly turned to her. "You really are the most beautiful woman here, you know." After following this with a quick kiss, he continued to pull her along with him.

She had the distinct feeling he was up to something.

CHAPTER 39

The dinner and speeches had come to an end. The orchestra members had returned to their seats and were ready for the dancing part of the evening.

His elbow on the table and his chin resting in his hand, Kevin reached for Abby's hand. His voice was low, for her ears only. "So, are you going to dance with me?"

She smiled at him. "You really like to dance? My goodness, you truly are every girl's dream."

He smiled. "Not every girl's dream, sugar. Just yours. And I don't mean to brag, but since I was forced to take dancing lessons when I was about twelve years old, I'm actually quite good at it."

She sighed. "As you may have already noticed, I'm not the most coordinated person in the world. I may embarrass you with my lack of dancing skills."

His mouth brushed across her jaw, his lips caressing hers. *"Aw,* sugar… you've just never had the right partner. Now, you and me? We'll be perfect together."

How in the world can you not respond to that?

It didn't matter where they were or who saw them.

Or if someone took a photo. Or even a million photos.

All that mattered was this moment and how much she loved him.

Her words were a soft murmur. "I love you so, so much." Her eyes closed, she pressed her mouth to his.

The sound of Chloe's voice brought them back to the present. She grinned, nodding at Sophie, who was seated next to her. "It's okay. They're allowed to do that. They're head over heels in love."

When everyone at the table laughed, Kevin grinned over at Chloe, giving her a thumbs-up. "Thanks, BFF!" He then leaned over to whisper in Abby's ear.

"Head over heels, over the moon, however you want to say it, I'm so in love with you, too."

The lights dimmed, a hush falling over the room. After the conductor walked over to the podium and waited for the applause to die down, he greeted the guests with a smile.

"Good evening, ladies and gentlemen. What a wonderful night this has turned out for the Children's Hospital. I've just been informed, through the generosity of everyone gathered here tonight, a record-breaking amount of money has been raised."

After a thundering round of applause, he continued. "This means it's time to celebrate with some great music and dancing. And once again, we're fortunate to have Amelia and Victor Porchini here with us tonight. Long-time supporters of this event, we're always thrilled when they agree to do a few songs with our orchestra."

Once Amelia and Victor came to stand beside him and the crowd had acknowledged them with even more applause, he continued. "But this year, it seems we have something a little special going on. Some-where in this room is a gentleman who has made a generous donation of ten-thousand dollars. In exchange for this, he asks only that Amelia and Victor sing his lady's favorite song for what will be their first dance together."

A thunderous round of applause and cheers erupted at this news. Again, the conductor waited for silence.

"We ask that you to give this couple some time alone on the floor for this dance. We'll let you know when you can join in."

He bowed, and with a wave of his baton, he nodded to Amelia and Victor. "So, if you're ready, let us begin."

As the orchestra began playing the instrumental introduction to the song, Alex groaned, dragging his hand over his chin. "This is *not* good, not good at all. This big-spender is going to make every other guy in this room look bad."

Lisa patted his hand. "I think it's romantic. Maybe you men could learn something from this."

"*Hmph…* I just hope it's not one of our guys." Then he zeroed in on Kevin, who had come to his feet. His hand going to his head, he groaned. "*Geeez…* Kev, you've got to be kidding. You? *Aw, man…* what are you doing to us?"

Abby turned, her breath catching in her throat when she saw Kevin was now standing behind her. He was gazing at her with a look of such love and tenderness, she could only shake her head.

Then she shook it again… and again.

A smile spreading across his lips, he held out his hand. "May I have this dance?"

Her eyes never leaving his, she didn't remember taking his hand, or that she let him lead her out onto the dance floor. It was only when she went into his arms and Victor began to sing the first lines of the song, everything became real. She buried her face in his shoulder.

> *"Never knew I could feel like this,*
> *Like I've never seen the sky before.*
> *I want to vanish inside your kiss,*
> *Every day, I'm loving you more and more."*

After a few moments, Kevin pulled away to gaze down at her. The tears slipping down her cheeks bringing on an emotional response he wasn't familiar with, he had to close his eyes. And even though he cleared his throat, he still wasn't able to hide the unsteadiness in his voice.

"Well… I must say, when I envisioned the first time I shared a dance with the woman I loved, my hope was it would be very romantic. She would be gazing up at me, all starry-eyed and as madly in love with me as I was with her." He chuckled. "And now, with this turning out to be such an expensive first dance, it would be nice to get my money's worth."

She shook her head against him. "I'm sorry. I'm so sorry." She gazed up at him, her laugh bordering on a sob. "But everything you do makes me so emotional. I can't help it."

When she began wiping the tears from her face with her fingers, he patted his pocket, shaking his head. "And now it seems I've gone and forgotten a handkerchief."

He sent an imploring look over at Alex, who leaned over to say something to Chloe as he reached into his pocket and handed her something.

She came running out onto the dance floor to hand Abby a handkerchief. After she got a hug from Abby, she turned to Kevin. "Daddy wants you to know you owe him. Big time. For both this crazy idea of yours and the handkerchief."

She turned to go. Then she stopped to give Kevin a-thumbs up. "I think you're the best prince ever. Great job, BFF!" After one more grin, she ran back to their table.

Back in Kevin's arms, Abby was clinging to him like she was never going to let go.

He chuckled. "Sugar, you aren't going to let me down, are you? Come on, let's wow them with our dancing skills. Just follow my lead. Like I told you before, we'll be perfect together."

As he began leading her around the floor, she relaxed in his arms. When Amelia began to sing, she gazed up at him. He was smiling down at her, and his eyes holding hers, he twirled her into another move across the floor. Caught up in each other's eyes, it was as if they were alone in the room, their love guiding each move.

"Suddenly the world seems such a
perfect place,
Moving with such a perfect grace.
Suddenly my life doesn't seem such a
waste,
Because it all revolves around you."

"Sing out this song and I'll be there by
your side,
Storm clouds may gather,
Stars may collide,
But I'll always love you until the end
of time."

The song was about to end. His hand moving to his jacket pocket, Kevin shook his head.

This wasn't right.

Instead, he rested his hand on her waist. After he twirled her around one more time, he bent her back against his arm and gave her a passionate and most fitting, song ending kiss.

Yes. This was right.

It was the perfect ending for the perfect first dance.

"Come what may,
Come what may,
I will always love you until my dying
day..."

CHAPTER 40

Sophie knew she should try to strike up a conversation.

But every time she even glanced over at Chester in the dim interior of his SUV, her mind went blank.

So she remained completely still, hoping he'd take her silence as a sign of how sophisticated she was.

When in fact, she was just about dying to talk about everything that happened during the evening.

She was also worried about how she was going to slip her shoes back on before they arrived at her townhouse. She had kicked them off as soon as she got in the car. Not a very ladylike thing to do, but her four-inch heels had her feet crying out for mercy.

Hmm... funny, this wasn't an issue while you were out on the dance floor.

A frown flitted across her face. During the evening, she had paid very close attention to the women competing for Chester's attention. With most of them looking like they'd just stepped out of a major fashion magazine, her confidence of earlier had slowly crumbled.

And now, it appeared to have left her for good.

She glanced down at the rose she was holding in her hand. Chester had pulled it from the centerpiece on their table as they were leaving, handing it to her without a word.

But that look had been in his eyes. Just thinking about this, her heartbeat jumped a notch.

She sneaked a quick peek over at Chester. His gaze catching hers, he smiled. This had her clutching the rose even tighter, her heart beating a little faster.

You do know, once he drops you off, the chances of ever seeing him again aren't looking good if you don't start talking.

"So, tonight was…" This coming out in an almost breathless whisper, she stopped to clear her throat. She didn't want him to think she was trying to flirt with him. Or trying to appear sexy.

Because there was no way she'd be able to keep that up. Nope, she wouldn't even know where to start.

She tried again, this time her voice coming out closer to normal. "I imagine the hospital is thrilled about the amount of money they raised tonight, don't you think?"

And this was the best she could come up with. But she was desperate. And it was better than nothing.

Chester smiled over at her, once again taken in by the sound of her voice. So breathy and sweet, yet at the same time, so seductive. He had a feeling in, *umm…* certain situations, it could easily drive a man wild.

It's already worked its magic on you, it seems.

He cleared his throat. "I'm sure they are. And everyone seemed to have a good time." A slow grin coming over his face, he nodded. "I know I did. Of course, this had a lot to do with the company I shared."

Now feeling more relaxed, she smiled. This was going a lot better than she'd hoped for. "I know. Our table was great. I loved sitting next to Chloe. Kids are so great at her age. They say what they think and they're always so honest."

He reached over to link his fingers with hers. "Well, if I may be honest like Chloe, I'd have to say it was your company I was referring to. Yes, everyone was nice, but you're what made the night so special for me, angel."

Staring down at their hands, marveling at how hers fit so well in his, Sophie almost missed what he said.

Oh, dear... he just gave you a compliment. So you need to say thank you or something.

"I had a nice time, too." This coming out all breathless again, she glanced over to see he was smiling as he pulled up in front of her townhouse.

Yes, Chester was feeling pretty good about how the evening had gone. In fact, he was already trying to think about a second date.

After he shut off the ignition, not quite ready for the evening to end, he shifted in his seat in order to see her better. Having already reclaimed her hand, he was a little intrigued by Sophie's behavior.

Staring down at their linked fingers, she had gone completely still.

This concerned him.

She wasn't afraid of him, was she?

Damn, this is the last thing you want.

He reached over to cup her chin in his hand, bringing her face dangerously close to hers. "Are you okay?"

Later she would claim his move was what made her do such a crazy thing. Before she could put a stop to them, the words came tumbling out of her mouth. Two little words, but together they had the power to change everything.

"Kiss me."

He stilled. Then gently tipping her face to his, his lips brushed over hers in a soft kiss. It wasn't what you would call an actual kiss, but the hint of passion was there.

Definitely...

When he leaned back, her eyes still closed, she didn't move.

Fascinated, he watched her lashes flutter open, and her lips curving into a smile, she looked right at him.

She sighed. "That was so nice. I knew you'd be good at it."

Flattered, but at the same time amused by her compliment, he chuckled.

This brought her back down to earth with a bang. Mortified, she began fumbling with the door handle.

He shot out of car and around to her side, taking her hand as she nearly spilled out onto the pavement when her feet tangled in the train of her dress. Keeping a firm hold on her, his fear she could take off and disappear right before his eyes, he reached into his SUV for her shoes.

He held them out to her. "Here, you should put these on."

She shook her head and turned to walk away. But he held her back. "Come on, you're barefoot. What if you step on something?"

When he saw the stubborn look on her face, he sighed. Before she could take another step, he handed her the shoes and scooped her up in his arms. After he carried her to the front door and set her down, he smiled at her flustered expression. "Sorry. But I didn't want to take any chances."

He watched her search through her purse for her key, only to drop both it and the rose at the same time. After he picked them up and unlocked the door, he turned to find she had her eyes closed, a look of desperation on her face.

His original plan, coming to him after her comment about his kiss, had been to take her into his arms and give her a kiss of an even more convincing nature. But this tragic expression on her face had him unsure. And judging by the unexpected wave of desire that barreling through him as he carried her to her door, he was treading on shaky ground.

So, he settled for reaching over to hold her hand.

Sophie was trying to keep herself together. What she'd imagined it would feel like to be in his arms wasn't even close to how it felt to experience it first-hand. When he'd set her down, she almost hadn't let go.

She opened her eyes, her smile tentative. "Would you like to come in?"

Would he like to come in?

Yes. There was nothing he'd like more. But he couldn't. It was too dangerous. Over the course of the evening, it had become clear, with her, it was different. There was something going on between them, and he wasn't quite sure how to handle it. So, he didn't want to do something foolish.

Hoping to soften his refusal, he brought her hand up to his mouth, lightly brushing his lips over her fingers. "No, I don't think so. But I'll call you about the tickets."

She nodded. "That would be nice. And again, thank you for such a wonderful evening."

She rested her hand against his chest, and rising on her tiptoes, she pressed the softest of kisses to his cheek.

Then she slipped inside her condo, closing the door behind her.

Still holding the rose in his hand, Chester stared at the closed door. Then he groaned, dragging his hand through his hair.

Well, you certainly didn't handle that very well, did you? No, you don't think so? Could you be any more of a jerk?

Before he could change his mind, he hit the doorbell.

The door opened as if Sophie had been right there, waiting. Which was exactly what she had been doing.

She gazed up at him, her blue eyes searching his so intently, he almost couldn't think.

He handed her the rose. "I forgot to give this back to you. And to tell you, I also had a good time. In fact, I had a wonderful time."

He took a deep breath. "I really want to see you again. It's not that I don't want to come in, because I do, more than anything. It's only that I think it would be better if we take things slow."

A soft laugh escaped him. "Because, *God help me,* angel... I don't know what kind of spell you put on me, but whatever it is, I know I don't want it to go away."

Suddenly looking shy, he shrugged. "I hope you understand?"

Her smile was brilliant, almost making him regret what he said about taking things slow.

Three times she nodded. And then she nodded again, her happiness reaching out to surround him with its warmth.

She watched as he began backing away, stopping to smile at her one more time before he turned and sprinted to his car.

She closed the door, and leaning against it, she slowly slid down to the floor.

Holding the rose to her lips, she couldn't stop smiling.
Her phone began vibrating in her purse.
She pulled it out to see there was a message.
It was from Chester.

Sweet dreams, Angel...

As she smiled down at the phone, almost giddy with happiness, she wondered...
Why does he call you Angel?

CHAPTER 41

Love, it's that calm serenity
that makes you want to hold her gaze,
not turn away.
~Anonymously Yours

Kevin drove down the street and turned into Abby's driveway.

Silently, he did this.

There was no roar of the engine or squealing of tires.

He glanced over at Abby. Her head resting back against the seat, her eyes were closed. Trailing his fingertips along the curve of her jaw, he watched as her lashes fluttered open at his touch.

She gave him a lazy smile.

He responded with a kiss. "We're home, sugar."

She smiled.

Yes, home…

Home would always be wherever he was.

Once they were in her condo and he'd taken Poppy outside, he slipped out of his jacket and threw it on the sofa. Undoing his tie and unbuttoning the top buttons of his shirt, he walked over to where

Abby was checking her phone messages. Gently removing the phone from her hands, he tossed it on the sofa next to his jacket.

He pulled her into his arms. "The phone can wait, sugar. Remember? Now I'm all yours."

She smiled up at him as she slowly began undoing the buttons down the front of his shirt. "It was Sophie. She wanted to let me know she had a wonderful time."

He gathered her hair in his hands, his lips traveling in a leisurely trail up her neck. "*Hmm...* that's good. I'm sure I'll get the details from Chester on Tuesday. But I don't care about any of that right now. I only want to get lost in you... in us."

His mouth coming down on hers in a deep kiss, he began moving them to the bedroom. When she stumbled, her feet caught up in the hem of her dress, he scooped her up into his arms.

In the bedroom, he set her down, watching as she continued to unbutton his shirt. When she started to pull the shirt down over his shoulders, he stopped her, holding out his hands.

"Cuff links, sugar."

She removed the diamond-studded cufflinks, and holding them in her hands, she studied them. Then she smiled up at him. "Very impressive."

He looked down at her hands. His gaze coming back to her face, he hesitated slightly before he spoke. "They were a gift from my mother when I graduated from college."

A look of pure panic on her face, she dropped the cufflinks as if she'd been burnt. Before she could pick them up, he stopped her. Framing her face in his hands, the look he gave her was one of pure love. "Sugar, I know what my mother did."

When she tensed against him, he pulled her close, whispering in her hair. "Why didn't you tell me?"

She closed her eyes, shaking her head against his chest. "I couldn't. I was so afraid of what would happen, and I thought the only thing I could do was let you go. But then I realized I'd made a mistake."

She gazed up at him, her eyes desperately searching his. "I love you too much. And I never want to be without you."

He wrapped his arms around her. "*Aw,* Sugar... I promise you never will. Not as long as I have a say. You have to know by now how much I love you."

At the reassuring look in his eyes, she began to relax against him. Her words were like a vow, her promise to him. "I love you, Kevin Kardell. I don't know what I did to deserve you, but I know that I'm never going to let you go."

She slid her hands under his shirt and down over his shoulders, pushing at it until it fell to the floor. "You're mine, every single inch of you. And now the only thing I want is for you to show me how much you love me, too."

Within seconds, their clothing was scattered across the floor and she was where she wanted to be, surrounded by him, his arms wrapped around her and holding her close. She closed her eyes, embracing the familiar rush of anticipation building inside of her. When he stilled, she opened her eyes to see he was gazing down at her.

He leaned down to rest his forehead against hers. His heart almost overcome with the knowledge she was finally all his, he didn't know if he could come up with the right words to let her know how he felt.

He only knew everything was good.

No, everything was perfect.

His words flowed through her like a vow. "This is what it's all about... you, me and how much love we have for each other. What we have is so amazing, sugar. And nobody will ever be able to take it away from us."

"Never..."

Then he was kissing her, a deep, passionate kiss. But the love between them that followed was gentle and unhurried.

They were home...

Together... and where they were meant to be.

They had fallen into a hazy, tranquil silence, the only light in the room coming from the moonlight that trailed across the bed. Her head on his shoulder and her eyes closed, Abby was almost hypnotized by the feel of his hand drifting over her, caressing her.

When she lifted her head to press a kiss to his chin, she found he was gazing down at her, a smile on his face. He smoothed the hair back from her face. "I love you."

"I know... I love you, too. So, so much."

He drew his arm out from under her. After leaving the bed, he smiled down at her. "I'll be right back. Don't go anywhere, okay?"

Closing her eyes, she snuggled into the warmth of the space he'd left behind, breathing in the lingering scent of his cologne, of him.

Then he was sliding back next to her, dropping a kiss to her cheek. In his hand, he was holding an envelope.

He reached over to turn on the lamp on the nightstand. After he settled next to her, he pulled a letter out of the envelope and handed it to her. "Now, I know you told me you don't need my help. So, if it will make you feel better, consider this a loan. Or I can be your silent partner."

He grinned, "I would even be willing to take on the job of official taste tester."

Then he was silent, watching as she read the letter informing her that the loan for her kitchen remodel had been paid in full.

She turned to him, her eyes wide. "But I don't understand. How did you know about this? I never told you... I never wanted you to do this. I can't..."

He stopped her with a kiss. "Yes, you can. I found the bill on the counter the night of the epic wine and cookie disaster."

He chuckled at the memory. "So, I took it with me."

When she looked down at the letter, shaking her head, he sighed. "Sugar, I expect nothing in return. I'm doing this because I love you. And because I think your cookies are the best damn cookies in Cleveland. Or in all of Ohio. What the hell, let's make that in the whole world."

She finally gazed up at him, her earnest expression bringing a smile from him. "I will accept this, but only on one condition. And this is you'll let me pay you back. Every single penny."

He studied her for a few moments before he reached over to tuck her hair behind her ear. "Okay. But I get to decide the form of payment. And it's not money I want. No, there's only one thing I want. And this is you, sugar."

Mesmerized by the sudden intensity of his gaze, she could only stare at him. When she opened her mouth to speak, he pressed his finger gently to her lips. "Let me finish what I want to say. But first, close your eyes."

After she did as he asked, he reached for her left hand. "I had planned on doing this tonight, right after we shared our first dance, but it didn't feel right. With all the publicity we've been dealing with, I wanted this moment to be only between you and me."

He slipped a ring onto her finger. Her lashes flying open, her gaze went to the ring, then to him. Pressing his finger to her lips again, he shook head.

His voice was rough, his smile slow and full of promise. "Abby, you're my world. You will always be the only woman for me and I don't even want to even think of spending my life without you. I want to have, to hold and to cherish you. And more than anything, I want to always be here to love you."

Here he stopped to press the gentlest kiss to her mouth before he added, "Until the end of time…"

He took a deep breath.

"Abigail Rose Evans, will you marry me?"

She had started to nod before he even finished speaking. Then, as the tears slipped down her cheeks, she just kept on nodding. And even after she threw her arms around him, she was still nodding.

This was a good enough answer for him.

Katy saw her phone flashing in the darkness. She picked it up from the nightstand, smiling when she saw it was a message from Kevin.

It was only three words.

She said yes.

CHAPTER 42

"*O*h, no..."

Making the turn off the freeway exit, Kevin shot a glance over at Abby. In the passenger seat, she was staring down at her phone.

"What's wrong, sugar?"

She wrinkled her nose at him. "Sophie sent a text. There's a new post on the Cleveland fan page."

After she found the page, she read it aloud.

> *To all of you Kevin Kardell groupies*
> *out there, it looks like it's official. He's*
> *definitely taken. As you can see in this*
> *photo, Kevin and his little redhead are*
> *now definitely a couple. A couple with*
> *a lot of class and flair, it seems. Any*
> *man who donates an astronomical*

amount of money, in exchange for their first dance alone on the dance floor, can only bein love. And yes, this actually happened last night at the Baseball, Babies and Teddy Bears fundraiser gala. So, we're thinking there's a ring in the near future for these two. We'll keep you posted.

The photographer had caught them at the end of the dance, when Kevin had dipped her back over his arm to give her that passionate kiss.

Kevin pulled up to a red light, and taking the phone from her, he studied it. He glanced over to see she was smiling.

He had only one word.

"Perfection."

Lost in each other's eyes, they continued to smile at each other until the light turned green.

Kevin put the car in park, and turned off the ignition.

He glanced over at Abby. "This is it, sugar. We're here."

A mix of excitement and apprehension on her face, Abby was peering over at the blue bungalow. Twisting the ring on her finger, she turned to him.

He gave her a reassuring smile.

Hers was lopsided in return.

After sending another glance back at the bungalow, she swallowed. "I'm scared. Maybe he's changed his mind, Or…"

He framed her face in his hand, shaking his head. "Everything is going to be fine."

At her skeptical look, his mouth twisted in a wry grin. "I know, I know… I've been wrong in the past, but this time I know I'm right. He's going to be thrilled when he opens the door and sees you standing in front of him. Trust me on this one."

He was sending her a look filled with so much love and support, any doubt she'd been holding onto began to fade.

Her words were a whisper. "I do trust you. And I love you so, so much."

"I love you, too. More than you could imagine." Then he smiled. "Now go. Go tell your dad how much you love him. I'll be right here if you need me."

She shook her head. "No, I want you to come with me." She grinned. "After all, if he's going to be a part of my life again, he will have to get used to you being around."

By the stunned expression on his face, it was obvious Abby was the last person her father expected to see when he opened the door.

It was Kevin's smiling face that had him sending Abby a tentative smile.

She smiled. "Hi, daddy."

The same smile he'd kept tucked close to his heart for so long, he held out his arms, his voice choked with emotion.

"Gabby Abby…"

With a small cry, she went right into his embrace. There were no tears—only a deep sense of relief.

And such unconditional love.

Just as Kevin had promised, everything was fine.

It was more than fine.

It was wonderful.

Abby stepped back and reached for Kevin's hand. The smile she gave her father was radiant. "Daddy, we've both come to ask if you'll walk me down the aisle."

EPILOGUE

Three Months Later

Cleveland won the World Series, beating St. Louis in the first four games of the final series playoff. Cleveland fans liked to think of it as a win—long overdue.

Kevin won Rookie of the Year for the American League.

And as he fought his way through the mob of cheering people on the field, he was searching for only one person. He finally spotted her. At the same time, a photographer leveled his camera right at him.

"So, Kevin… now that your team won the World Series, what are you going to do next?"

Pulling Abby into a hug, Kevin had to yell to be heard.

"Get married to the girl of my dreams."

He flashed another smile at the camera. Then he looked at Abby again—like the answer was always the same.

"After that… we have the rest of our lives to decide."

Confetti drifted all around them as he kissed her right there in the middle of the celebration, like he was never going to let her go.

You gotta love Cleveland…

LET'S DO SOME BAKING!

Abby's Favorite Sugar Cookies
(These have Sophie's five-star rating.)

Ingredients:
  2 3/4 cups flour
  1 teaspoon baking powder
  1 teaspoon salt
  3/4 cup butter, softened
  1 cup sugar
  2 eggs
  1 teaspoon vanilla
  1/4 teaspoon almond extract

Directions:
  Sift together flour, baking powder and
  salt; set aside.
  In large bowl, cream together butter and
  sugar.
  Add eggs, vanilla and almond extract;
  blend well.

Add dry ingredients and mix well.
Wrap dough and chill for at least 1 to 2
hours.
Preheat oven to 375°. Line a large baking
sheet with parchment paper.
Roll out dough to 1/2-inch thick on a floured
surface and cut with desired cookie cutters.
Bake for 8 – 10 minutes or just until set.
Yield: 3 dozen cookies.

* * *

Abby's Butter Cream Frosting
(So easy, but so good.)

Ingredients:
2/3 cup butter, softened
4 cups powdered sugar
1 teaspoon vanilla
2 tablespoons milk
1/4 teaspoon almond extract

Directions:
In medium bowl, cream together all ingredients until light and fluffy.

* * *

Chocolate Chip Coffee Cake
(Stephen claims this cake was one of the reasons he married Katy.)

Ingredients:
2 cups of flour
1 cup sugar
2 teaspoons baking powder

1 teaspoon salt
1 tablespoon grated orange zest
1/2 cup butter, softened
1 cup milk
2 eggs, slightly beaten
1 teaspoon vanilla
1 cup mini chocolate chips

Streusel Topping:
3/4 cup flour
3/4 cup sugar
1 tablespoon orange juice
1-1/2 teaspoons cinnamon
1/4 cup butter, cubed
1/2 cup mini chocolate chips

Directions:
Preheat oven to 375º. Spray a 13x9-inch pan
with non-stick baking spray.
For coffee cake, in a large bowl, combine the
first 5 ingredients.
Using a pastry blender or fork, cut in butter.
Stir in the milk, eggs, vanilla and chocolate
chips just until blended.
Pour into prepared pan.
For topping, mix all ingredients, using a
pastry blender or fork, until crumbly.
Sprinkle evenly over top of cake.
Bake for 35 -40 minutes. Serve warm.

ABOUT THE AUTHOR

L. B. Joyce lives in Chagrin Falls, Ohio. A freelance artist by day, with designing Christmas ornaments her specialty, she's also a writer by night. She loves getting lost in a good book, has redecorated almost every room in her house more times than she'd like to admit, loves baking up a storm in her kitchen, hates housework with a passion and will drive just about anywhere because of her fear of flying.

To keep up with the first eight novels of the series - *A Million Decembers* - *For the Love of July* - *February's Angel* - *Promise Me November* - *An Unexpected June* - *A January to Remember* - *September's Moonlight Serenade* - *Goodbye Heartbreak, Hello May March, a Song and a Dance* - (Along with - *A Grand Slam Kind of Christmas* - *the first book of the series Holidays in White Oaks Valley)* - *check out the* Twelve Months, Twelve Love Stories website/blog at:

https://www.lbjoyceauthor.com

Or go to Facebook at:

https://www.facebook.com/AuthorLBJoyce

Email:

lbjoyce12@gmail.com

Then, if you have a minute, check out the latest L. B. Bear Christmas Ornament designs and just about everything you ever wanted to know about Christmas at:

www.facebook.com/LBGlitterGirl

ACKNOWLEDGMENTS

Let's give credit where credit is due:

Can't Help Falling in Love ~ *lyrics and music by: George David Weiss and Patrick Joseph Vida*

Come What May ~ *lyrics and music by: David Baerwald and Kevin Gilbert*

Book Cover: Soxsational Cover Art

* * *